YOU MA
BOOKS
D1136036

Beauty Story

By the same author

Breach Candy
Atlantic

Beauty Story

LUKE JENNINGS

HUTCHINSON
London

1 3 5 7 9 10 8 6 4 2

This edition first published in 1998 by Hutchinson

Random House (UK) Limited)
20 Vauxhall Bridge Road, London SW1V 2SA

Random House Australia (Pty) Limited
20 Alfred Street, Milsons Point, Sydney,
New South Wales 2061, Australia

Random House New Zealand Limited
18 Poland Road, Glenfield, Auckland 10, New Zealand

Random House South Africa (Pty) Limited
Endulini, 5A Jubilee Road, Parktown 2193, South Africa

A CiP record for this book is available from the British Library

Papers used by Random House UK Limited are natural, recyclable products made from wood grown in sustainable forests. The manufacturing processes conform to the environmental regulations of the country of origin.

ISBN 0 09 180233 4 – Paperback
ISBN 0 09 180087 0 – Hardback

Typeset by SX Composing DTP, Rayleigh, Essex
Printed and bound in Great Britain
by Mackays of Chatham PLC

For Irwin and Cynthia Ebenau

1

Rain frets soundlessly at the Plexiglas window as the stewardess, nodding, counts us off to left and right. As the door sucks shut behind her, a synthesised version of 'Come Fly with Me' begins, at some random point in its course, to leak into the cabin from above our heads. It ceases abruptly, to be replaced by the more strident riffs prefacing the crash procedure video. Outside in the shining dusk the apron is a swinging blur of blue and orange. Slowly, then faster, the colours draw themselves backwards past the window.

When I was living here in London, I used to love assignments in New York. I would leave Heathrow in the evening and arrive at JFK eight hours later with the night still waiting. The flights themselves – the suspended summer twilights, the long unfolding of the Atlantic hours – were a gift, a time out of time. But this time the journey is different: this time I am not chasing a story, I am taking a story with me.

Beyond the Plexiglas, the city falls away. I loosen my seatbelt and reach forward for my briefcase.

'Pardon me, you're not going to use a . . . computer?'

I've heard the accent described as 'Long Island Lockjaw'. There is a certain space between my neighbour and myself, we are not shoulder to shoulder as they are in the less expensive seats, and I have registered little more of her than gilt-buttoned tweed and stale perfume.

'No,' I promise, taking an A4 envelope from the case. 'No computer. Just things I have to read.'

She raises a waxy hand bearing a large chrysoprase ring, the sort of piece you used to see in hotel display cases.

'Excuse my asking, but you know how certain people have a habit of . . .?' She shows teeth the colour of old ivory. The ring-bearing hand mimes a little stenographic dance.

'I know,' I reply. 'I hate it too. Turning everywhere into an office.'

I am saved from further conversation by the arrival of a steward with champagne. As I accept a glass, blotting the damp base on its circular paper mat, she peers suspiciously at the label on the bottle through amber-framed spectacles.

I sip at the cold champagne. For a moment I fear that she is interpreting the celebratory gesture as an invitation to further questioning, but then she responds in kind and lowers thin lips to her own tulip glass.

'Mmmm,' she murmurs, her eyes flickering to the cuttings in my lap. 'Rather tart.'

I search the armrest for the reading light.

Source: *NY Times*
Byline: ED LOVERT
Headline: FAREWELL MY LOVELY, or AU REVOIR?
Caption: Cooney: disappearance remains a mystery

Six months ago today, in circumstances which remain unexplained, the actress Dale Cooney vanished from a film set in Warwickshire, England. At the time of her disappearance Cooney was completing a cosmetics shoot at Darne Castle, one of Britain's oldest ancestral homes. On the final morning of filming the 21-year-old actress failed to present herself on set, and despite the best efforts of local and national police forces her whereabouts remains a mystery to this day.

Six months ago Dale Cooney was effectively an unknown, despite excellent notices for her first and only major film role (in Georgia Dionno's *Stillwater*). Since then, however, she has come to haunt the public imagination. Where is Dale Cooney? Is she alive or dead? Has she been abducted – or worse, murdered – or has she simply elected to retire from the public gaze?

Despite a raft of conspiracy theories, a bulging police folder of unconfirmed sightings and many hundreds of column inches of reportage, the important questions all remain unanswered. 'She appears to have been spirited away,' remarked one commentator, and the phrase is not wholly inappropriate. There was, or is, a transparency to Cooney's screen presence which lends itself to fanciful theories of this kind.

Perhaps it was this not quite corporeal quality which led to her selection last March as the new face of the Laurene Forth cosmetics empire, whose products include the Eternal Summer and Quatrieme ranges. Cooney's $6.5m contract with Forth is amongst the highest ever negotiated, but in the wake of publicity surrounding her disappearance the corporation's investment has been repaid many times over. While Forth has been criticised in some quarters for proceeding with the hugely successful Cooney campaign, spokespersons for the corporation have denied capitalising on the actress's disappearance. Says Forth's Nancy Waller, 'We wish Miss Cooney well wherever she is.' COPY ENDS.

Source: *Times* (UK)
Byline: STAFF REP.
Headline: BEACH WOMAN IS NOT MISSING ACTRESS

The body of a woman found on a Scottish beach ten days ago is unlikely to be that of vanished actress Dale Cooney, police confirmed today. It is now believed that the body, discovered at Culzean Bay, Strathclyde, was that of Sarah Carmody of Brentwood, Middlesex.

Miss Carmody, 21, a law student, was said to bear a resemblance to Dale Cooney, who vanished from a Warwickshire film set in June. It was this resemblance, combined with the fact that Miss Carmody was not reported missing for more than a week, that had led to inaccurate reports of the dead woman's identification as Cooney, said a Strathclyde Police spokesperson.

Positive identification by relatives is expected today. Mr Andrew Curran, procurator fiscal at Ayr, said on Saturday that a post-mortem examination of the dead woman showed that she had died by drowning. A fellow student of Miss Carmody's yesterday described her as 'depressive, a loner'.

Dale Cooney is known as 'The Face of Laurene Forth', and in the wake of her disappearance Forth products have achieved record sales. Spokespersons for the cosmetics giant, however, have denied capitalising on the event. COPY ENDS

There are several other pieces like these, all of them accessed from an on-line cuttings service. Nothing new, needless to say, but it is interesting to observe the process by which, over time, a story gradually slips its factual moorings and becomes free-floating, a vessel into which any old cargo of resentment, craziness or self-promotion may be lowered.

The final item, I am certain, will resist this drift. It is a twenty page fax copy of a galley proof whose origin, it is clear from the typeface and layout, is the offices of *Manhattan* magazine. There is no byline but a scribbled note in the top page margin indicates that the writer is Michael Vyshinsky and the publication date is February, a month away. The fax, like others that I have received from the same source, has been sent from the Plaza Hotel.

COPY STARTS

The idea of disappearance terrifies us. For all its bleakness, the word is generally employed with fearful euphemism; unwilling to dwell on the probable fate of the missing we make the matter subjective, switching the emphasis from their experience to our own, to their 'disappearance' from our sight. We all know what the missing look like – thoughtful, smiling, a little out of focus – and sometimes we can bear to look at the photographs and sometimes we cannot. For if there is one certainty, it is that the disappeared no longer bear any resemblance to these unfading images.

If we suspect a disappearance to be self-engineered, however, a part of us is enthralled, particularly when the missing person is – or has been – a public figure. When the British peer and alleged murderer Lord Lucan vanished from London in 1974 he left an irresistible mystery behind him. Few believe that his friends have told all they know; the whiff of aristocratic complicity lingers and the search continues. For beyond the puff of smoke – the *coup de théâtre* of the actual disappearance – resides a potent fantasy: that conventional ties of identity can be severed and a parallel life undertaken elsewhere. There are even those who subscribe to a unifying theory: that all such disappearances are elective, and that on some bath-chaired veranda beneath the turbid Paraguayan skies, 'Lucky' Lucan is enjoying a hand of bridge with Marilyn Monroe, Elvis Presley and Jimmy Hoffa.

> The Dale Cooney case, however, defies even the most basic categorisation. Was Cooney the architect of a brilliantly planned escape from the public eye or the victim of a perfect and apparently motiveless crime? Either way, it is becoming increasingly clear that at some vital, mortal moment at Darne Castle last summer, everyone was looking in the wrong direction.

I accept a second glass of champagne from the steward, light a 555 and manoeuvre a cushion into the small of my back. Halfway through the piece, I discover that I am hungry, and soon I am despatching course after miniature course – hard butter, cold cutlery, Montrachet – and wondering where the final pages of Vyshinsky's narrative will lead. The piece is well written and researched but I can already tell that he is not going to surprise us with a conclusion. I catch sight of my name on the next page. Beyond the stiff little airline curtain the sky is streaked with wild vermilion.

> . . . How are we to make sense of these events? The last person to see Dale Cooney alive, according to both her own report and that of the police, was the journalist Alison MacAteer. Perhaps because of her profession – journalists often hesitate to recognise their colleagues as 'real' participants in events – MacAteer has remained something of a shadowy figure in all that has been written about the Cooney case.
>
> In fact MacAteer, who is British, had been commissioned to write a report for *The Saturday Review* on the making of the Eternal Summer commercial. The magazine's interest had initially been sparked by Laurene Forth's costly replacement of their contracted 'face', the German model Karen Hassler, with Dale Cooney, at that time an all but unknown actress (the decision is said to have cost Forth in excess of $10m). Since the appearance of her report MacAteer has written nothing on the subject. Indeed a search reveals that she has made no statement about the case and her byline has not appeared in . . .

'That's Dale Cooney, isn't it! The girl who disappeared!' It is my neighbour, her eyes shining with exophthalmic excitement behind the amber frames. My heart sinks as I realise that she has been putting the thick lenses to good effect. She points with a stiff, slightly trembling finger to one of the captioned illustrations in my lap.

'And . . . and you're the other one, aren't you!'

The photograph in question has been much reproduced. Kees Reyntiens took it near the boathouse on the first morning of filming: Dale is half in costume, wearing the jewelled green bodice and lace sleeves over an old pair of jeans and Cuban-heeled boots (the skirt had to be taken away and ironed between each shot), and she is laughing. Consciously or unconsciously – she is fully made-up and her hair dressed with forget-me-nots – her posture and the disposition of her hands exactly mimics that of Robert Peake's 1599 portrait of Eleanor Duboys. I'm standing opposite Dale, mouth open and cigarette and notebook in hand, but all things considered not looking too bad. Behind us, at the side of the wardrobe marquee, a technician holds up a sound boom as if it were a tilting lance. In the background, at the lake's edge, camera track is being laid.

'It's you, isn't it?' She peers at the caption. 'Alison . . .'

'Yes,' I say wearily. 'It's me.'

The hand wearing the heavy chrysoprase ring traces Dale's face with a trembly finger.

'So sad,' she says. 'So pretty.'

'Yes,' I say, and she looks at me as if for the first time, her eyes following the long scars.

'I'm sorry, dear,' she says. 'I didn't mean . . .'

'That's OK,' I say.

'Can I . . .' She has the decency to hesitate. 'Do you mind if I ask you what happened?'

I smile. Does she mean what happened to me, or what happened to Dale, or what happened to the truth?

'It's all in the past,' I say. 'Really.'

'Part of you is still there, though, isn't it?' Her question is almost hungry.

I turn my face to the rain-streaked darkness. 'I'm sorry,' I say. 'It's not something I can talk about.'

Slowly, expressionless, the woman folds her glasses into their case and subsides back into her seat.

She is right, of course: part of me is still there at Darne, and there has not been a night in the last two hundred that I have not rewritten the script, not replayed the events of last summer. I have spent most of my professional life telling other people's stories; now, for better or for worse, I must consider my own.

2

I wasn't sure where to put my clothes. There wasn't so much as a chair.

Eventually I took the *Evening Standard* from my bag, opened it to its centre pages, and laying it over a stain in the carpet, undressed on to it. He didn't pretend not to watch me. It was already half-dark, and from beyond the vertical fabric-strip blinds came the irregular beat of rain. The radiator, over-hot, issued a dull knocking.

Dropping my bra, I turned to him, stood straight. He stared for a moment, retracted his lips into a tight, professional smile. The room was airless, as if sealed; my hands hung uncertain at my sides. As if from a great distance, the crawling hiss of the Baker Street traffic.

'Your . . . panties.'

'I'm sorry?' I asked.

'Could you take off your panties? Please.'

Panties? It occurred to me as I stepped out of them, wobbling on one leg, that I'd never actually heard anyone use the word out loud. Panties. The paired syllables became incomprehensible.

'For the unbroken line,' he explained, 'of the body.'

Framed certificates and an electric clock hung behind his desk. Behind me the radiator delivered itself of a particularly resonant knock, which in turn, it seemed, triggered a light on one of the telephones.

'Excuse me,' he said, eyes holding me. 'Yes?'

His voice, like his expression and his clothing, had a dully projected quality which made me think of insurance and daytime TV. I realised that I had forgotten his name.

'No,' he murmured into the receiver, 'no daylight till Wednesday. Absolutely not.' His tone hardened. 'Look, I've got a . . . Right, call me then. Yup. Good.'

His face swung back to me.

'Now . . . Alison, isn't it?'

'Er, yes.'

'Sure about that?' A tight, capped smile.

'Quite sure.'

'Well, Alison, let's have a little chat about your breasts.'

'Right,' I agreed.

'You're . . . how old?'

'Twenty-seven.' True, as of today.

'Someone . . . special in your life?'

I hesitated. 'Not really.'

He was silent for a moment, then tilted his head to one side. Touched a gold propelling pencil to his lips.

'And you'd like . . . bigger breasts.'

'Yes.'

'Can you tell me why?'

'I feel . . . they'd make me more . . . womanly. More of a woman.'

He nodded, seemed satisfied with the answer, and walked round to the front of the desk. His large dry hands and the minted decay of his breath reached me simultaneously. I concentrated my attention on the bookcase.

Beautiful Bratislava, I read, biting my lip as his thumbs brushed my nipples. *Scuba Magic. The Book of the Kilim.*

Bending his knees, he lifted each of my breasts in turn and peered at them from beneath. Again, the breath found my face. *Wall Hangings of North America.*

Nodding to himself, he stood back.

'You're almost there, Alison,' he said, leaning against the desk. 'Almost the . . . complete woman that you want to be. You've got a nice little body there, and you obviously take good care of it, but these,' he reached out again, 'could, as you say, be bigger. What's your bra size, exactly, 36B?'

'Yes.' *The Microwave Hostess.*

'Well, in my opinion you could certainly, and most attractively, carry a D.'

'I know I could,' I said. 'I just know it.'

This was not the first time I had posed as a potential customer for cosmetic surgery: we ran a version of the story at least once a year. As a woman of – as one of my male colleagues once put it – perfectly serviceable attractiveness, I had no need or personal wish to submit to the knife, the laser or the suction hose. My purpose, however, was to discover what the clinics would try and talk me into. Just how far they'd push me.

'Alison. Lovely. I'm Sonia.'

The dust-shadowed mouldings of the 'consulting room' gave an impression of uncertain purpose, of leases soon to expire. Despite the near-darkness and the rain outside, the elderly festoon blind remained unlowered.

Sonia, it seemed from her accent, had once been French; scalloped angora lapped her shoulders, and her spectacles hung from a gilt neck-chain.

'So, how did you find our lovely Doctor Bob?'

'Very . . . reassuring.'

'Most of our ladies fall at least a tiny bit . . . *amoureuse* of Doctor Bob.'

'I'm not in the least surprised; he's a real charmer.'

'You'll look so *wonderful*, I promise. So complete. Since Doctor Bob did mine, I've been so happy.' She parted the cashmere. 'Look.'

Carefully, holding it above and below as if a sudden movement might cause it to bolt, she tendered a pale hypertrophic breast.

'Fill it.'

'I'm sorry?'

'Here, Alison,' she took my hand, 'fill it.'

I felt it. Sonia's body exuded a heavy, chemically based perfume. Her eyes held me.

'Yours could be . . . so.'

'How do you think I'd look?'

'*Très chic*. Very desirable, very womanly.' She smiled, and as if absently, looped a strand of my hair behind my ear, watched it slowly refurl against my cheek.

'Let me tell you about our clinic.' From an oval-mirrored

dressing table she drew a printed prospectus. On the front was a photograph of a dark, gabled building surrounded by trees.

'Can I have a copy of this?'

'Of course, lovely. Is for you.'

She sat me down on a loose-covered sofa, offered me a gold-tipped menthol cigarette and subjected me to a soft blizzard of credit terms and accommodation details.

Sometimes, I thought, as the door closed behind me and the rain found my face, I really did earn the money I was paid. By the time I reached the car, which I had left on a meter in Crawford Street, my shoulders were damp beneath my coat and my feet cold and wet in my shoes. And I had a parking ticket: I was exactly seven minutes into penalty time.

Throwing my briefcase and the polythene-enveloped ticket on to the passenger seat, I gunned up the Capri and nosed out towards Gloucester Place. Rain drummed on the roof and the ice-blue bonnet of the car. Despite the fast-acting heater I couldn't stop shuddering; I wanted to lower myself into a hot bath, to wash away the cloying residue of Sonia and the dry handprints of Doctor Bob.

It would all add up to a strong piece, though. As I swung between traffic lanes I thought of the sad clutch of women in the waiting room, high-heeled and mascaraed for a wet Friday afternoon. There had been an avoidance of eyes, but at the same time a kind of slumped, round-shouldered complicity. I am sure that they had all, as I had done, rung round. They had all discovered that the unaccredited De Milo Clinic gave the cheapest silicone jobs in town. Not that cheap was *cheap*, of course. The figures were in thousands rather than hundreds.

Be the woman that you could be, was the message. Become the woman that you so, *so* nearly are. And the cost? Well, what price happiness? Or, as Sonia put it: 'Wud prize a penis, dulling?'

Clever enough stuff, of course. The other women, I was convinced, would all end up handing Sonia their credit cards and booking into 'Fairlawns'. Most of them would probably end up, for a month or two anyway, happier than before. Who knew? Who cared? Certainly not my readers.

I dragged the Capri out from behind a Green Line bus, and we bucketed northwards into Park Road. The days were getting longer now that March was here, but there was more than a memory of winter in the air. I shrugged deeper into my unsatisfactory coat.

The lift shuddered to a halt. Racketing back the gates, I unlocked the landing's single door into the grey darkness of my flat. Often, as tonight, I didn't immediately switch on the light, but moved with pale pleasure amongst the warm silhouettes of my possessions. Six floors below, mute beyond the glass, lay London: first the blackness of Regent's Park and then the hard, half-life glitter beyond. Kicking off my wet shoes, I drew the curtains. Around the walls the tiny liquid-crystal numerals of my hardware waited for me, flickering, clustered like fireflies. There was a dilute scented edge to the air that I didn't recognise. Sonia, I suppose. Her chemical traces on my clothing, in my hair ('*Of course, Lovely. Is for you . . .*'). The tape on the answering machine whirred, rewinding.

'Ali darling, happy *birth*day. Welcome to the over . . .'

I slid from the arm of the chair, felt my way to the bathroom and turned on the hot tap and the small tube-light over the mirror. A drink, I thought. Cigarettes.

'. . . about Sunday. Could you make it up here about twelveish? Orde's coming with um, you know, Wendy, so ring us if you're bringing anyone, I've got some lamb. Have a nice birthday. Love, Mum.'

She always signed off as if writing a postcard.

'Ali Baba, it's Bart. How did it go? Hope you didn't panic and sign up for new tits; yours are frightening enough as it is. Call me at the Death Star. Here till six thirty.'

'Ali, it's Orde. Listen, I'm not going to be in London on Sunday after all, Wendy and I are . . . Anyway, you'll have to make it home for lunch under your own steam. Are you bringing anyone?'

At that moment the tap coughed and the water, for some reason, packed up altogether. In the silence I thought I heard something, a half-breath, something suppressed.

'Who's . . .?' I started, but my voice was lost in a sudden rush of bathwater, and then, from my bedroom, came the unmistakable sound of a stifled laugh. My heart thumped at my sternum, my eyes froze, my fingers plucked at the lapels of my wet coat. Hyperventilating, and all but wetting myself, I shrank into the armchair. What burglar, who sane, would *laugh*?

And then they started singing 'Happy Birthday', and one by one, bottles in hand, my colleagues filed from my bedroom.

'You BASTARDS!' I screamed, relief swiftly giving way to fury. 'You BASTARDS.' My hand shook. 'How the *fuck* did you get in here?'

'Guilty,' said Bart Collier, lifting his arms in rueful surrender, a duplicate of my front-door key in one hand. 'Sorry we frightened you. It was supposed to be a surprise.'

'Surprise?' I said. '*Surprise?* I almost had a fucking *stroke*.'

'Well, dear,' said Ron Martinez, the paper's deputy editor, dipping forward for a kiss, 'you're not as young as . . .'

'Thanks,' I said, dazedly allowing him to sandpaper my cheek. 'Thanks a lot.'

I was clearly not going to get that bath.

'Happy birthday, glamorous older woman,' murmured Bart Collier ten minutes later, batting dark lashes at me over the Pol Roger that he had liberated from my fridge.

'Fuck off, Bart,' I said, still angry. 'Just fuck off.'

His eyes flickered round the flat. 'How was the De Milo Clinic?' he asked absently. 'I see surgeons with streaked hair and resort tans, soft peachy lighting, Pachelbel's Canon whispering from the cornices . . .'

'It wasn't a bit like that,' I said. 'The place was like a kind of bankrupt music school, as . . . *crepuscular* and dusty as it could be without actually frightening people away. The doctor – who had me stark naked for the best part of twenty minutes – is creepy in the extreme. And then there's this not quite clean-looking Frenchwoman who does the hard sell afterwards. I gave her your address, so expect some mail for a Miss Alison Littlechild.'

'Why Littlechild?' He raised his eyebrows at a petite, frosty-lipped sub-editor.

'I thought it might make me sound more pliant-seeming.'

'Pliant-seeming.' He touched his glass to his mouth, and lowered his voice. 'You see to your right?'

'Cheryl? The sub?'

'Yes, Cheryl. Did you know she's got a tattoo in her cleavage? She's got this fat little crimson devil sort of . . . stoking downwards with his trident. I've asked her to write a piece about having it done.'

'Women getting tattooed is hardly a new idea.'

'True.' He levelled his eyes amusedly at mine. 'I just thought it might be fun to have the whole process described – you know, the narrow stairs, the smell of surgical spirit, the giggling encouragement of the friends, the uncertain removal of the T-shirt, the needles going in and out, the beads of blood starting to the surface . . .'

'Why not just commission a report for your personal use?'

'You don't feel we have a duty to the wider public?'

'Body-customisation's just DIY for losers who haven't got property to fuck up? It's been done to death.'

'So have all the best stories. They're like nursery rhymes – repetition is all.'

He was silent for a moment. 'The De Milo people . . .' He ran a hand through his hair and frowned at the curtained window. 'Did you tape them?'

'Yes, from my bag. And I'd be writing it up now if you hadn't all . . .'

He jutted his lip like a Kuwaiti child bride denied a charge card.

'Don't be like that, Ali Baba. Don't be horrid. We're your friends. Your life. Your world.' He was still pouting when the opening chords of Maurice Jarre's *Fatal Attraction* score sawed through the flat, and a girl I didn't recognise knelt to adjust the volume. I had suddenly had enough.

'I want that key back *now*, Bart,' I said, my voice level. 'This fucking minute.'

'It's your birthday, Ali Baba. Be nice.'

'*Now*, Bart.'

'Children!' purred Ron, gliding between us, hands held before him in characteristic mid-aria pose. '*Ça suffit!* That perfume's too cheap for you, Alison, don't we pay you enough?' His fingers twitched at my collar. 'And you're *damp*, sweet child.' I glowered, and Bart, bored with my ill-humour, moved off towards the kitchen and Cheryl. Scenting an argument missed, Ron raised an eyebrow. I shrugged.

'Bart,' Ron observed in an exploratory sort of way, moueing Dietrich-like into an imaginary powder compact. 'You do have to admit, he's *wonderfully* preserved . . .'

'At twenty-eight,' I said, holding out my glass to a passing bottle, 'he fucking well ought to be . . . Who the hell are all these people, anyway? Who's that little nugget over there, for example?'

'Hywl Stern. Made that big fly-on-the-wall documentary series about the commissioning editors at Channel Four.'

'And that jail-bait thing with the hair, rifling through my CDs?'

'Jacinta? Our new feature writer. She's a LeQuesne.'

'Ron Martinez, you are so predictable. Can she write?'

'There's no particular reason to suppose so,' he patted an imaginary Jackie Onassis bob, 'but we've got good subs.'

'Including the doubtless soon-to-be-promoted . . .?' I nodded in the direction of Cheryl, who was crabbing towards Bart with a glass of wine in each hand and a pair of newly lit cigarettes in her mouth.

'She's not getting promoted by me. She's too useful where she is.'

'On Bart's face?' I asked, certain that he would repeat it.

'Exactly. *Galloping* into the night like Paul Revere.' He looked at me obliquely. 'Do you mind?'

'Not at all,' I said unconvincingly. 'Really not. There's something a bit unflatteringly . . . *serial*, though, about the way he goes from . . . I mean, honestly, look at her. Have you noticed how there's always this smell of cheap air-freshener round her desk? Like those Christmas tree things you get in mini-cabs?'

'Don't *ever* leave us, Alison,' said Ron, hectic with pleasure. 'You're *far* too venomous to lose.'

'I'm afraid that's not for drinking,' I said, swiping the last bottle of Pol Roger from Jacinta LeQuesne and replacing it with something Australian. 'Have some of this.'

'Thanks. Mmmm. Sorry.' She wiped condensation-damp hands on her skirt and batted away cigarette smoke. 'You're Alison, aren't you? I love your stuff.'

I unfroze a fraction of a degree.

'Thanks. I hear you've started writing for the paper?'

She dragged a thicket of feckless blonde tangle from in front of her face. 'I've filed one or two things.'

'Have they asked you to do anything on your father yet?'

'No. When I was on the diary page they got me to ring him for quotes a few times, but I don't think he's actually *totally* crazy about Ron. Not that they've met, but a couple of years ago Ron ran this horrid review of *The Garden of Reconciliation*. Daddy just calls him 'the spic' now.'

'The spic,' I said. 'Ron would love that.'

'Don't tell him,' begged Jacinta, throwing back the hair, 'or I'm *dogmeat*.'

'Oh, I'm sure he'll go on using you,' I said, kindly. She looked at me sideways, and in the ensuing silence I lit a cigarette.

'I've got some features ideas,' she said eventually, and I blew an interrogative plume of smoke over her shoulder.

'You'll probably think they're not desperately . . . It's just that there are some quite important issues, basically, that I think we should be addressing.'

'Tell.'

A little hesitantly, she told.

'Now why,' I whispered smokily into the honeyed tangle of her hair, 'don't you go and tell Bart Collier what you've just told me? The poor guy's been cornered by that ghastly girl over there – he's been sending up distress flares for the last twenty minutes. Rescue him and he'll love you forever!'

'Really?' asked Jacinta.

'Really,' I assured her. 'She's the sub-editor from hell. Wants to be a writer, can you imagine it?'

'Really?' murmured Jacinta, warming to my complicit tone. Arching an eyebrow, she launched herself and her hair in the direction of Bart and Cheryl.

'And what are you looking so pleased about?' asked Ron

Martinez, materialising at my shoulder. I looked around for an ashtray, and settled for an abandoned wineglass.

'Do you know, Ron, when I first started writing for the paper I used to imagine that you lived in the sacristy of a deconsecrated church on Haverstock Hill furnished only with a walk-in freezer full of virgins' blood and the coffin in which you slept.'

'Haverstock Hill?' said Ron. 'That's not me at all, dear, but talking of freezers, I very much want to do something on this upcoming Reg Garnett installation at the d'Arblay.'

'More sperm and dandruff?'

'He's thought rather bigger this time, my dear, in fact he's thought *biggies*. His new piece is called – wait for it – *Shit Pyramid*.'

'You're not telling me he's . . .'

'I am telling you, darling. He has. It's a thrillingly transgressive project. He's been collecting it for a year now, and freezing it. Each lump has a tiny label on it – date, place of expulsion, that sort of thing.'

'You boys. Whatever will you come up with next?'

He wriggled with pleasure. 'You know the best bit?'

'How can there possibly be a "best bit"?'

'The result is actually rather beautiful. The whole thing's been arranged inside a plate-glass cube, and the temperature is kept so low that it's all gone this wonderful glittering, crystalline, sort of . . . *sugary* white. Like one of those kitschy Nativity scenes. It sets up this fantastic tension between brain and eye. It's about time, it's about age, it's about fear of death, it's about the consumer society, there's a nod to the Pharaohs . . .'

'You've actually seen it?'

'No, it's not in place yet, the gallery sent slides. But there's no question, Garnett's going to be huge. He comes from Liverpool, the d'Arblay PR people promise he's hung on to the accent, and guess what, *his father was a sewage worker*, so there's this fantastic cross-generational . . .'

At this moment Bart, who had been talking to Jacinta, suddenly genuflected and swooped the volume of the hi-fi down to zero. There was an anticipatory silence, and drinks and cigarettes were suspended at half-port. Bart looked around him.

'Anyone by any chance give a flying fuck about the Eastern European refugee situation?' he asked conversationally.

The eyes of my colleagues met; their smiles were politely amused.

'Homeless teenagers?' Bart ventured reasonably, turning from face to face. 'No? No one gives a a toss about homeless teenagers? Deaths in custody, then. Surely someone cares about the DiC figures. *Black* DiCs then? No? No one at all?'

At his side, Jacinta LeQuesne touched her hair, lowered her eyes and fought to retain her smile.

'Sorry, old scout,' Bart said to her cheerfully. 'No cigar. Carry on, everyone.'

'Alison,' said Ron sternly, watching me watching Bart, 'I need my money's worth from that girl.'

'Of course you do,' I agreed. 'I must just ask you something, though, while I remember. What exactly is the origin of the word "spic"?'

An hour later, most of them had gone.

'Thanks for the party,' I said to Bart, who had helped himself to a packet of frozen profiteroles and several bottles of my best white cider. 'Could I have my key now?'

He was silent for a moment, his brow corrugated. 'I'm sorry about that De Milo Clinic article,' he said thickly. 'I shouldn't have sent you.'

It had never taken much with Bart. A few glasses were enough. I sat down at the table opposite him.

'What do you mean, you shouldn't have sent me?'

'I mean I shouldn't have sent *you*, not shouldn't have sent . . . anybody.'

'Why not me? I'd have said I was perfect.'

'No . . . forget it.' He waved the subject erratically away. 'I'm sorry, that's all . . .'

By the front door, one of the picture editors slowed almost to motionlessness in the act of pulling on his leather jacket; at the phone, Jacinta LeQuesne suspended her finger.

'Why don't you tell me some other time, Bart?' I said, advancing on the front door and bird-scaring the picture editor into the corridor as Jacinta, receiver in hand, mouthed me a question.

'Top bell,' I said. 'Park Mansions East.'

'You see,' Bart continued with the careful sincerity which always affected him when drunk, 'I think of your body with *great affection*.'

I saw Jacinta's eyes widen. Behind me, in the silence, I heard the tiny, suctioned gasp of the fridge door closing. This was everybody's birthday, it seemed, except mine.

'Bart, *please*.' I swept a trayful of glasses towards the kitchen. 'This is so *boring*.'

'No, let me finish.' He waved for me to stay. 'I feel bad, you know, really bad. I have respect for your body. *Respect*. It's not there to be . . .' He waved angrily, directionlessly. 'It's *real*, do you understand what I'm saying? It bleeds, it's real, it has functions.'

'So does Grosvenor House,' I snapped. 'Could I have my key?'

'I'll give it to you tomorrow morning,' he promised. He turned blearily to Jacinta. 'I loved your ideas. Really.'

'Didn't you just.' She smiled. 'I think I'll wait for my cab downstairs.'

I said nothing, and the door closed behind her.

'You're not staying, you know,' I told Bart.

'What do you mean, I'm not staying?'

'What I say: you're not staying.'

'Why not?'

'I want to be alone. And soon.'

'You know,' he drawled, 'it's a popular misconception that Greta Garbo said "I want to be alone." What she actually said was: "I want to be a lawn." And now she is one.'

'I'm calling you a taxi. Would you rather a black cab or take your chances with the Swiss Cottage crew?'

'Kiss me, Ali Baba.'

'Don't be disgusting.'

'Let me stay. I won't do anything.'

'What would be the point in your staying, then?'

'I could worship you as you slept.'

'I'd rather you worshipped me from Maida Vale, if it's all the same with you.'

'I love you.'

'Sure you do. And my cheque's in the post.'

Eyes closed, I listened to the sounds of the London night: the ebb and draw of the traffic, the grumble of the fridge, the even fret of Bart's breath. His eyes searched my body, scanning the eggshell freckles at my collarbone, the ghost-pale tan boundaries, the stubbled gathers at my armpits. 'Jupiter and its moon,' he murmured, touching the mole at the outer edge of the aureole of my left breast.

As always when he made the mistake of spending the night with me, Bart was bored. The thing that frustrated him, and I knew this because he had told me so several times, was that the slash-and-burn perversity – his words – that characterised my work was so decisively left behind at the bedroom door. Sex-wise, I was just too conventional. There was no dark-side stuff, no left-hand path, no worship of the Beast.

Drawing his fingers down my ribs, he traced the soft ridged bone. An inch above my hip was a faint Isle-of-Wight-shaped birthmark. For the moment, like my moon of Jupiter, like all my other affecting little puckers and asymmetries, this feature was almost a reason to love me, but by dawn, I knew – by the time the cigarettes had been smoked and we had slept – it would be be a reason to hate me: just one more reminder of the time-lapse corruption and the steady day-by-day dying that he would be embracing if he lashed his life to mine.

As we fucked I watched myself in the dressing-table mirror. Soon, the mirror was a window into another room, and my body that of a stranger. As the stranger rocked taut and gracile astride the headless form beneath her our eyes met in a faint collusive smile – a sad, friends-till-death smile in which, for a time, I was lost. And then we were in separate rooms again and her mouth was opening in a long, soundless cry and she was folding forwards from the waist, seeming to invert, was gone.

'Did you come?' I asked quietly, giving him the drowsy half-smile that instinct told me he feared and would never, as long as he lived, return. Perhaps there was some small cruelty in the question. Perhaps this was the stranger speaking.

He buried his face in the pillow. 'Gentlemen don't come,' he explained, his voice blurred by down filling and despair. 'They arrive.'

'This is *so* unfair,' I said to Bart the next morning. 'They've quoted me completely out of context. Why do all these so-called satirists hate women journalists so much? Why are we always "piss-poor hackettes"?' I had read the piece through five times. It was not due out until next week, but someone at the *Eye* had had the decency to send me an advance copy.

Bart leant heavily over my shoulder. ' "Crypto-fascist Little England intolerance",' he read out, breathing croissant crumbs all over the page. 'Hmmm. We must be getting something right.'

'But it makes me sound so shallow, Bart. And all that "bending the facts" stuff . . .'

'You are shallow, Alison. That's the point of you. The surface is where you operate best, and the surface – now more than ever – needs to be reported on.'

'I don't bend the facts.'

'Alison, this is me, right? You don't have to make excuses, just keep doing what you do.'

'I'm not obsessive, though.'

'You *are* obsessive. Your hates are many and varied and, I have to say, comprehensible only to you. You're the freeway sniper, the random thunderbolt, the slayer of the unrighteous. No one knows where you'll strike next.'

'I'm often very nice about people.'

'Of course. No one would talk to you if you stitched everyone up. It's the not knowing which way you'll jump that people read you for.' He poured the last of the coffee into his cup. 'And that I pay you for.'

I was carrying the percolator over to the sink when the intercom bell rang.

'Who's that?' asked Bart.

I picked up the receiver and listened. 'Courier,' I told him. 'I'll have to go down. Something I have to sign for.'

It turned out to be a Mail Lite bag containing a video and a folder.

' "The Forth Corporation",' read Bart. 'How come they've got your home address?'

'Because, you remember that profile I did of Karen Hassler? Well, she's the Forth Corporation's "face"; she advertises all their perfumes and cosmetics and I had to go through their PR department to get to her.'

'And you were nice about her? Is there some more coffee, by the way?'

'There is if you make it. And we're *always* nice about models. They're capitalism's cherubim and seraphim.'

'You were pretty nasty about little Miss Heart of Darkness.'

'I said she was a bitch. It was intended – and, I'm sure, taken – as a compliment.'

He lifted the coral-pink folder and leafed through the first couple of printed pages. 'They've dumped Hassler,' he said, after a moment. 'They've kicked her out. Listen to this. "The Forth Corporation have much pleasure in announcing that their new face . . ." It's embargoed, for Chrissake. Till *May*. You must have requested all this stuff.'

'I might have done,' I said.

He pushed his plate away from him and planted his elbow on the table and his chin in his hand. 'Who are you writing it for? I won't be angry, just tell me.'

'The Saturday magazine.'

'And you didn't think to ask me first?'

'It's a magazine story, Bart, not a newspaper story. And it's in-house. What's to ask?'

'I'm not going to have Lucy bloody Fane poach my writers, is what. Boozy old slapper. What's the story, anyway?'

I nodded at the folder. 'All I know is they've got a new girl and they'll be shooting a new campaign. Lucy thought it might be interesting to do a process piece: follow the whole thing from scratch.'

'I do just about know what a process piece is.' He scrabbled contemptuously through the folder. 'Dale Cooney.'

'What?'

'That's the name of the new Forth girl. Dale Cooney. Mean anything to you?'

I shook my head. 'Never heard of her. Where's she from?'

In answer, Bart slid the folder across the table and shrugged. 'Does it matter? This isn't a feature you'll be writing, it's a puff, a PR schmooze. You know how much Forth advertising the magazine carries?'

'Bart, I haven't promised I'll do anything for anybody. I just asked them to send me the stuff, OK?'

Bart nodded, and getting to his feet, turned to the window and the leaded roofscape beyond.

'Do you know why you stay with me?' he asked. 'Do you know why you put up with me bullying you and pushing you around and generally making your life unbearable?'

'No' I said. 'Why's that?'

'Because you know that I think you're special. Erratic, rude, antisocial, vindictive – all the signs of the dysfunctional literary spinster, in fact – but special. Do you know what animal you remind me of?'

'I'm sure you're about to tell me.'

'You remind me of a mink. Dark and shining and beautiful and viciously, senselessly destructive.'

For a moment I digested his words in silence. 'Do I shine?' I finally asked.

'You shine,' said Bart. 'I promise you, you shine.'

'People tell me I'm stupid to go on sleeping with you.'

'They're right,' said Bart. 'You are.'

'Can't you even *try* and be faithful to me?'

'I do try,' he said. 'It just doesn't work.'

'But Cheryl,' I said. '*Cheryl.* And that awful security girl from the lobby. And what was the name of that other one, who used to come round with the sandwiches? Kaylie, was it?'

'I can't help it,' said Bart. 'It's their cheap scent and their lower-class haircuts and their tiny little H. Samuel watches. I just get overwhelmed by this sort of *nostalgie de la boue*.'

I reached for my cigarettes. 'Well, I just want you to know that if I meet someone else that I want to do it with then I will too, and unhesitatingly and without consulting you. Deal?'

'Deal. The thing you're absolutely not allowed to do is write for anyone else.' Leaning over the back of my chair he put his arms round me. 'But I do love you.'

'Don't be ridiculous. And stop that this instant. And pass me that ashtray.'

'I do, Ali Baba, I love you. I invented you, after all. You're my creation. How could I not love you?'

3

The pavements were still galvanised with frost when I reached Camberley. I parked in Balaclava Road rather than block my parents' small drive, and walked round the corner to the house.

My father was kneeling on a plastic fertiliser sack on the frozen lawn, cutting back a rose bush. At his side lay a neat pile of cuttings, and on the red-brick garden wall the radio was relaying rugby news. At my approach he inserted his gloved hands into the base of the bush, effected a single judicious cut, and dragged out a long, trailing branch.

'Thorns we can do,' he observed, clipping the branch into pencil-sized lengths. 'Offshoots, that's a little harder.'

'If that's some kind of gnomic request for grandchildren,' I said, 'it has been duly noted.'

He nodded, and pondered the orange plastic handles of the secateurs. 'Come in the car?'

'No, Dad, I walked.'

'Ah'. He moved to the next bush, frowningly parted the stems. Over the years Dad's reputation as a gardener had grown apace, and his birthdays become an orgy of trugs, trowels and slug bait. That said, he had never really been a man for all seasons. He was unmoved by the drowsy blooms of summer; what he really liked was the bite of winter, the cutting back, the reduction of abundance to basic geometry. In the Far East, according to Mum, he never lifted a finger outside the house, although they had a large enough garden. But at that time, I suppose, he had his work.

My eyes drifted to Orde's silver Daewoo, and Dad nodded. 'Got here early.'

'And . . .?'

'Uh-huh.' The secateurs were deployed. 'Her too. The Wendy. Interesting-looking girl, in her way. She's inside patronising your mother.'

'How is Mum?'

'Oh . . . all right. She always gets a bit unhinged at this time of year, of course, babbling of green fields and so forth.'

'Why don't you let me buy you both a holiday? You could go to Singapore – stay with Jack and Dawn for a couple of weeks.'

'Doubt they could afford to have us. They live very quietly these days – no car any more, no more golf, no Philomena . . . And according to Dawn, Jack wets himself every ten minutes, poor old bugger. Apparently it's made things rather difficult at the club.'

'They should move back here.'

'That's what your mother told them. Jack's answer was that they've just had this new bathroom put in – special ramps and so on, the works, completely busted them – and they're determined to get their money's worth.'

'Well, why not a cruise then? Mum'd love a cruise.'

'Bingo and shuffleboard and cha-cha-cha at teatime? Charlie and Mavis Leathwaite went on one of those jaunts up and down the West African coast. They're both pretty ga-ga now, but Charlie swears they were the youngest on board by at least twenty years. People send their parents away on these equatorial cruises, you see, hoping they'll peg out at sea and save the expense of a funeral. Charlie's ship put ashore at Cabinda to take on a consignment of Black Forest gateau and it turned out the whole lot was infected with plague. He went on deck with a whisky one night and swears he found the crew tipping a pile of corpses in evening dress over the side to the sharks. Swiftian experience, apparently. Some of them weren't even dead.'

'Defoe. And does that mean no, by any chance?'

'We're not unhappy people, Alison. We lead full and, if I might say so, *varied* lives. I have my weeding and the bowls club. Your mother has the dog and her mail-order catalogues. It's a heady . . .'

'Oh, fuck off, Dad! I'll take Mum to the Seychelles for six months and we'll leave you here to rot in your mulch. Miserable old sod. What's for lunch?'

The secateurs were slipped into a pocket of his khaki slacks, the clippings rolled up in the fertiliser bag for burning at some later date. 'Lamb, I think. Come and meet the Wendy.'

'Dad, you behave yourself with her.'

He peered at me over the heavy yellow frames of his glasses, pretending senile myopia.

'And don't look at me like that; you know perfectly well what you're capable of.' Against the frozen white of the lawn and the drive the pebbledashed villa was a dull nicotine brown. We made our way inside.

After the clean cold air of the garden, the gas-fired fug was almost palpable. I hung my coat next to a brand new Barbour jacket with a pheasant brooch pinned to the collar, which had to be Wendy's. In the sitting room, Orde was toasting his corduroyed thighs at the red-brick hearth. Adjacent to him in her rocker-recliner my mother was a Crimplened sphinx, her ruined bulk loose-covered, her arms lying heavy along the arms of the chair as if awaiting electrocution. At her feet, his body intermittently shuddering with flatus, was the brindle-coated figure of Gunner, the retriever who – in my memory at least – had never retrieved. It was stiflingly, flush-makingly hot. Wendy was one of those biggish blonde girls you see in skiing-holiday photographs in other people's houses. She had been awarded the 'best' chair, a hideously uncomfortable Victorian creation upholstered in a kind of woven wire purpose-made to stab the thighs and snag the tights of anyone wearing anything flimsier than motorcycle leathers.

'Alison dear,' said my mother, raising a heavy, cigarette-bearing hand, 'Orde, darling . . .?'

Orde swallowed heftily, placed his Carlsberg can on the fireplace and gestured vaguely at the space between us. 'Mmmm, Wendy, sorry, this is my sister Alison; Ali, this is . . .'

She smiled uncertainly, made as if to stand, and I hurriedly waved her back to a sitting position.

'Has anybody given you a drink yet?' I asked her.

'Mmmmm!' Brighter now, she raised a tumbler of gin and tonic from the carpet and went into several seconds of pseudo-inebriate head-lolling and jaw-dropping, suddenly reassembling her features with a high-pitched machine-gun giggle.

For a moment nobody moved or made a sound, and then, mentally awarding her a straight ten on the Richter scale of unhinged nervous reactions, I offered her my 555 packet. She grabbed one – 'All the vices, I'm afraid!' – and released another shrieking volley of giggles. I turned to Orde for his reaction but he reared his chin like the Duke of Edinburgh and looked away.

Orde, a major in the army, was a press officer for the MoD, and looked older and tireder than his thirty-five years. It hadn't always been thus. When I was at university in Exeter he was a recently commissioned second lieutenant, and on the couple of occasions that he visited me caused a positively Pride and Prejudicial flutter in the chests of the Home County-reared princesses who were reading English with me. The princesses, in consequence – although this was not their wont with stroppy suburbanites who said 'toilet' and 'pardon' – cut me considerable social slack; and if I never had much to say to them, I was happy enough to lurk around the fringes of their summer Pimm's parties and country cottage weekends.

Mum was the only one of us who could lay claim to any kind of pedigree. The process of disguising it, I suspect, began that morning on the Changi Ferry when she agreed to marry Dad, who even then took a perverse pride in describing himself as 'not quite out of the bottom drawer'. She had expected family opposition, Carteret and Keene being very much a major concern in Singapore at the time, but to her surprise had encountered none. 'He's rather *plain*, dear' was the worst that her mother had found to say of the clever, awkward, bullish young Special Branch officer. 'But if you're sure . . .'

Being sure, as it turned out, was not quite enough. The world that they created for each other, my parents discovered, functioned perfectly for the two of them but very poorly indeed when anyone else was around. And Singapore being Singapore, someone else invariably was. Dad worked impossible hours, and was forbidden to discuss any of it, and wives were expected to pull together. There was a police social club, but Mum found she had little in common with the Port 'n Lemons, as she came to call them, and there were Dad's jazz evenings, but Mum couldn't see the point of jazz. She did her best to be a good police wife, but her abiding memory, she once told me, was of endless afternoons in the Serangoon Road clubhouse, playing halma and piecing together Lakeland jigsaw puzzles and listening to the rain drumming on the corrugated-iron roof.

At what stage her drinking reached problem proportions I never really discovered. From the stories that people like Jack and Dawn told it was clear that everyone used to put away a fair bit in those days, and you could collapse drunk every night for a year before anyone saw you as having a medical rather than a purely social problem. What was not in question was that it was her drinking which finished Dad's Special Branch career and forced him, via the backwaters of military liaison, into the dim, dull, no-questions-asked world of corporate security. And even then – early seventies it must have been – you could still see from the photos what a beauty she was before the eyes grew vague and secretive and the puffy booze-flesh overlaid the fine Carteret bones. Poor Mamma; looking back, I had the impression that she raised Orde and myself in something close to total silence. Perhaps she was terrified of transmitting whatever it was that had led her to lose control of her life. And looking at my brother through her eyes, immersing myself for a moment in her maternal fatalism, I could see that the suit-and-tie job at the Ministry had taken its toll. His collars had tightened, his rugger muscles had softened and the cavalry shine had departed him. And while I knew that he still went through the motions of working and playing hard, I suspected that his heart was no longer in any of it.

'In those days, of course,' Dad was telling Wendy, blinking as he polished his glasses, 'we made our own fun. For the long winter nights there was the wireless and my beer-mat collection, in the summer there were the stones on the drive to be whitewashed . . . It was a pretty hectic time, let me tell you!'

'I'm sure,' said Wendy, spoiling the deadpan response with a panicked whinny.

'So how exactly did you two meet?' I asked.

'Hoolie at Charlie Harrington's,' said Orde. He glanced conspiratorially at Wendy, who exhaled smoke.

'What happened,' she said, 'was that we'd been racing at

Sandown and got back and Charlie had made all these slammers, which of course . . . um . . .'

'. . . we drank,' suggested Orde encouragingly.

'We drank,' confirmed Wendy. 'And then I don't know whose idea it was but we all decided to get into our cars wearing nothing except our trilbys and drive round and round the drive?' She had that mannerism, borrowed from Australian soap operas and au pairs, of ending every sentence on an interrogative up-note. 'And then . . .' she went on, 'what's his name?'

'Roley?'

'Roley. Well Roley only goes into a handbrake turn, right? And I'm behind him, OK? And . . .'

'. . . And the next thing you know,' said Orde indulgently, 'your wheels are throwing up more turf than a polo pony and you're nine inches deep in Mrs Harrington's prize lawn.'

'Exactly,' said Wendy.

'Well, goodness,' I said. 'The lives you all lead.'

'Do they really give prizes for lawns?' asked Mum, very quietly, and I was suddenly aware of the Sunday sounds, of the bubbling wheeze of the fire, Gunner's twitching snores, the measured ticking of the clock. Wendy noticed these things too. I felt her gaze follow mine along the red-tiled mantelpiece, noting the seed catalogues, the Benares brass ornaments, the bound editions of Reader's Digest classics against the yellowing stucco walls. These things had been as they were for as long as I could remember. My father was not a man who espoused change for change's sake, and my mother was not one to venture an opinion on such subjects. The house, which had previously been owned by a dentist (the lounge was his surgery), had last been redecorated in 1980, the year that my parents moved in.

'I might get some gravy on,' said Dad, half turning to Mum. 'Have we still got a splash of that Valpolicella?'

'So what are you up to these days?' Orde murmured. 'Anything I should know about?' Not untypically, he had waited until Mum and Dad had disappeared into the kitchen and Wendy had gone for a pee before addressing me directly. Given the differences in our natures, we were a little self-conscious about our familial closeness. As a result we tended to ignore one another in small-talk situations, reserving ourselves for shorter, more intense face-to-faces.

'Usual,' I said. 'Nothing you'll get your chain rattled for.'

'Bloody hope not. That shore-leave article went down like a turd in a punchbowl. Hell d'you think you were doing?'

'I just went out with some sailors on a piss-up, Orde. I mean it's not as if people don't know that those navy boys like a pint or two. And it didn't involve you. I set it up direct.'

'Everyone knows you're my sister, for Chrissake, how stupid do you think those people are? You made them come across like serial rapists – all that stuff about first you trap it, then you . . .'

'I know, I'm sorry, they were rather too good to be true, weren't they? They just couldn't resist talking dirty in front of a girlie, and I'm afraid I just couldn't resist quoting them. But there was lots of positive stuff, it wasn't all trapping and shagging and pants-on-head.'

'What was there you could possibly call . . .?'

'That bit about how to cook a pizza in a trouser press, for example. That was sweet. And *vis-à-vis* trouser-related activities, is this love?'

'Is what love?'

'Miss Naked except for her Trilby.'

'D'you like her?'

'What's she do?'

'What d'you think?'

'I don't know. Estate agent? Business lunches? Tell me.'

'She's the women's national clay pigeon shooting champion. There, I thought that might shut you up.'

'I'm impressed. Truly I am. But doesn't that pouter-pigeon chest of hers . . .?'

'No it bloody well doesn't. Honestly, Ali.'

'So?'

'So what?'

'So is it love?'

'She's nice. We get on fine. And she's a big name in that world. Endorsements and stuff. Are you still . . .?' He drained his Carlsberg, belched, and covered his mouth.

'With Bart? Yes.'

'So what's the plan?'

'I've been working on various things,' I said, deliberately misconstruing his question. 'Profiles, investigations . . . usual stuff.'

'Cerebral as ever?'

'You know your sis.'

By the time I got back to London the light was almost gone. Strange knocking sounds had been coming from beneath the bonnet of the Capri, so I hadn't pushed it too hard round the M25. There were no urgent e-mails or phone messages waiting for me in the flat, so I percolated some Lavazza, put on Jerry Goldsmith's *Chinatown* score, kicked off my shoes and opened the Laurene Forth folder.

Despite Bart's disparaging comments I was sure that there was a strong magazine feature to be written about the construction and politics of a new beauty products campaign. It was models, money and movies rolled into one: a world to which – in my opinion, at least – the average reader would be only too grateful to be transported on a rainy Saturday afternoon.

Forth's new face, I read, was going to be an American actress called Dale Cooney. I'd never heard of her. There were two pictures of Cooney, so dissimilar that they could have been of different people. The first showed a slight, anonymous-looking girl with scraped-back hair and greyish eyes walking past a row of garment shops in – I would guess – one of the less upscale parts of Manhattan. She was dressed in tracksuit pants and a short-sleeved sweater and carrying a brown grocery bag, and looked annoyed to have been waylaid. The second picture was a studio portrait, full face, and here the angular planes of her face – almost feral in three-quarter shot – seemed to have been smoothed back to frame the level gaze. The ratty, home-blonded hair now fell shining and fluent around the heart-shaped face, and even her eyes seemed to have changed: the colourless side-glance was now a sure dark azure regard. In a curious way, however, the first picture was the more direct of the two. Even if unwillingly, she was addressing the photographer, the human being. In the second, the apparent blaze of intimacy was for the camera.

Was she attractive? Hard to say. She looked difficult, evasive, troubled, not sexy. 'A Beauty for our Times' they'd tagged her. Well, she was certainly camera-beautiful, and I could see immediately why Forth had gone for her. She had the sort of looks you could overlay with any amount of contemporary attitude; the classicism would always shine through. It was still a radical piece of casting, though. Beauty product faces were usually known to the industry, and usually brought with them a certain amount of reputation and connection and professional background. This girl was a complete outsider, and if I'd never heard of her, then the punters certainly wouldn't have. They didn't mention Karen Hassler's name in the press release, but it was clear that they'd got shot of their previous face mid-contract. What was the story there, I wondered. She would have taken them for serious money. You didn't diss Hassler and walk away unscathed.

Along with a video, Forth had also sent out an article from *Manhattan* magazine's recent Hollywood edition. This was useful: if I ever got round to writing the story there would be plenty of sleek copy I could plunder. The piece was headlined 'The Natural'.

The *Stillwater* girl runs deep, discovers CARLY GRUNEFELD.

The trailer parks around Eugene, Oregon, have gentle, melancholy names like Lonesome Fir, Arbor Fields, River Glade and The Cedars. Come home, these names seem to say, for here you will find rest. In truth there is little that is restful about such places; for all their self-containment, the parks tend to a shiftless and fractured disorder. People appear, stay awhile, and move on. Homes are regularly repossessed. The incidence of antisocial behaviour is high.

Havenwood, set on the otherwise featureless expanse between the Junction City railroad and the confluence of the McKenzie and Willamette Rivers, is typical of the area's smaller parks. Its homes, hunkering on brick-piles against the wind of the plain, give an impression of elephantine age, of having lined the cracked asphalt lanes forever. Step back for the wider picture and the park is all but lost, an insubstantial jumble against the white skies and the dull glitter of the rivers.

For all the park's invisibility, however, entire lives are lived here. In addition to spaces for a hundred and twenty trailers, Havenwood has a management and rentals office, a general store – Ray 'n' Eve's – and a laundromat. Until last March there was also a beauty salon called Laurette's. The salon burnt down – or was torched, nobody knows for sure – and has not yet been rebuilt. All that remains is a rusted angle-iron skeleton and two charred concrete support blocks.

The original proprietor of Laurette's was Laurette Cooney. Born of unknown parents and raised in a children's home, Cooney worked as a beauty salon assistant in Eugene before moving to Havenwood and buying an elderly single-wide trailer. There, she met Peter Lunev, a Vietnam veteran attempting to establish himself as a comic-book illustrator. They had two daughters: Dale, born in 1978, and DuToine, born a year later. One morning in 1982 Laurette awoke to discover that Lunev was gone. Neither she, Dale nor DuToine have seen or heard from him since.

Laurette borrowed $200 from a neighbour and converted the trailer to a daytime beauty salon. 'She put up a fancy mirror and lights,' recalls Jim Lusk, a long-term resident. 'They did facials, manicure, that kinda stuff.'

'The girls helped Laurette from the start,' remembers Ciss Levitt, a former neighbour. 'Dale especially – she was such a cutie-pie. I used to call her Cowboy.'

Dale and DuToine Cooney went to school in Eugene but the girls' attendance record was poor. In 1994, aged fourteen, DuToine gave birth to a son and moved to Eugene to live with the parents of the child's father. Dale remained to help her mother. One night in January 1995 a drunken Havenwood resident discharged an automatic weapon near the Cooneys' trailer. Four rounds struck Laurette in the head and chest, killing her instantly; Dale, sleeping two metres away, was unhurt.

'She took it hard,' says Ciss Levitt. 'Of course she did. But then she was one tough little stud. She buried her mother, gave evidence against Paulie (Paul Cvetic, the neighbour), and got right on with business.'

Business was variable. For two years Dale Cooney ran the salon single-handed. She was popular enough, but there do not seem to have been any boyfriends.

'Truth is,' says Jim Lusk, 'no one ever thought of Dale as any great Hollywood-type beauty. She kept herself looking nice – no tattoos, trailer-trash stuff like that – and one time I think she entered the Junction City beauty pageant. That was about the limit of it, though. What happened later no one could have guessed.'

What happened was that Hollywood came to Havenwood. Or rather, to Arbor Fields, a half-dozen miles away, where Georgia Dionno was shooting *Plains Song*. The film called for a scene in which police searched a trailer park for two teenaged thieves; Arbor Fields had been selected as suitable and a number of locals, Dale Cooney amongst them, had been recruited as background artists. During a break in filming Cooney made her way to the make-up trailer to enquire about training as a film make-up artist. At that moment Bradley Carver, a supporting actor, was having a wound section applied to his face, and Dionno was in attendance.

'I wasn't allowed to move,' remembers Carver, 'so I couldn't see all of what happened. I heard it, though.'

Dionno was looking for a character of Cooney's age to enact a brief non-speaking sequence, written into the film that morning, whereby a running FBI agent is deliberately tripped up by a friend of the young thieves he is pursuing. The script called for a 'gum-chewing, wise-ass, jailbait type'.

'Georgia asked Dale to test for the part,' says Carver. 'Which was kind of unusual for a thirty-second silent sequence. Dale was cool, though. She just said, like, yeah. No problem. I think her main buzz was that she would be getting paid actors' rates.'

A screen test was arranged, and recently I watched the three-minute sequence with Georgia Dionno in the edit suite at the director's home in Alpena, Michigan. The opening shot establishes a deserted avenue between two lines of trailers and worn-out cars; the avenue stretches to a hazy infinity. From behind a flatbed truck, Cooney moves into frame. In the bleaching midday light, she seems to waver, to shimmer. She approaches, striding towards us, but as a result of the foreshortening effect of the narrow-angle lens, she appears to get no nearer. At the same time, as she grows in the frame, something extraordinary happens. She seems to dissolve in the camera's regard; all tension lifts, all expression departs. The sky-blue gaze empties, becomes void, engages all and nothing before her. This is not the glib professional absence of the catwalk model – there is no haughty sublimation here, no vanishing into self-regard – but an instinctive process of elimination. I am becoming nothing, say those distanceless eyes, so that I may become whatever it is necessary for me to become.

'She was like glass,' says Dionno. 'Absolutely transparent. A natural.'

Plains Song was a modest success, and Cooney and the salon enjoyed a brief local celebrity. According to Jim Lusk it did not occur to Cooney to further capitalise on the experience. A year later, however, Georgia Dionno returned to Oregon to audition her for the lead in *Stillwater.*

'To be honest, no one expected great things of the project,' says Dionno. 'I was pegged as a competent director of small-scale pictures that would rack up polite reviews and earn out on video, so there were certain risks I could afford to take. Like hiring Dale, for example.'

Adapted from the novel *Thief River Story* by Jonathan Duelle, *Stillwater* is a courtroom drama. As Donna Shelest, the young wife accused of murdering her much older husband, Cooney assumes the taut, frozen luminescence of the Minnesota winter. Unconcerned at the possibility of conviction – wishing for it, even – her character refuses to assist her attorney with so much as a word, and gradually we understand that the question is not whether she killed her husband, but why. As the truth emerges, and with it the possibility of her acquittal, she seems to splinter before our eyes.

Only time will tell whether *Stillwater* enjoys a mainstream success or fades into obscurity. What is not in doubt, however, is that the film marks the emergence of a mesmerising new talent. Cooney's performance is unwavering in its certainty, and it is almost impossible to believe that, to all intents and purposes, this is her first film role. As well as an actress of startling promise, Dale Cooney is also that least definable of creatures, a true American beauty. 'What Dale Cooney has physically,' says the critic Paula Swenson, 'are all those abstract-sounding but actually very specific qualities of symmetry, proportion and line. It isn't a turn-round-and-stare thing, it's more something that gradually dawns on you. My God, you realise, she's absolutely perfect. And once you're in on the secret you can't take your eyes off her.'

David Eckhardt, the producer of *Stillwater*, agrees. 'Dale has a subtle kind of appeal on film which leads people to think that they – and only they – fully appreciate her. Her admirers are really quite secretive and possessive about her – women as well as men.'

Dale Cooney has never agreed to be interviewed, and according to drama coach Sam Bartelski, whose workshop she attends, the idea of talking about herself 'literally appals her'. 'Anything I have to say,' she once told Paula Swenson, 'I say on screen. I'm just an actor.' Off screen, Cooney evinces a sort of edgy vacancy. In photographs she tends to look wary, aggressive even. She has not revisited Oregon since the making of *Stillwater* and now lives in a small apartment on Manhattan's Upper East Side found for her by Georgia Dionno. Her friends – Dionno, Bartelski and the handful of fellow actors who make up her circle – are fiercely protective of her. Her agent, Merv Bergman at TCA, will neither confirm nor deny that Cooney is committed to any specific projects in the future. There is an almost palpable closing of ranks. 'It's as if she's armouring herself,' says one colleague. 'Making her privacy inviolable.'

'She knows that she's going to be a star,' explains Georgia Dionno. 'She knows that, for better or for worse, it's going to happen. And she's preparing herself.'

I replaced the article in the Forth folder. The video was of *Stillwater*. I guessed I was going to have to watch it.

4

As the cleaning lady hummed and hoovered around my feet I skimmed through the De Milo Clinic piece, ran a word-count, and e-mailed the copy to Bart's desk. This technology, which allowed me to earn a sizeable slice of my living in a Japanese dressing gown and bare feet, was easy to love. And if the persona which I adopted for the purpose was slightly less so, well, I didn't have to be her for too many hours a day. On my desk, in a rather nasty Perspex frame with the newspaper's name stamped along the bottom, was the photograph which appeared, postage-stamp size, alongside my byline. It had been taken at a Chalayan show three years ago (thoughtful, hair up, pen pressed to lips) and didn't look anything like me at all, but I kept it there to remind myself of the voice the readers expected to hear.

In the bathroom, I ran a comb through my wet hair, felt the blunt dark quills fall wet to my neck. Smearing a reflective arc on the mirrored wall, I regarded my pale, steam-blurred features. *Vogue* had rung me asking if they could feature me in a 'women in media' piece. There would be a studio session with DuChevalier, new clothes to keep, all the usual enticements. If I was going to say no – and I suspected that I was going to say no – it was because some tiny but insistent voice had always told me to remain a name rather than become a face, to let people construe whatever they needed from the inky little portrait that they saw in the paper.

Wrapping the kimono about me, I went through to the bed-room. The faint residual smell of cigarettes had been replaced by that of Windolene. A knotted black plastic rubbish bag stood by the door. Picking up the phone by my bed, I pressed one of the memory buttons.

'Tracey? It's Alison MacAteer. Are you free for lunch?'

The skies were heavy and the Brompton Road was dark with rain as I stepped from the taxi outside Harrods. It wasn't quite eleven o'clock but the day had already surrendered to the weather's overbearing chill, and I hurried for the warmth and the powdered comforts within.

Of all London's cultural establishments, the Harrods Cosmetics Hall is the most beautiful and the most atmospheric. With its low ceilings, etched glass panels and illuminated pillars the room has always reminded me of the salon of some great ocean liner. The dominant tones are oyster pink and black lacquer; silk pastel roses tumble from urns, gilded blackamoors and wood nymphs stand guard on plinths, and everywhere is a heady artifice. Indulge yourself, the room seems to whisper, this is the new Elysium: you need not die.

It was the customers, of course, who spoilt everything – as they always spoil everything – and many of them seemed to be dying even as I watched. Watery eyes flickered fearfully about them, sallow jowls trembled above cashmere coat-collars, liver-spotted fingers reached hesitantly for the latest rejuvenant salves and creams. Behind the counters the assistants observed them with a shrewd, doll-like vacancy from which, I noted, pity was not entirely absent. Perhaps they saw something of their future selves in the faces of their customers.

The Laurene Forth area occupied most of one wall. Above the display hung a huge illuminated transparency showing Karen Hassler dressed in a diaphanous shift and standing on a deserted beach over whose intense azure horizon distant clouds were forming. *QUATRIEME* read the legend. *GO FORTH.* To one side of this stood the Laurene Forth Treatment Room, a miniature pavilion sealed from the gaze of the curious by venetian blinds and containing a white towelling-covered day-bed. Half beach hut and half operating theatre, the Treatment Room was staffed by a team of white-coated female acolytes. It was a curious look: their uniform suggested the luxuriously paramedical, but their make-up had been applied as if for a *commedia dell'arte* performance.

'Hi,' said one lip-glossed Columbine. 'Help you at all?'

'Just looking,' I murmured. The air was heavy with the scent of Quatrième, with which a young man with a well-patted chin and an improbable moustache was spraying all who passed. At the counter behind him the various primers, toners, cleansers, serums, balms, masks, gels and emulsions stood translucent in their smoothly ground bottles against panels of cool white light.

'Why don't you sit down?' suggested Columbine, indicating an etched glass table and a leatherette chair. From the table's centre she raised a circular mirror, angling it so that an enlarged version of my face looked quizzically back at me, and for a full minute left me and my reflection in silent mutual contemplation.

By the time her carnivalesque features appeared beside mine I was hypnotised, for when I was not actually staring into a mirror, I used to forget – literally forget – what I looked like. I just couldn't summon up any kind of picture of myself in my mind. Whenever I was reunited with my image, in consequence, it was the occasion of a certain amazement.

How other people saw me I have no idea. My skin was London-pale, my hair dark, my face oval. Against the words 'Distinguishing Marks' in my old passport I had written 'None'. If I was being kind to myself I would say that I had the sort of looks which were susceptible to others' fantasies, by which I mean that I could be whatever they wanted me to be, and if I was being objective I would say that I looked completely anonymous. I wasn't the type that people turned round and stared at in the street, but I was nicotine-thin and I had my mother's bones; Bart and others before him had called me beautiful, but perhaps that's what men always call short-tempered girlfriends who show signs of wanting to go straight to sleep.

'Have you tried our new bio-tech and phyto-tech ranges?' asked Columbine.

'Tell me about them,' I said.

I didn't really listen, but then I suspect people rarely do. She talked about the virtual complexion, she talked about antioxidants and hydrators, she talked about lipids and silicas and sensories. And in the end I bought a heavy little glass-stoppered bottle of something or other; not because I needed it – I could have rung their press office and had them deliver a truckload – but because the act of purchase was part of the ritual which had begun when I had walked into the cosmetic hall in the first place. Only if I paid for it in person would this small, synthetic preparation be a meaningful gift to myself; only if the price-tag really stung would it represent a true token of self-love. Than which, let's face it, there's no greater intimacy.

At La Lupara I asked for a table by the window. The restaurant was not quite warm enough, and no more than half full, and as I waited for Tracey Decker I tapped my teeth with a breadstick and stared unfocused into the dull grey wash of Knightsbridge. Vaguely, I wondered whether to order wine. I was early out of professional habit, and Tracey was invariably late.

I lit a cigarette that I didn't particularly want and was suddenly irritated by the anticipation of her avaricious and self-centred presence. By the time she arrived, looking and smelling – as usual – like an unmade bed, the waiter was pouring my second glass of Frascati. In the course of slipping Tracey's chair behind her knees he stared long and hard down her front, which neither pleased nor displeased her.

'So, Alison,' she asked, holding out her glass straight-armed to the still-hovering waiter and looking around her in brittle, first-of-the-day anticipation ('Mmm, yeah, up to the top'), 'how's it all going, then? Sorry to be . . . I couldn't *believe* this fuckin' bus-driver . . .'

In retrospect, I suppose, and even if only because I was paying for the privilege, I should have listened more carefully to everything Tracey had to say. Once kick-started she had a tendency to flit, promiscuous of subject, but at the same time to become nervous if I bore down on her. I had found that it was easiest to let my attention wander but to remain reactive, like a telephone intercept, to certain key words and phrases.

As things were, it wasn't until she mentioned a new boyfriend that I really started listening, and it was at that point that I noticed that the waiters and the barman had formed a motionless tableau at the entrance to the kitchen and were staring at her in dream-like silence.

What exactly was it about Tracey, I wondered, that made men behave so oddly? Possibly it was to do with a curious impression that she gave of mistaken identity, of being an altogether different person than that suggested by her stale, overtight clothes and slept-in make-up. For overlaying her rank, skunkish sexuality was a curious silent-film quality, something sad and obliquely familiar of which she herself seemed unaware. Men were drawn to her with something like desperation. Bosses mostly, orderers of events. I think they sensed that there was something wrongly set about her, something that they wanted to first exploit and then correct. What I could also see was that when they failed (for Tracey's strength, and her weakness, was her absolute unreachability), they would want to hurt her, to slap her around, to leave her on a worse heading than before.

Until a year ago, Tracey Decker had been working flexi-hours on the men's toiletries counter in a department store in St Albans, where she had been spotted and given the chat by Howard Harvey, proprietor of HCM (Harvey Celebrity Management) Ltd of Wardour Street, London. Harvey was in St Albans for a promotional event involving a local football team, and impressed by his metropolitan manner and his lavish purchasing of state-of-the-art grooming products, Tracey had allowed herself to be schmoozed. She had attended the promotion at Harvey's side, and afterwards had been treated to the evening of her life in the town's premier night spot where, as she put it to me later, the tiger prawns and the cocktails flowed like wine. Early the next morning, in a motel off the M11 – where she had been particularly taken with the deepness of the carpet and the weight of the onyx ashtrays ('talk about four star!') – she had been bedded by Harvey. He had made it clear that a glittering future awaited her, had spoken easily of film roles, first nights, personal appearances . . .

That had been a year ago. Since then, things had not quite gone as Tracey expected. After that first night at the hotel, for example, Harvey had appeared to lose interest in her sexually. She had shrugged her shoulders about that, however, because professionally things had seemed to be All Systems Go. She had been summoned to the coral-carpeted office above the dry-cleaner's in Wardour Street, had been sat in the large top-floor room hung with framed celebrity photographs, and been given the name of the photographer who was to prepare her 'portfolio'. While she had been perched on the edge of the oxblood chesterfield, the PA had announced a call from Jack Nicholson in Hollywood.

'Tell Jack I'm in a meeting,' Harvey had airily dismissed her. 'He can try calling back in an hour.'

'Will do, Howard,' said the PA, who, Tracey had hardly been able to help noticing, could easily have been in the glamour business herself.

'Tell him,' Harvey added, as if as an afterthought, 'that I've got someone here he might well like to meet.'

That had done it for Tracey, really. The photo session had not been quite what she had expected when she borrowed the £350 fee from her parents (the 'glamour' poses, in particular, had come as something of a surprise), and the classes at The Actors' Studio seemed to be taking a longish time to arrange. But that said, no one could deny that she was seeing life. Several times a week a number of Howard Harvey's friends and clients would gather in the VIP suite at The Pinafore Club in Beak Street – an enterprise in which Harvey had a financial interest – and Tracey was always on the invitation list at the door.

She tended to a certain vagueness when describing these evenings to me. It was clear that as well as Harvey's 'celebrity' clients (Jack, as Tracey already thought of him, had not showed up yet, although Howard assured her that he always looked in when he was in town), there was a shifting cast of tabloid journalists, satellite TV presenters and the like, and that an inner circle usually 'went on' from The Pinafore to someone's town house or flat. Often they would make their way to the suite above Harvey's Wardour Street office, and there, said Tracey, without particular embarrassment, they played Pass the Parcel. Harvey's version of the game was a variation on the old car-keys-in-the-hat routine, and it never really came as a surprise to Tracey when she was led upstairs to the room with the foldaway bed and the box of man-size tissues. Because 'being a good girl', Harvey emphasised to Tracey, was necessary for her career. These people had major influence. They were 'big time players'. They could help.

Tracey, though, was not without a certain *farouche* cunning. In a desk drawer in Harvey's office she had seen a videotape labelled Decker/Vaughan. Since, two nights before, she had been the Pass the Parcel prize of Darren Vaughan, an up-and-coming show-biz astrologer, she guessed that their time together had somehow been taped. That night at The Pinafore she had told several of the other girls whose careers Harvey was handling of her suspicions. They laughed. 'Howard always watches,' they said. 'He always records it. Didn't you know?'

When she discovered the videotape, Tracey had called me by name at the newspaper. Interested, I had lunched her. At first, the scent of Ambre Solaire and piña colada already in her nostrils, she had wanted to sell me what she persisted in calling 'her exclusive' for fifty thousand pounds and a fortnight in Antigua.

Gently, I had put her in the picture. To nail Harvey, I explained, even though I personally believed her, we would need more than just her version of events. I told her about sworn affidavits, about copyright, about defamation of character; I mentioned Harvey's parliamentary contacts, and I told her exactly what an expert libel lawyer – and Harvey would certainly hire the best – would do to her in court.

She'd gone quiet on me then, as I knew she would. Why didn't we just keep in touch? I suggested. The drinks and the lunches would be on me, and if she put me on to any stories that made their way into print, I'd make sure she got a finder's fee.

And that was how it had been. We'd meet, she'd talk, I'd listen. It was painless enough; I already had half a dozen such arrangements up and running.

'So tell me about this new boyfriend, Tracey.'

'Yeah, I'm getting to that . . . Mm, this wine is really nice.' She raised her glass in a toast to the assembled waiters, chefs and kitchen porters who, together with their grandfathers, uncles, brothers and male cousins, were hanging purposefully around the entrance to the kitchen. '*Molto bianco!*'

I could have stripped stark naked and stood on my head and they wouldn't have noticed me. 'Go on,' I said testily.

'Yeah . . . where was I?' She turned to me suspiciously. 'Don't get *cross*, yeah, I'm telling you, OK? Like I said, two people have given me mobile phones in the last ten days. One of them was

Howard, and the other . . .?'

'The other?'

'The other,' said Tracey, with the uncertain triumph of the cat who after being kicked around the kitchen a few times has unexpectedly happened upon the cream. 'The other was Dan Fortess.'

There was a sudden emptiness behind my ribs, and I froze, my glass halfway to my mouth.

'Dan Fortess . . . the *actor*?'

'Don't look so surprised, Ali. Yeah, Dan Fortess the actor.'

*

When I was twenty, and just out of university, I rode shotgun with a photographer. At twenty-seven, Hal West was already one of London's big five paparazzi, and for the three months that we stayed together we had a lot of strange fun. He was a tall man, not handsome, but elegant in a loose-limbed, dishevelled sort of a way. He worked seven twenty-two-hour days a week, and our courtship, such as it was, consisted of me screaming at the back of his crash helmet as we wove through the West End traffic on his scarlet Ducati. He liked having me along when he was working because it meant that he could abandon the bike at a moment's notice and foot-follow his quarry. My job was to keep the F4s loaded up with colour negative and to make sure that the bike wasn't stolen or towed away while he was gone.

Life as a paparazzo, I discovered, was dislocating but curiously addictive. Every need and appetite was sublimated to the pursuit of the perfect frame, the naked moment, the big-money syndication shot. Meals were eaten on the run, sleep snatched only when all the drop-offs were completed and the next set-up was secured, sex scrambled blearily and forgettably between the two. The money came racing in but the money, as he was perversely happy to admit, was only a nominal motive with Hal. For Hal, the pursuit was the thing; although pursuit, I eventually realised, as I watched the Ducati disappear into yet another East London dawn, could look very much like flight.

Of our three months together – an amphetamine summer of afternoons collapsing into night and of nights bleeding exhaustedly into day again – one evening remains distinct. We were covering the royal première of *Faro's Daughter* in Leicester Square, it had been a beautiful midsummer day, it was still warm, and the light was just beginning to turn. We were in a good position outside the cinema – I'd chained our Texas Homecare stepladders in place at midday – and for once Hal seemed content to play it as it lay, to take his place in the photographic ranks. About fifty of us flanked the red-carpeted cinema entrance, while a privileged half-dozen, their names picked from a hat, waited inside.

The producers and the suits debouched from their taxis to the usual gauntlet of indifference, and then as the character players and B-list invitees started to arrive, the ratpack loosed off a few frames to warm up their motordrives. Photographically speaking, the evening's major item would be the film's young male lead, Dan Fortess, and the reason for the heavy-duty paparazzo presence was the rumour that he would be bringing Hermia Page. The two had never been photographed together but she had been sighted on the set of his new film at Shepperton, and he was rumoured to have been a semi-permanent backstage presence at the Paris couture shows. Hal, like most of the others, was hoping for a good two-shot of Page and Fortess for the morning editions; my rather less vital role was to cover the wide-angle group shots that the celebrity magazines occasionally picked up.

They arrived in a shining black limousine, and as the first white-out of flash broke over the car, I craned for a view from my stepladder. Hermia Page exited first, the long, bruise-dark eyes and slanting regard familiar from countless magazine covers and fashion editorials. Fortess followed – wry, broken-nosed, spare as a rapier – and was greeted by a ragged chorus of cheers and whistles and adolescent screams from behind the crash barrier. As I strained for a sight of them I was reminded, not for the first time, why I would never make the grade as a top-rank ratpacker. I didn't have the height, and I didn't have the weight. Cameras were shoved one-handed in front of my face, I was elbowed in the chest, and my turbo-quantum battery pack was jammed painfully into my kidneys. Far too late, I struggled to bring up the heavy Nikon, but my arms were trapped at my sides by the grubby, beery press of bodies. Within seconds, I could see only what was happening directly in front of me, and that only by standing on tiptoes.

Appearing to forget for a moment that she was not on the Givenchy catwalk, and leaving Dan Fortess standing by the car, Hermia Page began an unaccompanied sashay up the red carpet. Fortess, I think, must have called out to her, for Page then turned back, her hand flying apologetically to her mouth. At this point a broad denim-clad back swung in front of me, blocking my view, and when I could see them again Fortess had stepped forward into my window of vision and was offering Page his arm. Instead of taking it, however, Page tilted back her face and closed her eyes, and after a moment's hesitation, Fortess gently bowed his head and kissed her on the lips. It was a moment either of extraordinary and unscripted intimacy or of brilliant artifice – impossible to tell which – and it was greeted by the crowd behind the crash barriers with whistles and cheers. For several long seconds the couple just stood there, the summer air shivering with blue-white flash, and then, as they turned to go into the cinema foyer, Hermia Page glanced towards me. As the solitary woman in the phalanx, I probably stood out; you could even have said that there was some kind of parallel in our situations. She had changed her look since the couture shows, I noticed: in place of the Louise Brooks bob, her hair was now feathered starling-sleek to her head. She looked delicately, murderously triumphant. *I am I*, her look seemed to say, *and you are you. Thank you for accepting that this is how it must be.* I don't think I've ever loathed anyone on sight so completely in my entire life.

'Did you get it?' I asked Hal as we loaded the ladders into the back of a cab.

'The kiss? Yeah. I had a good angle on it. Shoreditch, please.'

We were on our way to Jonty's, otherwise known as Star Pictures, Hal's photo syndication agency and an unofficial club for the longer-serving paparazzi.

'What did you think of her?' Hal asked as he labelled up the rolls of negative.

'Who, Hermia Page?'

'Yes.'

'I don't know.' I shrugged. 'Another rich-girl model, I suppose. Even complexion, arms-dealer Daddy, shit for brains. Why?'

'Just wondering.' He looked up at me. 'Why do you hate people like her so much?'

'What do you mean, people like her?'

'I mean people like her. Well-connected women who do well for themselves. I've noticed you can't bear it, for example, if any other girl from your sort of background gets a piece in the paper or a job with *Vogue* or . . .'

'That's not true and it's not fair. What I can't stand is when some shrieking fuckwit gets a job just because her father's an MP or someone the editor wants to impress. And what the hell do you mean by my kind of background, anyway?'

'Well, private school. All that.'

'Look, the only reason I went to the school that I went to was that my mother's sister's husband – a man I never met – died of a coronary thrombosis on the other side of the world. Don't ask me how or why, but that fact somehow translated into my fees being paid at a convent in Surrey. There wasn't any money, or fancy clothes, or any of the other stuff that's supposed to go with being at a private school.'

'So you were the exception, then; the girl who couldn't afford a party frock?'

'Yes, if you like, I was the exception. I didn't have what the other girls had and they fucking well let me know it. Why are you giving me such a hard time about this?'

'Because I can see you racking up a hard time for yourself. If you're going to write about fashion, you're going to have to get used to the fact that the decks are stacked, that people like Hermia Page are always going to jump the queue.'

'Don't patronise me, Hal, I know exactly how the world turns for women like Hermia Page, and I also know that I don't have to like them if I don't choose to.'

'Of course you don't have to like them; all that I'm saying is that you shouldn't jump to conclusions. Not every woman born with a silver spoon in her mouth deserves to have it shoved straight up her arse.'

Advice from Hal, at that moment, was all that I needed. 'Don't tell me how to live my life, you sad voyeuristic *fuck*,' I screamed, stripping the exposed negative from my Nikon on to the floor of the taxi. 'Do you really think these spoilt bitches you wait for outside nightclubs at three in the morning actually *like* you?'

He laughed out loud. 'Oh, Alison, you are so *sweet*.'

From the street Star Pictures looked like a decidedly run-down concern. Its window held a ten-year-old print of a Page Three girl in a Father Christmas costume, and a dusty cactus in a pot. Inside, however, the business's prosperity was more apparent. The office walls were covered with glass-clipped prints of celebrities: celebrities startled outside nightclubs, celebrities showing their legs as they climbed from cars, celebrities displaying their cleavages as they blew out candles on birthday cakes. In the basement the processing, scanning and electronic dispatch equipment was brand new, and there were several rooms full of it. Star Pictures, which Jonty ran with his long-suffering daughter Little Brenda, stayed open twenty-four hours a day. Little Brenda, Jonty liked to confide to us, was being groomed. One day, when he retired to Cyprus, where he had leisure interests, Little Brenda would take over.

The frame that Hal finally selected was as perfectly composed as a 1930s film still. He had Fortess and Page three-quarter length and in profile, their expressions clearly legible. She appeared serenely, exquisitely absorbed; he evinced an almost courtly disbelief at her presence in his arms. Beyond them, beyond the bloom of flashlight and the crash barrier, vague spectator-figures strained, waved and shouted. It was curious to think, as Hal held up the 10″ by 8″ print, that the moment recorded was only forty minutes in the past, that its subjects were still sitting watching *Faro's Daughter* in Leicester Square. Other photographers' versions of the kiss-shot were being processed alongside ours, but of those that I saw, only Hal's conveyed the ambiguous tension of the moment, the uncertainty as to whose was the erotic surrender.

Jonty and Little Brenda agreed. 'That's the belter of the bunch,' confirmed Jonty, breathing the crumbs of his meat pie into my hair as he peered over my shoulder. 'Let's get it on to the wires.'

'Fuckin' A,' said Little Brenda. She turned to Hal. 'You goin' to the party?'

'It's a thought.'

'Which party?' I asked.

'The première party,' said Hal. 'It's in Bedford Square.'

''Cause if you *are* goin',' said Little Brenda. 'I've got to drive up West . . .'

'How do you know?' I asked him.

'How do I know what?'

'That it's in Bedford Square.'

'Everybody knows.' He winked at Little Brenda, who was loading up a pair of Leicas, and squeezed my waist. 'Shall we go?'

'I haven't got anything to . . .'

'That can be sorted. Jonty, have you got Enver's number, he's always got a frock or two about the place.'

'What is he?' I asked 'A drag queen?'

'Smudger,' said Hal. 'Fashion. Season or two and his stuff'll be everywhere. It'd be good for you to meet him.'

Jonty had the number. Enver turned out to be working, but said that we were welcome to come round to his Clerkenwell studio and borrow an outfit. Hurriedly, Hal changed out of his jeans and sweatshirt. Like several of the other paparazzi, he always kept a razor and a black tie outfit at Jonty's in case he had to crash something formal. We went in Little Brenda's Porsche.

Enver Kassapian's studio was on the second floor of a converted warehouse. Hal and I climbed the stairs; Little Brenda waited in the car. Enver's assistant met us at the lift, and ushered us into a vast open space whose perimeter was lost in darkness. Enver himself, a tiny figure in dungarees crouched over a Hasselblad, I at first took for a child. When he turned to us, however, I saw doughy features, heavy spectacles and a shaved head. He was photographing a sullen, muscular youth on a Biedermeier day-bed who, naked apart from a pair of oil-stained Y-fronts, was cradling part of a car's engine.

'Nice set-up!' said Hal to Enver, ignoring the youth. 'That's a Mondeo transmission, isn't it?'

'Wouldn't know, dear. Busy?'

'Oh, you know. Busy enough.' Hal ran his hands through his hair. 'Enver, this is Alison. Alison wants to write about fashion.'

'Very nice.' Enver looked up at me quizzically. 'And tonight you need the Cinderella treatment?'

I smiled, self-conscious in my shapeless motorcycle gear, and shrugged. 'Well, anything you can . . .'

'Come.' He led me slowly across the floor to a rail of very expensive-looking evening wear behind a long, golden Japanese screen. 'Tonight I play the fairy godmother . . .' he waved an imaginary wand at the bunched and glittering fabrics, ' . . . and you *shall* go to the ball!'

'Wow!' I said, dropping my crash helmet and reaching out disbelievingly to the shimmering lamés and taffetas and clouds of tulle. 'I can't possibly . . .'

'Are you in a hurry?' Enver called back to Hal.

'Not if you're not,' said Hal, and I heard him slap his pockets for his cigarettes.

'Right, dear,' Enver said to me, pointing to a door. 'Bathroom. Shower, wash all your bits, leave the hair damp. Call Oki when you're ready. He'll sort you out.'

Ten minutes later I emerged from behind the screen in a straight black satin skirt, black cap-sleeved lace bodice and black satin court shoes. Enver's assistant had stuffed tissues into the toes of the shoes, but otherwise everything fitted as closely and as lightly, somehow, as if it had been made for me. And standing there, I suddenly remembered something that my mother had said to me years before. It had been a thundery evening at the end of one of her brandy and soda days, Dad had been away on the mainland and she'd been picking tearfully through her jewellery box, telling me stories about the brooches and bracelets and rings and who had given them all to her. At the bottom of the box was a small manila envelope folded into four, and from this, into my damp young palm, she had poured several diamonds. 'They're so light!' I had said, rolling them around in my hand. 'You think they're going to be heavy and they're light as air.' At these words Mum had smiled and sniffed and blotted her puffy red eyes. 'Everything really beautiful's like that, darling. Everything. You'll see.'

'Ah,' said Enver, twinkling up at me approvingly. 'Chanel. Underplayed but sexy. Perfect for the gate-crashing *ingénue*.' He turned to the sullen youth. 'Isn't she scrumptious, Massimo? Couldn't you just eat her?'

Massimo pouted uninterestedly and turned away.

'I don't think he's hungry,' I whispered.

'He's disillusioned,' said Enver. 'Beauty and Truth mean nothing to him these days.' He raised his voice. 'You'll be telling us you don't believe in God in a minute, won't you, pet!'

In answer, Massimo swung his feet to the floor and, biceps quivering, walked heavily from the room with his gearbox.

'Don't take any notice,' said Enver severely. 'It's good for him not to be the centre of attention twenty-four hours a day.' He gestured me to the vacated day-bed 'Lie down. You need a dab of something.'

For five minutes I lay with my eyes closed as Enver pored over me with his powders and brushes and sponges. He smelt of some rich, dark old perfume overlaid with cloves. When he had finished he stood me up, stepped back a few paces and fired off a Polaroid.

'What do you think?' he asked, handing me the still-drying print.

I stared at it. 'Is that me?'

He hadn't done anything I could put my finger on. It didn't even look as if I was wearing make-up at all. What he had achieved, somehow, was to make me look like my unadmitted self, like the star of my dream-films.

'It's amazing,' I said, meaning Enver's work, rather than my own appearance, and then I realised with a stab of fierce satisfaction that I was no longer sure where the one ended and the other began. Enver, watching me closely, began to laugh.

'She's a virgin!' he cried, throwing up his tiny hands. 'It's her first time!'

'I wouldn't go that far,' said Hal.

'No, silly boy, not like that; I mean a *high fashion* virgin. Oh, I do so *love* to be the first.'

'Well, you are,' said Hal. 'Thanks.'

'Don't thank me,' said Enver, 'until you've heard the rules. The rules are that her stuff stays here and mine comes back tonight. The stylist's coming tomorrow morning and if it's not all here she'll go baresque, I kid you not. She's a dreadfully violent woman: her day's incomplete if she hasn't kicked a midget.' He turned back to me. 'Glass slipper nine a.m. tomorrow, OK?'

'OK,' I said. 'Promise.'

'Good girl. And Hal . . .'

'Yes?'

'See she folds that skirt before anyone fucks her.'

We squashed back into Little Brenda's silver Porsche, her Leicas heavy in my lap, her stepladder sharp at my shoulder. One of the cameras had a 400mm telephoto lens attached, and both were loaded with 1600 ASA negative, but for reasons of professional courtesy I thought it best not to ask who she was after.

'You look nice,' Little Brenda told me. 'Real nice. They won't suss you. Who's on security?' she asked Hal.

'Angus's boys,' said Hal.

'Few friendly faces about the place then?'

'Hope so.'

'If the security people know you,' I said to Hal, 'surely they'll chuck you out as soon as they see you?'

'Not if we're already inside. Once we're in – assuming we look presentable and don't start pointing cameras round the place – they're just making themselves look incompetent if they start trying to sling us out. Anyway, you look like the real thing. Very few paparazzi tip up to these affairs in Chanel.'

'You think I look like an actress?'

'Starlet, perhaps.'

'Thanks a bunch.'

'Don't take no notice of him,' said Little Brenda. 'You look brilliant.'

'That was a compliment,' protested Hal. 'Anyone can be an actress – look at *Spotlight*. To be a starlet, well' – he mimed pulling his shirt open – 'that takes serious talent.'

'Very funny. So how will we get in?'

'Bit of the old brass neck,' said Little Brenda. 'It works like this . . .'

*

Floodlights had been erected at the entrance to the gardens in Bedford Square, and the roped-off approach to the marquees within was guarded by several uniformed security men. Beyond the ropes a small crowd of fans waited with compact cameras and autograph books at the ready, while further away the less biddable – amongst whom a police constable and a WPC passed at good-humoured intervals – vainly searched the perimeter for an overhanging tree branch or an unguarded entrance.

Little Brenda had dropped us off at the corner of the square and slowly, hand in hand, Hal and I wound our way between the knots of onlookers at the railings until we were at the furthest point of the gardens from the entrance. Beyond the dark shrubs and the plane trees the marquees dispensed a soft lemon glow. The air was warm and the sky bright with stars.

'Wasn't this where the nightingale sang?'

'I think,' said Hal, 'that you'll find that that was in Berkeley Square. Somewhere between J. Walter Thompson and the Jack Barclay showroom. Are you ready?'

'Yes.'

'Then do everything exactly as we agreed, and do it fast, OK?'

'OK.'

Ahead of us, the flicker of the WPC's torch disappeared around the corner. Quietly, the silver Porsche drew alongside us and Little Brenda jumped from the driver's seat, leaving the engine running. From the passenger's side she and Hal pulled out the stainless steel ladder and walked purposefully to the railings. An amused buzz of comprehension rose from the dozen or so spectators.

'Let's move it,' said Hal, and as I kicked off the court shoes and reached for the waistband of the satin skirt I saw him run up the ladder and jump the railings. My fingers were shaking but a thousand pounds and change buys you a good non-stick zip and I stepped out of the skirt to a ragged volley of whistles and cheers. 'Hurry!' urged Little Brenda, and throwing the shoes and skirt over the railings I ran barefoot and all but bare-arsed up the ladder.

'Jump,' ordered Hal, and I jumped.

He lowered me to damp moss and sharp twigs. Behind me, as

we hurried away from the railings, I heard a spatter of applause, more whistles, and the scrape of Little Brenda disengaging the ladder from the railings. As I ducked behind the broad trunk of a plane tree and pulled the skirt back up my thighs, I heard the growl of the Porsche's ignition, followed by a screeching acceleration.

'How do I look?' I asked, wiggling my toes inside the shoes as we stepped over a rose bush on to a gravelled path.

'Fine,' said Hal. 'Fantastic. Just remember one thing: you're a star, a somebody, an A-list insider. Don't creep around, don't stare, don't behave as if any of this is out of the ordinary.'

'I could quite happily wear clothes like this every night.'

Hal looked at me thoughtfully.

'Yeah, well, I bet you could. Shall we join the party?'

'Fine by me. Have you got a camera, by the way? I mean, that is what we're here for, isn't it?'

In answer Hal patted his breast pocket.

'Isn't it?' I persisted. 'Or is this some kind of date?'

'Well, it is a beautiful evening,' said Hal, reaching up to touch one of the Chinese paper lanterns lighting the path. A couple approached us, the girl laughing as she teetered on the gravel.

'Hi!' said Hal, pinching his nostrils and blinking ruefully.

'Naughty things!' said the girl, waving a pretend-disapproving finger.

'The cocaine sniff,' said Hal, as the couple disappeared into the bushes behind us. 'The freemasons' handshake of the nineties.'

'Wasn't that . . .?'

'Yes,' said Hal. 'The amazing thing about her is that in all the thousands of column inches written about her, no one's made the connection between her obnoxious behaviour and the truly prodigious volume of Bolivian marching powder that goes up her nose. I've seen her in action at the shows, and frankly I'm amazed she can even walk in a straight line.'

'Tell me one thing,' I said, as we picked our way over the guy ropes of the principal marquee. 'If they're so valuable, why does Enver let these clothes out of the studio.'

'Owes me a favour.'

'Tell.'

'No.'

'Why not?'

'Because you are – or you're soon going to be – a journalist.'

'So?'

He stopped, and turned to face me. 'Knowledge is a commodity. If I tell you, sooner or later you'll use it.'

'I won't.'

'Well, you should do.'

'Well I won't. Besides, you adore me.'

'What gave you that impression?'

'Don't you?'

'It's a pretty creepy story,' said Hal, taking an unfiltered cigarette from a silver case.

'All the best stories are.'

He tapped the cigarette against the case and lit it. 'You know Sylvie Todd?'

'Yes.'

'Well, you know that she never wears see-through things, is never photographed topless, never shows her breasts on the catwalk like the other girls?'

'I didn't, but now you come to mention it . . .'

'It's her *schtick*, her little bit of mystery, and if you think about it it's quite a clever ploy. Anyway, eighteen months ago, when Sylvie Todd was absolutely the top girl, I got a call from Enver Kassapian, who at that point I hadn't met. No one really knew his work then, but he was popular with the models, especially Todd, and used to sit and gossip with them while they were being done up for the shows. He was like a sort of Toulouse-Lautrec figure, a sort of mascot, and you know what fag-hags models are. Anyway, one afternoon, backstage at the Salle Delorme after some show or other, Enver managed to photograph Sylvie Todd in the nude. He was using a concealed rig, but . . . *Wait*, you asked to hear this, so let me finish.'

'OK.'

'. . . But the picture quality was good. Sylvie was just goofing around, but the shot had a kind of no-one's-looking-so-fuck-me-quick look to it which, because it was her, made it a very serious commercial property indeed. Any other model it wouldn't have been worth sixpence, but Todd was on the want list.'

'What's that?'

'France, Spain, Italy, the gossip mags pay a lot of money for celebrity skin. They don't want posed stuff so much as grabs: tits falling out of dresses in nightclubs, long-range sunbathing shots, that sort of thing.'

'Why? Wouldn't it be cheaper to use regular, Page Three-type shots?'

'Sure, but the point about a grainy frame of a Monégasque princess or a supermodel topless on the beach is that it's been taken without the subject's consent. And for your average Mediterranean hand-jive artist who's never going to get within five hundred yards of a *plage privée* except to sweep it, that's an important consideration. What the sisters would call a power issue.'

'So?'

'So. Enver wanted to turn the frame into cash, but he didn't want his name anywhere near it – Sylvie Todd was his friend, after all. On the other hand, he didn't want to pass it over to some dodgy outfit and get ripped off. So he came to me, who he'd heard of, and I introduced him to Jonty and Jonty syndicated the frame and paid him fair and square and Enver bought his studio in Clerkenwell. *Voilá*.'

'With that one frame?'

'With that one frame. Sylvie, needless to say, hit the roof. Lawyers' letters flying right, left and centre. Nothing she could do, though. Never found out who got her.'

'You must have been proud of yourselves!'

He exhaled, and looked at me levelly.

'Do you want to take the clothes back?'

I said nothing, and flipping his cigarette on to the grass, he carefully ground it out with his toe.

'You know something, you'd do well to realise who your friends are. You want to run with the hounds, you'd better get used to the taste of hare.'

'Now there's a lovely, lovely metaphor,' I said.

In the Singapore days, when I was very young, we used to get invited to all the Carteret family gatherings, and for years afterwards I remembered these occasions as the very epitome of sophistication and privilege. Above all, I remember the smell. Patou's Joy and Havana cigar smoke were the dominant notes, but there were other elements too: the warm dampness of sprinkler-fed lawns, the breath-catching sweetness of frangipani and Marquise hair spray, the pallid cloy of rosewater and face powder and inadequately aired silk. I must have registered these early, for after my fourth birthday tea, at which I have a vague memory of my mother shouting and crying and throwing things, there were no more invitations to Easter-egg hunts at the country club or to cocktail parties at the house on Nassim Hill. Years later, however, I only had to close my eyes to recall those dizzying scents and to feel the cooch grass springy beneath my sandalled feet and to know, as if for the first time, the breathless intoxication of adult attention.

For some reason, perhaps it was the Chinese lanterns, perhaps it was the star-crowded sky, I expected to rediscover some of those same sensations that night. But I was no longer a child, this was nineties London, and the world that I remembered no longer existed, in Singapore or anywhere else. That evening in Bedford Square, it seemed to me, had a nervous, impatient edge to it; hard, intolerant laughter overlaid the plangent rise and fall of the string quartet, and I was aware of the constant flickering of eyes. These were not, I guessed, people who had had money in their pockets for very many years.

'Why's everyone so jumpy?' I whispered to Hal, and he shrugged.

'Coke? Ambition?'

'Pretty low-rent crowd.'

'There are levels. This is the outer level.'

'Can we move inwards?'

'In a minute.'

'Why not now?'

'I want you to acclimatise. At the moment you look as if you're about to be sacrificed to an Aztec god.'

'They're staring at me.'

'Who?'

'Over there.' I nodded to a loud, demonstrative group near the bar, amongst whom I recognised a TV lottery host and an elderly soap actress.

'They're worried because they think they ought to know who you are. Enjoy it. It's one of the sincerer forms of flattery.'

'I suppose so,' I said.

'It'd happen more often if you let it. There's quite an attractive woman behind that rude-girl front of yours.'

'Is that a personal or a professional opinion?' I asked, pleased.

'Professional,' said Hal. 'Personally, I like you vicious.'

It was the lottery host, a twinkling, matronly figure in dispatch rider's leathers, who led the group over. 'We want to know who you *are*,' he insisted. 'We've been watching you for ten minutes now and we're *convinced* you're someone and *we want to know who*!'

'Or *whose*!' said the soap actress, collapsing into the trilling shrieks which, a generation earlier, had been her trademark.

'Actually, I'm a writer,' I said modestly. 'For *Vogue*.'

'Really!' said a slight, balding man who was cradling a Pekinese dog. 'Which department?'

'Oh, you know,' I said, my heart thumping painfully behind my ribs. 'Features . . .'

'And who is the features editor at *Vogue* now?' asked the dog-man, whose breath reminded me of stale lobster.

'Umm . . . his name's Vronsky,' I answered wildly. 'You see I actually work for *Russian Vogue*.'

'But how thrilling!' said the lottery man. 'Venus in furs!'

'Cossacks!' shrieked the soap star. 'Say something in Russian for us.'

'Umm . . . *Oo vas yest'shto-neeboot' ot panos . . .?*'

'And what does that mean, dear?'

'It means I've always been an enormous admirer of your work,' I smiled.

'Bless you,' she said. 'Do you know, there isn't a day goes by I don't fall to my knees and thank God that I actually get *paid* for doing the *one thing* in the world . . .'

She looked around her for endorsement of this piety, and when it was not forthcoming, allowed herself to be drawn into a comparative analysis of Brighton-based clairvoyants. Any brief interest that I might have held for the group had evaporated. I turned to Hal, but he was listening glazed-eyed to a venture capitalist's description of a celebrity golf tournament in Chadwell Heath.

'What do you write about?' the dog-man asked me.

'Oh, fashion, film, the arts . . .' I glared at Hal, who inclined his head with a polite, self-deprecating smile.

'And who's the editor now?' my tormentor persisted, smoothing the glossy cranium of the Pekinese with a pale, ringed hand.

'Her name's Alexandra, um . . . Nevsky,' I said, draining my champagne and extending my glass to a passing waiter. 'She's perfectly brilliant.'

'Nevskaya, surely . . .' began the dog-man, and then, to my vast relief, we were interrupted. Someone was waving at us from outside the marquee.

'Oh, there she is at last,' said Hal, taking my arm. 'Excuse us.' He steered me rapidly in the direction of the waving figure whom I saw, with some surprise, to be Hermia Page.

'Hal, *angel.*' She threw her arms round his neck as I hung back, bemused. 'How *are* you? It's so wonderful to *see* you!' She beckoned to the tall, dark-haired figure who was standing beside her with his hands in his pockets, staring up at the sky. 'Dan, this is Hal West, absolutely one of my oldest friends, and . . .'

'Alison,' said Hal, drawing me forward. 'Alison MacAteer.'

'So how do you two know each other?' I asked, when the four of us were settled at a table in a smaller, rather more smartly appointed marquee from which the general run of invitees appeared to be excluded. Beside the table, two Dom Perignon bottles lolled in their silver buckets. For all my urbane front – or what I thought of as my urbane front – I couldn't restrain myself from sneaking glances at Dan Fortess. Half the country's female population was already in love with him and I suspected that the other half would be as soon as *Faro's Daughter* had been on general release for a week or two.

'School,' said Hermia. 'I was at Winkfield and Hal was at Eton. We used to have dances against them.' She placed a hand on Dan

Fortess's knee and crossed her eyes at me. 'Everyone was desperate to get off with Hal, needless to say. Much redder meat than his weedy class mates . . .'

'You never told me you were at Eton,' I said to him.

'You never asked,' he replied mildly, reaching over the table to refill Hermia's champagne glass.

'And before you start to wonder,' said Hermia, 'I was far too boring and mousy to warrant a dance with Hal, let alone a snog.'

'Or worse,' I added, proffering my own glass.

'Or worse,' agreed Hermia. 'Unlike Belinda-Jane Badenoch, the class nymphomaniac. Blow-Job had platinum-blonde hair at fourteen. Her parents took her to London every other weekend to have her roots done. God, I envied her.'

'Belinda-Jane Badenoch,' mused Hal. 'What on earth happened to her?'

'Oh, you know. Marriage, children, Wiltshire . . . How old are you, Alison?'

'Twenty.'

'You're a child-molester, Hal West!'

It kills me to admit it, but Hermia was charm itself, and anything but stupid. When Hal explained that we'd broken in with a stepladder she nodded as if it was the most normal thing in the world, and when he told her about me and the dog-man she laughed out loud and threw an arm round my shoulders.

'I was getting desperate,' I said. '*Fucking* man! I only had the Brothers Karamazov left.'

'Raskolnikov,' suggested Hermia. 'He could have been the lifestyle editor.'

'But you actually spoke to that woman in Russian,' said Hal.

'I went to Moscow with a party from university,' I explained, 'and was forced to learn that particular phrase the hard way. It means: "Do you have anything for diarrhoea?" '

Everyone laughed, including – I was pleased to see – Dan Fortess, who so far had hardly spoken. He turned to me and smiled and my heart soared into the unclouded blue stratosphere of his eyes.

'Do you get diarrhoea often?' he asked.

'Dan, *really*!' said Hermia.

'No, I only ask because I had frightful trouble in India, when we were making *The Siege of Krishnapore*. The studio gave me this pink stuff from the hotel chemist. It set like cement, and by the time we got back to Shepperton I was so bunged up they had to call in Dyno-Rod.'

He ran an elegant hand through his dark Regency curls and lowered his voice. 'Have you noticed how you never see those white dog-turds any more? When I was a boy they were everywhere. We used to put them in people's exhaust pipes.'

'Oh, that was you, was it?' I said.

'Yes, that was me. Me and a boy called Ripper Houlihan who was later banged up for interfering with farm animals.'

'He's a real charmer, isn't he?' said Hermia. 'If all those teenage girls actually got to spend fifteen minutes with him . . .'

'I won't hear a word spoken against my teenage girls,' said Dan. 'As long as they continue to park their gymslipped bums on the seats of cinemas showing my films.'

'Do you have a big gymslip following?' I asked him.

'Oh, he gets the moist gusset vote in a big, big way, don't you, sweetness?' laughed Hermia affectionately.

'Actually, I suspect I draw the Mills and Boon crowd more than the Blow-Job Badenochs of this world,' said Dan. 'More's the pity,' he added, rearing out of range as Hermia swiped at him.

'What was that film?' asked Hal. '*The Furtive Vice of Judith Hearn*? Something like that?'

'*Lonely Passion*,' said Dan. 'But yes. That sort of territory.'

'Dental hygienists?' I asked, draining my glass.

'In droves,' admitted Dan.

'Not my dental hygienist,' said Hal. 'Mine's called Ulla and looks like Eva Braun. She's thrillingly stern if you haven't been flossing. "You haff pluck, Hull," she tells me. "Knotty boy!" '

It wasn't even faintly funny, but everyone laughed in the way that people do when they have created an atmosphere in which they can safely talk complete nonsense. Dan, I noticed, was watching me in a covert sort of way.

'Do you remember a girl,' Hal asked Hermia, 'called Serena Rothesay . . . Rothwell . . . some name like that?'

'Serena Robertshaw?'

'Yes, that's the one. Do you know what happened to her, because I'm sure I saw her coming out of the Mirabelle with Charlie Fowey the other day . . .?'

Dan drained his glass, stood up and turned to me. 'Why don't we leave these two to their boaters and their bumfreezers and go and dance?'

Taken aback, I looked at Hermia.

'He might bore you,' she drawled amiably. 'But he's unlikely to bite. He's even quite a good dancer.'

'You *are* quite a good dancer,' I said five minutes later as Dan steered me fluently round the floor in the Regency-themed marquee where the chamber musicians were installed. They must have been playing from memory, for the chandelier that hung from the tented ceiling was dimmed to a point where it would have been impossible to read a score.

'There's always dancing in these period films,' said Dan. 'Minuets and cotillions and so on.'

'But not waltzes, surely, in *Faro's Daughter*?' Around us couples self-consciously ploughed through the approximate motions of the steps. Others watched us from the edges of the floor. I sensed Dan's eyes sweep the room over my shoulder.

'No, the waltz comes courtesy of RADA.' His arm tightened around my satined waist and he glanced at me sideways. 'So what did you think of the film?'

'I didn't see it, remember?' I said, and lowered my voice so that he had to lean closer to hear me. 'I'm just one of those . . . damp-gusseted little fans of yours.'

He drew his head back and looked at me in silence.

'D'you see?' I asked quietly.

'Yes,' he murmured, tightening his arm still further and blowing softly at a strand of my hair. 'I do see.'

I moved my shoulders so that my left breast, previously flattened against the lapel of his dinner jacket, pressed against his white shirtfront. He glanced downwards and smiled.

'The downside of being a film actor, Alice, is that people watch you all the time. If I were to do any of the things that I would like to do right now, it would be noticed and probably photographed.

These paparazzi get everywhere.'

'Don't they just?' I agreed, moving my hips against his. 'And it's Alison, in fact. But tell me, what exactly are these things that . . . that you feel very much like doing?'

'Oh,' he frowned, 'just things that ordinary people often do when they're dancing together. I'd like to take my right hand out of the small of your back and move it six inches lower down; I'd like to put my left hand over your breast, and perhaps kiss your neck and your ear and that little line of muscle that runs out to your shoulder . . . Nothing outrageous, for the moment.'

'And later?'

'Later I will go back to my flat with Hermia and you'll go back to wherever with . . .'

'With Hal.'

'Precisely. But then you are a journalist, aren't you? And I have, once in a while, been known to give interviews to journalists. And interviews can happen, well, anywhere, really. Privacy's the important thing, wouldn't you agree?'

'Absolutely,' I said.

To the visible gratitude of most of the other dancers, the waltz came to an end, and the musicians struck up one of those smoochy theme-music pieces that you can just drift around to. We drifted, if still a little formally.

'So tell me what might happen at such an interview?' I asked.

'Well . . . it might well take place outside London, perhaps at a small hotel near Bath – did you see *Persuasion*?' When he spoke, I could feel his breath warm and slightly alcoholic on my cheek.

'I've seen all Jane Austen's films.'

'Somewhere nice, anyway. Somewhere with a view. And of course the kind of an interview we're talking about might well occur during a week when the fashion calendar is particularly full. New York fashion week, perhaps.'

'I can see that it might.'

'And having ordered a bottle of . . . Were you enjoying the Dom Perignon?'

'The Dom Perignon was just fine.'

'Having ordered a bottle of Dom Perignon, and having particularly requested that the interviewer wear exactly what she is wearing tonight . . .'

'Go on,' I urged him.

' . . . I think that she and I would probably drink the Dom Perignon sitting on the balcony, looking out over . . . Would there be hills?'

I nodded. 'There would be hills.'

'Overlooking the hills, then. The journalist would take off her shoes . . .'

'Her Antonio Berardi shoes, perhaps, with the Kleenex in the toe?'

'. . . her Berardi shoes, complete with Kleenex, and she would put her pen and notebook on the floor. Her tape recorder would remain in her bag. It would never be switched on.'

'Why is that?' I asked.

'Because as she reached down for it I would stop her. I would reach out for her and place this hand' – he lifted it momentarily from my shoulder blade – 'on her left breast. I would feel . . . lace and a heartbeat against my palm.'

'If you put your hand over her breast like that,' I said, moistening my lips with my tongue, 'I suspect that she might turn to you, wanting quite badly and quite immediately to be kissed.'

'I would in fact kiss her at that point,' he agreed, 'and there would be a slight breeze from the French windows, which would be open. I would kiss her mouth and her neck and her throat and when I kissed the back of her neck her head would droop forward like . . . like a snowdrop. After a time, I would want to take off her . . .' His fingers plucked at the fabric of my sleeve.

'If she was wearing a Chanel guipure lace bodice,' I suggested, 'there might well be a row of little buttons down the back.'

His fingers brushed my back, flamenco-style.

'Yes, I would undo them.'

'I think that, for a moment, even with the buttons undone, she would hold this bodice thing against her.'

'I would kneel down and kiss the small of her back, just there.'

I smiled. 'She would still want to hold on to her top for a moment. Maybe it would seem that the bodice was warm and the breeze from the windows was cool.'

'She would drop it to the chair. Drop her arms by her sides, and stand by the window, waiting for him.'

'Do you think she'd do that? Don't you think that she might help him pull his shirt off and think how his body was familiar and not familiar, how she'd seen his body on the screen, separate from the man, but here were the man and the body in the same place – nowhere else but here, alone and with her?'

Again, he drew his head back and held me in his gaze. 'I hope that she would be thinking that. Because I would have been thinking about her from the moment that my agent rang me to ask if I wanted to do the interview. Because this, of course, is how the journalist would have made contact: through my agent. For all of that day I would have been wondering what she would feel like, how she would smell, how her skin would taste. I would have been wondering – as I'm wondering now – about her breasts; how they would look, how they would feel in my hands and beneath my lips. Tell me about her breasts.'

'Well, they are smallish,' I began, 'and at last count there were two of them . . .' It seemed that his arms had been around me for ever. Dimmed lights and pale faces swam past me.

'And if I drew my tongue over them and then stepped back so that they caught the breeze from the windows, would they . . .?'

'I suspect so,' I said. 'Nipples being what they are.'

'And tell me about these nipples: are they largeish, smallish, pinkish . . .?'

'Mediumish,' I said. 'You could safely cover each one with the top of a hundred-and-seventy-five-gram jar of Marmite. And a sort of dark cinnamon brown.'

'They would be beautiful. I would want to feel them against my lips and against my cheek.'

'Mmm.' I closed my eyes. 'She'd like that.'

'She's still wearing her skirt, of course, this journalist.'

Dizzy from the champagne, I opened my eyes again. 'There's a kind of clip arrangement at the side,' I said, 'and then a zip.'

'Perhaps she might undo it herself?'

'I think she might. It's sort of a girl thing. She would want the skirt safe and out of the way and over the chair and not having to be worried about. She'd wonder whether to take her knickers off too.'

'I would take them off for her.'

'Oh? Tell me about doing that.'

'She would be lying across the bed by now with her arms above her head and the scalloped elastic of her knickers tight across her hip bones and flattening her pubic hair. Her breasts and her armpits would be a little paler than the rest of her, her stomach would be marked by the tight waistband of the skirt, and she would not have shaved her armpits. She would smell of sweat, of the train and the taxi and the journey down from London.'

'Would that put you off?' I asked quietly.

'No, because that's how it would be. Her journey and its consequences would be part of it, in the same way that my waiting at the hotel would be part of it. Anyway, I would pull her knickers down over her legs and drop them over the edge of the bed.'

'She wouldn't move,' I said. 'She wouldn't cover herself up. She'd lie there with her legs open and let you look at her.'

'I would look at her. I would watch the way that her pubic hair, from being pressed flat by her knickers, would slowly lift from her skin. I'm right, aren't I, about her having this sort of crested tongue of dark hair . . .?'

'Yes,' I said. I felt my control of the situation ebbing, my body's rippling imperatives taking over from my brain.

'. . . This sort of long tongue of dark hair that makes me want to lick it into points and curls. Well, I'd put my hands underneath her buttocks, which would be cold from the afternoon sheets, and hook my thumbs round the front of her thighs . . .'

'Go on,' I murmured. My eyes were closed now, and I no longer quite trusted my legs to support me.

'. . . and bring my mouth down so that I could smell her smell and feel her hair prickling against my mouth . . .'

'Oh God,' I breathed. 'Please. Just take me outside and fuck me . . .'

The flash all but blinded me.

'Gotcha!' said Hal, and as the blue-white flare fell away into smouldering points of light and the tableau before me composed itself, I heard the sound of his and of Hermia's laughter. What had they heard?

'You buggers!' roared Dan, his metamorphosis instantaneous.

'Fucking sods. That's for the *Sun*, I suppose?'

'Highest bidder, mate,' said Hal, winking at me, and Dan laughed. My heart pounded painfully in my chest. People were staring at us. Everyone seemed to have stopped dancing.

'Are you all right?' Hermia asked me. 'You look as if you've seen a ghost.'

'Fine,' I managed. 'It was just a surprise, that's all.'

She looked at me quizzically, if not unkindly, and gradually my heartbeat slowed and a vestige of control returned to my legs.

'Pumpkin time,' said Hal, laying a proprietorial arm over my shoulder. 'Little Brenda awaits.'

'Perhaps you should leave a glass slipper,' said Dan. 'Or at least a Berardi court shoe.'

I curtsied, grateful to him for not pretending that the last half-hour had not taken place.

'What plots have you two been hatching?' asked Hermia, mock-severely, her birdlike head to one side.

'I'm afraid I've been bending Dan's ear about fashion,' I said apologetically.

'That's more than I've ever succeeded in doing,' said Hermia. 'I don't think I've met a man whose ears were less bendable on that particular subject.'

'I like the shows, though,' said Dan, placing a friendly hand on her bottom. 'Especially all that no-underwear stuff.'

'You're pathetic,' said Hermia, affectionately removing his hand. 'Truly pathetic.'

We made our way through the warm, lantern-lit darkness to the entrance, and waited out of sight of the photographers as Dan and Hermia's limousine was brought alongside.

'Hal, darling,' said Hermia, as kisses were exchanged. 'Ring us. And Alison, lovely to meet you. I'm sure we'll see each other again . . . professionally.'

'I've always thought you were fantastic,' I said.

'Thank you,' she offered me her cheek. 'That's really sweet.'

Their chauffeur reappeared at the entrance, and I took advantage of the diversion to push my hand down the front of my skirt and inside my knickers. When Dan turned to say goodbye I proffered him the hand, and as I had known he would, he raised it to his lips.

''Bye, Alice,' he said, looking expressionlessly down my arm into my eyes.

''Bye, Dan,' I said.

Hal and I followed them out through the flash-storm.

'Get the frame?' asked Little Brenda, as we squeezed into the Porsche's passenger seat.

'Yes,' said Hal, wearily. 'I got the frame.'

'Fuckin' A,' said Little Brenda. 'Let's go to work.'

The pictures made the morning editions the next day. All of them had Dan and Hermia's kiss, and most had the frame of Dan and myself as well. 'Who's That Girl?' wondered the *Daily Mail*'s diarist, while the *Express*, in more literary mood perhaps, captioned me as 'Dan's Dark Lady'.

The contrast between the two pictures was startling, and it was easy to see why the picture editors had used both. The earlier shot showed Dan as the public knew him: as the ardent, exquisitely mannered young lover. Kissing Hermia, his eyes were closed in a kind of rapturous disbelief, as if he could hardly believe his luck in winning such an exotic prize.

The later picture showed the man rather than the boy. His eyes heavy-lidded and unfocused, his fine-drawn features blurred and truculent with lust, he was leaning over me as if about to drag my skirt up and fuck me behind a pub. And where Hermia demurely received his embrace, her long eyes sliding from his gaze, my features were uncurtained by any kind of restraint at all: I looked mad for it.

On the first day, for most of which I stayed in bed in my Willesden Junction bedsit, blanketed by newspaper, nobody identified me. *The Evening Standard*'s 'Londoner's Diary' column offered dinner at the Criterion and free tickets for *Faro's Daughter* to anyone who could come up with a name, but nobody managed it.

'By my reckoning,' said Hal that evening, as we shared a microwaved Farmyard Pie and a round of teas with Jonty and Little Brenda at Star Pictures, 'the story's got legs for another twenty-four hours. Your best call now is to ring round all the tabloids first thing tomorrow, and say you're the girl in the Dan Fortess photo. Describe how you climbed over the railings – say you did it alone, don't bring me or Enver or Little Brenda into it – and how you met Fortess. Give 'em a bit of circumstantial – eyes across a crowded marquee . . . handsomest man alive . . . swept you off your feet . . . danced all night . . . dream come true . . . that sort of thing. Then let them all bid you up for the story. Better still, ring Howard Harvey or someone like that and get them to represent you.'

Jonty nodded his head in agreement. 'And if they want more pictures,' he said, jerking his thumb at Hal, 'tell 'em they've got to use laughing boy here. Or Little Brenda.'

'Fuckin' A,' said Little Brenda.

The next morning, the story was still running. Several of the tabloids re-used the 'Mystery Girl' frame alongside pictures of a pale-faced Hermia hurrying down the steps of Dan Fortess's Chepstow Villas flat. At eleven a.m., I made two phone calls. The first was to Dan's agent, whose name I had discovered from *Spotlight* in the local library. I had rung, I told her, to arrange a time and place for the interview that Dan and I had discussed at the *Faro's Daughter* première. Could she contact him and call me back?

My second call was to Lucy Fane, a newspaper features editor, to whom I began to explain – without giving my name – that I was the girl in the Fortess photo.

'How soon can you get here?' she interrupted me. 'Shall I send a car?'

'Half an hour,' I promised. 'And no, I'll take the bus.'

I dressed carefully and, insofar as my post-student wardrobe permitted, fashionably. Forty minutes later I was sitting in a small editorial office high above central Kensington. Opposite me, smoking, sat a cheerful, lightly intoxicated woman of about thirty.

'What I want to do, dear,' she told me, 'is to get one of our staffers to talk to you and write a first-person piece. "My night with Prince Charming", that sort of thing. By, um, whatever your name is, as told to . . . whoever. Then we'll photograph you looking gorgeous and' – she spread her hands – 'you can get on with being famous. How's that sound?'

'I'll talk to anyone you like,' I said. 'And I'll tell them anything they want to know. But there is something I want in return.'

Her smile hardened fractionally. 'And what might that be, dear?'

'I want a job,' I said.

She narrowed her eyes. 'A job? What kind of job?'

'In the fashion department. As an assistant. A coffee-maker. A go-fetcher. Anything.'

For a long moment she sat there in silence, looking from me to the picture on the front of the newspaper in front of her and back again.

'I'm an English graduate,' I added. 'If that doesn't count against me.'

'Wait here,' she said, eventually. 'OK?'

'OK.'

I got my job in the fashion department, and with a bit of help from one of the staffers, an ageless young man in a charity-shop suit, I wrote the gatecrashing-the-première piece myself. I didn't tell the whole truth, of course, but I wrote a lot more than Hal would have liked me to – about his being an old Etonian, for example, and about borrowing the clothes from Enver – and when the piece came out he stopped ringing me. Dan Fortess I described in conventionally breathless tones. He was swoon-makingly handsome, he was the dreamiest of dancers and we had talked about 'everything under the sun'. On the stroke of midnight, Cinderella-like, I had been rushed away in a Porsche.

'Selling newspapers is about telling people the stories they know already,' the ageless young man had explained to me over a late-afternoon lunch. 'And successful feature-writing is about imposing a familiar narrative structure on to the potentially terrifying chaos of real events. It's about providing comfort; it's about telling people that they don't need to worry. Do you know what BLT stands for?'

'Bacon, lettuce and tomato?' I hazarded.

'Well, yes,' he smiled. 'But in this business it stands for bright, light and trite: the three graces of feature-writing.'

'Do you think I've done the wrong thing going into fashion

rather than features?' I asked him.

'No, not at all. Fashion will teach you exactly the same lessons, because fashion is life in miniature. It has its own seasons and structures and narratives and these all have to be maintained, to be kept in play. Did you ever read the *Odyssey*?'

'Yes,' I said. 'Well . . . no. I haven't actually read it.'

'It's the story of Odysseus and his return from the Trojan War to the kingdom of Ithaca in Greece. For one reason and another this takes him ten years – you know how easily distracted we chaps are – and in his absence a number of suitors present themselves to his wife Penelope. Odysseus must be dead, they say; choose a new husband from amongst us. Penelope's answer is that she will make her choice when she has finished the tapestry that she is sewing. The suitors wait, but the tapestry is never finished because although she weaves away all day she unpicks it all again every night.

'Now you could easily say, as many have said, that these suitors must have been pretty dim if they didn't rumble her ruse. But just think for a moment. Imagine the situation. There they all are, these chaps. They've moved in, they've got their own rooms, they're being cooked for, the Ithacan staff see to the laundry, the weather's great and the whole situation's far too pleasant for serious rivalry. I imagine them spending long afternoons playing volleyball on the beach while Penelope sews away inside. After a year or two their wooing would have become a purely formal thing. They'd have rented cars, had their mail redirected, fixed themselves up with local girls . . . And just say that one night, tiptoeing down to the fridge for a can of Heineken, one of them had seen Penelope unpicking the tapestry, would he really have forced the issue by making a scene about it? I doubt it. Even if every single one of them knew what she was up to, and *she knew* that every single one of them knew, the tapestry would have gone on being made and unmade every day. And that's the job of the fashion journalist. Making and unmaking the tapestry.'

'Right,' I said.

I called Dan Fortess's agent from the newspaper that afternoon, and she promised to pass on my request for an interview. I gave my home number rather than an office extension, and for a week I monitored my messages several times a day. On the eighth day I called the agent back. Dan Fortess was not giving any interviews at present, she told me. Had she given Dan my name? I asked her. She most certainly had; I was the young woman who had written the article, was I not? I was? Then perhaps she might be permitted to offer me a word of advice. Certain stories, in her opinion – and Dan Fortess saw absolutely eye to eye with her here – had a very short shelf life. Once dead there was really no purpose in reviving them. Perhaps I would care to glance at tonight's *Evening Standard*?

I found a copy. The cover picture was of Hermia Page on a Milanese catwalk, shimmering and serene as the new moon.

*

'So,' I said. 'Dan Fortess. What's the score?'

Tracey Decker sniffed, hitched her sleeves up her narrow forearms, drained her wineglass and waited meaningfully. She made no further movement, but a waiter immediately materialised at her elbow and refilled her glass. As an afterthought, he offered the bottle to me.

'Well, it started, yeah, on this breakfast TV thing. Howard was on the show and there was that Countess Something that advertised her husband's Rolls Royce for ten quid in *Exchange and Mart* because he'd been seeing this woman from Egham, and there was Dan Fortess.'

'And you went along with Howard?'

'We'd been at the Pinafore the night before, yeah, because there'd been a birthday party for that Decky Spelvin as does the dog programme, and we'd gone on to this gay club in Soho. Flinch, it was called, but I'll tell you for nothing: I'm never going there again. There was this woman, right . . . I mean I say she was a woman, but . . .'

'You didn't go to bed?'

'No, not even to sleep! Just kidding . . . No, we didn't. We went straight on from the club to the TV place. Howard had a bit on board by then and, well, you worry, don't you?'

'So he asked you along?'

'Yeah.'

'And?'

'We got there and were shown into this, like, reception place with coffee and toast and that. The Countess was there too, and she was so pissed she couldn't hardly stand, all stains on her jumper and that . . . We were a right merry crew, I can tell you.'

'And Howard went on first?'

'Yeah. And then the Countess passed out, so they had to slap her around a bit, and then Dan arrived, yeah.'

'And you got talking?'

'Yeah.'

'And what did you think?'

'Well, I could tell straight away Dan fancied me, like you can, and when the TV people were helping the poor old Countess out to the ambulance and there was no one else there he asked me for my number. He rang that night.'

'And?'

'And I started seeing him.'

'You know he's married?'

'To that model, yeah. They've got two kids: Joe and Amber.'

'So how do things stand?'

Tracey shrugged. 'He says he's in love with me. He rings me from filming on the mobile. He's getting us a flat.'

'He's leaving Hermia Page?'

'Well, the flat's more for me. Gloucester Road.'

'And how do you feel about this?'

'Well, it's on the Piccadilly Line *and* the District and Circle . . .'

'No, Tracey, I mean how do you feel about the whole situation? How do you feel about *Dan Fortess*?'

She hesitated. 'He's ever so romantic, Alison, it's always flowers and that. And pants, he once got me. From Debenhams. La Perla.'

'So where do you meet?'

'At mine. His driver brings him. We can't go out, 'cause he'd be recognised.'

'So what do you do?'

She scratched her armpit thoughtfully. 'Well, he usually fucks me straight away and then when he's having a bath I ring for a pizza. And a beer: if you order a king-size pizza you get a free Italian beer. I cooked for him once but he said it was worse than school.'

'OK, listen,' I told her. 'Listen. You're going to start at the beginning, from the morning you went to the TV centre, and you're going to tell me everything, OK? Everything.'

'You're not going to write about it, are you, Alison?' she asked tremulously.

'Tracey, I'm not going to do anything you don't want me to do.'

'I've been told that before,' she said, toying with the stem of her glass.

'Tracey,' I said, 'this is me. I'm not going to . . .' I took her hand. 'I'm just going to turn this tape recorder on, OK?'

She hesitated, and finally, blankly, nodded.

'. . . I think he really loves me, don't you?'

'Yes,' I heard myself saying, 'I think he really loves you.' There was a click, and then the soft hiss of blank tape. Opening my eyes and removing the headphones, I reached for the power switch and flicked it off. Far below, beyond the double windows, lay the black-patched glitter of the city and the silent, glow-worm crawl of the streets. It was still raining. After a moment's consideration I switched the tape recorder back on, rewound the cassette and deleted the final exchange.

I ran a bath, added a few drops of stephanotis oil and then, naked, padded through to the kitchen for cigarettes and white cider. There was no need to close the curtains: the tower flat was the highest in the building, and faced the park. The front door was double-locked and on my desk I could see the amber lights indicating that the phone and fax were set to receive. Music, it occurred to me, might well assist logical thought: David Shire's score for *The Conversation* seemed appropriate, and I slotted the disc into the player. With the warm scent rising about me, I lowered myself into the bath and gently fitted my neck to its soft enamel curve.

After spending most of the day with Tracey I had just listened, or re-listened, to her ninety-minute account of her ongoing affair with Dan Fortess. Curious how much more you could hear in a person's voice when that person was not sitting right there in front of you. Tracey's flat estuarine vowels expressed her habitual bruised hopefulness and wary, life's-a-bitch stoicism in equal measure, but at no time, I noticed, did they express the slightest surprise that she, Tracey Decker of Kensal Rise, should be the object of a film star's erotic obsession. It was a curious absence, this lack of surprise. Perhaps it was common to all *femmes fatales*. For a fatal woman, I realised – fatal in the ruinous, ending-in-death sense – was what Tracey Decker undoubtedly was. Steam had clouded the mirror and the water was as hot as I could bear it, but an apprehensive frisson ran through me. Perhaps I was just tired.

And perhaps, in his way, Dan Fortess really did love her. Perhaps something in her cloying fatalism and imperfect physicality touched him in a way that beautiful, perfect Hermia Page could not. For Hermia had been beatified. Marriage, motherhood and a slightly longer than average modelling career – she was now thirty – had conferred upon her the status of national treasure, of official repository of the womanly virtues. She still worked, lending her gracious presence to selected campaigns and chosen products, but these days photo-spreads of Hermia were more likely to be lifestyle features than advertising. We had seen her unmade-up and floury-forearmed at the kitchen table, we had seen her dropping Amber and Joe off at school in the four-wheel drive, we'd seen her smiling the smile on the charity circuit. And in the background, smiling too but perhaps a little out of focus these days, husband Dan, doing his duty in black tie.

When Dan called Tracey on the phone he had given her – the phone whose number was known only to the two of them – he gave her certain instructions. He told her not to wash. He told her not to launder the sheets or make the bed. He made sure that she had not shaved under her arms. He needed her rank and undeodorised, with the brothel stink about her and the unwashed sheets beneath her. His lovemaking, Tracey told me, was desperate and agonised: he hurt her, he bit her, he left her scratched and abraded and sore. Sometimes he wept, sometimes he begged her forgiveness, sometimes he even prayed to her. There was some part of her, it seemed – some hidden essence of her – that he was trying to reach, trying to make flesh, trying to construct from the smell and the feel and the taste of her.

What could be the source of this desperate wanting? I wondered, as the rain wavered at the window and the speakers delivered themselves of Shire's melancholy cadences.

My guess was that Dan was one of those men who, metaphorically speaking, carried a suitcase around with them. In the suitcase was a theatrical costume. Every lover had to wear the costume, every lover had to play the same role in the same weary old repertory piece. The plot elements were the usual ones: the capricious selection of the prey, the passionate pursuit, her swift capitulation, his immediate boredom and distaste. But Dan was by no means stupid; he was certainly perceptive enough to identify himself as a serial romancer. He understood that his distaste was triggered by his lover's capitulation, and so he had introduced a subtly perverse element into the equation. What he had sought and found in Tracey – and what, perhaps he had once hoped to find in me – was someone who, for all her blank physical submissiveness, was unable to truly give herself. Since she could not give herself, and thus allow him to despise her, the release that despising her would provide would always remain just beyond his reach. No matter how much he degraded her, he would never be able to free himself of her. She was his *cantharides*, his Spanish fly, the itch at which he would tear until he was bloody. Perhaps, I mused, that was a kind of love.

It wouldn't read like a love story, though. It would read like these stories always read: like a celebrity kiss-and-tell piece. I wouldn't write it myself; I'd call in a couple of favours and auction the whole package – tapes, surveillance photographs and an introduction to Tracey – through an intermediary. Some tabloid hack could run with the story and take the byline. They'd give it the front page and, at the very least, a double spread on two and three. I'd make quite a lot of money – certainly enough to pay off the flat – and so, one way and another, would Tracey. The 'Cinderella' story would get reprised again – it was all there in the cuttings files – but otherwise I wouldn't be associated with the story in any way. Bart, for example, would never know.

*

One of the accusations regularly levelled against journalists is that they catalyse events, they make things happen that otherwise would not have happened. But this is not how it works. How it works is that stories reveal themselves: you become aware at a given moment that a narrative is in play, and that you are one of the players. It is as if, having thought that you were standing still, you looked around and saw that you were being transported to perspective infinity on one of those moving airport walkways. Travelators, I think they're called. Around you, being carried forward on their own travelators, are the other players. Relativity ensures that these other players remain in focus but that everything else becames a blur, falls away. It is a dreamtime moment, this perceptive shift, but once it has occurred you cannot unmake it, cannot move against the narrative flow. And as I leant from the cooling bath to extinguish the night's final cigarette I admitted to myself what I'd known from the moment Tracey first spoke his name: that this was personal. The story lines had been drawn, and it was entirely appropriate, in the Aeschylean sense, that I should be the narrative's instrument. In many ways, my hand had been forced. You could have described me, not unreasonably, as a victim of circumstances.

5

Hal rang my bell at nine thirty a.m. It had been six years, but he was looking more than six years older than I remembered him. We greeted each other a little awkwardly, and I offered my cheek for a kiss. His face was cold.

'You've done well for yourself,' he said, rubbing his hands together.

'So have you, I'm told.'

He shrugged. 'I still love the work. I see you made "Hackwatch" in *Private Eye*.'

'Oh, that, yes. I'm quite proud of it, actually.'

He laughed. 'Well, you're in good company. Who's the target today, then?'

'Dan Fortess.'

'Dan? You're kidding. I saw him and Hermia up in Thame a fortnight ago. What's he been up to?'

'Guess.'

Hal nodded. He looked tired. 'Girl? Boy?'

'Girl.'

'And we're off to her place, yeah?'

'We are. I'll pay you your day rate now, or your rate and a half post-publication. Plus the same again for all negatives in my hand.'

'Is the story a definite runner?'

'Definite.'

'Post-publication, then.'

'You're on.'

I briefed him en route. It was a bitterly cold day, and despite my thermal clothing I was grateful for the van's heating system.

By ten, we were in place, and within minutes of switching off the engine the van's interior was once again a refrigerator.

My calculation had been that from the TV Centre, where Fortess was filming, his driver would approach the Harrow Road from Scrubs Lane before turning left into Kilvert Avenue, which was where Tracey lived. Hal agreed that this was the logical route. Accordingly, we tucked ourselves into a space some forty yards north of her front door and on the opposite side of the road.

'She says he'll probably be coming around midday?' asked Hal.

'Yup.'

'Is she in now?'

'Let's see,' I said, and pulled out my mobile. Tracey answered on the second ring and I cut her off.

Taking off his gloves, Hal set up the shot. The back of the van was fitted out like a miniature photographic studio, with backward-facing seats and wind-down windows. He mounted a 35mm Canon on a tripod, and attached a heavy telephoto lens.

'Wow.'

'Nice piece of glass, isn't it? Look through the viewfinder.'

Tracey's front door looked close enough to lean out and touch. We would probably have no more than a second or two when they were both in frame, but the definition was amazing: I could see every detail of the brass leprechaun knocker, and all but read the names on the bells. The mobile rang in my pocket and I jumped, almost overbalancing the camera.

'Hello?'

'Hello, who's that?'

'Tracey?'

'Alison. You rang, yeah?'

'Sorry, Tracey, it was a mistake, I meant to dial someone else. How's things?'

'Oh . . . OK. Bit itchy, actually, but can't have a bath 'cause You Know Who's coming round.'

'Tracey, you're a grown-up. If you want a bath, have a bath.'

'D'you think?'

'Of course I think. And when he rings the doorbell, just wrap a towel round yourself. No man can resist a pretty girl in a towel and . . . Have you got any of those fluffy slippers?'

'I've got some Doctor Scholls.'

'I don't think they send quite the same message. Perhaps you could have a rose in your mouth?'

'I'd prick myself.'

'You take the thorns off, Tracey.'

'Yeah, well . . . I think I'll leave it. Ta-ra, Ali.'

'Ta-ra, Tracey.'

'Why haven't you told her you're doing this?' Hal asked, and I mimed a chattering mouth with my fingers.

'But presumably she'll sell the story when the piece comes out?'

'She's one of Howard Harvey's girls, so I have to assume so.'

'This is going to be nasty, Alison,' said Hal, loading up a 35mm Nikon and clicking in a lens. 'Dan I don't give a monkey's about, but it'll destroy Hermia and the kids.'

'Running with the hare, now, are we?'

Hal looked at me in silence for a moment. 'Why did you hire me in particular?' he asked. 'London's full of smudgers.'

'Because you're the best man for the job, Hal. It's as simple as that.'

He nodded thoughtfully.

'OK?' I asked quietly. 'No problems?'

'No problems.' He smiled, and handed me the Canon's electronic shutter release. 'You've seen how I've framed the shot? Well, when I give you the word . . .'

'I press,' I said. 'Presumably.'

'And keep pressing. You've got seventy-two frames in there.'

'Understood. And what are you going to do?'

'I'm going to hand-hold this one,' he answered, holding up the Nikon. 'Just to make sure we're covered.'

We settled into the bucket seats. With the windows open it was very cold indeed, and our breath condensed in front of our faces. I zipped my fleece top up to my chin and pulled down my skiing hat.

'Can I smoke?' I asked.

'No.'

'Did you bring any coffee?'

'In the Thermos. Just pour out an inch at a time. I don't want any spilt if we have to move fast.'

I drank an inch of coffee. Twenty minutes passed. My hands and feet ached with the cold.

'This is a shit job, West,' I said.

'I know,' said Hal. 'But it pays well.'

For the next half hour we sat in silence. Every time a car drove up the street Hal followed it through the Nikon's viewfinder. At a little after eleven Tracey opened her front door to put out the rubbish. She was dressed in a cheap quilted dressing gown and had a towel wrapped turban-style around her hair. Grabbing the Canon's electronic cable release from my lap, Hal fired off a half-dozen frames.

'You're slowing down, MacAteer.'

'Sorry. Yes, you're right.'

If everything worked out as planned, even frames like these would be important. The tabloids often ran surveillance shots as a time-coded sequence.

'Looks like she's washed her hair,' said Hal. 'Either that or she wants to hide the state of it from the neighbours.'

Five minutes later the bulky figure of a uniformed policeman swung in front of the rear windows.

'Morning,' said Hal levelly.

'Some nice gear you got there,' said the policeman, peering inside. 'Very nice. You're not job, are you?'

'Matrimonial,' said Hal.

'Matrimonial my left bollock! Two of you and ten grand's worth of kit? Come on mate, we're all supposed to be . . . what do they call it? Inter-agency co-operation and all that.'

'Have it your own way,' said Hal equably.

'Excuse me.' I smiled what I liked to think of as my dazzling smile. 'I wonder if I could ask you to . . .' I waved him gently from the window.

He side-stepped smartly. 'Sorry, ma'am. Anything to assist Her Majesty's . . . whoever!' He winked. 'I'm all for co-operation, me!'

'Some people watch too much TV,' murmured Hal, as the cop ambled out of earshot.

'Why didn't you say we were press?' I asked.

'Because one press photographer often leads to fifty, and that's a traffic and obstruction issue. He'd want to know the score, probably have to radio in. It's never worth telling an outright lie – photo-surveillance is perfectly legal – but if he thinks we're Box or Customs he'll know there won't be any fuss. It'll go in his notebook, but that'll be the end of it.'

'I hope so,' I said. 'God, I'm cold.'

'Watch,' said Hal. 'Concentrate.'

At twelve forty-five a dark-green Rover pulled up outside Tracey's house. 'Here we go,' said Hal, motordrive whirring. 'Press!'

Dan was dressed in a brown leather jacket and baseball cap; his face was muffled to the point of unrecognisability by an Arab scarf. He stood head down on the doorstep, hopping from foot to foot with the cold, his body angled away from us. The door opened just wide enough for him to slip inside. There was no sign of Tracey. In the road, the Rover glided past us and away. I lifted my thumb from the shutter release button. 'Fuck!'

'How long does he usually stay?' asked Hal.

'How long does it take?' I answered bitterly.

'I'll reload.'

'Did you bring any sandwiches?'

'In the box. Tuna for me, cheese and onion for you.'

'You remembered!'

'I remember your breath.'

Dan Fortess stayed for half an hour. At the end of that time the Rover drew up in front of the door and the driver jumped out and jabbed at the top bell. As Dan hurried out I loosed off another flurry of shots, but the scarf was still obscuring his features. Once more, Tracey remained invisible. The Rover disappeared into the Harrow Road.

'Well, that's that,' I said, dropping the release cable to the floor of the van. 'We're stuffed. Do you think he's lucky, or just very switched on?'

At that moment there was a tap on the van's windscreen behind us. Outside was an unmarked four-door Ford with a serious-looking aerial and three obvious plain-clothes policemen. All the doors were open.

'Stay here,' said Hal, zipping the Nikon lens into its bag. 'Let me deal with this.'

Morosely, I lit a 555. From outside the car I heard strained fragments of conversation. How much, I wondered, had the day cost me? How much more was it going to cost me to get the two-shot? It had to be a two-shot, and both Dan and Tracey had to be clearly recognisable.

And then, as I flipped the cigarette end through one of the open back windows, my heart began to pound. The green Rover was back, and Dan, scarfless now, was jumping from the passenger door. Desperately batting at the smoke, I grabbed the Canon's cable release. At Tracey's front door, Dan pressed the bell. He looked round impatiently and I squeezed off a single frame. How many had I got left?

The door opened. It was Tracey, in the dressing gown, holding up what looked like a sheaf of papers, a script perhaps. I waited, my thumb suspended over the button. Stepping back from the door, Dan reached for the papers. But something had displeased Tracey – his peremptory manner perhaps – and she whisked them behind her back. I lowered my eye to the viewfinder and read her lips.

'Say *please*,' Tracey was saying.

Testily, Dan stepped forward again and reached behind Tracey's back, blocking her face. She transferred the papers to her other hand, and with both faces finally in shot I pressed the release button. *Chakka chakka chakka.* Three frames and the motordrive was silent. We were out of film but Dan was halfway to the car by now and Tracey's front door was closing.

Yes, I thought. Yes, yes, yes, yes, *yes*.

Hal's face filled the window. He hadn't noticed the Rover, Dan, Tracey, anything. He looked stressed. 'They want to know who you work for,' he said.

I found an ID card and passed it out. One of the suits glanced at it and frowned back at me.

'We're not doing anything illegal, are we?' I asked.

'No, love. Just that one of our lads reported what he described as a Security Services watcher team on our patch, and these days we like to be told about that sort of thing in advance. What's the story?'

'Actors,' I said. 'Two-in-a-bed love tryst.'

He nodded. 'Bollocks to 'em. My sister married an actor once. Complete waste of fucking space. You warm enough in there?'

'Yes, thanks.'

He gave me a card. 'You need anything, love, you give us a bell.'

'I will,' I promised.

'I'll print up straight away,' said Hal, pulling into a resident's parking space. He smiled slyly. 'My, um . . . wife'll get us some tea.'

'Your *wife*?'

'Er, yes. My wife. It was OK for me to get married, wasn't it?'

'I'm sorry, Hal. I don't know why I assumed . . .'

He ushered me through the narrow front door of a perfectly restored Georgian house. There were long shadows, dark walls and the faint odour of lavender furniture polish.

'This is . . . amazing.'

He shrugged and smiled. 'Ill-gotten gains. Spitalfields is one of the oldest and best-preserved parts of London. I've become quite a bore about it.'

'Some other time, perhaps?'

'Some other time. Ah, here she is.' A slight figure was descending the crepuscular stairway. Hal glanced at me sideways, checking my reaction.

'Hello, darlin'. Long time no see!'

'Little Brenda! I don't believe it. You're . . .' I pointed interrogatively at Hal.

'Yes,' she smiled. 'I am. How's our Cinderella?'

'Not so bad,' I said. 'Not so bad. So now you're Little Brenda West, for heaven's sakes! Wonders will never cease.'

She looked at Hal and they smiled one of those married-couple smiles.

'Actually,' she said, 'it's *Lady* Brenda West.'

'I didn't know you had a title, Hal.'

'When did you ever hear of a paparazzo with a title?' he asked reasonably.

'Yes, I see what you mean. Blimey, though. Lady Brenda West. Very Evelyn Waugh. How's Jonty?'

'Dad died. Massive heart attack.'

'I'm sorry,' I said. 'I guess it wouldn't have been like him to have had a minor one!'

'I 'spect you're right,' said Little Brenda. 'Anyway, I run Star Pictures now, so if you ever . . .'

'I might well,' I said. 'I might well.'

Behind Little Brenda a small fair-haired boy was making his way down the stairs. He came to a halt on the bottom step, and I went down on one knee.

'Hello,' I said gently. 'Who are you?'

'This is Archie,' said Hal, proudly. 'He's three.'

'Hello, Archie. Goodness, aren't you a handsome boy. Just like your dad.'

Hal and Little Brenda smiled another of those married-couple smiles.

'Fuckin' A!' said Archie.

Back at the flat I drank a couple of white ciders straight out of the fridge. The elation of the successful stake-out had worn off, and the encounter with Hal had depressed me. Time's winged chariot, I supposed, but there was something else, a sense of things falling away. I had always thought of Hal as a true believer.

In order not to prolong things, I had rung Dan Fortess's agent as soon as I'd seen the prints, and she'd called me back on the mobile within half an hour. Dan would be very happy to do an interview with me, she said. Why didn't I go down to Thame for Sunday lunch?

Sunday was two days away, and now that the encounter was inevitable, I longed for it to be over. It had to be me, though, who confronted him. Partly because of the money – the more complete and watertight the package, the more money I'd get – partly, in some contradictory sort of way, for Tracey's sake, and partly because I needed to draw a line beneath my own Dan Fortess story.

On a more cheering note, I'd returned to find a message from Suki Mott at the Laurene Forth press office offering me exclusive access to the new campaign shoot if I could secure a guarantee that the story would run at feature length. I'd called Lucy Fane at the magazine and she'd OK'd it immediately, and wanting to wrap the whole thing up, I'd rung Suki and caught her in her car, stuck in a Knightsbridge traffic jam. She was pleased to hear I was covering the shoot – we had met on the Karen Hassler piece – and promised to send me exact dates within seven days. The shoot was two and a half months away and the location a closely guarded secret, but she promised we'd all have a lot of fun. Fun, in this context, was code for a no-holds-barred entertainment and hospitality spend, and I told Suki, quite truthfully, that I was looking forward to it. Had she met this new girl? I asked her. No, she said, but they were all going to New York next week to do just that. Had I watched *Stillwater* yet? She promised I'd be blown away. Literally blown away.

The intercom rang as I replaced the phone. It was Orde and Wendy, and I remembered with a rush of exasperation that I'd asked them to come over for dinner when we'd met up for lunch in Camberley.

I buzzed them in. Wendy folded me in a giggly Fracas-fragrant embrace and handed over a tissue-wrapped bottle of something red in a Europa bag, while Orde, in late recognition of my birthday, awkwardly placed a small polythene bag of CDs on the kitchen table. The best two of these were Bernard Herrmann's score for *Fahrenheit 451*, which I had been looking for for ages, and Artie Kane's *Looking for Mr Goodbar*. Perfect bed-time music for a single girl, all in all, and I thanked him, touched.

I gave them what I always gave my dinner guests: cook-from-frozen Trawlerman Pie and champagne. I had a freezer stacked full of Trawlerman and Hearty Crofter pies, the joy of these products being – apart from their cook-from-frozen status – that their integrated vegetable content obviated the need for any peeling and steaming. Very few people complained about the taste.

'Do you always drink champagne?' asked Wendy. She giggled apologetically, and made a cross-eyed Bugs Bunny face. 'Not that I'm complaining, of course!'

'That and white cider,' I said. 'I don't really like many other sorts of wine. I had Dom Perignon at a party when I first moved to London, and that was it, really.'

'Whose party?' asked Orde.

'No one you know.'

'Not . . . your Prince Charming, by any chance? Not Dan Fortess, divine dancer and – what was it – brilliant conversationalist, in whose strong arms . . .'

'Oh God, here we go,' I said wearily.

'You don't know him, do you?' asked Wendy. 'I think he's gorgeous.'

'I'm sure Orde will tell you the story of me and Dan Fortess,' I said. 'He's most amusing on the subject.'

The story, or Orde's version of it, got us through the meal. When we had finished the Jack Frost Lemon Flurry, I made a cafetiere of Lavazza and loaded the *Stillwater* video into the VCR.

'Here's the main feature,' I told them. 'It's not out in this country yet. I'll tell you why we're watching it afterwards.'

It wasn't bad at all. I'd expected self-indulgent and over-extended bleakness, but actually it moved pretty fast. The title sequence shows the arrest – for murder – of Donna Shelest, played by Dale Cooney. Inside the remote lakeside house lies the body of her much older husband, a kitchen knife planted in his back.

The case looks cut and dried. The DA has political ambitions, as DAs always have in these pictures, and needs a surefire conviction. Enter Rob Wells, the inexperienced young lawyer appointed by the court to handle Donna's defence. His task looks hopeless. To begin with – for the first half of the film, in fact – Donna will not speak, will not defend herself.

Inexorably, the DA builds his case. Rob, however, is convinced that there is more to the story than meets the eye, and despite the fact that he is recently married, he finds himself increasingly attracted to the mysterious Donna. Certain that she is holding something back, he travels to the small town where she grew up. There he finds people unwilling to talk, gets nowhere, and frustrated, returns to the city.

On the penultimate day of proceedings, however, a deaf and dumb young man whom Rob has befriended in Donna's home town arrives at his office and presses a crumpled document into his hand. It is a copy of a birth certificate. The next day, in court, Rob calls Donna to the stand. Is it true, he gently asks her, that the man to whom she was supposedly married was in fact her father? Yes, says Donna, tears streaming down her cheeks. A sad tale of long-term sexual abuse comes to light and a verdict of justifiable homicide is brought. Donna departs the courtroom a free woman, but alone.

'Very neat,' said Orde, standing up, bear-like, to stretch. 'Did you guess?'

'About halfway through,' I said, flicking the rewind button on the remote. 'The plot left itself nowhere else to go. What did you think, Wendy?'

'Wouldn't have guessed in a million years,' she said, clutching at Orde's rugger shirt as she followed him to her feet. 'Whoooo. Dizzy girl! Needs her bed!'

'What did you think of her?' I asked. 'The Donna one?'

'Liverish,' said Orde. 'Looked like she could do with a few press-ups, bit of fresh air. Although did you notice how it never really got light there, what was it called, Rainy Lake? It was always this sort of grey . . .'

'Pretty, did you think?'

'She had this sort of . . . do-I-fancy-her-or-don't-I-fancy-her quality. Kept you on the jump.'

'And bottom line?'

'Bottom line I didn't, really.'

'Wendy?'

'Thought she was fabulous, actually. Kill for those cheekbones.'

'You said you'd tell us why you were showing us the film,' said Orde.

'I'm writing about her. She's the new Laurene Forth girl.'

'Who was the old one?' asked Wendy.

'Karen Hassler.'

'Now *she's* gorgeous,' said Orde. 'The Kraut with the Pout. Why did they bin her?'

'I guess because they're trying to sell cosmetics to Wendy rather than to you,' I said.

'So what did you think of this . . . whatever her name was?'

'I don't know,' I said.

6

I wasn't looking forward to my day's work. People thought that it was easy, what we did, and that it took no toll, but they were wrong. It wasn't easy and it got harder as time passed. When I first started in features I was loosed almost daily into environments of grief and betrayal; a woman – or a woman's voice – was felt to be less intrusive, more likely to produce a forthcoming response. 'Send the girl in,' they'd say, and I'd be slipped in like a ferret. I'd nod and I'd listen and I'd seem to do nothing and at the end of the day I'd return like one of Fagin's pickpockets, my bag stuffed with quotes. I didn't greatly enjoy it, but I knew that I was good at it.

Dan, his agent had told me on the phone, was very much looking forward to seeing me again, as was Hermia. I wasn't particularly worried about Dan, but now that the day had come, I had to admit that I didn't feel altogether comfortable about what I was going to do to Hermia. If she had any memory of me at all, I mused as the train rattled through Goring and Streatley, it was as the twenty-year old *ingénue* in borrowed clothing who tried to steal her boyfriend and then added insult to injury by selling the story to the press.

I had tried to dress with dark metropolitan precision, to make no concessions to the rural fantasy that I assumed we were about to enact. I had no intention of striking the right note or playing the game, and I certainly didn't want Hermia Page to think of me even for a minute as a potential friend. Rather, I wanted to convey an impression of unadaptability, of lonely containment in my work. Given what I was about to do to them, this seemed the least insulting approach, although in the end it didn't make much difference: they were both going to hate me. The Capri would have provided a fast getaway but the Capri, frustratingly, was in the garage with transmission trouble. I had thought of hiring a car for the day but in the end had settled for a first-class rail ticket.

Dan met me at Oxford station with Amber, who was six, and Joe, who was four, and a largeish dog.

'Alison,' he said easily, as if I popped round every other day. 'Hi. Let me take that.' He reached for the briefcase containing my tape recorder, my notebook, my cigarettes, an audio cassette marked Tracey D. and the packet of 10″ by 8″s printed up for me by Hal West.

'It's fine. I'll hang on to it. How are you, Dan?'

He had changed and he hadn't changed. The wry regard had sharpened a little, but the eyes were the same vertiginous blue.

'Terrific,' he said. The dog strained at the leash and Joe tugged at his coat. On the train I had harboured the dim hope that the whole lunch business could be dispensed with; that I could buttonhole him there and then, put the questions to him that I had to put to him, and take the next train home. With the children there, however, this was impossible. Dan's presence caused considerable – if decently muted – excitement in the ticket hall. Everyone recognised him, and it was clear that while he made a show of ignoring this he was in fact quite appreciative of it.

The drive, in a newish Cherokee Jeep, took about twenty minutes, of which the first quarter-hour was motorway. Dan apologised for this, as if fearful that I would take the landscape personally. 'We get off in a minute,' he kept saying. 'Just a couple of miles more.' The children sat in politely spooked silence in the back.

When we did finally leave the motorway Dan's demeanour became expansive, proprietorial. A minor road wound through a small village, and the entrance to Kingham Lodge lay between tall banks of yew. The house itself was large, and of stone. Dan led us round the outside to a sunlit garden with an orchard and tall grey trees. Hermia was visible at a kitchen window; she waved, and I raised a hand in hesitant response.

'Can I show her where we saw the eel, Daddy?' asked Joe, more confident now that he was on his home turf.

'Sure you can,' said Dan. 'And her name's Alison, not "her".'

'Alison,' said Amber experimentally. 'We don't need wellies, do we?'

Dan glanced down at my Manolos.

'The ground still looks pretty frosty,' I said. 'I think I'll be OK.'

We crunched over the hard ground to the stream which bisected the front lawn. The reeds were hoar-frosted, and jagged sickles of ice edged the running water.

'It was there,' said Amber, pointing. 'Just in that deep bit there.'

'I saw it too, Alison,' said Joe, taking my hand. 'In the deep bit, there.' Trusting the absolute security of my grasp, he suddenly leant right out, pointing, over the stream. To counterbalance myself I had to take a step forward, straight through the icy crust of the mud. I gasped with the cold of it; Dan grabbed Joe, pulling him back from the bank, and I felt my leg sink deeper.

'Here,' Dan took my wavering back-stretched arm. 'Pull.'

The mud released me with a loud, sucking glop, and I fell backwards, my leg black to mid-calf, my shoe ruined. Amber giggled uncontrollably but Joe, shocked, started to cry. I picked myself up, and tried to brush off the mud and the little bits of twig that had attached themselves to my clothes. 'It's OK,' I said to Joe. 'It's OK.'

'I'm . . . what can I say?' said Dan, pressing Joe against him. 'I'm mortified. Your *shoe*. We must get you inside.' Behind him, Amber was pinching her nose so as not to giggle.

Hermia, rubbing cream into her hands, met us at the door. 'Oh my God, Dan, *really*!' she expostulated. 'Alison, darling, *what* have they done to you? Dan, *honestly*!'

Swiftly, she took charge of the situation. The children were dispatched to the playroom, and Dan was instructed to carry me up to the bathroom. This last, I guessed, had more to do with the preservation of their cream stair carpet than with any possibility that I might have injured myself.

'Such a fair burden,' murmured Dan.

'Watch it, buster,' said Hermia, following us up the stairs.

Dan parked me on the edge of the bath, and hurried guiltily

downstairs. Hermia pulled off the muddy shoe and dropped it into a basin.

'Trousers.'

'They're fine, Hermia.'

'They aren't. Come on. Off.'

I took them off, she threw them in the basin with the shoe and told me to wait. She returned with some velvet trousers – the Gucci price tag still attached – and a pair of brand-new ankle boots. 'Ferragamo, I'm afraid, not Blahnik,' she apologised. 'But you can keep them if they fit. They're just too tight for me. You know what big ugly feet we models have.'

The trousers were a couple of inches too long but the boots could have been made for me.

'They're wonderful,' I said. 'I'll turn these up an inch or two.'

'One of these days,' she smiled, 'I'm going to see you in your own clothes.'

Penitently, I closed my eyes. 'I'm sorry,' I said. 'I was twenty. And very gauche.'

'You know, I never said, but I saw you earlier that night. Outside the cinema. You were wearing a sort of dispatch rider's jacket. Yours was the only face without a camera in front of it and you were staring at me with those wild eyes of yours like . . . like some kind of *angel of death*. I wondered about you all the way though the film. And then when you turned up at the party looking absolutely drop-dead divine . . .'

She laughed, and shook back her hair. 'I gave Dan real hell when your article came out. I mean, *real hell*. I flew to Milan and didn't return his calls for forty-eight hours. And when I finally deigned to speak to him, the first thing he asked me was if I would marry him! So I've actually had rather affectionate memories of you ever since.'

'I think I'd rather be remembered as Cupid than an angel of death,' I said. 'Do you mind if I snip these tags off?'

'No. Here. You're not married, are you?'

'No. I go out with someone in my office. Pathetic really.'

'Married?'

'Him? No. I wouldn't put up with that.'

'Alison, forgive me for asking this, and I'm presuming on seven years' acquaintance here rather than ten minutes, but why do you look so unhappy?'

'Do I look unhappy?'

Reaching out to the broad Victorian washbasin, she took a brass-framed shaving mirror and held it in front of my face. For more than a minute, I regarded myself in quizzical silence, but saw nothing beyond the incurious gaze of my own eyes. The heavy base of the mirror dripped on to the bathmat.

'I'm tired,' I said. 'I probably work too hard.'

'What else do you do?' she asked, replacing the mirror.

'Apart from what?'

'Apart from work.'

'I read. Go to films. Listen to music.' I wriggled my toes inside the Ferragamo boots. 'These are so beautiful.'

'Do you go out much?'

'Well . . . restaurants, clubs and things, all that tends to be work. So, no, I don't go out much.'

'You just sit at home and wait for this guy? He must be pretty special.'

'I stay at home because I have everything exactly as I want it there. If he rings, he rings. Usually I don't let him come to my flat. I go to his.'

She looked at me with gentle pity. 'Modern love, huh?'

I shrugged. 'Call it that.'

She took my shoulders in her hands and frowned intently into my eyes. 'Alison, is that really the best you would have wanted for that beautiful creature who stopped the show at the *Faro's Daughter* party?'

'You thought she was beautiful?'

A momentary laziness touched the oblique, powder-burn eyes. 'Still do, kiddo. She was a one-off. An original.'

I stood up abruptly. 'She'll have her day.'

'Promise?'

I forced myself to smile. 'Promise.'

Walking down the stairs, the full knowledge of what I was about to do to this very likeable woman came flooding back. I'd been through the stitch-up routine before, but I'd never felt quite so disinclined to do what – as night followed day – had to come next. Soon they would be picking over the details of my visit. And all the time, they would be thinking. *And all the time* . . . It had never been quite like this before. My guts were like an unthawed chicken's: jagged hand-shredding blocks of ice.

Lunch was excruciating, and despite Hermia's skilful work with mortar and pestle and garlic press – she made her own pasta and pesto, needless to say – I tasted not a single mouthful. I sensed that Dan and Hermia were looking to me to pay my way for the interview with conversation, with witty, pro-active insider stuff, but I was monosyllabic, writhing on the pin, my observations trailing into irrelevancy.

The incident by the stream seemed to have cowed the children, too. They sneaked glances at each other but there were no giggles, no whispers. Dan, who was under the impression that mine was to be a broad-sweep profile, was simultaneously playing the ironic father and teasing me – flirtatiously, but well within the guidelines – about the 'hatchet job' that I was shortly to perform on him. He was very sure of himself, very confident that he had me on-side and within bounds, and so far, by dint of non-specific blather about mid-career appraisals and 'the life of the working actor', I had evaded the question of the article's hook. Vanity and common sense must have been slugging it out, I guessed, for there was nothing on his current professional horizon on which a major profile might reasonably have been hung.

The truth was that Dan Fortess's star had waned since our first meeting. He had dazzled for a couple of years – mostly in period pieces – had become the favourite brooding aristocrat of a million teenage girls and bulimic Jane Austen fans, had been overpraised, lured to Hollywood, miscast in a couple of straight-to-video clunkers, and slung back in the pool with the rest of the jobbing cuff-shooters and trilby-tippers. For several years, things had been slow. The overseas mini-series market had picked up a little of the slack but in Britain he had been viewed as a quintessentially mid-nineties phenomenon, not yet susceptible to reinvention. As Hermia Page's husband, however, he had remained in the public eye, and the press had lost no opportunity to punish him for his earlier success. Where they had once been happy to use studio publicity stills, picture editors took to running unflattering grab-shots. The story was the oldest in the book: her on the up and up, him on the slide.

Casting him as a villain was a masterstroke, for by then, as the B-list-at-best consort of the regally A-list Hermia Page, Dan Fortess was beyond PR redemption. In the eyes of the public he was a villain already, a vampire battening on the sweet bounty of the Lady Hermia. In *Wirral A&E*, as the cold but brilliant Dr Belvoir, he had been persuaded to capitalise on this negative image, and the result, if a little camp to the finely tuned eye, had been described as compulsive viewing. The series presently in production was the third, and for Fortess it would be followed by a Royal Shakespeare Company season at the Barbican in which he would alternate the roles of Angelo in *Measure for Measure* and Vendice in *The Revenger's Tragedy*.

An interesting enough professional history, certainly, but not so interesting as to make the jump from the arts to the features pages. Deep down, I suspected, Dan knew this, and was telling himself that I had set up the interview in order to see him again, and that my inarticulacy was the result of my having carried a torch for him for so long.

I was pretty sure that Hermia didn't think that, though. She was canny, Hermia, she knew I was up to something. That was why she was so happy to get me into her Gucci pants. You can't stitch people up when you're wearing their clothes, when you've eaten their pesto, when their children have shown you where they saw the eel.

'"There is something sinister about Dr St John Belvoir,"' I read from the photocopied TV review, '"something decadent. You can tell that he is intimately versed in the darker arts of the boudoir . . ."'

Dan laughed. 'Yes, I remember that piece. I remember we were having a read-through on the first day of rehearsals and the director said to me . . .'

We were sitting at the top end of the lawn on an Edwardian bench whose iron members had been cast to resemble sentimentally knotted branches. Around us, in their shaped beds, heavily pruned rose bushes stood in frost-hardened compost. Beyond the rose garden was a stand of poplars whose shadows, untouched by the winter sun, were a crisply silvered blue.

It had been Hermia's idea that I should interview Dan outside. Five minutes earlier she had brought us coffee and carrot cake on a Chinese lacquer tray and this now sat decorously between us on the bench. My tape recorder was on the tray, my briefcase on the ground at my feet. I had drunk most of my coffee but Dan's, as he warmed to his theme, was growing cold. I didn't listen to his answers; I barely listened to my own questions. Eventually he fell silent, and I asked if I could smoke. Reaching for my lighter and 555s, I flicked on the Acu-Sonic micro-recorder in the breast pocket of my coat. I felt better than I had earlier. Despite the cold, my fingers were quite steady.

'So, Dan Fortess,' I said brightly, 'would you say, today, that you were a happy man?'

He threw an expansive arm along the top of the bench and gave me his actor's face, his blank, open-book, child-on-the-threshold-of-eternity face. 'How could I not be? I have all this, I have a career which, fingers crossed, seems to be back on the rails, I have two wonderful children, I'm married to the woman who, by general agreement, is the most beautiful in the world . . .' He shrugged self-deprecatingly. His eyes were the blue of the winter sky. 'Yup. I'm a happy man.'

I gave him my best, bird-curious, Joan Bakewell look.

'So why are you fucking Tracey Decker?'

Eternity passed. Motes swam in the cloudless azure sky. A bird sang in one of the poplars. Slowly Dan Fortess reached for the tape recorder on the Chinese lacquer tray and switched it off. More time passed.

'This is . . . because I didn't ring you back, what, six, seven years ago? Is that what this is about?'

The role was that of Everyman, the honest seeker after truth, struggling to comprehend an unreasonably abstruse point of philosophy.

'This is nothing to do with me at all. I'm just curious.'

His eyes searched the landscape before him. He extended his fingers, brought them down on his knees as if about to play

Rachmaninov. 'Alison, we can still . . .'

'Still what?'

'Christ, you're merciless, aren't you? And all because . . .'

'Please,' I said. 'Understand me. This is nothing to do with me. This is about you.'

'You're kite-flying. Making it up. Who is this Tracy Whatever-her-name-is? I've never heard of her.'

In answer I trod out my cigarette, pulled the yellow print envelope from my briefcase, and handed him the 10″ by 8″ pictures in sequence order. There was Tracey in her dressing gown putting the rubbish out, there was the car pulling up, there was Dan's dash to the front door, there was Dan, recognisable, pressing Tracey's bell, and finally there was Dan with Tracey on her doorstep, his arms encircling her, their faces inches from each other, the background a velvet lagoon of differential focus.

'So what does this prove? Me talking to another actor?'

In answer, I ejected the cassette from the Sony and replaced it with one from my briefcase. Tracey's voice was immediately recognisable: '. . . so he's round at mine, yeah, and he's fucking me, yeah, and he goes, like, "I'd die if I couldn't see you, Tracey, I need you that much" and I go, "Why's that?" and he says, right, "Because you *are* me, Tracey; your body's my body, your . . ." '

His gaze emptied; the skin around his eyes and mouth seemed to grow old. I replaced the cassette and the photographs in my briefcase.

'Those are copies?'

'Those are copies.'

He nodded. Folding his arms across his chest, he rocked backwards and forwards. I watched him. Time passed.

'Who knows?'

'People know. Tell me why, Dan.'

'You tell me why, Alison. Why are you doing this?'

'Because this is the story. This is what I do.'

He stared at me. 'What have you . . . become?'

'This isn't about me.'

'I think it damn well is about you. I think it's a hundred per cent about you. What can you possibly gain from destroying my family?'

'You're a public man. In return for all this' – I gestured about us – 'you have to expect a level of . . . interest in your doings.'

'You've got the story wrong. You've got it on its head.'

'Still stands up, though. Do you deny that you and Tracey Decker have a sexual relationship?'

'No comment.'

Got you. No comment was a reaction. Legally, you could go to print with a no comment. Perhaps he knew this.

'Why Tracey Decker?'

'If you can give me a good reason why you're doing what you're doing to my family, I'll tell you . . . why Tracey Decker.'

I had what I had come for. Anything else was a bonus. More rope. I lit another 555 and offered him the packet. 'OK. I'll tell you why I'm doing this. Do you know the story of the scorpion and the tiger?'

'No.' He took a cigarette and extended a hand for my lighter.

'The scorpion wants to cross the river. The tiger's about to swim across, so the scorpion asks him for a ride. "No," says the tiger, "you would sting me." "Why would I do that?" asks the scorpion. "We would both drown." Persuaded by the logic of this, the tiger agrees. They set out, but when they reach the middle of the river, the scorpion stings the tiger. As they are swept downstream towards the waterfall the tiger turns to him. "You've killed us both," he says. "Why?" "Because," says the scorpion, "it is in my nature so to do." '

Dan nodded, and smoked in silence. Behind us I heard the crunch of twigs. The children were creeping up on us, playing Grandmother's Footsteps. I turned and smiled down at them.

'Mummy says do you want any more coffee?' Joe asked me. Biscuit crumbs surrounded his mouth. He had his mother's eyes.

'Tell Mummy no,' said Dan to Amber, who was wiping her hands on the seat of her jeans. 'You can take the tray, though.'

'I want to take it,' said Joe.

'You take the sugar bowl,' said Dan.

'OK,' I said, when they were out of earshot. 'Tracey Decker.'

'You'll probably think I'm crazy.'

'Tell me, Dan,' I said. Here it all came. The love-as-recognition riff, the Jungian anima defence. I wasn't sure I could bear to listen. From behind us, as if in answer to my thoughts, came the slow crash of bone china. We both turned. Neither of the children was hurt.

'Is there anything I could say which would make any difference to what you're going to do?' he asked. 'Would ten thousand pounds make any difference?'

'I'll get a lot more than that for this story.'

'How much more?'

I told him. Behind us, Hermia was investigating the tea-tray shunt. She was pretending to be cross. 'Well, Daddy *shouldn't* have told you to!'

'Fifty thousand,' said Dan, very quietly.

'You're offering me fifty thousand pounds to kill this story?'

'Yes, I am. Now listen to me. Don't speak, just listen, OK? I've got a dollar account that Hermia doesn't know about. If you agree to put the originals of all material relating to myself and Tracey Decker in my hands, I will give you a cheque for the dollar equivalent of fifty thousand pounds. When the cheque clears, you give me the stuff.'

I said nothing. Folded my arms. Felt the little Acu-Sonic in my pocket.

'Ask yourself why you're doing this story, Alison. There's no conceivable public interest benefit; you're doing it for the money. That's a given. Now you just might be able to auction the story for more than I'm offering you, but are you really prepared to destroy my family – my children – for the difference? I know you, Alison. I've known you from the first second I set eyes on you because you're exactly like me: a calculating, opportunistic shit. But you're not completely heartless. Like most truly selfish people – like me, again – you've got a broad sentimental streak, and that's why you're not going to destroy my children's life just for the hell of it.'

I said nothing. On the still air, behind us, I could hear the tiny plinkings as Hermia gathered the broken china pieces.

'Let me tell you what's going to happen,' Dan continued, his voice absolutely level. 'I'm going to drive you back to Oxford station, and before you get on the train, I'm going to give you that cheque I told you about. Tomorrow, you're going to go to any of the American banks in London, and you're going to open an account and deposit the cheque. It'll take a week or two, and then you'll get notification that it's cleared. At that point you're going to ring me, and we'll arrange to meet. I'll tell Hermia that you were ringing to say the story you came to do today has been spiked. And we'll meet and you'll hand over the photographs and negatives and tapes and everything else and we'll look each other in the eye and that will be that. And *then* . . .'

'And then?' I said.

'And then you and I have unfinished business of another kind.'

A breeze rustled the poplar trees, and I hunched into my coat and closed my eyes.

At this point, my memory begins to get patchy. I have no recollection, for example, of replying to Dan's suggestion. The conversation must have ended, however. We must have made our way back to the house. I must have said goodbye to Hermia and the children.

There is about a minute of absolute clarity. Dan had helped me into my coat, I could feel the black satin lining cold at my wrists and neck, and as he stepped away I lifted my hair from beneath my collar and turned to the dark rectangle of mirror. Before me stood a pale, grave-eyed stranger, the stranger I had sometimes seen making love in the early morning; the stranger whom, seven years before, I had glimpsed in Enver Kassapian's Polaroid.

A long blank, and then I was being driven at speed along a road overhung with trees. I was in an open car, my hair flicking at my neck and cheeks, wind-tears streaming backwards from my eyes. My hands were clutching something, my briefcase perhaps, and my feet were braced against the floor. The dashboard was veneered wood and the seats were of hard, shiny leather.

And then a low steel-flanked vehicle – a farm trailer, perhaps – was sliding backwards into our path. I seemed to have a moment of choice, to accept what was to come or to resist it, and I closed my eyes – as I have always closed my eyes – in calculated acceptance. If I am obedient, I remember thinking, perhaps I will not be hurt. If I am obedient, perhaps I will be loved.

I was six years old when I fell into the swimming pool at the

Tanglin Club. It was evening, the palms were still and the mosquito-repellent candles were burning. I didn't struggle, I simply fell through the blood-warm water. Minutes seemed to pass and then I was rising through the deep-water silence, my arms flat to my sides and my hair sleek to my head. As I broke the surface, the water leapt phosphorescent before me, an ecstasy of spray which hung suspended for a moment and then drop by brilliant drop, fell away. Arms reached for me. I had never been held closer.

This time, however, there were no anxious arms to gather me from the water. This time they let me go, they let me return to the silence. Others were there. Familiar faces crowded around me, whispering of my new beauty.

'You look so wonderful,' said Sonia. 'So complete.'

'You shine,' murmured Bart, touching my cheek with his finger.

'Where am I?' I murmured.

'Stillwater,' whispered a slight, fair-haired figure.

I slept until they moved me, and while the sleep and the darkness were infinitely gentle – were love itself – the lights and the pain were worse than anything that I had ever known or imagined. The lights and the pain robbed me of the years that I had lived. I was new-born in pain.

When they began to cut my clothes off, I woke again, frightened now. Perhaps acceptance had been the wrong course. I wanted to ask them to stop, to say that with a little help I could take the clothes off myself, but their hands were fast and sure and when I tried to speak I managed only a fluttering and soundless exhalation. Breathing through my mouth was suddenly difficult, metallic-tasting snot webbed my throat and the tube from my nose made swallowing uncomfortable. *I'm sorry*, I wanted to say, *I'm really not usually as disorganised as this* . . . Cold shears slid from my collar to my breastbone, and I felt the fabric part. *I'm sorry*.

A face-shape swung between my eyes and the light. 'Well, we know she's Catholic,' a woman's voice said at my ear.

'How?' came a male voice from near my feet, where unhurried blades were scissoring through the soft Florentine leather of my boots.

'Lourdes medal,' said the woman briskly. 'Hurry, she's not looking good.'

'Thank you very much,' I murmured, but no one paid me any attention. *My Ferragamo boots*, I thought, and began to cry.

'Hello, stranger,' Hermia whispered, deftly snipping through the gold chain at my neck.

'I'm a one-off,' I murmured, the tears coursing warmly towards my ears. 'An original.'

'You're the Angel of Death,' said Hermia.

The shears raced through the wiring of my bra, nosed beneath the waistband of my trousers.

'Aha.' A pause. A suction at my upper thigh.

'What've you got?'

'This. Straight through the femural vein.' The sound of glass rocking on metal. 'Pressure dressing, please.'

'Didn't the ambulance crew . . .?'

'Obviously not, they thought the face and chest were the limit of it. Mother of God, this velvet's like a sponge.'

'Have you . . .?'

'Yes. Eight units. They'll be at least half an hour, though. How much unmatched have we got in the fridge?'

'One up, three ready.'

I felt a wet slither beneath my bottom, and as my pants and the upper part of my trousers were pulled away I was spitted on the ragged blades of a pain so intense that, for a moment, it was unrecognisable even as pain. The darkness came flooding back, wrapped me like a flag.

When I woke, the pain had withdrawn, but I sensed it waiting nearby. A male voice, not the voice of the pain, was asking why I was so shocked.

'Could be intraperitoneal bleeding,' said the woman. 'We'll need a DPL. Pulse?'

'Hundred and forty. Thready.'

'Blood pressure?'

'Seventy systolic.'

The first voice, tired-sounding now, spoke with exaggerated clarity.

'Alison, you've got to help us. Can you hear me?'

Of course I'll help you, I wanted to say. I'll do anything you want. Anything at all. But first – *first* – just let me sleep. Right now, I need sleep more than I've ever needed anything.

There was the faint breath of a swinging door.

'Blink twice if you can hear me, Alison.'

I tried, but my eyes wouldn't close. The faces swam beyond a cracked ochre varnish. I was baffled by the unreasonability and complexity of their demands.

'Alison . . . *Alison!* Sally, lose the saline and get some more blood up. Quick, we're losing her.'

Peonies of light bloomed silently before my eyes.

'Come *on*, Alison!' The first voice was urgent now, but seemed to be coming from much further away. 'Stay with us.'

At my ears was the drawing back of a great tide. 'Fight, Alison,' the voice implored, '*Fight!*' But the whisper died away, was lost to the breaking wave. I was a spectator now. Below me, attended by three women and two men, the naked, light-bleached body of a stranger lay on a hospital trolley, her eyelids fluttering faintly in the smashed vermilion mask of her face. Glass fragments studded her upper body, and temporary pressure dressings had been applied to a transverse gash from her right hip bone to her left breast and to a deep laceration on her upper left thigh. Her pale skin was slick with blood, red and shining around the principal wound sites, a dull beef-brown elsewhere. From the side of the trolley, held in place by her body, hung stiff, blood-caked strips of underwear and clothing. Others had fallen to the floor. The attendants in their green pyjamas and bloodied plastic aprons slumped like exhausted butchers, their gloved hands at their sides.

7

I lay weightless on the rushing oceanic night; below me the world turned. I could see nothing, but I sensed the earth's rotation and the dark infinity against which I drifted.

Iceland, Viking, North Utsera, South Utsera, Finisterre, Trafalgar . . . My passage and its co-ordinates were announced without emotion, but I knew that I was being drawn downwards from the night, my body reinvested with weight. *Valencia, east-north-east, six, one hundred and twenty-five, falling slowly* . . . I met curtains of gauzy light, wavering drifts of spray, the vast indifference of the sea. Below me, waves hurled themselves against a desolate shore. *Boomer, calm, mist four miles, one thousand and twenty-eight, falling* . . .

And then the curtains were a mosquito net plucked by a monsoon breeze. A faint powdery scent lingered in the bedroom, and I could feel the hand smoothed across my forehead. . . . *becoming cyclonic in the north, thundery showers* . . .

I wanted to sit up, but found that I was unable to move, that I was pinned to the bed by a crown of bayonets that had been driven through my womb. I am so greatly loved, I thought, reaching for the blades, and a scarlet flower of pain burst inside me. The National Anthem was playing. The pain spread like a stain – it was a living thing now, swelling with the music – and after a time it was impossible to remain silent, as I had promised to try and do. Then the music snapped off, to be replaced by a voice.

'Alison . . . Alison? Can you hear me? Alison?'

When I eventually understood that the voice was addressing me, I was unable to make any sound at all. My lips were numb and unresponsive and seemed to be several times their usual size. I could see nothing: some dark, fuscous varnish seemed to have been painted over my eyes. From my crotch rose great dumbing waves of pain.

'Hang on, love, I won't be a . . .' – the sound of a cellophane packet unwrapped, a finger flicking against plastic – '. . . I won't be a minute.'

The needle slid into my arm – purest love, purest release – and I fled away.

'I thought I was dead,' I whispered. The room, or such of it as I could see through my swollen eyelids, was white. Pale sunlight barred the walls and ceiling.

'You nearly were,' said the doctor, his voice tired. 'You lost a lot of blood. And you were very profoundly shocked. Not to mention the hypothermia, of course.'

'What happened?' My voice, breathed through numb, sutured lips, was that of a failed ventriloquist.

'You were in a car accident,' he said. 'You weren't wearing a seat belt, you went through the windscreen face first, and you ended up in a frozen ditch at the side of the road.'

'I'm sorry,' I said. Tears burnt my cheeks. 'Why did you bring me back? It . . . hurts *so much*.'

'We saved your life.'

'I wasn't cold.' My tongue was dry as wood. He had to lean towards me to hear me. 'I was . . . fine.'

'You were dying,' he said levelly. 'The crash team saved your life. Don't you want to know where you are?'

The pain came in waves, raping me. I shut my eyes.

'No. Later. It hurts in my . . . can you . . .?'

'Soon. Try and breathe.'

'Please,' I murmured.

I heard the door close.

'Please,' I said, hours later.

'Like it, do you?' The nurse's voice was amused. 'You wouldn't be the first.'

As she withdrew the needle I had an impression of freckles, of pale-lashed eyes.

'Diamorphine,' she said. 'Heroin to you and me. That's why your mouth's so dry.'

'Where am I?' I whispered.

'No one's told you? God, this *place*. You're in B Wing of the John Ackroyd Hospital in Aylesbury, Bucks., and my name's Tara Lewis. I was on your crash team.'

'My . . . face?'

She took my hand. 'Ssssh. Your face'll be OK; I cleaned you up myself. It's very swollen and contused at the moment, and probably a bit sore, but . . .'

'How will I . . . look?'

'Your eyes are fine, and . . . and the rest will heal, OK?'

'OK.'

The pain gradually withdrew, gathered itself at a distance. I closed my eyes. 'Do you need me?' I murmured.

'No, love,' she said gently. 'You can pop off now.'

Later, the family came. Orde brought Wendy. It was a bad time, the pain was edging its way back, grinding and jagged, and there were just too many people to apologise to. They looked appalled at my appearance, and all that I could manage was tears. After a minute or two, Tara hurried them away.

'Can I have a mirror?' I begged her when she came back into the room. 'Please.'

Tara wiped my eyes and my nose with a tissue, glanced down at the watch pinned to her blue uniform shirt and pursed her lips.

'Please,' I said. 'I saw how they looked at me. I have to know.'

'Alison, trust me, OK?'

'Can I have a mirror?'

She pulled her cardigan tighter across her shoulders and looked at me appraisingly. 'Don't you want to know how your friend is?'

'Dan?' The truth was that I hadn't given Dan a thought. And even now that Tara had mentioned him, I couldn't bring much concern to bear. The world in which he lived and played seemed a galaxy away.

'How is he?' I asked.

'He's fine, as it happens,' said Tara. 'He was concussed when he came in yesterday, but he's fine. Not to mention gorgeous, of course. I was the envy of the hostel.'

'He's all yours,' I said.

'He's all his wife's,' said Tara, with something like awe. '*God*, but what a beautiful woman she is. The skin on her, and those enormous eyes. She's just the most . . .'

'Tara,' I whispered.

'Mmm?'

'Get me a mirror.'

She waited until she had given me the next shot, and then held a make-up compact in front of my drowsy and barely comprehending eyes. My scalp was bandaged and such hair as I could see had been cropped to a stubble. My face seemed to have been replaced by some gashed and over-ripe tropical fruit: I saw purple bruises, crusted planes of scabbing, the raw, red-black tacking of sutures. One jagged scribble cut straight through my lips from my chin to my right cheekbone. Others, like crazed Apache war-markings, tore outwards from my eyes.

After a moment I looked down from the square of mirror to the neat satined puff on its shimmering disc of powder. It was a Laurene Forth compact, I noticed. The sight calmed me, made infinitely more sense than the demented horror above.

'A week,' said Tara, snapping the compact shut, 'and you won't know yourself.'

'Was it glass?'

'Glass, ice, the car, the road.'

'And you . . .?'

'I cleaned you up, yes. Debridement, it's called.'

'Tell me.'

'Tweezers first, for the glass, then soap and water and a stiff nailbrush. You scrub until everything's out. Quite tiring it can be, sometimes.'

'I'm sure. And . . . down below?'

'Umm . . . You've got a fractured pelvis, I think.' She moved to the foot of the bed and picked up my notes. 'Yes. Two breaks, the sacro-iliac joint at the back and the pubic ramus in front. Various cuts and bruises but it's the orthopaedic stuff that's giving you pain. What they've done is pinned you, put in these rods to realign the bones.'

'Rods?'

'Sort of Meccano, except made of this rather nice satin-finished steel. They're called fixators. Don't move now.' She pulled back the sheet; I struggled to look downwards but found myself unable to lift my head. Frustrated tears welled in my eyes.

'Rods through my skin?'

'Pins going into your bones. The rods connect them.' She bent over my groin. 'Mmm. This all looks . . . on course.'

It hadn't been a nightmare, then. I was literally nailed to the bed.

'So I can't move, or . . .'

She replaced the sheet. 'Don't worry. You'll be fine. We've popped a catheter into your bladder, and as for the other, you'll be constipated for a fortnight with all the analgesics you've had, so we'll worry about that when the time comes. What you've got to do now is rest. Would you like me to leave you my radio?'

She came back with a battered, paint-spattered Roberts. 'My boyfriend's doing up his house,' she said. 'Bugger that he is. What d'you fancy?'

'Can you get Radio 3?'

'I've never tried. What's this?'

It was Scriabin's *Poème de l'exstase*, and overlaid the heroin nicely.

The injections, I discovered, came every four hours, with the brief rapture of the pain's retreat giving way to an easeful, frictionless calm. I would sleep, and the pain would bide its time.

Tara went off soon after it got dark outside, and was replaced by a silver-haired young man called Colin. Colin wore trainers and expensive aftershave, and his approach was silent. To begin with I was rather afraid of him, but his fingers were steady as they went about the long and tiresome business of changing my dressings. As regards his maleness and my nakedness, I was a long way beyond caring.

The first time Colin spoke to me – on the morning of the second day, it must have been – he was laying squares of tulle gauze on the line of stitches running from my right hip to my left breast. Mendelssohn's *A Midsummer Night's Dream* was playing on the radio. The pain was crouching in the corner of the room, waiting for Colin to go, waiting to get me alone.

'I saw Pauline Faull dance this at the Apollo the other day.'

'Dance it?'

'It's a ballet as well as an opera,' he explained, lifting another square of gauze with the tweezers. 'She was Titania.'

'Was she good?'

'She was vicious. I adore her.'

'Tell me.'

'There's a little group of us goes to everything she does. My friend Josie's the worst. Before the curtain goes up she runs around the auditorium spraying Arpège everywhere. That's Pauline's favourite perfume. Josie's awful.'

'You're a ballet fan.'

'You could say. Can I just . . . That's it, chin up. Good girl.'

'And do you meet all the . . . this Pauline and so on?'

'Oh, Josie's very intimate, she's been to the house and got the signed pointe shoes and everything. The only time I met Pauline was in an off-licence in Barons Court: she was buying a twelve-pack of Red Stripe. The tone was calamitous.'

He chattered on. It kept the pain at bay. A point occurred to me: 'Colin,' I said, 'did they save any of my things? My briefcase, for example?'

He looked in my locker.

'There's no briefcase,' he said. 'There's some cash, a packet of 555 cigarettes, a plastic lighter, some kind of miniaturised recording device – what are you, a spy? – a holy medal . . . No briefcase, though.'

That afternoon, Dan and Hermia came in to see me. Dan, stubbled and sweatshirted, looked none the worse for the crash, and for the hundredth time I asked myself the same question: *Why wasn't I wearing a seat belt?*

Hermia, dressed entirely in white as if in homage to the medical environment, came straight over to my bed. Her footsteps slowed as she approached, and I watched her flinch as the shock of my appearance broke over her. As I'd anticipated, a hand stole for a moment to her own face and a finger traced the mirror-images of my deeper lacerations.

'We prayed for you,' she began. 'Me and Joe and Amber.'

'Thank you,' I said. 'It worked.'

She smiled and shook her head. 'Honestly, when I saw you there . . .' Her voice wavered and her eyes brightened and Dan came up behind her and put an arm around her shoulders.

'I'm sorry,' she said, wiping her eyes and blowing her nose on a tissue from the box on top of my locker. 'Really. I'm the last person who should . . .'

'You saw me?' I said.

She nodded.

'When?'

'You didn't hear what happened?'

'Nothing.'

She turned to look at Dan, who nodded.

'You're sure you want to hear this?'

'Please. And sit down.'

'OK. Well, about an hour after you and Dan left for Oxford, I got a call from Dan saying he was at a place called Gumber Farm on a . . . a side road off the A418. He said there'd been an accident and that he'd wrecked the Alfa. There was a certain amount of other stuff besides – he was obviously confused – so I told him to stay exactly where he was. I found Gumber Farm easily enough on the map and drove there in the Cherokee with the children in the back; Sunday, you see, so no nanny. I found Dan in the kitchen, having a cup of tea with Mr and Mrs . . . what was their name?'

'Norton,' said Dan.

'Mr and Mrs Norton. Right. Well, Dan was extremely pale; obviously very shaken and a big bump on the side of his head and shocked and so on, but alive, and no bones broken, and Mr Norton told me what had happened. Apparently he'd been backing a tractor and trailer into the road from one of his fields and a car had skidded on the black ice and smashed into the trailer. When he got down from the tractor, he found Dan looking groggy but otherwise OK in the smashed-up Alfa. The doors were crushed so he undid the seat belt and pulled Dan out through the windscreen, or where the windscreen had been.

'Anyway, he'd played rugger for Saracens or someone and he recognised the signs of concussion, so he sat Dan down against the hedge, wrapped him up in an old coat he had in the tractor-cab, and tried to get the trailer out of the road and back into the field. Well, the car had somehow got tangled up with the trailer so he didn't get very far, but he did manage to drag the wreckage off the road. It was a very cold day, as I'm sure you remember, so rather than leave Dan where he was he walked him down to the house, several hundred yards away, and put the kettle on. Dan then phoned me on his mobile and Norton rang the police saying accident, black ice, no one seriously hurt but car smashed up, etcetera.

'Anyway, I got there at the same time as the police and the ambulance. We found Dan like I told you – in shock, basically – so they bundled him into the back of the ambulance, and I followed them in the Cherokee with the kids, the idea being that after he'd been checked out at the hospital, I could drive him home.

'Well, we set off down the road, and passed the remains of the car and the trailer, and something seemed wrong. And then I realised. All the time I'd been assuming that Dan had been on his way *back* from Oxford when he hit the trailer, but from the position of the car and the trailer it was clear he'd been *on his way there*. And that being the case, where the hell were you?

'I went crazy. I flashed my lights, hooted the horn, did everything, but the ambulance didn't stop. The siren wasn't on, but it was taking that lane at a fair pace. All I could do was tell the children to hold on tight and follow. Eventually we reached a T-junction and I managed to slew round and block them. The driver jumped out – really angry, as you can imagine – but before she could have a go at me I yelled at her that there had been a passenger in the wrecked car.

'Well, she ran round the back and asked Dan if this was true, but Dan' – and here Hermia put her arm around his shoulders – 'just stared at her and said he couldn't remember. You were completely out of it, weren't you, sweetheart?'

'I don't know what to say,' said Dan quietly. 'I just don't know what to say.' He opened his hands and looked down at them. 'I'm sorry.'

Behind him the door opened and Tara leant in. 'Cuppa, anyone?'

'That would be lovely,' said Hermia. 'Tea, Dan?'

He was staring at me, expressionless. 'Yes. Thank you very much.'

'Where was I?' asked Hermia, when Tara had gone. 'Yes, anyway, I persuaded them to drive back to the scene of the crash, and we all jumped out and there you eventually were, face down in this frozen culvert at the side of the road. It was quite deep and there was this sort of hedge and thick bramble bushes and people had chucked . . . you know, fertiliser bags and . . . I don't know, but there you were, down the bottom, sort of . . . twisted up in that black coat. And so still. I was sure you were dead. The police who checked out the scene of the accident hadn't seen you, but then I guess they weren't expecting to. They would have been on the other side of the road, looking at the car.'

She hadn't said it in as many words, but I had been dying in a rubbish-strewn ditch. The reason no one had noticed me all twisted up in my black coat, I guessed, had been that I had looked like more rubbish.

'I'm afraid at that point I left you to the ambulance people. There was nothing I could do and I didn't want the children to see you like that, so I got back into the car and drove them home. And then, in the distance, just as we were turning into the drive, I heard the sirens starting up. That's when I knew you were hanging on, that you were still alive. And that's when we started to pray.'

I stared at her.

'I was put in the room opposite,' said Dan. 'They kept me in overnight. Apparently they radioed Oxford when they found you and Oxford sent us here, as being closer.'

Hermia nodded. 'The ambulance came rocketing back past the house, foot down, sirens on . . .'

'And the press?' I asked.

'We were lucky there,' said Dan. 'Someone from the tow-truck firm apparently rang the tabloids saying I'd been involved in a crash. The tabloids got on to the police, who at that stage thought no one else was involved, then on to Norton, who was under the same impression, and finally they rang Hermia, who said that I was fine. There were a few column inches yesterday morning – "Actor Unhurt in Smash", that sort of thing – and then after lunch Hermia and I did a sort of photo-call for today's editions with Norton at Gumber Farm. No mention of you at any point, which I assume' – he raised an ironic eyebrow – 'is what you wanted?'

'Yes,' I said. 'Thank you. Thank you both.'

'I wish there was some kind of apology I could offer you,' said Dan, continuing to look me straight in the eye. 'But I really wouldn't know where to start.'

'It's OK,' I said.

The silence was broken by Tara's entrance with the teas.

'I've warned the others the wicked Dr Belvoir's back!' she announced brightly. 'We're all great *Wirral A&E* fans. You were so awful last night; that poor Nurse Beal! Milk and sugar?'

Colin came on duty at seven p.m. With an hour to go before my next injection, I was at a particularly low ebb.

'How are we this evening?'

'Pain's bad. Talk to me.'

'Hmmm.' He folded the sheet back and peered up at my thigh. 'Let's just have a look at . . . You don't want to hear about *my* troubles . . .'

'Do. Tell. Anything.'

'Did Tara give you a bed-bath?'

'Yes.'

He returned the sheet. 'Talk to you. Well, mmm, OK. I've become . . . *enmeshed*, as they say, in a web of lies. I've met this guy, right.'

'Go on.'

'Well, he thinks I work on a market stall.'

'Why?'

'Well, I told him I did.'

'Start from the beginning, Colin. Who, what, when, where, why.'

'OK. Right. Well, I met him in the Aylesbury Duck last

weekend, and I'd been doing some decorating and things and was looking pretty rough; anyway, he came over and obviously liked what he saw and gave me the chat and that's what I told him I did. Gave it a bit of the WC accent . . .'

'WC?'

'Working class, bit of the old "Cor, fuckin' 'ell", which is obviously what he wanted. Anyway, long story short, we go back to his. Tone very high – tortoiseshell snuff boxes, recessed spotlights, all the business – one thing leads to another, and I stay the night. Fine – more than fine, very nice indeed in fact – but now we're stuck with the Eliza Doolittle story line.'

'Ah.'

'Wait, the plot thins. This morning, I come back to Josie's – you know I share with Josie – and there's a message: he wants to come over. Now, one look at the place – all the ballet data and the Pauline memorabilia – and he's going to know I'm not a barrow-boy.'

'Tell him.'

'I couldn't. He'd just think I was some sad queen. And I know what you're going to say, that I'll be living a lie if I don't tell him, but sometimes . . .' He glanced at his watch. '*Sheisse*, I must get on, I'll see you at eight.'

'I want to know what happens.'

'You and me both, dear.'

'Eight, then?'

'Don't worry, I'll be here.'

'Me too.'

The next day, I received a brief visit from Mr Gupta, the orthopaedic surgeon who had operated on me and whom I vaguely remembered meeting on my first morning. He flipped back the sheet, frowned at the scaffolding around my crutch, nodded to himself and left the room without speaking. Shortly afterwards, Tara came in to tell me that I was to get no more diamorphine. From now on, she said, I would be on oral pain control.

I pleaded that I was not ready, that I needed more painkiller, not less, but she was adamant; the doctor had made his pronouncement.

'He's a nasty fucker, that Gupta,' I mumbled.

'He's one of the best orthopaedic surgeons in the country,' said Tara reprovingly. 'We're lucky to have him. He's not so much one for the bedside manner, perhaps, but . . .'

'He hates me. He thinks it's all my fault.'

'He thinks what's all your fault?'

'Oh, I don't know . . . The assassination of Gandhi . . . My not wearing a seat belt . . .'

'What nonsense, Alison. Really. You're just another patient as far as he's concerned. If we keep you on the diamorphine any longer you'll get addicted, and we're not out to turn you into a junkie.'

'One more,' I begged. 'One more won't . . .'

'One more just might. No, it's Volterol and Coproxamol from now on.'

A thought occurred to me. 'Is this a private room, Tara?'

'It's what's known as an amenity room. You get it if it's available, or you particularly need it. Otherwise, yes, it's private.'

'So how long can I stay here?'

'You were moved here to begin with because it was free. A patient . . . left earlier than expected. Now, normally we'd pop you into a general ward, but as it happens we've just had to close a couple of those and there aren't any beds available. So for the moment you're safe in here.' She looked down at her watch. 'Can I ask you a question?'

'Go ahead.'

'Why *weren't* you wearing a seat belt?'

'I don't know,' I said. 'I really don't know. I always . . .'

'Perhaps it broke,' said Tara. 'Oh, and I forgot to say, you've got a couple of visitors this afternoon.'

It was Bart and, of all people, Jacinta LeQuesne. Bart surveyed me for a moment before planting a careful kiss on the tip of my nose – I could smell the liquor from his expense-account lunch – while Jacinta hung back, short-skirted and cat-smug. I read the plot at a glance.

'You're a star, MacAteer,' said Bart, turning away from me to pace the floor. 'Everything on the line for the story. What a player.'

'Breaking you in, is he?' I asked Jacinta, and she had the grace to look away.

'And what a story!' continued Bart, as if I hadn't spoken. 'The actor, the supermodel and the gold-digging scrubber. A classic of the genre.' He swung round to me and smiled. 'I mean, I am right in assuming, aren't I, that despite its frankly tabloid bent, that story was for us? I am right in assuming that, aren't I?'

I said nothing, and he slapped his wrist playfully. 'Silly me. Of course I'm right. I must be, because by the terms of our contract, we have first refusal on all your work.' He swiped the water beaker from the top of my locker. 'So it must have been for us. Drink?'

I said nothing, and he sucked some lemon barley water through the straw. Behind him Jacinta folded her arms.

'Well, we're running it anyway. Jassy's here to debrief you, while I . . . keep a weather eye on things. We'll need your expenses to date, of course, and while we're here we should sort out some sort of fee for you. A buyout, to include the photos and the tape. How does two and a half sound?'

Again, I said nothing.

'I know what you're thinking,' said Bart. 'You're thinking: now how did they manage to get hold of those photos and that tape? How did they get on to this? I mean, obviously you were going to bring the story to us when you were ready – that goes without saying – but just how did they . . .?' He smiled, stooped forward and forced his hands deep into the charcoal trousers of his suit.

'Well, I'll tell you, laughing girl. I'll tell you. We got a call from a Mr Ray Inskip, of Thame, Oxon., who operates a twenty-four-hour breakdown and vehicle recovery service, and Mr Inskip had rather an interesting story for us. It seems he had been called by the police to clear a crashed Alfa Romeo sports car from the scene of an accident, and had been given the owner's name: one Daniel Fortess. Inskip, of course, knew who Dan Fortess was, and he inspected the car . . . well, let's just say he gave the contents rather closer attention than he might otherwise have done. Amongst these contents was a briefcase, which yielded your ID card, a packet of photographs and a C90 audiotape.

'Well, Inskip did what any public-spirited citizen would have done. He looked at the photographs and he listened to the tape, and he rang the number on your card and the switchboard put him through to me. He should really be handing this stuff in to the police, he explained, but . . .'

Bart shrugged. 'So I sent Jassy to see him with a bag of pocket money. By lunchtime yesterday we'd found the tart and an hour later I was head-to-head with Howard Harvey. And respect where respect's due: the man may be the sleazeball's sleazeball, but he does know his business. He gave me the story for nothing, knowing that we'd break it respectably and he could still auction Decker off to the tabloids for the salacious details.'

He paced in and out of my field of vision. I said nothing.

'I know what you're thinking, Ali Baba. You're thinking how can we break this story respectably? It's still a celebrity kiss-and-tell, you're thinking, which is why you were going to take it down to Wapping. Except that it isn't. Or at least it is, but it's more than that. There's a side to this story that I don't think you know about.'

I turned my eyes away from him. Stared at the wall.

'But let's just talk about your fee. We're not legally obliged to give you anything – we've got Decker, and she's singing like the proverbial canary, so we don't really need the tape. And the photographs? Well, they're good, but they're not really us. We don't really need grubby nylon dressing gowns, if you know what I mean. No, I think we'll dress Miss Decker up in Galliano, get Enver Kassapian or someone to photograph her. What do you think, Jassy?'

Jacinta, eyes lowered, flicked dust from her jacket.

'But we should give you some kind of finder's fee, Baba, even if your name doesn't appear anywhere near the piece. And let's face it' – he picked up the chart from the end of my bed – 'you're not going to be earning for a month or two with, what's this . . . a displaced pelvic fracture anterior and posterior. Ouch, sounds nasty!

'So, it's something or nothing, really. Two and a half did I say? Let's make it three. I'd call that a pretty good deal, all things considered.'

He bent over me and I closed my eyes.

'Look, Alison, you tried to put a tabloid package together

single-handed, and like many others before you, you fucked up. I'm sorry that you're lying here in hospital instead of banking a cheque for fifty grand, but those are the risks you take. Big boys' games, big boys' rules. Now, I'm trying to be a good sport about this. Take the money, take your time, pay your mortgage, and when you're better, come and see us. Jassy?'

Jacinta opened her briefcase, and handed Bart a commissioning form in triplicate. Bart held it in front of my face. The figure was three thousand pounds. Slowly, isolating the movement so as not to disturb my spine or pelvis, I brought my arm from under the sheet, took the form and placed an edge between my teeth. Biting hard, I tore the form in two, and dropped the twisted pink, yellow and white A4 sheets to the floor. A strip of paper stuck to my lip, and I tasted warm blood.

Shaking his head, Bart slowly drew back the sheet from my body. Taking his time, he surveyed the discoloured dressings, the long, tacked laceration from hip to breast, the clotted gouge of my inner thigh, the seepage at the fixators' entry points around my pubis.

'They've shaved you,' he mused. 'And there was a time I might have found that interesting. Right now, I have to say, you're one of the most repulsive sights I've ever seen.'

He paused. 'Oh, and I nearly forgot.' He dropped a hand into his trouser pocket. 'The key to your flat.' He flipped it indifferently at my groin.

As he moved away, Jacinta dropped her briefcase and stepped determinedly towards the bed. Pale-faced, she reached for the key, brushing me with an unsteady hand, and placed it on the locker. Then she drew the sheet back to my chin.

'I'm sorry,' she whispered, and stooping for the briefcase, followed Bart from the room.

'Your temperature's up,' said Tara severely. 'I hope your friends haven't got you overexcited.'

'They're not my friends,' I said. 'They're work. And they won't be coming back.'

'Alison, are you sure you're all right? You're not to be worrying about your work, you're in no fit state.'

'Tara, please, do me a favour, lend me a phone.'

'There's a plug-in one somewhere on the wing,' she answered 'But there's usually a bit of a queue. Is it important? Will it stop you worrying?'

'It is important, Tara. Sorry.'

She brought me one ten minutes later. Hermia had left me the Thame number on an envelope, in case there was anything I needed, and she answered, sounding tired, on the second ring. Was Dan there? I asked.

For several seconds, Hermia was silent. 'Alison,' she said eventually, 'what did we ever do to you except offer you our friendship?'

For a moment I heard the sound of my own breathing in the mouthpiece, then the line went dead.

'Is everything all right?' asked Tara.

'No,' I said, closing my eyes. 'Nothing's all right.'

'You're not to worry about things,' she scolded me. 'It's not good for you. Now, I'm just going to pop this phone back to Mr Maxwell and then we're going to take these stitches out of your face.'

I almost welcomed the distraction.

'I told him,' said Colin that evening, testing the temperature of the bed-bath with the back of his hand.

'Sorry, told who?' I asked. 'What?'

'That *guy*,' said Colin. 'You remember I told him I worked on a stall in the market and you said I should tell him the truth?'

With an effort, I dragged my concentration back to the here and now. 'Sorry,' I said. 'Yes.'

'Well, it was just like you said. It was fine. I told him I'd lied and that I was a nurse and all that, and he just laughed and said he'd guessed I wasn't a barrow-boy from my hands, not to mention my accent. I'd never make it on to *EastEnders*, he told me – here, I'll just lift that arm up . . . gently does it . . . and now the other – but I was a natural for *Casualty*. So anyway, all hunky-dory in the meat-packing department. Like I said to Josie, you can't . . . Is that painful there?'

'No worse than usual,' I said. 'So now you're an item?'

'Well, it's funny, you know, because I was staying round at his, and I went to the bathroom, and he's got like these *cabinets* full of face cream and toner and bronzing sticks and God knows what, and to be honest, I do find all that a bit . . . queeny. Do you know what I mean? I mean, I don't want to be unkind, Alison, but do you know what I mean?'

Dan, pale with anger and strain, came to see me on the Saturday; Tara looked nervous as she showed him in.

For a minute or two he said nothing, just stalked round the room nodding to himself.

'I've come today,' he began, 'because apparently the article's coming out tomorrow. We're leaving tonight for . . . well, it's none of your business where we're going; we've taken the children out of school for the rest of term, anyway.'

He sat down in the room's single chair and raked his hands exhaustedly through his hair. 'What happened, Alison, tell me. I thought we had a deal, for God's sake.'

From the corridor outside came the rattle of a tea trolley and the muted squeak of crêpe soles on linoleum. Further away, a telephone rang unanswered.

'A deal?' I said, measuring my words. 'What kind of deal?' He had offered money, I remembered. A lot of money. I might even have recorded him doing so.

'You know perfectly well what I'm talking about. You agreed to . . .'

'Dan, there's a lot that's gone from that afternoon, but if you're on the receiving end of some press attention right now it's because you chose to drive us into the side of a farm trailer at sixty miles an hour.' And I explained about my briefcase and its contents.

'Oh, I see,' he said, clasping his hands together to control their shaking. 'I see. It's my fault that my wife, my children, my parents, Hermia's parents . . . that scores of perfectly decent people are going to be put through complete hell by some poxy Sunday newspaper just to bump up their sales a half-point. That's my fault, is it?'

'Well,' I said mildly, 'you could have kept it in your trousers.'

He pounded his forehead with his fists, stood up and continued his pacing. 'You are fucking . . . unbelievable. Genuinely evil. You lie there like some kind of run-over rattlesnake, all broken up but still completely poisonous. I should just' – he shook his head, searching for the words – 'just stamp on you and walk away. I don't give a fuck if it's your name on the piece or that snotty, patronising little cunt Jacinta's, or whose it is. Can't you people ever understand that it's not intentions that matter, it's consequences?'

'Look, I don't want to fight with you about this, Dan, but I repeat: you started this. You started it the day you picked up the phone and called Tracey Decker. From that moment onwards, all of this was inevitable. If Tracey hadn't talked to me, she would have talked to someone just like me. The only question was when.'

He looked at me in amazement.'But Alison, don't you . . . know?'

'Know what?'

He leant over the bed towards me and searched my face with a kind of tender revulsion. 'You don't know, do you?' he said wonderingly. 'You really don't.'

'I don't know what you're talking about now, no.'

He slumped back down in the chair.

'How much can you remember about that car journey? Before we crashed into Norton's trailer?'

'Nothing. Which is why, by the way, I'm giving you the benefit of the doubt about leaving me to die of hypothermia and blood loss in that ditch at the side of the road.'

'Alison, look, I swear, I would never . . . I would *never* . . . Can I tell you what happened in that car? What really happened?'

'I'm listening.'

'Right then. We'd had our conversation, in the course of which you'd agreed to kill the Tracey story and to give me all the negatives, prints and tapes relating to it, and I'd said I'd run you into Oxford in the Alfa. A minute or two out, I stopped the car in a lay-by and wrote you out a cheque for seventy-five thousand dollars. Now, I don't know what you meant to do with that cheque; whether you were actually going to deposit it or whether you just wanted to see me go through the motions of writing it, or what the hell you wanted. But you took it, and you pocketed it, and the conversation proceeded to certain unfinished business between yourself and myself, at which point all sorts of extremely wonderful things started to happen. Now, unfortunately that car of mine is pretty well known in that neck of the woods – was pretty well known, I should say – and we were only about half a mile from the house. Wherever the hell we were going to end up that afternoon, it wasn't in that lay-by. We agreed to go into Oxford, find a hotel, and . . .'

He closed his eyes and shook his head.

'You looked, in your funny, angry way, really quite beautiful that afternoon. Radiant. I think Hermia noticed it too. You were so grim and tight-lipped when you arrived but I honestly think that – I don't know whether it was the cheque or the knowing that you weren't going to . . .' He shrugged. 'It was like you'd had a death sentence lifted, you were really quite fey. And when I put the car in gear and started up, you were sort of stretching like a cat, clothes all undone, and I had no intention, believe you me, of wasting any time. I wanted us between the sheets in the Randolph Hotel, and I wanted us there fast.'

'And I didn't get my seat belt back on,' I said blankly.

'You were . . . fixing yourself up.'

'You swear this is the truth?'

'You can't remember any of it?' he asked wryly.

'I can remember saying goodbye to Hermia. I can remember seeing the trailer and feeling the brakes locking on the ice and knowing we were going to crash; even accepting it, in some curious way, but the rest . . .'

'Is it so hard to believe?'

'Look, if I took that cheque – whose existence I doubt, frankly – it would have been as evidence that you'd tried to buy me off. As for this scene of passion which is supposed to have followed, well, I only have your word that it ever took place at all.'

He regarded me dispassionately and spoke quietly. 'Alison, I don't care whether you believe me or not. My reason for telling you all this – from which, by the way, I have nothing to gain, and literally everything to lose – is that I want you to know something about yourself. I want you to know that when your so-called journalistic principles were actually put to the test, you folded. One whiff of the money and you rolled over like a bitch on heat. You're compromised, Alison MacAteer, and the next time you're giving some poor bastard a faceful of your professional righteousness I want you to remember that fact.'

'Hate me all you want,' I said, attempting to keep my voice as level as his. 'You've actually made me feel rather better about all of this.'

'Hate you?' he said incredulously. 'I don't hate you. I don't feel anything for you; I mean, look at you, for heaven's sake.' He stood, and turned contemptuously away.

'Yes, look at me.' I heard my voice rise suddenly and uncontrollably to a scream. '*Look at me, you fucking* . . . A week ago, according to you, you were so desperate to get me into bed you couldn't even wait until I was . . . Well, you've got me into bed all right now, you bastard.'

The pain came flooding back then, and the tears, wave after racking wave of them. I sobbed like a child, and every involuntary heave was agony. I wept for the past, for all that I had destroyed in myself, and I wept for my torn, broken present. I had never known such desolation, never felt so unutterably alone.

After a time I felt Tara's hands on my shoulders, holding me still. She said nothing. Behind her I heard the door close.

That night I barely slept. The light above my bed stayed on all night, and every time I dozed off I was awakened by the rattle of trolleys or the windy flapping of the double doors in the corridor. At one point, outside my room, an argument broke out between a porter and a security guard; later a phone rang interminably.

The article came out the next morning, and caused considerable excitement amongst the nursing staff who had seen Hermia and Dan come and go over the last week. The newspaper was passed amongst them, and by the time it reached Colin, who was now on the day shift, it was almost eleven a.m. When it was handed to him he was removing the stitches from my chest and thigh.

'Are Hermia Page and Dan Fortess very close friends of yours?' he enquired tactfully.

'No,' I said. 'I've just met them a few times.'

He nodded to the paper. 'And did you know about all this business?'

'I've no idea what it says,' I answered truthfully.

'Well, just let me finish unpicking your seams,' said Colin, drawing a short section of surgical nylon from beneath my left breast and dropping it into a kidney bowl, 'and I'll read it to you. I've always been a huge fan of hers, and I wouldn't kick him out of bed, either.'

Five minutes later he was perched on the end of the bed, ready to jump to his feet should the stern tread of authority make itself heard. ' "Marriage à la Mode",' he read. 'By . . . how do you pronounce this? . . . Jacinta LeQuesne?'

'She is a bit of a mouthful,' I agreed. 'Go on.'

'Right. Here we go:

> ' "To outsiders, Hermia Page and Dan Fortess would seem to have it all. She is the supermodel who has been described as the popular face of British fashion; he is an in-demand actor and the star of a top-rated TV series. The couple have two children, and divide their time between a restored seventeenth-century manor house in Thame, Oxfordshire – recently photographed for *House and Garden* magazine – and an elegantly appointed pied-à-terre in London's fashionable Notting Hill. Both Page, thirty, and Fortess, thirty-two, have confirmed their commitment to their six-year-old marriage. 'Sure it's hard when you both have international careers,' Dan Fortess recently told *Hello!* magazine, 'but where there's a will – and a Concorde terminal – there's a way!' 'We Pages are like swans,' Hermia Page told an interviewer last year. 'We mate for life.'
>
> ' "The reality, however, is somewhat different. Dan Fortess's close friendships with several of his female co-stars have been an open secret in show-biz circles for some years now, and last week Hermia Page admitted to me that she is having an affair with model agency proprietor Claudine Le Besque. 'Yes, I have a lover,' Page told me yesterday, as Amber, six, and Joe, four, played on the lawn outside the £850,000 Thame home. 'And yes, my lover is a woman.' "

Colin glanced up at me. 'You look shocked. I thought you journalists were beyond all that?'

'I'm just . . . surprised,' I said. 'Aren't you?'

'Oh, she's always been a major icon in our community,' said Colin. 'You know, her strength, her suffering . . .'

'Her *suffering*?'

'Well, you know what I mean. The husband living it up with starlets in Malibu, and her saintly and alone in the kitchen with her Delia recipes, rolling out the pastry and generally being fantastically brave and strong. Shall I go on?'

'Please.'

'Right. Here we go:

' ". . .Claudine Le Besque, thirty-six, who has a reputation as a tough negotiator, bought the Prima agency five years ago from the Paris-based Bidault group. Within eighteen months she had lured the world's brightest modelling talent to the agency's Mayfair HQ. Hermia Page, who defected from New York's prestigious Elect agency, has been described as the jewel in Le Besque's crown.

' " 'Mutual appreciation turned to love,' a close friend of the couple told me, shortly after Page's arrival at Prima, when Le Besque invited the twenty-five-year-old model to dine *à deux* at her £1.5m flat in Little Venice, West London. 'I ended up staying for a week,' Page is rumoured to have told a colleague.

' "The agency boss is not thought to be the Gloucestershire-born model's first female lover. 'But Claudine is special,' Page has confided to a fellow model. 'She fills a void in my life. She understands me in a way no man could understand me . . .' " '

'Go on,' I urged.

'Oh, there's the usual stuff about truth and honesty and the effect on the children not being a major problem and so on. I'll leave the article with you, I just want to . . . yes, here we go:

' ". . . While Fortess continues to live with Page and to act as a father to their children, he has made his own romantic arrangements, and his present companion is vivacious blonde actress Tracey Decker, 20.

' " 'Dan never talks about Hermia to me,' Decker told me when I visited her studio flat in Kensal Rise, West London, 'and he's certainly never said anything about her and another woman.' She and

Fortess met, Decker explained, during the recording of *Starchat*, a daytime TV show. 'And things just grew from there. We were best friends before we were lovers, we had so much in common.' Did it trouble her that Fortess was a married man with children? 'No,' Decker affirmed. 'I'm confident that he loves me.'

' "Recently, Decker auditioned for a part in Channel Four's *Wirral A&E* hospital series, in which Fortess plays a starring role. 'I should hear from them soon,' she told me hopefully.

' "Decker was encouraged to speak to me by her agent, Howard Harvey of Harvey Personal Management. 'Tracey has nothing to hide,' says Harvey. 'She is a very honest person, as well as an exceptionally talented performer. At the moment I'd say she's just bubbling under star status, but naming no names, certain people in Hollywood are watching her career very closely. I'm very happy to be handling her interests.' "

'Here,' said Colin, arranging the newspaper so that I could hold it in front of me. 'Take your time over the rest of it; I must go and slave over a hot bedpan.'

Bart had done it cleverly, I had to admit. He'd obviously been sitting on the Hermia/Claudine story for months, and he'd seen his chance. Every editor had material like that: privacy-violating stories which, as they stood, were unpublishable. That a contemporary saint like Hermia Page was sleeping with a thirty-six-year-old female executive was a difficult story anyway, flying in the face of the established narrative as it did.

Bart had circumvented this – with my unknowing help – by adding Tracey Decker to the equation. With Tracey's preparedness to be named, the narrative could proceed intact. Tracey could be cast as the scheming starlet and Dan as the serial adulterer, in which lurid context Hermia's affairs would appear little more than fragrant, semi-mystical episodes in a journey of self-discovery. The photograph of Claudine Le Besque helped. Reading between the lines of Jacinta's prose I could easily imagine Hermia's long fingers at the velvet collar of the Frenchwoman's suit, easily imagine Hermia's dark, amused eyes meeting that quizzical, intelligent regard. And for all the apparent crassness of those property prices, the piece did make it clear that the couple's embraces took place in fine and tranquil surroundings, that the windows overlooking the canal were tall, that the wallpaper was hand-blocked, that the furnishing fabrics were expensive.

The picture desk, meanwhile, had gone to town with Tracey's makeover. Dressed in pretty much nothing except a slash of lipstick and a calculating stare, she had clearly been dispatched direct from Bitch Central. In Jacinta's article, hours of quotes had been edited down to the merciless few which would establish her as the archetypal scheming harlot, and Howard Harvey's endorsement of her talent – obviously included as a thank-you to Harvey for the unpaid use of Tracey – only made things worse. Everyone knew what kind of 'actresses' Howard Harvey handled. Dan Fortess was not quoted and had obviously refused to speak to Jacinta. His photograph was a still from *Faro's Daughter*, showing him moody and silk-chemised in some gambling hell.

And just in case anyone should mistake all of this for some tabloid-style sex-scandal spread rather than a serious sociological enquiry, Bart had enlisted the witch doctors. A celebrity therapist wrote of the Probable Effect on the Children, a radio rabbi opined about Marriage and the Millennium, and a Whipsnade behaviourist mused on the subject of lesbianism amongst chimpanzees.

The story, inevitably, was picked up by the tabloids. Through Howard Harvey, Tracey Decker sold the serialisation rights to her story, and made, at a guess, two or three times what Dan had offered me to kill the piece. According to Dad, who came to see me on the Wednesday and had taken a keen interest in the case, Tracey also appeared several times on TV. On the Thursday a couple of titles ran long-lens shots of Dan and Hermia shopping with the children in Los Angeles, but that appeared to be the story's last gasp.

My face and chest were healing, if slowly and achingly. My pubic hair was growing back and my groin itched unbearably. I told Colin, and the next evening he brought in a little plastic skeleton hand on a stick, which I was able to poke between the steel fixators and scratch myself. 'For itch relief only,' he explained sternly. 'No monkey business.'

On the Saturday I was given a proprofol sedative, moved from my bed to a trolley via a low-friction slide and taken to the operating theatre. There, under general anaesthetic, the fixators in my pelvis were adjusted. I woke retching, and in renewed and horrible pain. I swore at Mr Gupta, and – less forgivably – at Tara. The following days and nights were almost as bad as the first week, but without the diamorphine to escape into.

Slowly, however, a month passed. My world was the white room and the bed and the swinging of doors in the corridor outside and the distant bleeping of pagers. In the mornings spring sunshine striped the wall, at night I lay in a pale corona of electric light. The door was usually left ajar, and I would hear half-conversations, snatches of diagnosis, fragments of bewildered complaint. Misdirected strangers would step into the room, regard me for a moment, and leave without comment.

Most nights I listened to Tara's radio, drifting between transcontinental sports commentaries and the reminiscences of forgotten actors and hours and minutes of shallow sleep. When I woke, I would reach for the tuning dial and shiver the air with a Bavarian polka or that sad Middle European jazz that they broadcast in the hours before dawn.

I started to read several of the American political thrillers left by my father, but soon found myself confusing the plots and the characters. After the first week, Dad was my only visitor; he came on Saturdays, as if to give the impression that he worked during the week. Tara asked why none of my colleagues came to see me and I explained that I had always worked alone, that I hardly ever saw them anyway. Would that nice couple be coming back? she wondered, meaning Bart and Jacinta. I told her that I rather thought not. She never asked about boyfriends, and it occurred to me that because she had only ever seen me in my scarred and broken state she probably did not think of me as someone who could ever have been wanted by a man.

As if in confirmation of this assumption, I gave up on my appearance completely. I was sponge-bathed once a day, and once a week Colin or Tara washed my hair into a portable basin arrangement which fitted behind my neck, but I could no longer face looking at myself in Tara's mirror. I felt hideous, grotesque, mutilated beyond repair. Because the crown of my head had taken the impact of the windscreen, most of my hair had been scissored away when I was admitted. After a month – and two readjustments of the extensors under general anaesthetic – I could feel a lank half-inch crop growing back over the scar tracks on my scalp. The hair finally grew back elsewhere, too. 'We're bushy-tailed again, as well as bright-eyed,' Colin announced archly one morning, as he pulled back the sheet. Bright-eyed I wasn't, though, except with occasional tears of frustration and self-revulsion. I passed entire days too wretched to eat, speak or even smile. The white room and the bed, at these times, were not only everything, they were forever.

Colin and Tara knew when to leave me alone, but when I encouraged them they talked. Both seemed to understand that by offering me information about their lives without asking me questions about mine, they were going some small way towards assuaging the utter helplessness that I felt. By allowing me to withhold knowledge, they granted me a tiny pretence of power. And I think that in their tough, professionally distanced way, they were almost fond of me. I was the longest-term patient either of them had ever cared for – double pelvic fractures were extremely rare, apparently – and I'd always been a good listener.

Colin's private life, I soon learnt, was chaotic. He was a one-man soap opera, the objects of his restless desire succeeding each other on a weekly or sometimes even a daily basis. He liked butch, straight-acting men, but however promisingly his liaisons started it was never long before the loved one displayed an inappropriately detailed knowledge of the recordings of Maria Callas or let slip that he'd seen *Yentl* half a dozen times, and then a new pursuit would have to be undertaken. I suggested to him that while gay clubs and ballet auditoria remained his hunting grounds, the prospect of his happening upon Mr Right was, at best, a distant one. 'It's the journey,' explained Colin, who had a penchant for the well-tried aphorism, 'not the arriving.'

Tara's romantic life was rather more stable, and like several of her colleagues she was going out with a policeman. Dave, her steady, was a big man with scarred knuckles and a ready wink. Tara described him as 'just a big softy', but I wasn't so sure. I'd been around policemen a lot over the years – seen them without their PR veneers – and I'd yet to meet one you'd describe as a softy. Tara seemed to have Dave licked more or less into shape, however: they were saving up to get engaged, and spent such off-duty hours as they shared staring into high street jewellers' windows.

I suggested to Colin that perhaps Tara's Dave was the real man he'd been looking for all this time, and he readily concurred. 'Wasn't it Jean Muir who said that all you needed in life was something simple in dark blue?'

A month after my admission the fixators in my pelvis were adjusted for a second time, and shortly after I had come round from the anaesthetic I was told that I had a visitor.

It was Lucy Fane, in an expensive black suit, and for a long moment I watched her trying to match my damaged face to the one she knew.

'It sounds ridiculous to ask how you are . . .' she began, and I said nothing.

'It's the hair,' she tried again. 'It's the short hair that makes you look different . . . Oh hell, Alison, I'm sorry, love, I'm just no good at this. You look *terrible*.'

'Bart Collier wasn't very impressed either,' I said quietly. 'He said I looked repulsive.'

'No, dear, I don't mean you look terrible *terrible*, I mean you look terrible like you badly need a glass of Roederer Cristal and a saunter down Sloane Street with a credit card and a couple of hours' attention from Nicky Clarke; *that* sort of terrible. Don't wilfully misunderstand me, dear. And fuck Bart Collier, for heaven's sakes. Who cares what he . . .'

'How are you?' I asked.

'As ever, dear. I just thought I'd look in and see how you were . . . getting on.'

'Badly,' I said. 'As you can see.'

'Are you in, um, pain?'

'I've messed up my pelvis. I'm kind of pinned out down there, and every couple of weeks they tighten the screws. I was cut up a bit, too, as you can see, but that doesn't actually hurt any more, just aches.'

'How many more . . . screw-tightenings are there?'

'Two, all being well.'

'Then you're out?'

'I guess so. What brings you up here, Lucy?'

'I came to see you, dear, see how you were . . .'

'Lucy . . .' I said threateningly, eyeing her suit.

'Well, funeral, dear, actually, but *miles* away. Other side of Oxford.'

'Anyone I know?'

'Did you ever meet my father?'

I stared at her.

'Oh, don't worry,' she said. 'He was the most frightful shit. No, to be honest, what I really came for was to make sure you were on course for this . . . beauty story thing?'

'Beauty story thing,' I murmured.

'You know,' she said. 'This Laurene Forth campaign. They've sent me all the stuff – there's probably a ton of it waiting for you at your flat – and I must say it all looks just fabulous. It's costing . . . I wouldn't like to say how much it's costing, but millions, certainly. Charles Sheldrake's directing the filming, it's all taking place at this *amazing* sixteenth century sort of miniature Elizabethan palace that no one's ever seen, someone called Inigo Jones is doing the clothes – you must try and talk to him – this Cooney girl is completely *extraordinary* . . .' She threw her hands in the air. 'What can I say? You're going to have the most fabulous . . .'

'Lucy,' I interrupted her. 'you're going to have to find someone else. I'm not going to be able to do it. Could you press that button there?'

'Sure, what's it do?'

'Calls the nurse. I'm going to be sick.'

She walked to the window, her heels soundless on the flame-retardant carpet. 'I get that sometimes,' she said absently, 'although usually a bit earlier in the day. The thing that I've found is that if you get a half-pint of really good lager – Lowenbrau or Starpromen or Grolsch, something like that – and just knock it back cold, straight from the fridge, as soon as you get out of bed . . . Are you all right, dear?'

While Tara cleaned up my face and changed my pillowcase, Lucy stared through the vertical blinds at the car park and made tiny galloping sounds with her fingernails on the top of the locker.

'Look, Alison,' she said, as soon as Tara had gone, 'we're leading with this story. You've got the cover and you've got four thousand words – four, not three five – and you've got the fee you asked for plus a pro rata top-up. You're going to have *fun*, Alison, do you remember what that means? Suki Mott's fixed it so that you'll be staying in this castle place with the production team and the cast – there's not just this Cooney girl, apparently, they're also using Gina Tagliaferri and Fiona Duff and, I'm sure, any number of *heavenly* men – and you can just use the place like a sort of luxury rehab centre; you know, wear a big straw hat, drink champagne, snooze in a chair on the lawn, chat to Charles Sheldrake and the Cooney girl from time to time, take the odd note, help yourself to one of the model boys if the sunshine gets you antsy, and write it all up when you get home. It's not exactly a high-pressure assignment, darling, now is it? I mean, we're not talking Snipers' Alley here. We're not talking the Fall of Saigon.'

'Lucy, please, I'm not ungrateful. I'd have loved to do it if . . .'

'If what?'

'Lucy, look at me.' My fingers traced the long welts of scar tissue slashed across my face. 'You're asking me, looking like this, to live on a film set for a week or however long it is with some of the most beautiful women in the world. Do you really think that they'll want someone with a cut-up face, of all things, hanging around? It's one thing just being an ordinary person they can patronise, it's quite another being the embodiment of their worst nightmare. Believe me, Lucy, I know these people. They'll avoid me – quite literally – like the plague. Can't you get . . . I don't know, London's full of writers who . . .'

'It's your take on it I want, Alison. No one else's.'

I suddenly understood. 'Ah, right, this is all part of it now, is it? Send in the girl with the damaged face to report on the beauty industry. She was scratchy enough before she went through the windscreen; just think what she's going to be like now. She'll be unravelling right there on the page.'

'You're one hundred per cent wrong,' said Lucy, her patience audibly ebbing. 'I just want you to get better and to get back to work.'

'Not on this story. Please.' Tears stung my eyes. 'Lucy, I'm sorry, I just came out of surgery and I'm full of drugs and . . .'

Turning on her heel, she snapped open her handbag.

'Can I smoke in here?'

'No.'

She nodded, unhooked her bag from her shoulder, slung it into the chair and turned to face me.

'OK, Alison, listen to me. Do you remember the day you came to see me with your Cinderella story and asked me to get you a job?'

'Mmm.' I closed my eyes. Nausea swam at the edge of my consciousness.

'When I looked at you across my desk that day, I knew straight away that you'd be good. You had nerve, timing, curiosity, single-mindedness . . . all the things, in other words, that you can't teach. You also had an English degree, if I remember rightly, but we soon laid that ghost to rest.

'My one hesitation was that you came to me with a story that was basically all about you. Some people can never write themselves out of the picture, and while this is fine for an experienced columnist, it's not a good sign in someone just starting out. But then you said you wanted to start in fashion, and I thought, well, OK. That'll damp down that pert little ego of yours.

'And then before I know it you've done your time and you're a feature writer with your name in caps and a byline photo. And for all your success and your drooling boardroom admirers I saw that I had been right: every word you wrote was about yourself. Now, I'm not saying you should have adopted a Manhattan-style Opinion Zero neutrality, but I am saying that a slick prose style and a preparedness to fillet alive anyone who displeases you is not – ultimately – enough. You turn into one of those venomous middle-aged freaks who's wheeled out to vent her bile at the target of the day and then, having done her turn, is locked up in her cage again.

'The point I'm making, Alison, is that you can do better.

You've got a cool observational eye, and that's what this piece needs: the ability to see what's really happening. I don't want one of your centre-stage revenge slayings; I want you watching from the wings. A shadow beneath the trees.'

'A pretty badly disfigured shadow,' I murmured, longing for Tara to come and take her away.

'Darling, you can't hide for the rest of your life. And you're exaggerating, anyway. You're not disfigured, you've just got a couple of scars across your face. It's as if you've . . . I don't know, fought a duel or something. And let's face it, Laurene Forth is one of the world's biggest cosmetics manufacturers and they're going to have their best make-up people right there on the set. If they can't get you looking presentable . . .'

I turned my head away. 'Please, Lucy. Leave me alone. I'm not even sure I want to go on writing, let alone . . .'

'You need a good hairdresser, dear, that's all. I'll have someone sent round. And I'll courier you the location details for the shoot. In the meantime,' she stood to go, 'you get yourself sorted out.'

'Lucy . . .'

'Mmm?'

'I'm sorry about your father.'

'Oh, don't mention it.' She glanced at her watch. 'I hope that bloody driver hasn't gone off for lunch. I'll call you, OK?'

'I'm not doing the piece,' I whispered, but she was already no more than the lingering odour of nicotine and Madame Rochas, and the diminishing clip of her heels.

8

Darne Castle in Warwickshire was built *c.* 1580–85 as a hunting manor for Sir William Duboys, whose descendants occupy the estate to this day. The house, a near-perfect example of the Elizabethan chivalric style, has been tentatively attributed to the master mason Robert Smythson. Mullioned and transomed bay windows display stained-glass armorial bearings, 'typed' stair-towers stand at each wing, while the central porch, in the words of Falconer's *Great Houses* (1870), 'offers a confident and classically ordered frontispiece in the manner of Serlio'.

Queen Elizabeth I (who, in a memorandum to Penelope Rich, expressed her admiration for the house's 'pleazynge smallnesse') is known to have been a guest at Darne on several occasions, most notably in 1594 when it is recorded that a masque 'of an incredibl cost' (Samuel Daniel's *The Triumph of Vertue*) was presented. The house has other literary associations: in 1620 Philip Massinger penned *The Wyldegrave of Darne*, a dramatised version of the legend of Herne the Hunter. The manuscript has survived (unlike any description of Daniel's masque), and is in the possession of the British Museum in Bloomsbury, London.

As the train racketed and swayed through the outskirts of Warwick, I replaced the Laurene Forth file in my briefcase and took final stock of myself in the mirror. Before leaving the London flat I had spent more than an hour applying make-up to the scars on my face, smoothing and brushing and dusting until the angry suture tracks were no more than faint, silvered welts; the result, perhaps, of some gentle toxic hand drawn across my features. After ten weeks in a hospital bed my skin had an almost moon-like pallor. There were dark shadows at my eyes, and the bones showed.

I had dressed minimally: plain white cotton shirt, black Daryl K trousers, buff Sigerson-Morrison flats. Lucy Fane had been right, I had to paint myself out of the frame. It wasn't the writing that terrified me, it was the people: the blasé, dead-eyed perfectionists who made up the beauty crowd. I wasn't ready for them. I just felt too taut-wired and vulnerable to take them on.

Lucy, however, had not been prepared to countenance my refusal. Why she was so insistent I have never been quite sure. It's possible that she felt responsible for me in some obscure way and thought that total immersion in work might speed my recovery, but then it's equally possible that she just wanted to antagonise Bart. Either way, blithely ignoring my protests, she had sent me reams of information concerning the shoot, and two days before Dr Gupta finally withdrew his fixators from my pelvis, she had dispatched her Mount Street hairdresser to attend to me. Beneath his flickering scissors my brutalist surgical crop was transformed into a neat, close-fitting style which I wouldn't have chosen for myself but which I had to admit I didn't actively dislike. And in my biddable state, Lucy's gesture achieved its desired effect. I rang her at her office to thank her, and despite all of my apprehensions found myself agreeing to write the article. It seemed like the course of least resistance.

Since leaving the John Ackroyd Hospital I had seen no one that I knew. My clothes – and Hermia Page's – had been cut off me in Casualty two and a half months earlier, and I took the train to London in a tracksuit and plimsolls bought for me in Tesco by Tara. It was summer, I discovered, and in the late May sunshine the post-institutional lassitude and disorientation that hung about me began to lift. Over the next few days I paid the bills, went for walks in Regent's Park, listened to music, caught up on my smoking, and slept. On the seventh evening, a Sunday, I collected the Laurene Forth material and read it to the accompaniment of Lennie Niehaus's score for *Bird*.

It was Monday morning now, a hot midday approached, and as the train pulled in to Warwick station I felt a thudding apprehension. I was still, I knew, very shaky. I couldn't bear to be stared at – I had had to change seats twice on the journey from Paddington – and since my discharge from hospital I had found my eyes filling with tears at the slightest provocation or the smallest kindness. I constantly heard myself apologising to people.

Braced against the weight of my suitcase, I stepped out on to the station forecourt. Beyond the exhaust-haze of the taxi rank shimmered a large silver Mercedes. As I lowered the suitcase to the pavement, a figure rose from the car's open rear doors and stepped briskly towards me across the cobblestones. For a flickering moment, as she registered my imperfectly healed features, her eyes widened.

'Alison MacAteer? Hi there, I'm Nancy Waller.'

Wiping my palm on the seat of my pants I took the offered hand and murmured appropriately. My first impression of Laurene Forth's PR director was of pallor and fine-drawn brownness, of ivory and cinammon and écru. She was not what I would have called attractive, she was too rangy and diet-drained for that, but she managed a certain etiolated Manhattan chic.

'I'm late,' I said as a wiry, suntanned man in a Laurene Forth T-shirt hurried my suitase to the car. 'Sorry.'

'You're not late at *all*,' Nancy insisted, squeezing my hand reproachfully and fixing her pale brown gaze between my eyes. 'Really not! And it's so fabulous to meet you. Just fabulous. I know we're going to do *great* things on this story. Everyone's just dying to . . . But how was your journey?'

'Fine,' I said. 'Fine. Thank you.'

'I must try your trains,' she murmured without obvious irony. 'I believe they're marvellous.'

Behind us a cab ground its gears and impatiently sounded its horn. Nancy made placatory gestures at the driver and we hurried across the cobbles and climbed into the Mercedes' air-conditioned, white-leathered interior. This was not my first time in a car since the smash; I had deliberately taken several taxi rides in London. The first of these, an unhurried cruise around the park, had left me so obviously distressed that the driver had offered to buy me a cup of tea, but by the second or third outing my panic had subsided to a prickling, sweaty-palmed apprehension. Now that we would be negotiating fast country roads rather than London's traffic-sclerosed arteries, I hoped that I could face the journey ahead of us with something like composure.

'No, as I was saying,' Nancy subsided gratefully against the heavy German upholstery, 'everyone's dying to meet you – we're just thrilled to have your magazine on side for this one. And I promise you' – the pale hands chopped downwards in grave parallel – 'I *promise* you, this is all going to be just so . . . great! Fletcher Walsh, that's our marketing head, well, I've never seen him so fired up. And Charles Sheldrake?' She spread her palms as if spot-checking for stigmata. 'Alison, the man's quite simply a genius.'

'I saw most of the *Sword of Honour* series on TV. And of course *Love's Labours Lost*.'

'Don't you just love Shakespeare?'

The guilelessness of the question silenced me for a moment. 'Sure,' I said. 'I mean, yes. Definitely.'

'You know it was originally going to be filmed here, at Darne?'

'*Love's Labours Lost*?'

She nodded. 'Charles eventually had to make it in France because of uncertainty about the English weather. The producers were worried about over-runs, continuity, stuff like that.'

'And you're not?'

She shrugged. 'We can wait, within reason. But hey!' She gestured to the fleckless blue sky and the unexceptional suburban landscape beyond the sealed windows.

'Do you have a long-range forecast?'

'Set fair. What I guess you'd call a heat wave.'

'So when do you start principal photography?'

'Tomorrow morning, all things being equal.'

'And what things might not be equal?' The question flicked out like a whip; for a moment I was listening to my old self.

Nancy raised an eyebrow and turned to me, surprised. 'We're expecting Dale today.'

'She's not here yet?'

'She's on her way. Some things got rescheduled.'

At this moment the driver cornered fast, strafing the chevron road sign with gravel chips, and my arms flew to protect my face.

'I'm sorry,' I said, blinking and feeling foolish. 'I recently had a . . .'

'I know you did. I heard from Suki Mott.' She gave my forearm a brief squeeze and leant forward to the driver. 'Tony, there's no hurry. Take it slowly, OK?'

'I'm really sorry,' I whispered. 'It's just . . .'

'Well, hey!' said Nancy, squeezing again as I blew my nose into a fistful of tissues. 'It's no problem. No problem at all.'

I dabbed surreptitiously at my eyes and wondered how much further we had to go. We were driving along a straight road into the sun and I was aware of my face throbbing and of a nervous tic starting near my right eye. I felt in my bag for my sunglasses.

I glanced at Nancy; in the streaming midday light her flaxen-fine hair was transparent, the skull's form dark against the plate glass. In front of her the driver reached up for the sun-shield and I noticed that his arms were blued with old tattooes. MUM, I read. BRITISH MOVEMENT. LONGING FOR THE CRUCIBLE OF WAR.

The roads narrowed, there were no more villages, and we seemed to be gaining height. For a time we were more in shadow than in light, and then an avenue of poplars drew broad sun-stripes across the grey-tinted windscreen.

The purpose of Nancy's silence, I guessed, was to allow the preliminary elements of the Darne landscape to take their effect on me, and despite my fragile mood the ploy was not entirely unsuccessful. It had been some minutes, I realised, since we had seen another car. Without warning, we turned off the road and climbed an unmetalled track through a plantation of young beech trees. Silence and the forest closed around the silver Mercedes, the pale, translucent leaves of the beeches lending the scene an almost sub-aquatic calm. After a short while, during which I was conscious of Nancy watching me, the track looped back on itself, and I saw the gatehouse. Of old, dark-patterned brick and lichened stone, it reared with forbidding suddenness against the light-shot green of the forest. At its far corners stood twin octagonal towers, their leaded cupolas cresting the tree tops.

Leaving the car idling, the driver disappeared into the

shadowed archway. He returned a moment later, and slowly steered the large car through the double gates within. Standing by the open gate, unmoving, was a tall, dark-skinned figure, clad entirely in black. For a brief moment I thought he was wearing some kind of period theatrical costume, but a second glance told me that the garment I had taken for a jerkin was a padded waistcoat of some synthetic material and that his sword-belt held carpentry tools. Unsmiling, arms folded, he was staring straight at me.

'Stephen Faulds,' said Nancy. 'Whom you'll meet.'

From the gatehouse we exited into a small clearing. I looked back; from this aspect the sun-washed brick was a weathered rose colour. Beds of lavender pressed at the foot of the wall and purple wisteria climbed one of the towers. A towel and a pair of Bermuda shorts hung from a clothes-line over the tiny lawn.

Slowly, we nosed forward into the dimness of the forest, beech nuts and acorns popping quietly beneath the tyres. The path forked and the driver directed the Mercedes into a low, olive-painted hangar containing a tractor, several old-fashioned mowing machines and a heavy 1960s-vintage motorcycle. The driver swung my suitcase from the boot of the Mercedes and indicated that I precede him.

I stepped from the garage into a warm silence. The air was earth-scented, and beneath the thin leather soles of my shoes the mossed turf was springy and a little damp. The trees were older here, their layered canopies far overhead, their massive grey trunks some distance from each other. About fifty yards in front of us, like a dark curtain drawn across the prickling brightness of the forest's edge, stood a high stone wall. I turned questioningly.

'Just follow the path,' Nancy ordered me, smiling.

'I'm beguiled,' I admitted.

'You will be,' she promised.

The path led alongside the wall, which had crumbled in places, to a stone gateway. At one time this must have been an imposing feature, but brambles and ivy had reclaimed it and the armorial motifs surmounting the piers had been worn to near-unrecognisability by the elements. The ironwork hinges had been recently oiled, however, for the gate opened at a touch. I stepped through, and for a long moment – oblivious of all but that which lay before me – stood speechless.

Beyond the wall, the ground fell away into a vast, dizzying bowl of green, into whose stillness, it seemed, poured all the sunlight of England. It was as if I had stepped into a sixteenth-century painting, but one whose artist had been deliberately careless of perspective and scale in the interest of effect.

Darne Castle stood on the far side of the valley. At that moment the building appeared almost depthless, its bays and towers shimmering as if the light passed straight through them, its roof pavilions insubstantial against the blue of the sky. The distance across the valley was hard to judge – a curious foreshortening effect seemed to obtain – and for a long moment it seemed that I could reach out and lift the building like some jewelled toy from its hilltop.

I had never before been moved by a landscape in the way that, those first moments, I was moved by Darne. There was a feeling of recognition, a sense of knowing the place from another time, a correspondence to some deep longing. I wanted to be contained forever within its airy regularity, to submit for all time to the serene and timeless safety of its order. As it was beautiful, so I would be made beautiful. I raised my hand through the whirling particles of light and, ravished, let it fall.

'Well?' asked Nancy.

'It's wonderful,' I said. 'I'm entranced. All those windows. "That purest sky for brightness they dismayed . . ." '

'I'm sorry?'

'Spenser,' I said. 'One of our Elizabethan poets.'

'Fabulous,' said Nancy. 'Just fabulous . . . You know, this place isn't in any of the books, or with any of the agencies. It's a completely virgin location. They don't even know for certain who built it.'

'So how did you come to . . .?'

'Be using it? Well, first off, Charles Sheldrake is a friend of Phoebe Duboys, who's the . . . I guess you'd say she's the daughter of the house. Charles knew the place from visiting with Phoebe, and there was the whole history of his trying to make *Love's Labours Lost* here. What really did it for us, though, was something else that Charles brought to the party, something so unbelievable that . . .' She smiled to herself and shook her head. 'Well, you'll see when we get there.'

She took a pair of sunglasses from her straw bag and led off down the track which wound through the park. The driver followed with my suitcase.

'Don't worry about any of this background stuff,' said Nancy over her shoulder, 'because I've scheduled a meeting for you with Charles and Fletcher – that's our marketing director – after lunch. They'll tell you exactly how all of this happened; take you through the whole thing step by step.'

'Fine,' I said, catching up with her. 'Are we looking at the front of the house from here?'

'Yes. There's a drive and an entrance on the other side, but this was the original approach. Visitors would have come through the forest like we did, and seen exactly what we see now.'

It was true, there was nothing in view that would not have been there at the end of the sixteenth century. I imagined William Duboys and his companions pausing here for a moment on their return from the hunt – a little out of breath, perhaps, their horses sweating and fidgeting beneath them, the smell of the gutted stag heavy in the air – and surveying the broad sweep of greensward and the bright towers beyond. Perhaps, on occasion, the scene would have been lent profounder significance by the Artemisian presence of the Queen.

'Thanks,' I said. 'I'm glad we came this way.'

'Hey. Don't mention it.'

We started the descent. The tyre-furrowed track bisected a long swath of grassland which had never, I guessed, served any particular function beyond the decorative. Elms, beeches and oaks stood at intervals in the meadow grass, with deer disposed in their shade. As we walked down towards the river and the low stone bridge, the house seemed to rise above us, its buff and silver-grey insubstantiality resolving itself into details, into lead and glass, into drainpipes and lightning conductors, into hard old brick and stone.

The river was broader than it had looked from the forest, and ran dark and heavy beneath the stone bridge. Its surface was of an almost viscous brightness, and in the shadow of the arches I could see slow-waving weed like emerald hair. Some distance to my right the river passed beneath a second stone bridge and broadened into a lake whose far shore was shadowed by forest.

'You can't really see it from here,' said Nancy, as we leant over the rough mossed parapet, 'but when the house was first built, the lake was laid out in the shape of the crescent moon.'

'Amazing,' I said.

'Chub,' said the driver, speaking for the first time.

'I'm sorry?'

He nodded downwards. 'Fish. In the river.'

'I bet,' I said.

'Tony,' said Nancy, 'why don't you take Alison's things on up? It's the blue room, next to Miss Cooney's.'

He hurried up the worn stone steps in the direction of the house, and Nancy and I followed at a more sedate pace. I was hot now, my legs were beginning to get shaky and my shirt clung wetly to the small of my back. As we climbed, the grassland became formal garden, paved and terraced. We reached a small lawn, and I took the opportunity to sit down on a stone bench beneath a fig tree.

'I'm sorry,' said Nancy. 'You must be tired. I didn't think.'

'I'll be fine,' I promised. 'The doctor said I should walk every day; get my strength back.'

'Well, there's plenty of room to do that,' said Nancy, folding her arms over her narrow chest. 'Only a short way now, though.'

I looked back in the direction we had come; beyond the swath of deer park the forest enclosed us completely. Ahead of us, the steps climbed to an ironwork gate. Wordlessly, I followed Nancy upwards and through the gate. To my relief, I saw that we had reached the final level. The gate led into a formal topiary garden, the hedges and colonnades standing a little taller than head-height, the shadowed avenues closely mown. Niches for statues had been cut into the dark yew, and in one of these a stone bird reared; in another a mermaid writhed.

'You must explore the garden later,' said Nancy, as we passed through the silent green corridors.

'I will,' I promised.

I followed her round a last buttress of yew and found myself facing the soaring bulk of the house. The porch, surmounted by a shield carved with a stag's head, stood on a terrace above a whitened flight of steps. Inside was a large entrance hall and a sudden coolness. Despite ceiling-high stone windows the room seemed dark after the brightness outside. A set of chairs had been stood against the walls, and tripods, cables, light stands and the aluminium cases used to transport film equipment were strewn about the patterned flagstoned floor. Painted ancestors regarded me equivocally from the walls. There was a faint smell, which I would come to associate with the house, of dampness and yeast and furniture wax.

Nancy led me up a wide stone staircase to a small, rather austere first-floor room, with painted walls and velvet curtains of a faded French blue. A single painting, a Restoration portrait of a young girl, hung above the narrow iron bed, and a heavy Victorian washbasin was braced against one wall. My suitcase stood in the centre of the floor.

I pulled off my shirt, ran the water until it was cold, washed my face and slicked back my hair. In the mirror my face was pale, and there was a nervous brightness to my eyes. The scars, hectic against the pallor, throbbed angrily. The longest of these, a long slash from the left side of my chin to my right cheekbone, had laid both my lips open, neat as jelly. My mouth had healed, more or less, but a swollen and irregular tightness remained. A second flourish had been cut across the upper surface of my cheekbone, parallel to the lower wound, and a third, symmetrically matched by a gash over my left eye, flared upwards and outwards through my eyebrow. The moment of the crash was inscribed on my face forever.

I was pulling on a clean white shirt when there was a knock at the door. It was Nancy, asking me to go down to lunch. I had hoped – badly hoped – to have time to re-do my make-up, to neutralise the glaring scar tissue. It was clear, however, that Nancy was going to wait outside my door until I came out. Perhaps, I thought, it was better this way, better to get the worst over all at once. I would sit before them and let them stare at me, let them gorge themselves on my injuries. They were, after all, professional voyeurs.

Turning up the collar of my shirt against the sun, I followed Nancy down the wide stone staircase and through a series of smaller hallways and unlit corridors to a side exit of the house. She seemed impatient now, no longer in a mood to explain things as we went. We stepped out into the sunny warmth of a kitchen garden and I reached in my bag for my sunglasses. A path led past netted raspberry bushes and a long white Victorian greenhouse to a small wrought-iron gateway. Some distance beyond it stood an immense old cedar, its wide-spreading boughs acting as an irregular shade for the twenty or so figures seated at a long, white-clothed table on the lawn beneath. I had an impression of heads bowed over food, of straw hats and shirtsleeves, of sharp green light. Nancy and I walked towards the tables, our footsteps silent on the carpet of needles, and one by one, with the polite expectancy of an audience, the faces lifted towards me.

Nancy effected the introductions, and everyone was charming. No one flinched, no one stared, everyone smiled. But even as the sun splintered through the heavy cedar branches, a darkening rain-cloud of self-doubt enclosed me. The last few days, I realised, had given me a false sense of security; I could deal with strangers one at a time, but in these numbers they were quite simply terrifying. For most of the next half-hour I either stared wretchedly at my plate or surreptitiously watched others talking. When spoken to, I responded in monosyllables. My farouche and unprofessional behaviour horrified me, even as I knew myself powerless to correct it. Three months ago I would have looked forward to an occasion like this; now it was as much as I could do not to get up and run from the table. I succeeded in chasing a salad around my plate and swallowing a couple of glasses of white wine, but tasted none of it.

Eventually, the wine had its effect, and I began to wind down a little. By then, I think, people had realised my distress, understood that I wanted to be left alone. Their eyes glided neutrally past me, seeing and not seeing. A cup of coffee and a cigarette gave me something to do with my hands.

Seated directly opposite me, locked in conversation with his lighting cameraman, was the director, Charles Sheldrake. He was a spare, dishevelled figure of about forty whose features were shadowed by a wide-brimmed panama hat. At first glance he cut a benign, almost whimsical figure, but then he raised his head and I saw the hard watchfulness around the eyes. Film directing, I remembered Dan telling me on the occasion of that never-to-be-forgotten Sunday lunch at Thame, is the opposite of diplomacy. The essence of diplomacy is compromise; the essence of film directing is getting your own way at whatever cost.

Seated between Sheldrake and the cameraman, and implicitly if not actually involved in their discourse, were two models, both of whom I recognised. Fiona Duff, a Home Counties English rose, was making a show of participating in the conversation, switching her regard from speaker to speaker like a Wimbledon spectator; Gina Tagliaferri, dark, mobile-boned and Milanese, was staring straight ahead, absently stirring a cup of coffee. As our gazes crossed, a smile touched the corner of Tagliaferri's mouth.

'It's terrible,' she said, her eyes holding mine so that I was forced to return her gaze. 'It's always the same in England. The location is beautiful, the food's fine, and then they bring the coffee.'

'Seems OK to me.'

'You're here to write about us, is that right?'

I nodded.

'So what's the story?'

I shrugged, and she raised her eyebrows.

'I'm sorry,' I apologised. 'I'm being very rude. I've been . . . out of circulation.'

'What happened?'

'Car accident. I was booked to do this piece first, otherwise . . .'

'Otherwise?'

I searched her face for signs of condescension, but found none. 'Otherwise I wouldn't have done it,' I said.

'You don't like it here?'

'It's not that; of course I do. It's just that the last thing I need right now, frankly, is a celebration of . . . of female beauty.'

'Look, believe me, your face will heal; I've seen much, much . . . You smoke, don't you?'

'Yes.'

She reached down to a bag at her side and pulled out a soft-pack of Nazionale with a book of Quo Vadis matches stuffed inside the cellophane. 'Could you smoke one of these for me?' she asked. 'I've given up, but I really, *really* miss the smell.'

'Sure,' I said. 'Why not.' The match's sulphurous flare was unwavering in the warm midday air. The loosely packed cigarette crackled.

'In my face, could you?'

I blew a slow plume of smoke towards her.

'My father died last year,' she explained, closing her eyes and inhaling. 'Nazionale was his brand. How long did you say you were in that hospital?'

'Ten weeks. Almost a record, apparently.'

'And now you feel . . .?'

I shrugged. 'Physically OK. Otherwise . . .'

My lip quivered, and snatching a linen napkin, I blotted furiously at my eyes. Gina watched me, but said nothing, and trying my best to keep a steady hand, I finished the cigarette. When I stubbed it out, Gina raised her hand in valedictory salute to the last drifting curl of smoke.

'*Ciao*, Papa . . .' She smiled. 'I'm a veteran in this business, you know. Twenty-eight.'

'I remember when you started,' I said quietly. 'I'm twenty-seven.'

'Well, we babushkas must stick together.' She flipped the Nazionale pack over the tablecloth and into my lap. 'Will you be my official smoker?'

'Sure.'

'Fantastic. My guess is we're all going to be here for some time. Dale Cooney hasn't even left New York yet, as far as I know. So you might as well take it easy for a day or two, because everyone else will. In fact . . .'

'What?'

'Nothing. It's just that I've had an idea. A surprise for you.'

'Everyone seems to have surprises for me today. Can I ask what it is?'

'It would hardly be a surprise if I told you, would it?'

'I suppose it hardly would,' I replied.

*

'Alison,' said Nancy, breathless. 'Hi again.'

I opened my eyes. Lunch had been cleared, and exhausted by the morning's walking, I had escaped to a deckchair beneath the cedar.

'Sorry,' she said, rolling her eyes. 'ET phone home. Everyone's coming out of their breakfast meetings in New York and the wires are red-hot. Let me get Charles and Fletcher for you, I know they . . .'

She came back with Sheldrake and a smooth-jowled Madison Avenue type, immaculately attired for leisure.

'Why don't we walk?' suggested Sheldrake, when formal introductions had been added to the handshakes that we had exchanged on my arrival at the lunchtable. 'Then we can bring you up to date and show you something of the place at the same time.'

'You OK for that?' Nancy asked me.

'I'm fine,' I assured her. 'Really.' The dark cloud of doubt seemed to have lifted and the sun was warm on my face. 'Do you mind if I bring my tape recorder?'

'Not at all,' said Sheldrake, bestowing a calculatedly charming and reassuring smile. 'Let's go and sit in the boathouse.'

The lawn fell away to a grouping of lime trees, beyond which lay the lake that I had seen earlier. We walked down to the water's edge, where a pillared loggia stood in the shade of a huge old copper beech. Inside the loggia were stone benches and a dark, damp coolness; in the flooded channel between the benches an elderly punt was moored.

Fletcher Walsh darted a quick smile at me from behind his tortoiseshell spectacles. 'It's quite a place, isn't it?'

'It's extraordinary,' I said. 'I've never been anywhere like it.'

We settled ourselves against the stone walls, and I pressed the record button.

'OK,' began Walsh, steepling his fingers, 'let me give you the background to what we're all here to do. You probably know a lot of this already, but I'll reprise it.

'Eighteen months ago – the Christmas before last – Laurene Forth launched Quatrième, a new female fragrance line. Our face was Karen Hassler, and our stills and stories were shot over three weeks in the Marquesas Islands in the Pacific. The fragrance was great, the images were strong, the buzz was good, and pre-launch we were cautiously upbeat.

'But Quatrième didn't connect. It's still out there in the stores, obviously, but it's never really . . . It wasn't the fragrance, our researchers told us, it was the campaign. The look of the moment was edgy and urban and waifish, and Karen Hassler – who had originally been contracted by my predecessor – was your basic catwalk überbabe. Reviewing the campaign in the UK, the *Sunday Times* style section described her as looking 'like a rich German on holiday', and while I guess you have to be European to get the full timbre of that, we were forced to admit that we sort of knew what they meant.

'So we regrouped, and I went into a huddle with my team. Ten days passed, cabin fever was setting in, and I decided to give everyone the afternoon off. To cut a long story short I ended up in an arthouse in the Village watching the film version of *Love's Labours Lost*.

'Well, I watched it twice through, and what really struck me – what really blew me away – was the look of the piece. There was a kind of painterly quality to it; the whole thing was bathed in this romantic, northern European light. You could tell from the landscape that you were somewhere that . . . that it rained in the spring, perhaps, but where the summers were glorious.

'The next day I had the whole team watch the picture and buy copies of the play, and by the end of the week we had the conceptual basis for a new female fragrance line. The slate-grey, neo-existential tendency, we all agreed, would burn itself out, as these extreme trends invariably do, and the new descriptives – words like "Arcadian" and "metaphysical" – would relate to a subtler and much more optimistic raft of possibilities. The new colour – every fragrance has its colour – was the hazy forest green of Charles's film landscapes. That night I hit the phone, and after a little trouble I was connected to . . .' He gestured courteously towards Sheldrake, who was gazing up at the vaulted ceiling of the loggia.

'It had been a difficult morning,' said Sheldrake. 'I was filming a drama series called *A Family and a Fortune*, various things had gone awry, and everyone on the set was pretty scratchy. We were just setting up a shot when someone brought me a phone. There was this American, I was told, he'd rung five times and he wouldn't take no for an answer. So I took the call, explained I couldn't talk and suggested he call me back in a couple of hours. If, as he said, he was calling from New York – where I calculated it was about three in the morning – I thought that the delay would probably put him off. It didn't, needless to say, and he rang back exactly two hours later. He explained who he was and why he was ringing and we had this long conversation about *Love's Labours Lost*, in the course of which I explained that my principal influences *vis-à-vis* the film's lighting and colour had been the English Renaissance painters.'

'What he's trying to say,' explained Fletcher Walsh with a small, fastidious smile, 'is that I made him miss his lunch. What he should have done was tell me to call his agent and to check out the Tudor portraitists in the public library. But he didn't, he gave me his time – for which I will be eternally grateful – and by the end of our conversation I knew that I'd found our director. He agreed to come to New York, and I promised I'd make up for that missed lunch.

'Meanwhile, the fragrance still needed a name, and we needed to turn our concept into a brief to send out to the fragrance houses. It was actually the youngest, least experienced member of the team who finally got it. It was about midnight and I'd just come back from the Met and a première of the new *Don Carlos*. The opera had been bad and dinner had been worse and I was generally feeling far from terrific when a fax started coming through. It was from Justine, working late at the office. The message was headed "NFFL Brief", and began:

' "Shall I compare thee to a summer's day?
Though art more lovely and more temperate . . ."

'It was, of course, Shakespeare's eighteenth sonnet, and Justine had underlined the first line and the eighth, which, as I'm sure you remember, reads:

' "But thy eternal summer shall not fade".

'Well, the more I read the poem, the more exactly I thought it expressed everything we wanted the NFFL to say.'

'NFFL?'

'New female fragrance line. For security reasons we never use new product names prior to launch. Anyway, as I was saying, the sonnet set me thinking. There was all that youthful, green-leaf, Shakespeare-in-the-Park stuff, but there was also a air of poignancy, of mystery. What Justine had realised – and what I myself realised as soon as I read it – was how perfectly the sonnet translated to the architecture of a fragrance. The first notes – the first hit, if you like – would be a dazzling, dewy emerald, scintillant and sharp; these would dry down to a floral main accord, and this main accord gradually give way to a series of darker base notes composed of all those haunting, half-remembered twilight scents . . . What we could create, I saw, was a fragrance which celebrated beauty but which also expressed something of its transitory nature, something of the melancholy truth that "summer's lease hath all too short a date".'

He blinked self-consciously, and I realised that he was holding his glasses in his hands. Perhaps he found it easier to express abstract ideas to a blur than to my quite possibly sceptical face. In my new Acu-Sonic recorder – the old one was an insurance statistic – the cassette clicked quietly to a stop.

'Is any of this making sense?' Walsh asked.

'Absolutely,' I said. I flipped the cassette, and sat back.

'OK. By morning, Justine had a brief roughed out for the fragrance companies. A couple of the older guys dug their heels in' – Walsh rubbed his eyes regretfully – 'but we eventually talked them round. We had to: any trouble and they'd have crossed the street to one of our rivals. And at that stage, of course, the whole project was top secret.

'The brief went out to half a dozen carefully selected fragrance houses, and a series of raw samples came back. The one that our panel of testers finally chose was created by a nose in Grasse, southern France. By then, back in New York, we'd agreed on a name: Eternal Summer. Well, it would take us a year and a couple of thousand adjustments to get the fragrance just right, but by then we knew exactly what we wanted and I was able to get on with finding a face and building a campaign. My first call, as I'd promised, was to Charles. I bought him a Concorde ticket, flew him to New York and gave him the lunch I owed him at Balthazar. There, he completely stunned me by telling me that he not only had the perfect location for the Eternal Summer film, he also had the perfect face. Perhaps, Charles, you'd like to . . .'

Sheldrake looked out at the lake. 'I always intended to shoot *Love's Labours* here at Darne; it would have been appropriate at all sorts of levels.'

'Even though the play was actually set in France?' I interrupted him.

'Yes' he said. 'Do you know it?'

'A bit. From university.'

'Ah,' he looked at me with very faint interest. 'Where were you?'

'Exeter.'

'Did you know Tom Warwick?'

'Yes, he was my tutor. How do you . . .?'

'We were at Cambridge together. And I used to teach English myself.'

'Where did you do that?'

'At a school in London, for a bit, and then back at Cambridge . . .' He fell silent for a moment, as if in memory of those days. 'Anyway, back to *Love's Labours*. To cut a long and very tedious story short, we weren't able to film here. All the locations were exteriors, and the money people were worried about the weather causing over-runs. We eventually shot the whole thing in the Périgord region of south west France, where needless to say we walked straight into the wettest summer for sixty years. In fact, for all the disappointment of not being able to use Darne, the rain turned out to be on our side in the end, and gave the Dordogne countryside precisely that intense, steamy freshness that Fletcher was talking about earlier.

'Anyway, to cut to the chase, you can imagine how amazed I was to hear that my film had helped to inspire a new perfume, of all things. And then to be offered the commercial to direct, well, it was irresistible. Fletcher didn't even come with a script; he just handed me a single A4 photocopy of Shakespeare's eighteenth sonnet. He didn't have a location, he told me, and he didn't have a face. I, on the other hand, knew straightaway that I had both.'

'I can see how you chose Darne,' I told him. 'But why Dale Cooney?'

'Can I answer that?' asked Walsh, and Sheldrake nodded.

'Right. Like Lauder, Lancôme and the rest, Forth manufacture a vast range of beauty-related products, of which the most visible and glamorous are the fragrance lines, OK? Now, as you know, all of these products are marketed using faces. A lot of European corporations mix and match their faces; they use actresses for their fragrances because fragrances are supposed to be about personality, and they use photographic models for their cosmetics because cosmetics are supposed to be about perfection. In the US, however, where perceptions of these things are slightly different, we tend to contract a single face to market all of our products. Laurene Forth is a single-face corporation, and until very recently that face was Karen Hassler. She featured in our fragrance ads, she featured in our cosmetics ads, she featured in everything we did.

'Unfortunately, it's become increasingly clear that Karen's day is . . . Well, let's just say that she's starting to look a little mid-nineties. And so when Charles tells me that one of the conditions of his directing the Eternal Summer film campaign is that the face of the fragrance is Dale Cooney, I realise I've got a serious decision to make. The question I have to ask myself is not if Dale's the right face for the fragrance – Charles has already persuaded me of that – but if she's got what it takes to be the new face of the Laurene Forth corporation. If I say yes, I've not only got to find enough money to persuade Cooney to sign an exclusive contract with Forth, I've also got to buy off Hassler, whose lawyers are going to scream that I've publicly humiliated her, destroyed her career, et cetera. And all of this in the wake of the failed Quatrième campaign. It's going to cost well into eight figures.

'Having said that, we have a sensational product. Quatrième was good, but Eternal Summer is quite simply glorious, and to do it justice we have created a new kind of beauty story. We are going to create the most intelligent, complex and visually ravishing campaign ever. Not to mention the most expensive.'

'And if it fails?' I asked.

'If it fails, well, the corporation goes into . . .' He made a tail-spinning motion with his hand. 'We can't fail,' he said.

'Does your press office know you're telling me all this high-rolling finance stuff?' I asked.

Walsh shrugged. 'I haven't told you anything that you wouldn't figure out for yourself sooner or later. You need attributable figures, I'll give you attributable figures, because frankly I'd rather you spent your time watching us work than digging through our company files. I don't mind the world knowing we're going for broke on this one.'

There was a short silence, Sheldrake looked from Walsh to me and back again, and then the Acu-Sonic clicked off.

'Sorry, Charles,' said Walsh, 'I seem to have rather dominated . . .'

'Look, I'm sorry,' I interrupted him, glancing from one of them to the other, 'but there's something I still don't understand.'

'Which is?' asked Walsh.

'What made you both so sure that Dale Cooney – an all but unknown actress from, let's face it, the middle of nowhere – was the right face for the Eternal Summer campaign?'

A glance flickered between the two men.

'I think,' said Charles Sheldrake, lifting his broad-brimmed panama hat from the stone bench and placing it carefully on his head, 'that it's time to walk up to the house and introduce Alison to Eleanor Duboys.'

I followed them along the shore of the lake and then along the banks of the river until we reached the path that we had taken that morning. At the bottom of the steps climbing to the gardens I asked if we could rest. We stood for a minute, and I smoked a 555.

'You have lumbar problems?' asked Walsh.

'Pelvis,' I said. 'Double fracture.'

He nodded in apparent sympathy.

'And comparatively rare, apparently; I was the object of not a little surgical interest. At one point I was photographed for a textbook.'

'I hope they paid you well.'

'You know us orthopaedic supermodels,' I said, burying my

cigarette end in a lichened stone urn. 'We won't get into bed for less than ten grand.'

He smiled and inclined his head, and we began the ascent. At the top of the steps the wild garden ceded to more formal arrangements and we paused in a grass-carpeted avenue between two walls of clipped yew.

'You almost expect Madame de Tourvel to step from behind one of these hedges,' I said to Walsh.

'Madame de . . .?'

'Michelle Pfeiffer,' I explained. 'In *Dangerous Liaisons*. Or maybe Anne Louise Lambert in *The Draughtsman's Contract* or Marisa Berenson in *Barry Lyndon* or, at a pinch, Delphine Seyrig in *Last Year in Marienbad*. I'm very keen on topiary movies.'

'Then you're going to enjoy ours,' said Walsh. 'Let's go inside.'

I followed the two men through the knot garden into the entrance hall and up the wide stone staircase. On the first-floor landing, Walsh indicated that I precede him down a shadowed corridor hung with landscapes and portraits. The floorboards were uneven, and at one point Sheldrake had to take my arm to prevent me turning an ankle.

At the end of the corridor – we were now in the west wing, I calculated – was a Tudor doorway carved with a linen-fold design. I lifted the heavy iron latch and the door swung inwards to reveal an empty oak-panelled chamber. Pale afternoon sunlight streamed through a pair of deep, uncurtained bays, illuminating the dead-leaf browns and faded blues of the tapestries which hung to right and left of the fireplace.

I paused in the doorway for a moment, and then stepped into the lavendered stillness. Motes whirled in the disturbed air and long fingers of light reached for me, drawing my shadow across the dark old boards of the floor.

On the opposite wall, dominating the chamber, hung an Elizabethan portrait of a young woman. As I approached it, I sensed Walsh and Sheldrake watching me. ' "ELEANOR DUBOYS in the character of a Nymph of Diana",' I read from the gilt cartouche, deliberately not looking at the painting. ' "ROBt PEAKE pinxit".' And then, raising my eyes, I stopped dead, and everyone and everything vanished except myself and

Eleanor Duboys. She had been painted in a green dress with lace sleeves and a deep-cut bodice trimmed with scarlet. A silver crescent moon gleamed at her forehead, a bow and quiver were slung over one shoulder, and in her long unringed hands she held a single dark-feathered arrow.

It was her face, however, which held me transfixed. Not so much its beauty – though beautiful she undoubtedly was, with her subtle half-smile and her elusive sapphire gaze – as the fact that this was a face and an expression that I knew, had puzzled over, had even attempted in some measure to decode.

'You asked why Dale Cooney,' said Walsh. 'That's why Dale Cooney.'

'It's just amazing,' I said, shaking my head in disbelief. 'She's the absolute living image . . .'

Sheldrake smiled in quiet triumph and reached inside his linen jacket. 'Who's the living image of who, though? That's the question.'

He handed me a couple of folded sheets of paper. 'This might be a good place and a good moment for you to read the film treatment. Why don't we leave you alone to do that? There should be some tea outside on the lawn when you've finished.'

With that he and Walsh left the room, closing the heavy door behind them. Their footsteps receded down the corridor, and I seated myself on the ledge of the bay adjacent to the painting. The sun washed my neck and the leaded glass and deep oak panels enclosed me as if I was in the stern of some great landlocked galleon.

TREATMENT – NFFL

The principal sequence opens in the present day. In the panelled tower-chamber of a country house a fashionably dressed young woman is standing by a bay window, examining an ancestral portrait. We see that the subject of the portrait is also a young woman, and that despite her sixteenth- century apparel, she bears an extraordinary resemblance to the figure regarding her. A transposition takes place, and now it is the young noblewoman who is standing by the window. All traces of the twentieth century have vanished.

The young woman steps from the house into the gardens. There is an elaborate parterre, stone steps, a bridge over a stream. She descends. It is a summer's morning; there is dew on the grass, and deer are disposed around the formal parkland. She passes with proprietory grace between the shadowed walls of an *allée* of clipped yew and pauses by a statue. She appears to be searching for something – or someone – and her fine, pale features express a longing.

And then, at the dark edge of the forest beyond the gardens, she sees a figure. The distance is too great to establish more than that he is tall, and dressed entirely in black. He waits in the shadows, unmoving.

It is midday; the sun is high in the sky. The young woman, languorous now and with her eyes half closed, reclines in a narrow, gilded boat on a lake. Her long fingers trail in the olive water, the forest is dark beyond. A figure, of whom we see only a black damask sleeve and a narrow hand, propels the boat with a pole. The pole slides through his fingers, dropping water like jewels, soundlessly piercing the lake's surface.

It is afternoon; she sleeps. Her bed, or bower, is a grassy bank studded with wild flowers. Above her is a spreading oak, before her a stream. A shield rests against the tree, bearing the device of a winged heart rising from flames.

It is twilight. At the lakeside the household sit feasting as masquers in fantastical costumes approach in procession. Amongst their number, in the costume of a nymph, we recognise the daughter of the house. She leads the masquers into a formal dance, the music being provided by lutenists, flautists and hautboy-players on an island in the lake. The tempo quickens, torches are lit, and there is general dancing. The nymph is claimed by a dark, black-clad figure and briefly, before she is whirled away into the darkness, the flames illuminate her cheeks. The scene dissolves in a shower of sparks, and once again a young woman is standing before a four-hundred-year old portrait. She smiles, and the copy line ('Thy eternal summer shall not fade . . .') is whispered in voice-over.

Whatever I had expected, it was nothing like this. The château or country house setting was hardly a new idea in the world of beauty product marketing, but most campaigns shot in those kinds of locations relied on atmosphere rather than story. The models might drift past honeysuckled statuary or wander through summer rose gardens or be glimpsed, briefly, in the dim interiors of ballrooms, but I had never known them play out complex allegorical narratives of this sort. Tall, dark figures were pretty much par for the course, but formal masques and mystical emblems were a definite departure from the idiomatic norm.

Not that, as a former student of the period – even if a dilatory one – I didn't recognise Sheldrake's sources easily enough. The moon goddess Diana, huntress and patron of chastity, often served as a metaphorical stand-in for the Virgin Queen; in allowing herself to be depicted as a nymph of Diana, therefore, Eleanor Duboys was simultaneously proclaiming herself virgo intacta and a loyal subject of the crown.

The meaning of the shield bearing the flaming heart was harder to divine. It was an *impresa*, one of those esoteric symbols so beloved of the Elizabethans through which they conveyed their more secret allegiances. This particular *impresa* was borrowed from Isaac Oliver's portrait of Lord Herbert of Cherbury. The painting shows the baron reclining by a brook in a woodland setting in an attitude of fashionable melancholia, the shield on his arm bearing the flaming heart and the motto 'Magica Sympathia' – Sympathetic Magic. Again, the image was a well-known one, and I had not been the only English undergraduate to have a poster of Oliver's painting on my wall. Thomas Chatterton had been the number-one hall-of-residence pin-up, but the moody baron had run him a close second. The *impresa*, as far as I could remember, referred to the necessity of purifying the soul in order to attain heavenly wisdom; something like that, anyway.

None of which got me any closer, however, to divining why Charles Sheldrake should have introduced these frankly arcane themes and emblems into a perfume advertisement. I would have asked him, but the arrogance of his manner disinclined me. I was also aware of a hint – or more than a hint, perhaps – of a challenge. You can take all of this as you find it, he seemed to be saying, or you can try and decipher its real meaning. He was behaving, in short, like an Elizabethan.

Before making my way down to tea, I decided to explore. A

narrow, iron-studded door set into the side wall of the chamber seemed as good a starting point as any, and folding Sheldrake's film treatment into my trouser pocket I lowered myself from my perch in the window bay and tried the latch. The door, which was unlocked, opened on to a dark spiral stair-tower. The walls were windowless, but the light from the chamber revealed stone treads worn to a shine.

I hesitated for a moment, and then, as my eyes grew used to the dimness, became aware of daylight above me. Leaving the chamber door open, I climbed upwards towards the light, and a half-minute and several spiral turns later found myself in a low octagonal space lit by a ring of grimed glass panes. A door secured by a galvanised steel bolt barred access to the light; the bolt was stiff and new, but I managed to work it loose, and stepped out into the brightness of the roof.

The octagonal area I had just exited, I saw, was surmounted by a leaded cupola rising to a tiny, pennant-shaped weathervane. An identical stair-tower stood at each corner of the flat roof, and around these a low balustrade had been raised, forming an enclosed promenade. It took me some time to get my visual bearings, however, for grouped around the roof was a whimsical profusion of architectural forms. There was a pavilion with a fish-scaled roof, there was a miniature pyramid, there were columns, obelisks and spires. The effect was of some perverse, overbearing dreamscape; it was as if, up here on the roof, the designer had secretly assembled all the decorative elements that he had withheld from the house's exterior. Perhaps it was a subversive architectural joke, a placing of the building's fashionable minimalism within inverted commas. I took the Acu-Sonic from my bag, put in a new cassette, and pressed the record button.

'Darne's secret roofscape,' I murmured. 'Late-sixteenth-century irony. Case perhaps to be made for the quasi-post-modern Elizabethan sensibility . . .'

'Ssshh!' hissed a voice, female. 'Get down.'

I almost jumped out of my skin, and worse, almost threw the Acu-Sonic dictaphone over the parapet. Turning, I saw a sharp-featured woman of about my own age sitting cross-legged in the angle of the stair-tower and the balustrade. Her shoulder-length hair was greasy, she was wearing filthy jeans and a crumpled lace and velvet shirt, and she was rolling a joint.

'Down here,' she whispered. 'Quickly.'

Doing my best to avoid the cobwebs, I hunkered down beside her.

'You must be the journalist,' she said. 'No one except a journalist would talk shit like that.'

'Guilty,' I admitted, embarrassed, my knees cracking.

'People are always saying they're guilty,' she mused, taking my chin between her fingers and turning my face to hers. 'I'm not guilty at all. You, on the other hand, my dear, are quite . . . seriously fucked up, aren't you? Physically, I mean. Quite sexy, though, those scars, in a *belle sabreuse* sort of a way. I'm Phoebe Duboys.'

'Alison,' I murmured, dazed. 'Alison MacAteer.' She smelt of body odour, Lebanese hash and very expensive perfume. Tearing the flap off her Rizla packet, she made a roach and pushed it into the liquorice-paper joint.

'I'll light this in a minute,' she said. 'First, look over there.'

I followed the direction of her outstretched finger, but at first, so many were the obstacles on the roof, I could not see what she was pointing at.

'Look, stupid,' she hissed. 'Over there.'

It was Sheldrake again, his hands in his pockets, talking to Fiona Duff, who was listening attentively. They were out of earshot, and I guessed that they had come out of the stair-tower opposite us.

'So?'

'Figgy's rather keen that Charles interfere with her,' Phoebe explained. 'And if we keep out of sight they just might . . .'

'I should go,' I said, half rising.

Phoebe grabbed me painfully by the skin of my upper arm, and pulled me down. 'Stay,' she said. 'You're a journalist, aren't you? I thought this was what you people did?'

She had a point.

'Watch Charles,' Phoebe whispered. 'Watch him hedge his bets, the fucker. On the one hand he's flattered that she wants him to . . .'

Genuflecting, I peered through the grove of columns. Fiona Duff was half sitting, half leaning against an Ionic chimney stack; Sheldrake was facing her. Another inch or two and their bodies would touch. It was clear that she expected him to kiss her.

'. . .On the other he doesn't want to actually do it, because when all's said and done . . .' Phoebe jutted her lower lip.

'What? What's the problem? She's very pretty.'

'It's more a class thing. Men like Charlie Sheldrake can't really cope with the Figgy Duffs of this world. She's probably got some frightful Rothmans-smoking mother holed up somewhere off the North Circular.'

'He doesn't seem to be doing too badly,' I said, as Sheldrake lifted Fiona Duff's long brown hair and let it fall.

'Well, let's see.'

In silence we watched as he reached a hand out to her red silk mandarin jacket and unbuttoned it. It fell open, and the director regarded her body thoughtfully. Eventually he looked away.

'That's all he needs, you see,' said Phoebe. 'To know that he could have had her if he'd wanted to.'

Fiona straightened, and walked to the front parapet. Still unbuttoned, she folded her arms beneath her breasts. The posture was curiously void of effect. Like most models she sexualised herself by putting clothes on, rather than by taking them off.

'You seem to know him pretty well,' I said.

'Well, he used to interfere with me on a fairly regular basis. He even wanted to marry me at one stage, would you believe it, before wiser counsels prevailed.'

'His or yours?'

'Mine. It wasn't *moi* he fancied,' she turned her sharp, sallow little face towards me, 'it was the bloodline. He was always looking at the pictures, trying to find a likeness. I used to tell him there's only one, and that's the Zuccaro drawing of the Lady with the Weasel in Mummy's bedroom. I'm the weasel.'

'You've got a very nice face,' I said, embarrassing myself even as I spoke, and Phoebe bared her teeth at me.

'Nice? Fuck *nice*.' She felt in her pocket for a lighter, and lit the joint. 'I'm like you, looks-wise: very much a specialist taste. Not for all men.'

She took a long drag, held her breath, sipped air through her lips to stop herself coughing, and passed the joint to me. On the other side of the roof I watched Sheldrake usher Fiona Duff into the stair-tower and close the door behind them.

'But then ask yourself what sort of men actually go out with girls like Figgy,' Phoebe continued when she had exhaled. 'Bright men are intimidated by beautiful women – even by very stupid ones – because they tend to . . . to hold beauty itself in high esteem. You see them freeze up, try and reinvent themselves so that they can cope, and it just doesn't work.'

She reached out her arm for the joint, which I had allowed to go out.

'And who do the world's most beautiful women end up with?' She flipped the lid of her Zippo and the Rizla paper crackled. 'The boneheads, basically. The brain-dead. The guys who are just too vain and stupid to doubt themselves.'

'What about Dan Fortess and Hermia Page?' I asked, on impulse.

'Well, no one's exactly keeping the Nobel Prize warm for Dan Fortess, are they? Although that's a more complicated situation, because . . . Don't you want any of this?'

'I'm supposed to be working,' I said. 'I've got ninety minutes of tape to transcribe.'

'I was at school with Hermia,' said Phoebe thoughtfully. 'You don't know a woman called Jacinta LeQuesne, do you?'

'I know who she is,' I said guardedly.

Phoebe flipped the remains of the joint over the parapet. 'I think I might ask them down here: Hermia and Dan, that is. They've been having a bit of a rough time recently.'

I stood up and dusted the seat of my trousers. 'I'm just going to have a look round,' I said. 'If that's OK.'

'Be my guest,' said Phoebe, closing her eyes.

From the roof, I saw just how isolated we were. At the front of the house, bordered by the oak and beech forest, were the gardens, the lake and the deer park. At the rear, the woodland pressed much closer, bearing down almost jungle-like on the circular lawn and the rhododendron-lined drive. A long removals truck, I saw, was parked outside the back door. As I watched, men and women in brown overalls carried several heavily laden clothes-rails out of the back of the truck and into the house. When the job was finished, I watched the vehicle's hesitant progress as it ascended the forested drive and finally disappeared amongst the trees.

To the east side of the house was the walled garden and the grey-green spread of the cedars. Beyond the trees the lawn descended to the lake, and I saw that the dark expanse of water retained, with a little imagining, the shape of the crescent moon.

'I'll have the Lapsang,' I said. 'Thanks.'

There were half a dozen of us sitting at the table under the cedar. Gina Tagliaferri was reading a book, Charles Sheldrake was making notes on a script, and Fiona Duff was rather blankly addressing a cucumber sandwich. She'd changed from her red mandarin jacket, I noticed, into a dove-grey poorboy.

'So how's it all going?' said Nancy.

'I could almost write the piece already,' I said. 'I'm going to have to be pretty selective.'

'That's good, isn't it?'

'Oh yes, definitely – thanks, one sugar, no milk. I see the costumes have arrived?'

'That's right. John-Paul's just checking them now, jewel by jewel.'

'Remind me who . . .?'

'Louise Tallis. She was Charles's designer on *Love's Labours Lost*. These costumes are based on paintings by . . .' she consulted her folder, '. . . here we are, by Alonso Coello, Hans Eworth – am I pronouncing that right? – Nicholas Hilliard, Isaac Oliver and Robert Peake, and on masque designs by Inigo Jones. They're to die for, basically, just these *rivers* of lace and chiffon and seed pearls, and so *sexy*! Put them on a Paris catwalk and you'd bring the house down. Anyway, I thought you could meet with John-Paul tomorrow morning, perhaps – he's in charge of the costumes – and also with Sabrina, who's doing hair, and of course Carlton, who heads up our cosmetics division.'

'Everything but the girl, then,' I said mildly, stirring my tea.

'I'm sorry?'

'Do we have an ETA for Dale Cooney?'

Nancy's smile tightened perceptibly. 'Tomorrow, according to our best reports. Can I say nine a.m. to John-Paul?'

'Try saying "youth" with a Jamaican accent,' interjected a slender young man in a black frock coat, to whom I hadn't been introduced.

'I'm sorry?' said Nancy, startled.

'It's not Hans E-worth like e-mail,' he explained coldly to her, 'it's Eworth. But no matter.' He turned to me, effectively cutting Nancy out of the conversation altogether, and held out a long, thin hand. 'I'm Oliver Duboys.'

'Phoebe's brother?'

'The same. Have you met her?'

'Sure have,' I said. 'I'm Alison MacAteer.'

'The journalist?'

'The journalist.'

'You must have one of these sandwiches, then, Miss MacAteer. The English may have fallen behind in other respects, but we still lead the world in tomato sandwich making. The trick is to blanch and peel the tomatoes, and then, having sliced them, to blot the slices on kitchen paper so as not to make the bread soggy. After that, crusts off and salt and pepper only.'

'Naturally,' I said. 'So are you older or younger than Phoebe?'

'Both younger and comelier, as you will have observed. She's a rouged and farded thirty, I'm a fresh-faced twenty-eight.'

'And what do you . . .?'

'I restore paintings, mostly.'

'Here?'

'I've got a studio here, yes.'

In the glancing afternoon light his skin was pale almost to the point of transparency. His eyes were the same sea-grey as his sister's, and his fine red-gold hair, which he wore long, was tied at the nape of his neck with a black ribbon.

'Did you restore the Peake portrait?' I asked him.

'Eleanor?' he said gravely, addressing himself to his teacup. 'Well, not really. Six years ago I was the indented slave of a London restorer named Cornelius Sharpe, who's pretty much the *éminence grise* as far as paintings of this period are concerned, and I persuaded Bill – that's my late father – to have Eleanor cleaned by Sharpe at the Courtauld Institute, so that I could watch. It turned out to be a rather uncomfortable feeling – not unlike watching a relative having plastic surgery – but I learnt a lot. Since then I've worked on a number of medieval paintings, mostly *in situ*.'

'What are you restoring at the moment?'

'Something I've just bought. You must come up and have a look; it's actually a bit of a puzzle.'

'I'd love to,' I said.

'Come up tomorrow, then, when I'll have it set up for cleaning. I'd like your thoughts on it.'

'My thoughts!' I said, surprised. 'I don't know anything about picture restoring.'

'You're an outsider,' he said, raking me casually up and down with his eyes, 'and I could use an outside opinion. Shall we see you at supper?'

'I guess so. A girl's got to eat.'

'Eight, then. We don't dress.'

Leaving me to deconstruct this final statement, he climbed to his feet, inclined his upper body towards me in a vestigial bow, repeated the gesture to Gina Tagliaferri, who fluttered her fingers, and turned towards the house.

'Hey, Alison, you're honoured,' said Nancy dryly, when he had disappeared from view. 'Dinner with the family.'

'Doesn't everyone . . .?'

'Absolutely not. We eat in the Hall or outside, the family eats in the dining room.'

'And who does the cooking?'

'We do. I mean, our people do. All the Duboys' household staff and gardeners have been given a two-week vacation.'

'So you're what, cooking and cleaning and generally keeping house for them?'

Nancy shrugged. 'I guess.'

'The family are going to be in the film,' said Charles Sheldrake abruptly, looking up from his script.

'Where?' I asked. 'I mean, how?'

'In the masque,' said Sheldrake. 'The family will represent . . . themselves.'

'Themselves four hundred years ago?'

'Themselves,' said Sheldrake, returning to his script.

I drained my tea. At the far end of the table Gina Tagliaferri folded her sunglasses into their case and raised a conspiratorial eyebrow. I mimed smoking a cigarette and she nodded.

'Presumably,' I said to her ten minutes later as we walked round to the front of the house, 'saying that we don't dress for dinner is a polite way of saying that we do change for dinner.'

'Something like that,' she confirmed, drawing her hand along the low hedge bordering the path. 'Although you can never really win with the English aristocracy. They asked me to eat with them a couple of days ago and I wore this plain black Palmiro dress, and when I got downstairs to the dining room there was Oliver dressed as an extra from *Dracula*, Bridget – that's the mother – in floor-length Valentino and Phoebe looking – and pretty much smelling – like an unmade bed. Not that any of it mattered, really, because in general they treated me like some sort of mute au pair, just there to listen to them and maybe pick up some table manners and some basic English. At one point, my being Italian, Bridget asked if I'd been to the River Café, but that was about the limit of it, conversationally. So take your pick, really.'

'I can't wait,' I said, exhaling Nazionale smoke, 'Tell me something, Gina, and don't take this the wrong way, but where *did* you learn your English?'

'The short answer, I guess, is the London School of Economics.'

'You graduated from the LSE?'

'Yes.'

'So how come you . . .?'

'I responded to a demand curve. Now don't you take this the wrong way, Alison, but are you OK for something to wear tonight? We're pretty much the same size.'

'Yes,' I said. 'For once in my life, I think I am.'

Back in my room I found a pen and notebook, jacked the Acu-Sonic into the mains, stretched out on the narrow iron bed and started to listen to the afternoon's interview with Walsh and Sheldrake.

I doubt that I managed ten minutes. When I woke up, disoriented, there was a line from the headphone cable across my cheek and a damp place on my pillow where my mouth had been. It was almost eight o'clock, and the light had gone from the sky.

I had stripped to my underwear before I remembered that I had no idea where the bathroom was. Pulling on my kimono and taking a towel from beside the heavy Victorian basin, I stepped out of my room. Instinct told me that bathrooms lay at the ends rather than in the middles of corridors, and that their doors were often distinguishable from others by some subtle difference of architrave pattern, lock furniture or degree of inset. An examination of the doorways yielded no clue, however, and then I remembered that Nancy had told me that my room was next to Dale Cooney's. She, surely, would have an attached bathroom. I opened the left-hand door a crack, and saw a tan-coloured suitcase with little wheels attached that somehow could only have been Nancy's. Behind the right-hand door, however, I discovered a broad, shadowed room dominated by a vast four-poster bed. A curtained exit in one corner admitted me to a small Victorian bathroom, and twenty minutes later, more or less presentable, I was asking one of the caterers the way to the dining room.

It was a feeling that I would experience many times over the days that followed: that I had arrived late at a play in which everything depended on the initial exposition.

The dining room was a miniature version of the entrance hall, with the same bistre-painted woodwork and sea-green curtains. A long oak table set for five stood on a Persian carpet in the centre of the pale stone floor, and the sense of entering a stage set was heightened by the fact that the players already present were disposed about the room in tense, unmoving silence. Oliver and Phoebe were seated opposite each other in one of the window bays, a thin, taut woman in a lilac cheongsam was hovering near the sideboard, and a fourth figure, military in bearing, was staring out of the second window.

They all turned to me as I came in. 'You must be Alison,' said the thin woman flatly. 'How lovely. Oliver, would you offer her a drink?'

'Of course,' said Oliver, rising distractedly to his feet and walking slowly towards me. 'What can I get you?'

The tray held five bottles of whisky, all opened, and a decanter of something rust-coloured and sedimented. 'Perhaps a whisky?' I suggested.

'Any particular one?'

'That one,' I said, pointing at random.

'Don't have that,' said Oliver. 'It's sort of a joke one we give to the Americans. I think they make it somewhere near Stevenage. Have the malt, unless you'd prefer a Malibu or something.'

'Oliver!' said Phoebe.

'Well, I don't know,' said Oliver. 'She might have done.'

'The malt's fine,' I said.

He handed me a tumblerful, and I took a sip. The advantage of expensive whisky seemed to be that it tasted slightly less strongly of whisky than ordinary whisky did.

'Ice?' asked Oliver testily. 'The film people have probably got ice.'

'Oliver,' said Phoebe. 'Either be nice to her or . . . go and sort yourself out.'

In answer, waving like a song-and-dance-man as he went, Oliver left the room. I was surprised; he'd seemed quite friendly at tea.

'I'm sorry,' said the thin woman, whom I assumed to be Bridget Duboys. 'He just gets a bit tired.'

'He's just acts the cunt,' said Phoebe. 'More to the point.'

For the duration of the drink-pouring routine, the figure by the window waited with his hands behind his back. It was the tall, dark-skinned man I had seen earlier at the gatehouse, only this time around, instead of a tool-belt and overalls, he was wearing an expensively tailored Italian jacket and flannel trousers.

'Stephen Faulds,' he said, extending his hand. He had a Sandhurst accent, a painful handshake and the unblinking regard of a bird of prey.

'I'm Alison,' I said. 'The journalist.'

'Yes,' he said, a faint smile touching the raptorial features. 'I saw you arriving.' He took my tumbler, and without spilling a drop, poured its contents back into the bottle. 'Now, what would you really like to drink?'

'A glass of cold white wine, please.'

'Chablis?'

'That would be perfect.'

'Get it, would you, Phoebe?' he ordered quietly. 'And bring some glasses.' He returned the whisky tumbler to the tray and stoppered the bottle. 'You mustn't let them bully you. This, for example – although she not untypically neglected to announce the fact to you – is Bridget Duboys, châtelaine of Darne.'

I inclined my head.

'Stephen is our conscience,' whispered Bridget, touching the diamond brooch at her shoulder as if it were the relic of a martyr, and staring at my empty whisky tumbler.

'I can take any amount of bullying,' I confided to Faulds when we were finally seated. 'You know what they say about the pen and the sword.'

'Oh, I'm sure the pen is a wonderful instrument of revenge,' he replied. 'But in the short term, my money's on the sword every time.'

For ten minutes now, Bridget, Phoebe and Oliver had been locked into a family discussion, leaving Faulds and me to forage, conversationally speaking, as best we might. 'I knew the whole thing was impossible as soon as I saw her duvet cover,' Bridget Duboys was saying in her flat, expressionless voice. 'But you just have to let these things take their course.'

Suddenly indifferent to the opinion of everyone around me – I had drunk at least half a bottle of Chablis on an empty stomach – I fished an ice cube from the water jug in front of me and ran it over the burning scars on my eyes and mouth. As I wiped my face with my napkin I saw Phoebe watching me with frank, voyeuristic interest.

'Was it a car crash?' she asked, addressing me directly for the first time that evening.

'Yes.'

'Painful?'

'No, a positive pleasure,' I said. 'Can you pass the wine?'

Smiling, she pushed the bottle towards me in its coaster. 'Where do you actually come from, Alison?'

'Well, I was born in Singapore.'

'That's sort of like Guildford, isn't it? Except with prickly heat?'

'Don't tease her,' said Oliver. 'Or she'll write horrible things about us.'

'He's right,' I said. 'I will.'

For one brief moment there was silence, and everyone at the table stared at me. My lips were burning, and I was unable to prevent myself dabbing at them with my linen napkin. I looked down, but there was no blood. When I looked up again, they had all resumed their earlier conversations. The exception was Stephen Faulds, who was watching me.

'So,' I said brightly, 'you're Phoebe's boyfriend?'

'That's one way of putting it, I suppose.'

'And you're in the army?'

'Used to be. Is that so obvious?'

'It is to me. Which bit were you in?'

He smiled again.

'I'm a landscape gardener now,' he said. 'Not a soldier. I watch over the grounds.'

'Watch over them?'

'I keep an eye on things. Coffee?'

'*Allora*,' said Gina. 'How was it?' We were sitting on a bench in the knot garden, and although all colour had fled the neat arabesques of box and turf, the air was still reverberant with the day's events.

'Awful,' I said, crushing my cigarette end into the watered gravel. 'Unspeakable. They practically ignored me. Talked about me as if I wasn't there. Except for Stephen Faulds.'

'Phoebe's boyfriend?'

'If that's what he is, yes. Although they seem an odd couple, frankly.'

'Did you like him?'

'He has a kind of . . . lethal charm, I suppose.'

'Where's he from?'

'Father English, mother Jordanian. That's as far as I got. And used to be in the army. Some technical bit.'

'Fancy him?'

'Gina, really!'

'Well?'

'No. I don't.'

She looked at me, expressionless, and we both laughed. The sound, like my cigarette smoke, seemed to hang in the twilit stillness.

'I don't, Gina, honestly. And especially not if he's some kind of *thing* of Phoebe's.'

'So how did you get away?'

'The meal finished, Stephen bowed to me like Sir Walter Raleigh, and they all just . . . fucked off.'

'Well, I doubt you'll have to do it again.' She closed her eyes and inhaled the night air. 'It's so beautiful here, isn't it?'

'Gina,' I said hesitantly, 'I just want to say something to you and I want you to tell me if it makes sense, OK?'

'Sure.'

I touched my lip with my tongue. 'When I went home to my flat in London after being in hospital for ten weeks and I looked in the mirror and I saw this damaged, altered person, I felt . . . *I don't belong here*. I've got this picture on my desk that was taken for my byline in the paper and I thought: these things are hers, not mine. I can't eat her food, I can't drink her drink, none of her clothes fit me. It was . . . it was like walking into a dead person's flat, and trying to work out who she was from her possessions. Because I don't know who she was. Honestly, Gina, *I don't know who she was*. And as for who I am . . .' I ran my hands nervously through the short buzz of my hair. 'Well, this has been Day One.'

Gina looked around her, at the walls of clipped yew and the black bulk of the cedar against the sky. 'So how has it been, your Day One?'

'Strange.'

She nodded, her expression unreadable. 'Yes. That makes sense.'

9

Breakfast was served on the lawn, beneath the cedar. I arrived a little before nine, by which time the dew and the chill of the morning had evaporated and the further reaches of the estate were already swimming in the pale heat haze. Gina and Fiona were there, as were Walsh and Oliver Duboys, but by tacit agreement the coffee-drinking and croissant-tearing and cigarette-smoking were conducted in silence.

Afterwards, the models and I made our way upstairs to the Long Gallery on the first floor, which John-Paul, the production's wardrobe master, had transformed into his domain. Uncovering the clothes-rails, he revealed a shimmering array of embroidered satin bodices, transparent chemisettes, gauzy camisoles, silk chiffon slip dresses, petticoats, partlets and flounces. Trestle tables had been erected, and on these were laid out the jewellery and the accessories: the carcanets and aigrettes, the necklets and the trellises of pearls, and the various headdresses, biliments and attires. Each item was numbered, and related to a series of costume specifications which, together with the designer's sketches, were displayed on boards.

'While you're here,' John-Paul said to Gina and Fiona, 'I wonder if I could just ask you to slip into these frocks?' He was a large, hesitant man with a shaved head, delicate of gesture. Reading from the list, he assembled the various elements of the two costumes.

Fiona was one of those forgettably perfect blondes who took up the bulk of the editorial slack in the upmarket glossies. You saw her everywhere, but you'd walk straight past her in the street without recognising her. 'What am I supposed to be?' she hissed to me, unbuttoning her white Dead Zone shirt as John-Paul directed her to her costume.

'One of those,' I said, pointing to the Inigo Jones drawing of an ethereal dancing figure. 'A nymph of Diana.'

'Oh,' said Fiona. 'Right. Lovely!'

It was indeed lovely, and as it was her job to do, she looked effortlessly wonderful in it. The costume, very light and simple, consisted of a bodice of olive-green silk seeded with pearls and a two-tiered pleated chiffon skirt. The bodice was cut to fully expose her breasts, which were covered only by the transparent gauze of her chemisette.

'Blimey!' said Fiona. 'This is a bit cheeky for prime-time, isn't it?'

'Shoes,' said John-Paul firmly, handing her a pair of rosetted silk slippers, 'And your biliment. Hold still.' Carefully he manoeuvred a gold filigree headband into her hair, which she had arranged at his instruction into a flat chignon.

'Right, ladies,' he said, as Gina – similarly transformed – wriggled her toes in her rosetted slippers. 'Shall we walk?'

Slowly, their pace conversational, Gina and Fiona promenaded down the gallery. As they did so the fragile costumes seemed to warm around them, to come to life, and as they reached the first of the window bays, the morning light turned their streaming gauze mantles to white fire.

'It's a wonderful thing to see,' said John-Paul, taking a threaded needle from the cushion on his wrist and deftly turning back the cuff of a lace sleeve. 'Inigo Jones first drew these costumes four hundred years ago and there they are, just as he imagined them.' He smoothed soft hands over the stubbled cannonball of his skull and lowered his voice. 'But they're very good girls, these; it's much harder than you'd think to respond imaginatively to period costume. You've got the two types, you see. That Gina, she's a thinker, she's intelligent, she thinks herself into the part. Figgy Duff, now, she's as daffy as the day is long – wouldn't know a Stuart masque from a bite in the arse – but she's instinctive. Put her in the clothes and her body will respond.'

At the end of the gallery the models swung round and returned to us.

'Thank you, ladies, I think we're suitably stunned.' John-Paul pursed his lips. 'I wonder if I should get Charles Sheldrake along to look at these.'

'He's gone to London,' said Fiona. 'Went off early.'

'Well, I hope he brings our girl back with him,' said John-Paul.

'Does anyone know where she is?' I asked.

Fiona shook her head.

'She doesn't look the acting-up type,' said Gina. 'Maybe she's sick.'

'So where's the crew and everyone?'

'On standby at their hotels, I guess. Waiting for the word.'

'Boring for them,' I ventured.

Fiona shrugged. 'The longer it takes, the more cash they make. They're all on top-dollar rates.' She smiled and raised a quizzical eyebrow. 'Like you, I expect?'

'I'm paid by the story,' I said. 'Piecework.'

'What *is* the story, exactly?' asked Gina.

'I'm not sure yet,' I said.

'Alison, could I trouble you?' asked John-Paul, touching my shoulder.

'Sure,' I said. 'What?'

He pointed to a costume of ivory silk that he had arranged on a table. 'Would you mind trying it on?'

'I'd love to,' I said. 'Whose is it?'

'Well . . . yours, actually.'

I stared at him. 'You're kidding.'

'I had a word with Charles,' said Gina triumphantly. 'I thought you needed cheering up. He said yes immediately. He loves using real people.'

'I'm real enough,' I said.

I took off my shirt and trousers and pulled on the buff silk petticoats. The costume was fuller and more elaborate than the masque dresses, and a small bolster lay coiled beside it on the table.

'A French bum-roll! I've always fancied one of these.'

John-Paul looked at me curiously. 'Where did you learn about French bum-rolls?'

'University,' I said, gasping as he pulled the laces of the bodice tight behind my back. 'I was supposed to have been studying the literature, but I got diverted by the fashion.'

I tied the bum-roll around my hips – high at the front, low at the back, as was the 1590s vogue – and John-Paul, kneeling, knotted the farthingale skirt and flounce over the top. The effect was startling. I now had a cleavage that would have stopped traffic and a waist as waspish as that of the Virgin Queen herself.

'Cool?' I said, twirling. 'Or what?'

'Cool!' Gina confirmed. 'Definitely.'

Five minutes later, with chiffon sleeves covering my arms and silk chopines on my feet, I was an Elizabethan lady of quality.

'One last thing,' said John-Paul, and passed me a black velvet mask with silk ribbons. I tied on the mask, which covered most of my face, and stepped in front of one of the mirrors.

'How do you feel?' asked Fiona.

'I'm ready for my close-up,' I said.

When we were finished I made my way up to the roof promenade, pausing briefly en route to renew my acquaintance with the portrait of Eleanor Duboys. I stepped from the gloom of the stair-tower into the splintering glare of the open sky, and quickly sought the shade of the small central pavilion. There, unclipping my phone from my belt, I dialled the number of Orde's paging service. The reception on the roof, as I had hoped, was good, and I sent a three word message – 'MAGAZINE PROFILE WENDY?' – followed by my mobile number.

By the time I had smoked a cigarette, my phone was ringing.

'What do you want?' demanded Orde. We never used names on these occasions.

'Wendy'd make a good subject,' I said. 'Girls with guns and all that. I'm sure she'd photograph well.'

'What do you want?' he repeated.

'Some background on a name.'

'What for?'

'Personal,' I said. 'I'm being taken an interest in.'

This, I knew, was the only acceptable answer that I could have given. Although neither of us had ever put it into words, both of us knew that Orde felt a kind of vestigial responsibility towards me. If he could think of it as family duty, he was occasionally prepared to stretch a point, if not actually to break the Official Secrets Act.

'And the profile?'

'I can guarantee seven hundred and fifty words plus half-page picture.'

'Spell out the name,' he said, and the phone went dead. I called his pager service, and spelt out FAULDS, STEPHEN, approx. 35.

From the back of the house came a dull, damped banging. I walked to the parapet and saw that several Nissen huts were being assembled around the circular driveway. Two more removal trucks were parked there, and crates were being unpacked. One of the unpackers saw me standing on the roof and waved, and I walked back to the front parapet and settled myself against a column. As soon as Dale Cooney turned up, I guessed, everything would change. The place would be crowded with film crew members, technicians, carpenters, extras and all those bossy, baseball-hatted, walkie-talkie-toting types who seemed to proliferate around film sets.

Somewhat to my surprise, I realised that I was not particularly looking forward to her arrival, and that despite the weirdness of the Duboys family, I was beginning to enjoy myself. I was even beginning to feel a little less self-conscious about my face. For better or worse, no one here had known me any other way, and if I could cope with models and beauty professionals – and it seemed that I could – then I could cope with just about anyone. And I was lucky; my facial injuries could have been worse. There was no rough patching or grotesque torsion, as there so easily might have been, just those cursive slashes at the mouth, cheeks and eyes. With something like surrender, I turned my face to the sun.

When the phone on my belt rang, I was almost asleep.

'Yes?'

There was a lot of background noise, and Orde sounded strained. 'Ring me tonight, OK?'

'Is there a problem?' I asked, but the line was already dead.

Holstering the Motorola, I looked down over the estate. In the park, the deer were all but invisible in the low shadows beneath the trees. To the left of the park the lake gleamed its dark invitation, and I decided that what I wanted more than anything else was to be by water. It was too hot to sit in my room and finish the transcribing; too hot to expand upon the few scribbled notes that I had made about the costumes; too hot to write up my reaction to the news that I was to play a role in the film myself.

Slowly, hatless, I made my way across the lawns to the lake. Some kind of white blossom had fallen from the bushes at the water's edge, and drifts of this hung motionless in the surface film. Beneath the copper beech tree, beside the loggia, was a small rowing boat, with its oars shipped. After a moment's hesitation I undid the mooring rope, climbed in and shoved off from the tree roots. Soon the boat was gliding across the lake, stripes of reflected light rocking and glancing in its wake. I rowed parallel to the bank for a few minutes and then, my wrists tired, pulled for the island which lay some thirty yards from the far shore.

Circling the island I found an overhanging willow, tied up to it, pulled in the oars, lowered myself into the reclining passenger seat and lit the last of Gina's Nazionale. Precisely what, I wondered drowsily – now that everything was so unaccountably but so absolutely different – was I going to do with the rest of my life?

After a while, the proximity of the lake and the unanswerability of the question became too much to bear, and making a neat pile of everything except my T-shirt and knickers, I lowered myself over the side of the boat into the olive water.

The drop-off around the island was acute, and although I duck-dived down as far as I could – until the water was dark and cold around me – I could not reach the bottom. I breast-stroked slowly around the island for a few minutes and then, curious, struck out for the far bank. This was guarded for most of its length by dense thickets of elder and bramble, but as I swam closer I saw submerged stone steps, an iron mooring ring and a tiny landing area, from which a narrow footpath led obliquely into the forest. It was an arrangement of some elegance, and invisible from more than twenty yards' distance.

I sat on the grass bank for a minute or two, dripping and catching my breath, and watched as the ripples of my approach died away. I was aware of an insect drone, of the sour-sweet stink of rot and blossom. Where, I wondered, did the path lead? To the deer park? The gatehouse? I took a few paces, rounded a spiked sloe bush and stopped dead. Half-submerged in a cascade of dog rose and bramble, its arms raised in silent greeting or perhaps warning, was the stone figure of a bear. Weather and the passage of the centuries had blurred its contours, but the animal features were still clearly recognisable. At one time, I supposed, before this tidal wave of plant life had overtaken it, the statue would have formed part of the grand design of the lake; perhaps others were so concealed.

Beyond the statue of the bear the thorn bushes became a tangle of nettles and bindweed and then a dim colonnade of trees, their topmost branches converging overhead to form a threadbare canopy only thinly pierced with light. I was conscious of my apprehensive heartbeat, of the close, fungal scent of the forest, of the path growing cooler beneath my bare feet. I continued for about fifteen minutes, telling myself a little nervously that I could turn back at any time. The insect hum gave way to silence, dark branches of yew and cypress brushed my arms, and moths fluttered palely about my face. And then, cresting a small rise, I stopped for the second time.

Below me, and about fifty yards ahead, the forest's roof parted to admit a downpouring of sunlight into a small grass-floored clearing, at the exact and emerald centre of which, cross-legged, sat Phoebe Duboys. Her head was turned away from me, but there was no mistaking that feral, watchful presence.

Slowly, my feet silent on the moss, I walked down between the trees. A stream crossed the clearing, and its whisper grew increasingly audible as I descended. I saw that Phoebe was rolling a joint, and not wanting to startle her, I paused before entering her chamber of light. She looked up, however, unsurprised.

'It's my *belle sabreuse*,' she said. 'Hello, Belle.'

'Hello, Phoebe,' I said, stepping towards her. She was wearing another of her velvet-trimmed tops – green, this time – over a suede skirt and plimsolls, and looked like an extra from a very low-budget film about the Ancient Britons. Lighting the joint that she had been preparing, she handed it to me.

'No transcribing today?' she asked wryly. 'No interviews?'

I took a drag, and held the smoke down until I felt my lungs heave, felt the first prickle of anoxia. Scarlet pimpernels, I saw, studded the grass like drops of blood.

'What's to transcribe?' I asked eventually. 'Who's to interview?'

'You could interview me.'

I lowered myself to my knees beside the stream, dropped in an oak leaf, watched it whirled away over the shining pebbles. 'This is strong stuff,' I said, handing her back the joint.

She smiled. 'Yes, it is. We've got a greenhouse full of it. Well, half full, anyway; every other plant's a tomato.'

'I'm think I'm going to lie down,' I said. 'It's made me feel quite dizzy. No snakes around, are there?'

'None,' said Phoebe. 'I promise.' She sat back on her heels. 'You should take your T-shirt and pants off. I'll put them to dry on the bush.'

I hesitated, and she smiled. 'Don't worry, nobody ever comes here except me.'

'Not Oliver?' I asked. 'Or Stephen?'

'They have their own places. This is mine.'

I peeled the clothes off. Swimming in and out of my consciousness was the image of clothes spread over a bush. A painting, perhaps? A photograph? I closed my eyes, dazed by the stillness and the sudden warmth of the sun, and Phoebe put the joint to my lips.

I sipped at the cool smoke. 'OK,' I said. 'I'll interview you. Why . . . why were you all so vile to me last night?'

'We're difficult,' she said, after a time. 'I admit.'

'Is that it?' I asked. 'Just . . . "We're difficult"?'

'I'm sorry,' she said, holding the joint to my mouth. 'We behave like we do because we can. We behave like we do because we've got nothing to lose by doing and saying precisely what we please. How's that?'

'Honest enough, I suppose.' I opened my eyes and blew a thin plume of brown smoke at the sky. Without warning, Phoebe swung one leg across my chest and knelt astride me, holding down my arms. She smelt of patchouli and of her own vulpine body smell, and the lace of her pants was scratchy against my stomach.

'Alison,' she whispered, her face inches from mine, 'do the same. Do what you want to do. Say what you want to say. Stop worrying what people will think, OK?'

'All right,' I said, irritated, and half twisting, dropped the remains of the joint in the stream.

'I'll make another,' said Phoebe, climbing off me and busying herself with her tobacco tin. I looked around. My eyes were attuned to the clearing's jewelled brightness, and the forest beyond was impenetrably sombre.

'There could be a thousand eyes watching us,' I said.

'There could be,' agreed Phoebe, flipping her Zippo. 'Does that idea excite you?'

'It doesn't terrify me,' I said, taking the joint from her. 'Which is strange, me being me. Or until recently, anyway.'

She bent to examine my stomach, her thick hair trailing me. 'I've marked you with my knickers, look.'

'I'm marked already,' I said, exhaling, and she touched a finger to the grey-pink cord of scar tissue on my thigh and then, very slowly, very gently, followed her finger with her lips. Sensing my body's involuntary reaction, and that my consciousness was beginning to slip its moorings, I raised myself on to one elbow.

'Miss Duboys,' I said carefully, 'are you trying to seduce me?'

'Not particularly,' she said, plucking a scarlet pimpernel and placing it carefully in my navel. 'This is all just . . . circumstantial.'

I tried to answer, but found it impossible to speak and listen to myself at the same time, so gave up. Taking the joint from me, Phoebe flipped it into the stream, where it hissed briefly. Tiny points of light bloomed and burst before my eyes. I tried again.

'The *impresa*,' I said.

'Ah,' she said. 'The *impresa*.'

'The painting,' I said. 'Action and reflection. "Magica Sympathia". The painting and the play are the same.'

'Go on,' she urged softly, but the images and the logic were fading.

'I'm losing it,' I said.

' "Sympathetic Magic",' said Phoebe. 'Hold on to that.'

Almost absent-mindedly, she began to undo the green velvet buttons of her shirt.

Naked, there was a kind of changeling wildness about her. Crouching at my feet, she dipped her finger into a hole in the stream bank and began to anoint her upper thigh with wet clay, some of which caked in the dark tangle of her pubic hair. Moving thoughtfully upwards, she drew a shining trail from her left hip to her right breast, and I belatedly understood what she was doing.

'Draw the rest,' Phoebe said, and I ran a clay-dipped finger across her mouth, her cheek and her eyes, forging on to her sharper, darker features the familiar signature of my wounds. In the heat the pale clay dried within seconds to a ghostly, reflective silver; she looked like an Iceni warrior, cat's-eyed and demonic.

'You're me,' I said. 'My mirror image.'

'Of course I'm you,' she said. 'Who else would I be?'

We were kneeling face to face now, and raising my face to the light with both of her hands, she drew first my upper and then my lower lip into her mouth, exploring the uneven ridges of scar tissue with her teeth and the point of her tongue. The sun beat a shining blood red at my eyelids, and I tasted the clay on her mouth.

She released my face, and I felt her fingers take easy possession between my legs. 'You're hurting me,' I heard myself say – although she wasn't, especially – and twisted to the ground, so that she had to follow me or withdraw her hand.

'No one's hurting you, Belle,' she murmured, arranging herself beside me. 'No one's here; only you.'

I moved hard against her hand, covered it with my own, felt her stiffened fingers' fluent suck and slide. She brought me off fast, holding her fingers inside me until my gasps had subsided, and then, after a last interrogative flutter to confirm that I was done, slid them out from beneath my covering hand. Disgorged of her a heartbeat too soon, I turned my cheek to the grass, saw through half-closed eyes the casual wipe of her hand against her thigh as she slouched to her scattered clothes.

When I awoke, ravenously hungry and with sunburn prickling at my shoulders, she was gone. Beyond the clearing the path continued into the forest, and that, I felt sure, was the route she had taken. My T-shirt and pants were dry, and pulling them on I padded back through the dim woodland towards the lake. The journey, taken fast this time, took less than ten minutes, and I raised a hand in wry salutation to the bear as I passed. From the landing area, the house was just visible through the trees on the lake's far shore, and beside it, beneath the cedar, tiny uniformed figures were shaking out the tablecloths for tea.

I slipped into the water – why had I bothered to dry my clothes? – and swam slowly towards the boat, which lay motionless beside the island. I did not attempt to analyse the afternoon's events; they begged an infinity of questions, and for once it seemed preferable to submit to the narrative – to allow it to reveal itself in its own time – rather than to try and make it coherent.

In the boat I wrung out my T-shirt, pulled on my trousers, aligned the prow with the copper beech tree, and cast off. Drifting through the outer fringe of branches a few minutes later, I discovered Nancy Waller and Fletcher Walsh deep in conversation on the bank. Both were holding satellite phones.

'Hi!' I said brightly, and for a moment they stared at me.

Nancy was the first to recover herself. 'Well, hi, Alison. How's it going?'

'Just fine,' I said, poling myself to the bank with an oar. 'Just fine. Isn't this weather the purest bliss?'

She smiled tightly. 'The purest,' she agreed. She was fully and flawlessly made up, her clothes were impeccable, her hair had that honeyed, moneyed Park Avenue sheen. She didn't look like a woman who wanted to be thrown a wet mooring rope, and something told me that she didn't want to be asked questions about Dale Cooney, either.

'Any news of Dale?' I asked, swinging her the rope.

'Yes,' said Fletcher, catching it adroitly and drawing the boat alongside the tree roots. 'She's on her way.'

I threw my shoes ashore, climbed out and made fast to a root.

'You're looking very . . . outdoorsy,' said Nancy, taking in my sun-flushed face and damp, dirty T-shirt. 'And a little happier than yesterday, perhaps, am I right?'

'I'm looking forward to being in the film,' I said, stepping into my shoes. 'That should be a laugh.'

'It will be,' said Fletcher, fervently. 'And more than a laugh. A lot will be written about this campaign in years to come.'

'Do you both love it?' I asked. 'The beauty business, I mean?'

They looked at each other as if to say: who's going to deliver the line, you or me?

'Beauty is life,' said Nancy. 'It's that simple.'

'That's five cucumber sandwiches,' said Oliver Duboys. 'I've been watching you.'

'I'm hungry,' I said. 'I didn't have any lunch.'

'Working?'

'Walking,' I said. 'Exploring parts new.'

At the end of the table Phoebe flicked Silk Cut ash into her saucer and ignored me, as she had done since I sat down. Oliver, on the other hand, although as pallid and tautly drawn as ever, was being solicitous and amusing, and was far more animated than he had been at dinner the night before. Between them, John-Paul was sewing tiny jet beads to a gold and velvet biliment and a man with a viewfinder hanging around his neck on a cord was making notes in fine-nibbed Pentel on a shooting script. Sheldrake, I gathered, was still in London. There was no sign of Fiona or Gina.

Given Oliver's changeable moods, it seemed a good moment to follow up on his suggestion of the day before.

'You said you had a puzzle,' I said. 'A painting you had just bought.'

'So I did,' he said. 'Would you care to see it?'

'Very much.'

'I've started working on it today,' he said. 'It's all set up. If I tell you how to get there, will you come up in five minutes?'

Oliver's studio, it turned out, was in the east wing, opposite and a floor above the Oak Chamber and the portrait of Eleanor Duboys. The room's original character was hard to divine, however, as some heavy, buff-coloured material – raw linen, perhaps – had been hung from batons over the walls, and synthetic brown flooring strips had been laid over the broad elm boards. A small refrigerator pulsed in one corner, a dozen or so unframed canvases rested against the walls, and there was a faint smell, not unpleasant, of solvents and varnishes. At the centre of the room, in front of the window bay, stood a tall wooden easel.

'Sit down,' said Oliver, indicating a dust-sheeted armchair at the far end of the room, 'and I'll tell you a story.'

I sat, and he paced, narrow-shouldered and austere. Despite the lingering heat of the day, he wore the sleeves of his white cotton shirt double-buttoned at the cuff.

'You asked what I do; well, one of the things that I do apart from restoring is buying and selling paintings. Mostly on behalf of the family, but occasionally for friends, collectors abroad and so on. I specialise in early English masters – Peake, the Olivers, Gower, Johnson, Larkin, the usual suspects – but a lot of less important stuff comes and goes too: school of, circle of, et cetera.'

'Now,' he went on, inclining his head so that his eyes vanished into their shadowed sockets, 'have you by any chance heard of a novelist and playwright called Guy LeQuesne?'

'Yes. Wrote *Smoothing the Ice* and *The Garden of Reconciliation*. Phoebe was asking me yesterday if I knew his daughter, Jacinta.'

'That's right. She's a journalist of sorts, and recently wrote a rather vicious and gratuitous piece about some friends of ours. Anyway, the story goes that until very recently Guy LeQuesne – that's the father – had set his heart on becoming a member of the Garrick Club, and had found people to propose him, second him and generally shoehorn him in. Now, I haven't read his books, but apparently, despite fairly heavy sales, they're, um . . .?'

'Very, very bad indeed?' I suggested happily.

'Getting on that way,' he agreed gravely. 'Which wouldn't matter a bit, needless to say, if he was a genial sort of a bloke, but by all accounts he's a thumping snob, totally humourless, and if not quite a statutory rapist, then certainly a man whose interest in the school-leaving generation has been known to exceed the avuncular, if you get my drift.'

'So not very . . . What is it they say? Not very *clubbable*?'

'To put it mildly. Anyway, a couple of months ago his number came up for election and a cabal of insiders – led, so word has it, by a journalistic colleague of yours – saw to it that he was blackballed. There was the usual teacup storm: a couple of letters to the *Spectator*, a snigger or two on the books pages, a ripple of amusement at Radio Four. You probably . . .?'

'I was in hospital at the time. I'm afraid it rather passed me by.'

'Of course, yes, as it would have done.' He ran a hand through the long red-gold hair and darted a pensive glance at me. 'Flashback, then, to a newspaper party last Christmas, where Guy LeQuesne is simultaneously schmoozing the books people and trying to scare up a job for the daughter. He falls into conversation with some pearly, impressionable-looking girl and tells her – amongst other self-regarding guff – that he's just bought a marvellous, rather mysterious old painting named *Perdita*, apparently of an actress playing that particular role in *A Winter's Tale*. He's just about to become a member of the Garrick, he goes on, and when his membership goes through he intends to donate the painting to the club; to bring it with him as a sort of dowry. He doesn't – in the way that those kind of people don't – bother to ask the girl what she does. Which is a big mistake. The pearly girl isn't quite the Fulham airhead he thought her; in fact, she works on the paper's diary page and notes down the conversation, just in case it should come in useful. Which it does, of course, as soon as the Garrick blackball story breaks. The moment she sees it, the pearly girl gets on to her spies at the auction houses, and sure enough, *Perdita* is handed over a saleroom counter within the week.'

'The painting's no use to him any more?'

Oliver shook his head.

'So where did he get hold of it in the first place, and why?'

'He bought it from an antique shop in Burford, in Oxfordshire: one of those places that sells overpriced heritage tat to tourists. It wasn't a very good painting, and it was unsigned and undated and completely without provenance, but it was old and it appeared to have this rather odd Shakespearian connection. I suppose LeQuesne thought it an interesting theatrical piece and the sort of thing that a well-connected playwright ought to have at his disposal. Once the Garrick had given him the cold shoulder, needless to say, he couldn't get shot of the painting fast enough. It must have mocked him and his social aspirations every time he saw it.

'Anyway, "Londoner's Diary" ran a bitchy little piece that

night about LeQuesne dumping *Perdita* in the wake of the blackballing, and dropped in a picture of her. I was in town, saw the piece and the picture, rang LeQuesne the next morning and offered him his reserve price plus ten per cent. He agreed, and sounded only too happy to withdraw from the sale; he obviously didn't want to give the media a third bite at the cherry.'

'But hang on a minute, how did you find out the reserve? And his number, come to that?'

He shrugged. 'Like everyone else, I have my people.'

'So what made you buy it?'

Standing, he walked over to the wall, and lifted a small oil-painted panel that was resting there. Carefully, he carried the painting to the easel, fixed it in place, stepped back and beckoned me over.

'Come and have a look.'

The panel, measuring perhaps twelve by eighteen inches, was a miniature version of Robert Peake's portrait of Eleanor Duboys. In the bottom right-hand corner of the panel the word 'PERDITA' was inscribed in tiny gold-leaf capitals. In comparison to that of the Peake, however, the workmanship of the panel was crude. The figure, although competently enough modelled, had a lifeless quality about it, and the face was a stereotypical mask.

'OK,' said Oliver. 'Just off the top of your head, what do think this painting is? What do you think its function was?'

'Well, without knowing anything about painting, I suppose that if some actor-manager, say, was decorating his house with paintings of the great Shakespearian roles, and commissioned some jobbing painter to knock them up for him, and the painter had access to the Peake portrait . . .'

Oliver watched me steadily.

'No,' I admitted. 'I guess that theory doesn't really hold water. The point of all those Garrick-type theatrical paintings is that they celebrate performers rather than roles. Sarah Siddons as Boadicea, or whatever. And they're all much, much more recent than this could possibly be. How old is *Perdita*?

'Old,' said Oliver. 'Seventeenth century, at least.'

'OK, forget the green-room portrait idea, but given the name, it's hard to believe it's not connected to *A Winter's Tale* in some way. As some sort of an advertisement, perhaps? But if so, why not name the '

'It's a puzzle, isn't it?' smiled Oliver.

'What do you know about it?' I asked, staring at the painting as if to unlock its secrets through sheer concentration.

'I know that at some stage this painting has been fairly extensively mucked around with.'

'How can you tell?'

'Several things. I thought I'd have some fun with it, clean it up a bit. It's got a very dark old varnish on it which its previous owners left on, probably because it hides a lot of the weaknesses of the painting, and when I . . .'

'Before you go any further,' I interrupted him, 'how much is this thing actually worth?'

Oliver raked his hands through his long hair. 'In saleroom terms, not much. The Burford gallery probably took a couple of grand off LeQuesne – maybe even three – but the London hammer price would be less.'

'Despite its age?'

'Old doesn't necessarily mean good. Pieces like this wash backwards and forwards all the time: bought, re-framed, re-attributed, flogged on for a small margin. Those fake-posh country house hotels are full of them.'

'So you've cleaned it, you were saying?'

'No, just a fraction of it.' He pointed to a small matt area in one corner. 'It's a very slow business and I had a lot of other work to get through first. When I did get round to it, though, I discovered something rather unexpected. Look at this.'

From a table next to the easel he lifted a spill, like a long matchstick, wound around with cotton wool so as to form a swab. One edge was flattened and brownish.

'When you talk about cleaning a painting,' Oliver began, 'you're mostly talking about removing old varnish which has got discoloured. To dissolve the varnish we use alcohol suspended in a decelerant. It's a highly controlled process; go one molecular level too deep and you're lifting off the artist's original paint or, equally damagingly, his glazes. With practice, though, you can feel the difference. Varnish, and especially recent varnish – last hundred years – seems to slip off, but paint sort of . . . drags. Now you'd think that the older the painting, the more vulnerable the paint surface, but it doesn't quite work like that. The Elizabethans, for example, were masters of the chemistry of painting. They used pigments like tin-lead and lapis lazuli and cinnabar, and layered them in such a sophisticated way – binding them in complex glazes and so on – that for the most part they've set to this jewel-like hardness. The result is that they're actually much easier to clean than a lot of more recent work. Providing you're using a gentle enough solvent, you can just lick the varnish off the top and leave the glazes and pigments intact. But check this out.'

Taking the swab, he dropped two or three drops of clear liquid on to it with a pipette. 'Here,' he said, handing it to me. 'Hang on to this.'

I held the swab gingerly as he lifted the painting from the easel and placed it face up on the table in front of the window bay. 'Right,' he said. 'Go to work.'

'Me?'

'You. Draw it gently across this bit here. That's it, don't be nervous, that's surgical-grade cotton wool, you won't . . . And again, that's good.'

He lifted my hand. The working surface of the swab was a dark, opaque, brownish colour. 'That's varnish,' Oliver explained. 'Probably coach varnish. In the eighteenth century, when the man came round to waterproof the coaches for the winter, you'd bring the paintings out into the drive so that he could slap some varnish over those too. Now go over that bit again.'

I did so, and felt the surface draw at the cotton wool. Worried, I examined the swab.

'That's pigment,' said Oliver. 'Paint. Ivory black, at a guess.'

Horrified, I stepped back.

'Don't worry,' he said cheerfully, turning the swab a half-revolution between my fingers. 'It's not contemporary with the painting; it's far too soluble. Scrub on.'

Carefully, I continued, until the swab was lifting no more black pigment from my square centimetre of panel.

'Bedrock,' said Oliver. 'You're down to the reign of Good Queen Bess. Let's just arrest the process there. May I?'

I moved out of the way and he bent over the panel. 'So what exactly was the paint I was taking off?' I asked.

'A cover-up,' said Oliver, straightening. 'At some point between the painting of this panel *circa* 1600 and its revarnishing a couple of hundred years later, some thoughtful soul blacked out the background.'

'It looks as if it was black anyway,' I said.

'You're right, but probably with an inscription or a coat of arms painted on to it.'

'And why would anyone want to paint those out?'

'Your guess,' said Oliver, lifting the painting and angling it to the light, 'is as good as mine. My professional instinct, though, says that the Perdita inscription is original. I'd also guess that there was originally more to it.'

'What might be missing?'

'How are your Latin verbs?'

'Mostly forgotten, I'm afraid.'

'*Perdo, perdere, perdidi, perditum*?' he hazarded. 'Third declension regular?'

'To lose,' I said. 'I can remember that much. Hence Perdita, the lost one, abandoned on the shores of Bohemia.'

'In the play of *A Winter's Tale*?'

'Well, not in the David Essex song.'

'So you think Perdita's a name,' he mused, 'and not a past participle?'

'Now I'm lost,' I said.

'You and me both,' said Oliver, his gaze suddenly absent. 'I'm sorry,' he said, cranking his forearm as if to work his bicep. 'I've been wasting your time.'

'Not at all,' I said, trying to make sense of the hanging threads of the conversation. 'It's been fascinating. Will you tell me what you find on the panel?'

'It'll probably be nothing,' he said, glancing around him, his concentration visibly ebbing. 'Shall we see you at dinner?'

'I think I'll probably be eating with the film people tonight.'

He nodded, not listening, and raised a pale hand. 'Whenever, then.'

I lay in Dale Cooney's bath for an hour, with the stone-framed windows thrown wide and the scent of the gardens below and the cool water lapping around my chin. The events of the morning already seemed hazy and distant, their exact sequence hard to recall. What on earth had possessed me, apart from Phoebe's drugs and her not very clean hands? Had it been the place itself, green and secret in the resinous pine-needled silence? Had it been that downpouring of sunshine in which, like a wasp in syrup, I had found myself fatally, luxuriously suspended? In retrospect, it all seemed to have curiously little to do with Phoebe, who was a little less present each time I revisited the memory. 'No one's here,' she had said, 'only you.' But she had been there, of course, and I only had to close my eyes to smell her, to feel her fingers' probing.

Sliding underwater, I ran my hands through my inch-long buzz of hair. The tracks and welts on my scalp seemed to have subsided a little, and I could no longer feel their insistent pulsing. Time and sunlight were also beginning to smooth the scars at my lips, my cheeks and my eyebrows. Scar tissue doesn't tan, Tara had told me before I left hospital, so avoid too much sun. I had always done that anyway, I had told her, because I'd always been fair: a winter baby, a child of storm, a daughter of the monsoon.

Right now, though, the cool bathwater and the summery flush at my face and shoulders and the open-ended nature of the story were combining to produce a hesitant new optimism in me. I would accept my new facial couture, I told myself; I would assume absolutely the character determined for me by the random passage through my flesh of exploding windscreen glass and splintering fascia and sheared chromium trim. Except that it was somehow impossible to believe that the result was random, that it was not intended; because mine was designer damage, of that there was no doubt. It had the asymmetry, it had the line, it had that authentic death-crash chic. The challenge was going to be living up to it.

I dressed for dinner in a black Bilquis Kwai slipdress and a garnet choker that had been my mother's, and as I walked across the lawn to the long, linen-covered tables it seemed to me for the first time that I was not entirely separate from these beautiful, slightly terrifying people, that to any new arrival I would appear to be one of them. It was the time that film-makers call the magic hour. The hazing glare of the day had given way to a saturated luminescence, and stillness ruled; below us the lake was molten gold.

As I approached the group around the tables I sensed that everyone had been touched with the same inchoate sense of occasion. It was as if we had dressed up for no better reason than to celebrate the day's passing. Nancy was holding glittering court with John-Paul and the models, and it occurred to me that this was probably the last evening before the arrival of Dale Cooney. Cooney's presence, of course, would change everything. Her newness to England, the millions she was being paid, her celebrity-in-waiting status, her supposed beauty; all of these factors would in their various ways relegate the other players to the shadows. Gina and Fiona certainly knew that, and perhaps that was why they had chosen tonight to dress their hair with rosebuds and sapphires, to wear midnight-blue Valentino and silver Givenchy, to shine.

Beyond them, back from London, Charles Sheldrake was making a series of forceful points to Fletcher Walsh. I couldn't hear what they were talking about, but Sheldrake appeared more animated and fired by purpose than I had ever seen him.

No member of the Duboys family was present – a fact which may well have contributed to the evening's easy, excitable mood – but Stephen Faulds was there, and made it his business to attend to me, steering me towards the champagne table on my arrival and ensuring that I sat next to him at dinner. For all the impeccability of his attentions, however, I found him strangely unreadable. His courtesy and formal good manners exceeded by some degree the usual officers' mess veneer, and sprung, it seemed, from some private absolutist code. I was reluctantly forced to admit to myself that he would probably have offered the same consideration to any woman in my situation.

'So why landscape gardening?' I asked him, as our plates were set before us.

'It's to do with the imposition of order,' he said, frowning at his plate. 'It's an opportunity to subject nature to the tyranny of an aesthetic ideal. Will that do?'

'As a job description, or an answer?'

'Both, I hope.'

'It's not easy to see you as a bedding plants man.'

'I'm not a bedding plants man, but then neither were the Elizabethans, particularly. They didn't have a twentieth of the floral varieties you can get now; just violets and cowslips and kingcups, that sort of thing, semi-wild stuff. But then the Elizabethan garden wasn't so much a series of flowerbeds as an extension of the house, built rather than planted. All those avenues and *allées* and knots and walks, they're like secret rooms joined by secret corridors. And all that mysterious emblematic statuary . . .' He smiled, and looked down at his hands. 'If it seems strange to you that I wish to spend my life tending such . . . such fine and private places, perhaps I should remind you that I'm half Arab, and for Arabs, Paradise itself is a garden.'

'Staffed by houris,' I couldn't resist adding. 'With eyes like gazelles.'

'Quite so,' he agreed, his gaze rising to meet mine. 'With eyes like gazelles.' He drained his glass. 'And now may I ask in my turn . . . why fashion?'

'Oh, that's easy,' I said. 'It's my opportunity to subject my bank account to the tyranny of an ever-changing aesthetic ideal.'

He smiled. 'I can understand why you buy it, but what made you take up writing about it?'

I thought for a moment. 'When I was seven,' I said, 'my family moved here from Singapore and I was sent to a convent school in Surrey. Part of the uniform was a blue cardigan, and after a time I noticed that there were two kinds that people wore. The first kind – the regulation one – was a bright, primary-coloured acrylic-mix thing from John Lewis. There were a handful of girls, though, who didn't wear the regulation ones, because they had the second kind, which I suppose must have been lambswool. These were subtly different: they were slightly duller-textured, a slightly greyer blue, and they could be pulled up the forearms in a grown-up, vogueish sort of way, and you could leave the buttons undone and they'd hang just so, and you'd look like someone in a French film.

'Well, I never got one of the second sort. I wanted one more than anything else in the world, but I was lucky to be at the school in the first place and my parents certainly weren't about to suggest by word or action that the uniform wasn't quite up to the mark, so I had to lump it. There were certain things, though, that I never understood. The lambswool cardigans were all the same colour and pattern, so did a select handful of parents get a special clothes list, or did the smarter mothers simply agree amongst themselves that acrylic was beyond the pale and make their own arrangements at Harrods or wherever? I never found out. What I did discover, though, was the way that certain brands and products were employed . . . emblematically.'

'It seems that we both have a taste for codes,' said Faulds quietly.

'It seems we have,' I said. 'Tell me about the statuary.'

'Well, there's the pelican. Have you seen that?'

'If it's the one I'm thinking of, almost hidden in a hedge . . . or is that a swan?'

'It's a pelican, and because legend used to have it that pelicans fed their young on their own blood, the bird became an analogy for the Virgin Queen, whose sacrifices on her subjects' behalf – so it was said – knew no limits. William Duboys would have made sure that the Queen was promenaded past the statue, and its presence would have been duly noted. In one of the nearby *allées* there's a statue of a phoenix, too, but no one's quite sure if this refers to the Queen and her Madonna-like talent for reinventing herself, or to William Duboys' sympathy for the Catholic cause, which to survive was going to have to rise from the ashes to which the Queen and her father had reduced it.'

'Sounds as if he liked to sail quite close to the wind, then, your girlfriend's forebear.'

He pursed his lips at that, but let it go. 'I guess so,' he said.

'And talking of bears,' I went on, 'what about the stone bear by the lake? What does that signify?'

'I really don't know,' said Faulds. 'The fact is that we've lost the key to all but the most obvious of these emblems.'

'The bear,' Charles Sheldrake pronounced loudly and a little unsteadily from the end of the table, 'is the agent of Female Nature. Didn't Tom Warwick teach you that?'

'I'm sure he tried,' I said.

'Isn't it possible that a bear is sometimes . . . just a bear,' suggested Faulds, mildly.

'Don't be absurd, Stephen,' said Sheldrake belligerently. 'When was a bear ever just a bear?'

I left them to it, and switched my attention to Fiona and Gina's account of their visit to Stratford-upon-Avon. They'd been invited backstage at the theatre, apparently, and been made a great fuss of, and then eaten too many scones at tea.

'People think it's a really glamorous life looking good all the time,' Fiona was protesting, 'but it's not. It's really hard work.'

'Sing it for us, sister,' said Gina.

The shadows had lengthened and faded by the time I carried my coffee down to one of the stone benches overlooking the lake and rang Orde.

'What are you doing with this Faulds character?' he immediately demanded.

'Nothing,' I said, lighting a 555. 'He's just working here. Why, what have you got?'

'Well, not much really. Born '65, commissioned Royal Engineers '85, usual tours of duty, left with rank of Major in '92. Run of the mill stuff. I've had to report your enquiry, though, because his file's flagged.'

'So what does that mean?'

'Probably that he's stayed in the game in some capacity; as a contract officer or a consultant or something.'

'So my speaking to you will get back to him?'

'Might, might not.'

'Thanks a lot.'

'No choice, kid. See you soon.'

'Hang on. One more thing, does the name of the late Bill Duboys mean anything to you?'

'Sure. He owned D-Tech. That's a matter of public record.'

'And what does D-Tech do?'

'What *did* they do? Security consultancy, basically. They were one of the bigger UK players.'

'So Duboys might have employed Faulds at some point?'

'It's perfectly possible; why don't you just ask him, for heaven's sake? It's all very touchy-feely these days.'

'Thanks, Orde.'

'For nothing.'

'No, you've helped. And my love to Miss Double Barrels.'

'Over and Under actually. Much more fun. She'd love you to fix up that magazine profile, by the way. And while I've got you on the line, could you try – please – and visit the parents. I was there last weekend and Mum was being very doomy, saying it wasn't worth investing in a new fridge-freezer at this stage in their lives and one more stair carpet should see them both out. They need cheering up a bit.'

'You think a few hours' interface with their crazed spinster daughter would do the trick.'

'They were worried about you, Ali. I've never seen Dad as upset as the day we first saw you in hospital. Go down and see them, OK?'

'I will,' I said.

'Promise?'

'Promise.'

'Is everything OK?' asked Gina, sitting down beside me as I slapped down the aerial.

'Family,' I said.

'Ah,' said Gina. 'Family.'

'Do you think she'll come tomorrow?' I asked, and Gina scented the still, twilit air and smiled.

'Why are you doing this assignment?' I asked. 'I mean, you're a big name, Tagliaferri. You don't need to play second fiddle to anyone.'

'I'm twenty-eight, Alison,' she said gently. 'I'm lucky to be here, making this kind of crazy money. And I'm glad to be here, too: I'm glad I met you. I have the feeling this is going to be a shoot we're all going to remember.'

'In a good way or a bad way?'

'That I can't say yet. But look around. Look at this place. You don't feel there's the sense of something . . . waiting to happen?'

'It's happening already, as far as I'm concerned. I could stay here forever.'

I looked around me, at the formally dressed men and women disposed like chesspieces about the lawn, and realised that my last statement was no more than the truth. For all the strangeness there was an order here, and an aesthetic, to which I found myself almost viscerally responsive.

It was almost as if, in some way, I belonged here.

10

I woke early: the alarm clock showed ten past five. I would have turned over and tried to go back to sleep, but some impulse – some dream-related curiosity, perhaps – drew me from the narrow iron bed to the window. The dawn was a misted, vaporous grey, the horizon no more than a faint wash against the half-lit sky, the silence absolute. While the household slept, I decided, I would claim the domain as my own.

I dressed quickly, pulling on a sweater against the cold and stuffing the Acu-Sonic into my trouser pocket in case of inspiration, and crept to the stone staircase, squeaky-soled baseball boots in my hand. Washing would have to wait.

The front door was locked, but the bolts slid back without protest and the heavy key turned quietly in my hand. The air was damp but sharp, mutedly resonant, dense with the day ahead. Lacing up my Converse boots, I descended the fan of steps to the terrace, where a heavy dew overlaid the parterre and the knot garden. It was as if a watery veil had been drawn over everything: the lawns, the gravel, the dark geometries of yew.

Silently, I paced the corridors of topiary, my footsteps dark behind me. I discovered corners I had not yet visited, and further emblems in stone: a coroneted hound, a gauntlet holding a lady's glove, a porcupine. Returning to the gravelled central *allée*, my canvas boots drenched, I turned back to look at the house. It had a sealed, forbidden air, its stones cold, its glass as dark as lakewater.

The central path to the deer park was more direct than the lateral approach through the gardens, but the ascent was steeper, which was perhaps why Nancy had avoided it on the day of my arrival. Balustraded stone stairs led all the way down to the river, and at any point on the journey one could turn, if so disposed, and seek reassurance of the supremacy of the human will over brute nature from the sight of the house's classically ordered porch. At the bottom of the steps, thus reassured, I lit a 555, savouring the faint dizziness as the first smoke hit my lungs. Wood pigeons called; below me, in the river, the long green tresses rolled in the current.

Slowly, wet to the knees now, cigarette in hand, I ambled through the long grass towards the lowest part of the valley. This was marked by a giant oak, beneath which I could just make out the silver-brown shadows of fallow deer. Perhaps, I thought, if I was quiet, and didn't rush, they would allow me to approach them. I had covered perhaps half of the distance when the deer rose as one and scattered.

I thought at first that I had frightened them myself, and then a tiny insect pulse began to beat the air and the toy-like form of a bubble-nosed helicopter appeared in the vagueness above the treeline. As I watched, the helicopter grew larger and larger until it was all that I could see and hear and the grass was flattening crazily in the rotor wash and the sparks were flying from my cigarette.

The helicopter touched down twenty yards away, the near-side door opened, and a slight, fair-haired figure jumped to the ground. For a moment the girl was inseparable from the disturbance of her arrival, inseparable from the urgent swish and pulse of the rotor blades, and then, as the helicopter rose into the air behind her, hovered for a moment and swung back towards the treeline, she seemed to have nothing to do with it at all, and was just there.

A dazed near-silence followed, during which the girl looked around her and I listened to the slow prickle of the grass. She was wearing jeans, baseball boots like mine and a T-shirt reading 'MY MUM AND DAD WENT TO SEATTLE AND ALL I GOT WAS THIS LOUSY T-SHIRT!'.

'You're Dale,' I said, eventually.

'Yes, I am.' She was squinting up at the house, framing some imaginary composition with her fingers. She didn't seem to have any kind of bag. 'Who are you?'

'I'm Alison,' I said.

'Alison.' She tried out the name as if she had never heard it before. Her voice was so soft I had to strain to hear it. 'You from Forth, Alison?'

'I'm a journalist. Writing a piece about the campaign.'

'That's nice,' she said, turning to look at me.

'I woke up early,' I explained. 'I was walking.'

She pushed the dark-blonde hair away from her face. 'I was kind of surprised to see you,' she admitted. 'You think anyone else knows I'm here?'

I shrugged. 'There's a security team. I'd guess they might just have noticed a helicopter arriving.'

'I was hoping for a quiet hour or two before I have to see people,' she said. 'Is there any place you can take me?'

'Yes,' I said. 'If we're fast there is. Head for that bridge.'

Her fast was a lot faster than my fast. By the time we reached the bridge, squelching in our grass-seeded boots, I was exhausted.

'Sorry,' I gasped. 'I've been in hospital. I'm out of shape.'

'Why were you in hospital?' she asked, immediately interested.

'Car crash,' I said. 'Messed up my back. Come on, this way.'

We crossed the bridge and I led her as speedily as I could manage along the riverbank to the lake. When we were well concealed beneath the copper beech tree, I looked up. Two men were half running, half walking round the outside of the house: one of them, I saw, was Tony, who had carried my suitcase on the day I arrived.

'Climb in,' I said, indicating the boat. I shoved off hard, forgetting to warn her to duck, and a branch clouted her on the back of the neck.

'Sorry,' I said. 'Drowning you isn't part of the service.'

'Oh no?' she smiled. She trailed her fingers through the dark lake water. 'This is beautiful, though. You don't think anyone'll come?'

'They can't get to you even if they do come,' I said, allowing the boat to drift. 'I'm taking you to the island.'

She nodded. 'Great. Thank you.'

By the time I had tied up, pulling the boat well out of sight beneath the trees, my back was screaming in protest. It was with some relief that I helped Dale from the boat and subsided against a tree trunk.

'I'm dead,' I said.

'And I'm grateful,' said Dale, folding her arms. She scratched at her elbow and seemed to consider for a moment. 'Are you going to want to . . . interview me?' she asked.

'I wouldn't mind,' I said. 'At some point.'

'Could we just, like, meet up and talk?' she asked. 'Kind of as friends. Could we do it like that?'

'Of course.' I shrugged. 'Whatever.'

She nodded slowly. 'Swear to me one thing, though.'

'Which is?'

'You'll never record my voice or do any of that shorthand, stenographer stuff.'

'OK,' I said, conscious of the recorder in my pocket.

'And no notebooks, OK?'

'I wouldn't want to misquote you,' I said.

'Look, we'll talk, we'll hang out, we'll do what we do. Afterwards, well . . . you just write what you like.'

'Can I just ask you one question now?'

'Uh-huh.'

'Why that T-shirt?'

'Oh, this.' She smiled. 'It was a gift from my sister DuToine. When she gave it to me she'd crossed out all the words except "MY DAD WENT TO SEATTLE" with a marker pen. First wash, though, the marker came out.'

'I'm sorry.'

'That it washed out?'

'About your father. How old were you when he went?'

'Oh . . . it was a long time ago.' She looked around her and then back at me. 'Thanks again.'

It was a dismissal. I hauled myself to my feet.

'Am I leaving you here, then?'

'Can you give me an hour? Come back for me at, say, quarter after seven?'

'Sure. Mind if I have a cigarette before I go? Steady my rowing arm.'

'No problem.' She smiled, closing her eyes and allowing her

head to incline against the tree trunk. The morning vapour was beginning to lift from the lake.

I lit up. Outside the house, four or five hundred yards away, the caterers were laying the tables for breakfast; otherwise there was no sign of activity. That the unremarkable-looking girl opposite me was at that particular moment the highest-paid model in the world – even if only through an accident of facial similarity – seemed beyond all belief. That I was about to maroon her in the middle of a Warwickshire lake and deny all knowledge of her presence seemed, in contrast, almost plausible. Twenty minutes later, a cup of coffee at my elbow, I was lying in her bath.

'So what's she like?' whispered Gina, waving an early wasp away from the marmalade.

'Smaller than she looks in the film, thin, blue eyes, sort of heart-shaped face . . .' I strained to remember. 'Quite easily forgettable. And as far as I can make out – and in the nicest possible way – completely off her trolley.'

'And you just left her there?'

'What else could I do?'

A shadow fell over the white linen tablecloth. It was Sheldrake, in a sort of Via Condotti village cricketer outfit.

'What are you two sirens plotting?' he demanded, rubbing his hands together. 'Ah, Cooper's Oxford, they remembered, *bueno*. Gina, love, when you're ready, could you see Carlton about hair and make-up, I want everyone on full stand-by for eight o'clock.'

'Are we shooting today?' asked Gina, raising an eyebrow at me.

'All things being equal,' said Sheldrake, throwing his deconstructed jacket over the back of a wrought-iron garden chair.

'I'll tell Figgy,' said Gina.

'She knows,' said Sheldrake, taking a bleeping phone from his pocket. 'Yes, Fletcher . . . Yes, I heard . . . No, she'll be here somewhere, it's just her way of . . . Yeah, sure, in her own time.'

He folded the phone away. 'We have our errant star,' he said. 'A helicopter touched down an hour ago. The crew'll be here any minute.'

As if in confirmation of his words, a distant hammering started on the other side of the house, the sound reaching us as a series of damped ricochets on the still air. Gina and I said nothing. I was relieved that my silence was not going to be responsible for half a million pounds' worth of delays. Sheldrake watched us.

'This picture – I promise you, ladies – is going to be an event. We are going to enjoy ourselves; we are going to gorge ourselves on beauty.'

Sensing that a mission statement was about to be born, I took the Acu-Sonic recorder from my pocket, laid it on the table and flicked it on.

'I mean, what a fantastic challenge,' continued Sheldrake, his voice assuming broadcasterly orotundity as he addressed the little tape recorder. 'To make a fully rounded feature film, complete with plot, character development and so on, lasting only forty-five seconds . . . It's like being asked to paint one of those jewel-like Elizabethan miniatures.' He looked up. 'Do you know the work of Nicholas Hilliard, Alison?'

I nodded.

'What would you say was the defining characteristic of his work?'

'Smallness?' I ventured.

Sheldrake regarded me expressionlessly, and I suddenly knew exactly what sort of teacher he had been.

'Englishness,' he said. 'Late-sixteenth-century Englishness. No other time or place could have produced Nicholas Hilliard, any more than any other time or place could have produced Shakespeare or Spenser or Peake or Smythson. There's a wonderful shining grace about the art and the artifice of those Elizabethans. Look at this . . .' – he swept his hand proprietorially upwards – 'at this exquisite sugared conceit of a house. Look at Hilliard's palette, look at all those vermilions and emeralds and bright cerulean blues. Look at Peake's portrait of Eleanor Duboys, for heaven's sake. Because that's what I want, I want that brightness. I want to catch it before it falls from the air.'

He was silent, and turned his attention a little self-consciously to his breakfast. Although certainly rehearsed, it had been a not unimpressive performance.

'You're sure she won't mind my coming?' asked Gina, as we

walked down towards the lake.

'Wouldn't have thought so. All things being equal, as Charles Sheldrake might say.'

We were overtaken by a miniature tractor drawing a trailerful of camera track to the lakeside.

'Have you ever thought what a meaningless phrase that is?' mused Gina. 'As if all things could ever be equal.'

'Perhaps he subscribes to the view that the material world is all illusion,' I said. 'And that all things are thus equal in their insubstantiality.'

'If that's the case,' said Gina, 'it probably wouldn't make much difference to my health if I were to smoke one of those illusory 555s of yours.'

'Quite possibly not,' I said, handing one over. 'But shouldn't you be exfoliating, or putting on your foundation, or whatever it is you supermodels do for a living?'

'Oh, you know how difficult we are. We're always late. Light me, please.'

By the time I had got Gina into the boat there were half a dozen technicians unloading gear on the bank. The somnolent atmosphere of the last few days had evaporated with the dew on the grass. Even Gina seemed to be assuming some sort of professional persona. 'Could you row, possibly?' I asked her.

'Hands, darling,' she said, regretfully extending her long, cigarette-bearing fingers. 'No can do.'

'Watch that branch,' I said, just a moment too late.

On the island Dale was meditating, or at least doing something which involved sitting cross-legged with her eyes shut. As I shipped the oars and lowered my blistered hands into the water, she opened her eyes.

'Alison,' she said. 'Hi. And I recognise you – you're Tagliaferri, aren't you?

'That's right,' said Gina, a note of surprise in her voice.

'I had a beauty salon at home and we used to follow all the models. I had your picture on the salon wall. You were wearing this fitted black jacket, and these *deep black pearls* . . .'

'My first *Vogue* cover,' said Gina. 'Jacket by Richard Tyler, pearls by Jenny Matsui, foundation by, as it happens, Laurene

Forth. That was a while back.'

'So were my salon days,' said Dale, almost wistfully. The pistol-shot hammering suddenly stopped, and the sound of ribald laughter drifted across the lake.

'They know you're here,' I said, and Dale smiled, and I suddenly and absolutely saw the point of her.

'Yeah,' she said. 'OK. Let's do it.'

Dale rowed. As we stepped from the boat a crewcut woman from the technical team murmured into a headset, and a minute or two later, as we ascended the sloping lawn towards the house, I saw that a delegation was moving down to meet us.

In appearance they were not a homogenous group. Nancy Waller was draped in her usual silks and cashmeres, but next to John-Paul, whose pale bulk had been casually poured into an Arsenal football strip, she looked over-costumed, an exaggerated representation of her type. Fletcher Walsh's white three-piece suit, meanwhile, was somehow more Mandingo than Manderley, an effect not lessened by the presence at his side of Carlton, Forth's make-up supremo, whose muscled black limbs shone beneath denims so ruthlessly slashed as to be little more than cobwebbed seams. All four, however, were marching decisively in step, and I had a strong impression of common purpose. From the further reaches of the lawns, other figures began to converge.

I excused myself, leaving Dale with Gina, and continued up to the top of the slope. Beneath the cedar, Sheldrake was leaning back in his chair, legs crossed, contemplating the remains of his breakfast. I joined him, and poured myself a cup of coffee.

'So,' he looked up, 'the queen's on the board, finally. You've delivered her.'

'I'm sorry,' I said, embarrassed. 'She just wanted somewhere to . . .'

'Don't worry; I understand. *Pain au chocolat*?' He could be charming enough when he tried.

'No. I mean, yes, OK, thanks.'

'So what do you think?'

'Seems like a nice girl,' I said.

He nodded.

'Yes, she is that.' He dragged a linen table napkin across his mouth and crumpled it absently on his side plate.

'So what will you be filming today?'

'We're starting with the garden this morning, and then moving inside for one or two of the interior set-ups. You're welcome to come and go as you please, but I'd rather you didn't ask me questions during the actual filming. Fair enough?'

'Of course.'

'I'll introduce you to Kees Reyntiens, who's doing the stills. He'll fill you in on any technical stuff you need.'

The group containing Dale approached, and Sheldrake looked up as if taken by surprise.

'Dale, my love!' he said, addressing her as if she were alone rather than surrounded by at least a dozen people. 'Hello again! You're looking wonderful.'

'Well, thanks,' said Dale, smiling faintly.

'We were just going to show Dale her room,' said Nancy brightly, 'and then . . .'

'Can we be ready to turn over at eight?' asked Sheldrake abruptly, turning to Carlton and John-Paul.

'OK by me,' said Carlton. John-Paul nodded.

'Right, everyone,' said Sheldrake. 'I want two minutes alone with Dale and then we go to work.'

I went indoors to change my shoes.

Carlton had set up his stall in a glass-roofed conservatory at the back of the house. A long trestle table ran the length of the glass exterior wall, and on this were arranged an extensive array of make-up, a tray containing Carlton's brushes and instruments, and several vases of cut flowers, amongst which freesias and tulips predominated. A air-conditioning unit purred in one corner, and muted choral music issued from a pair of wall-mounted speakers.

At the exact centre of the room, her eyes closed, Dale Cooney lay back in a reclining white leather chair. Her hair had been pinned back, and her face cosmetically smoothed to a pale, translucent ivory. Slowly, Carlton swivelled the chair from side to side, attentive to the play of the light.

'Watch,' he said, 'and learn.'

Once again he angled her face away from the direct sunlight, but this time it seemed to me that the turning planes of her brow and her cheekbone retained a faint luminescence even as they moved into shadow. A moment, and the illusion had passed. 'No,' I said. 'I'm imagining things.'

'Watch again,' said Carlton.

He repeated the movement, and I saw the same suspended glimmer. It was subtle as a breath, but it was there.

'It's what we call "slow fade",' he explained. 'Kind of a particle physics thing.'

'I'll take your word for it,' I said.

'You do that. We made up this particular colour especially for Dale – check it against the portrait of Eleanor there – but in September we're launching a full range of photo-reactive cosmetics.'

'Fletcher didn't mention that.'

Carlton shrugged and checked one of his coded blow-ups. 'Fletcher's a fragrance man, and I guess there are times when he doesn't see the bigger picture. But why don't you check out some of our new products yourself? I'll put a collection together for you.'

'I don't really use cosmetics these days,' I said, as he hovered over the trestle table.

'You don't miss that fine interplay of the synthetic' – he ran a clear lipstick over the back of his hand and held it up to the light – 'and the intimate?'

'Not really.'

He nodded, and taking a sable brush, began to paint the lipstick on to Dale's mouth.

'Is she asleep?' I asked.

'No, child,' said Carlton. 'She's a professional.'

'Underskirt first,' said John-Paul, twenty minutes later. 'That's it – just let me tie the tapes – now the overskirt.'

We were in the Long Gallery, and Dale, fully made up, was putting on her Eleanor Duboys costume. Further down the gallery, Gina and Fiona were being helped into their own costumes by John-Paul's assistants.

'It's so light,' said Dale. 'I was thinking they'd be these great heavy dresses, but it's so light.'

'It's English silk,' said John-Paul. 'Made by the finest mulberry-fed Pewsey silkworms. Now, my love, this little chiffon nonsense is your chemisette, which goes on like so, and then the bodice goes on top. So now, if you could just brace yourself against something solid . . . Perhaps, Alison, you wouldn't mind . . .'

Dale gasped and dug her fingers into my shoulders as John-Paul hooked and eyed the bodice down her back.

'I can hardly breathe. I'm suffocating.'

'That's good,' said John-Paul. 'Suffocating is good.' He took a pair of jewelled lace and chiffon sleeves from the table. 'Now, these button on here, under these shoulder-pieces, like so . . . And then we have the double tier of pearls, we have the ruby earrings, the hair is loose . . .'

'And the ring,' said Dale.

'You're right,' said John-Paul. 'We've forgotten the ring.' Rummaging on the table, he found a gold signet ring, which, consulting one of his enlargements of details of the Peake portrait, he slipped on to her wedding finger. It was much too large for her, and as Eleanor had done in the portrait, he attached the ring with a black string which he then tied around her wrist.

'Elizabethan women loved the contrast,' he said. 'The black against the white skin.'

'Was Eleanor married?' I asked.

'I wondered that,' said John-Paul. 'But the unbound hair suggests not. Besides, her name's still Duboys.'

'Yes, of course. Stupid of me.'

He handed me the 10″ by 8″ enlargement of Eleanor's hand. 'And have a close look at the ring.'

I carried the photograph to the window. The crest on the ring, I saw, was a stag's head, similar to that which, in more complex form, surmounted the porch.

'So,' I said, 'her heart still belonged to Daddy.'

'That sort of thing,' said John-Paul. 'Yes.'

'I want to see her,' said Dale, lifting her skirts and slipping her feet determinedly back into her baseball boots. 'I want to see her now.'

John-Paul turned to the stack of photographs on the trestle table, but Dale was already halfway to the door. Raising an eyebrow at me, and taking Dale's silk chopine slippers from the table, John-Paul followed her out of the Long Gallery. Turning to glance at Gina, who shrugged, I followed John-Paul and the squeak of Dale's rubber soles on the floorboards.

Although to my certain knowledge she had never been taken there, Dale made straight for the Oak Chamber, and, slowing, came to a halt in front of the Peake portrait. Thoughtfully, and with a certain fastidiousness, she stepped from her Converse boots, and John-Paul, kneeling, slipped the silk chopines on to her feet. For several minutes she stood there, unmoving, as John-Paul and I waited behind her. Then, as if performing a kind of minimalist ballet, she undertook a series of subtle alterations, first to the set of her head and her shoulders and her arms and then to each finger, each lock of hair, until she mirrored Eleanor Duboys exactly.

Gesturing that I should stay where I was, and that if possible I should keep Dale there too, John-Paul slipped from the room, and a moment later I heard the murmur of his voice in the corridor. When he returned, still carrying Dale's Converse boots, it was with Sheldrake, Fletcher and Nancy. Dale hadn't moved.

'Dale,' said Charles Sheldrake quietly.

She turned. Her expression, and in some curious way the carriage of her body, had changed utterly. And her eyes. It was as if she saw us but saw through us, as if we were insubstantial, there but not there. What we were witnessing was no more and no less than an actress at work, but even as I reminded myself of this fact, it seemed to me that she was calling on experience far beyond her own, that her gaze traversed not just this small room, but centuries.

'Eleanor?' whispered Sheldrake.

She looked up at that, frowning for a moment as if trying to remember something, and then gathering up her skirts, swept smoothly to the door. It was Nancy who realised that she expected it to be opened for her, and who even murmured an apology as she did so.

Watching her go, Charles Sheldrake turned triumphantly to Fletcher Walsh.

'She's going to do it for us,' he said.

'Yes,' Walsh answered. 'I think she is.'

11

'Say what you like about the glamour of film-making,' said Phoebe, rolling lazily on to her back, 'it's a fucking boring process.'

It was the third morning of filming, and along with such members of the production team as were not needed at that moment, we were sprawled on the sloping lawn above the lake. Below us a small marquee had been erected, outside which Dale was pacing back and forth, watched a little nervously by Carlton and Sabrina, the production hairdresser. Dale had returned her silk skirts to Jean-Paul, who was re-ironing them, and had changed back into her jeans, over which the jewelled Elizabethan bodice sat strangely but prettily. At my request Kees Reyntiens had rowed out on to the lake to photograph the scene for the magazine, and was crouched over his Hasselblad twenty yards from the shore.

Moored some distance beyond him was a longer boat, a gilded, high-prowed vessel in which Dale's stand-in – a torpid blonde from Upton-on-Arrow – reclined on her cushioned seat, smoking. The boat, which like the masque designs had been copied from drawings by Inigo Jones, had been delivered by truck an hour earlier and physically carried to the lake by the crewcut woman and her acolytes. The idea was that whilst appearing to be poled along, the boat was actually to be drawn across the water on a rope. At infrequent intervals this process was rehearsed. An order would be given, the rope-men on shore would commence their trudge, and the camera, remotely monitored by Sheldrake, would begin its slow progress along the track.

It was barely nine o'clock, but the sun had already lifted the dew from the newly mown grass and a heavy silence overhung the valley, the silence accentuated rather than diminished by a loud-hailer's occasional reverberant calls. Something about the impatient heat of these last mornings reminded me of Sports Day at the convent, of my mother unsteady in her summer frock, of raspberries and melting ice cream.

It had been an interesting but ultimately frustrating two days. With typical perversity – although somewhat to my relief – Phoebe had taken off for London on the morning of Dale's arrival, leaving me to get on with my work uninterrupted. As a result I had most of the material in place and in order, but with a single important exception: I hadn't got a single usable quote from Dale. She answered me if I spoke to her, she appeared to like my company, and sometimes she even sought me out. But she never, ever said anything I could use. There were only certain topics of conversation, I think, that she even listened to. If I mentioned the world beyond the boundaries of Darne – Oregon, for example, or New York, or London – her face went blank. Her absorption in her silent film role was absolute, and she clearly did not want to step outside the experience for a single moment. Attempting to joke her into a response, I had suggested that with the money that she was earning from this job she could probably buy an Elizabethan stately home of her own, complete with crescent-shaped lake and island, but she had just looked away. And yet I was positive that she wanted to talk to me. This was not wishful thinking; I knew the signs well, recognised the hesitations, the hangings about, the sudden hurryings away. We had sat together at dinner the night before, and as the shadows lengthened beneath the cedar and the night drew down she had questioned me in minute detail about my crash, about my morphine dreams, about the colour of pain, about the kindnesses and the random cruelties of strangers. I told her everything that I could remember – told her until my food was cold and my cigarette a column of ash – but I didn't know what she really wanted to hear, didn't know which questions were the important ones, and which ones were being asked merely for form's sake.

I liked her, though, and I suppose that I wanted to please her. Her beauty fascinated me, and most particularly the way that it was constructed from absence. She had no habitual expressions; at rest, her face simply emptied into flawless vacancy. I stared at her quite openly, but she didn't seem to mind. Perhaps she didn't notice. Perhaps she was used to it.

Everybody, I noticed, was very kind to her. The technicians offered her chewing gum and Coca-Cola as if she was a child, and when she gently refused these, along with their halting attempts at conversation, they took to tiptoeing around her as if the sound of their shoes on the grass might disturb her delicate equilibrium. They didn't look like people who were easily impressed, but they were impressed by Dale.

'So. Is she gorgeous, then?' asked Phoebe, squinting at me from under her arms.

'Why don't you go down and meet her?' I said. 'They're obviously going to be ages setting up. And she is supposed to be playing the part of your ancestor, after all.'

'Later,' said Phoebe. 'I'll meet her later. She's probably being a tree or a peanut or thinking in Middle English or whatever these American actresses do before they go in front of the cameras.' She peered down at the marquee. 'Besides, she's being mobbed up by all those hair and make-up queens, and I can't be doing with homosexuals this early in the morning, so just tell me about her.'

'OK, then. No, if you want my personal take on Dale Cooney she isn't gorgeous; gorgeous is the wrong word, it suggests something much more fully blown. What she's got, though, as Eleanor clearly had, is this very private, very subtle, very guarded beauty. It's as if . . .' I plucked at the short, mossy grass, searching for words, '. . . as if it can only be displayed in secret, very briefly and intensely, and then has to be locked away again.'

'That was very cutely put.'

'I'm trying to work out what I think; I've got to write several thousand words about this girl, remember?'

'You sound smitten, *sabreuse*.'

I raised myself up on one elbow. 'You've got me wrong, Phoebe. I'm not, as it turns out, smitable in that particular way.'

'And what particular way might that be?'

'You know. Like what happened in the woods the other day.'

'Why, what did happen in the woods the other day, Belle?'

I closed my eyes and collapsed on to my back. 'I give up,' I said.

'Now we're getting somewhere,' said Phoebe, touching my nose with a fingertip. 'Have you had breakfast?'

'Well, no, now you mention it.'

'Let's go and get some.'

'I think they've cleared away.'

'Not up there; we'll go to the gatehouse. Stephen'll fry us something; he's very good with a pan.'

'A strong coffee and a fag will do me.'

'I'm sure we could manage that.'

'I think I should stick around and watch.'

'Nothing's going to happen for at least half an hour, and even then they're just going to pull her backwards and forwards in the boat.' She looked at me calculatingly. 'Wouldn't you like to see inside the gatehouse? I've seen you treating Stephen to your follow-me-home-and-fuck-me routine.'

'Oh, please!'

'Oh please yourself. You've hardly been discreet.'

'That's unfair, Phoebe!'

'*That's unfair, Phoebe*,' she imitated me. '*That's unfair*. You were all over him at dinner the other night, as you well bloody know. And I can't imagine you've been wasting your time while I've been away, either.'

That, in fact, *was* unfair. The truth was that I had barely spoken to Stephen Faulds over the last couple of days. True to Charles Sheldrake's philosophy of using 'real' people, Stephen had been co-opted into the film, to play the mysterious, distantly viewed figure in black. So that his time would not be wasted, Stephen kept his costume at the gatehouse. When he was needed for a shot, he would be telephoned with the co-ordinates of the wood or the hilltop where he had to stand, and a few minutes later we would see him racing across the fields on his motorcycle, his rapier at his side. Sheldrake would direct him by phone, and then, true to the spirit of the role, Stephen would return as he had arrived. I'd never even seen him close up in his costume.

'Tell me something, Phoebe,' I said, breaking the bad-tempered silence as we walked along the riverbank towards the bridge. 'What do you actually know about Eleanor?'

She kicked at the path. 'To be honest, I've kind of had it with Eleanor. Ever since I was a child I've had people peering at me, trying to spot a resemblance to fucking Eleanor. "There's something about the mouth" they'd say, or "She's definitely got Eleanor's nose" or whatever. Not to mention all the ghastly art queers and historical detectives one's expected to be polite to. I've half a mind to take a match to the little cow. She costs us a fortune in insurance.'

'She's earning you a bit now, isn't she?'

'In the short term, maybe. In the long term all that it will mean is more art queers and Eleanor perverts. It doesn't bear thinking about.'

'Why historical detectives?' I asked.

'Oh, there's some piece of business about a Latin inscription and about Eleanor's not being buried where the rest of the family is. Like I said, I can't be doing with it. Why are you so interested?'

'Because I've got to write about the campaign, and Eleanor and the portrait are very much part of it. I also have a suspicion that Dale's going to keep herself pretty closed off, so there's a limit to how much I can make the whole thing a profile of her. So the more background I can get . . .'

'You know, Belle, a very hard, glittery look comes into your eyes when you talk about your work.'

'Perhaps that's because it matters to me,' I answered her. 'My entire life – my clothes, my car, my food, my phone, my flat – is paid for by my work. Strange as that may sound to someone in your position.'

'My position?'

'You know what I mean.'

'As it happens, I do work,' said Phoebe. 'In my fashion.'

'And precisely what work do you do?' I asked, making a mental note to remember to ask Oliver about the inscription.

'I paint,' she said. 'Is that good enough? I mean, does that count?'

'I'm sure it does,' I said. 'And I'm sorry. I'm being a bitch. Why don't I just go back to the lake?'

In answer, Phoebe flung an arm round my waist, hitched her thumb through one of the loops of my belt and stepped in front of me so that we both tripped and fell on to the sloping riverbank. Pain lanced through my back and groin, and for a moment I was unable to move or speak. As Phoebe hauled her legs from beneath mine a second flash of pain spitted me, nettles stung my cheek, and I felt my hands clasping and unclasping at a clump of reeds. Beside me, on her knees, Phoebe froze.

'Oh my God, Alison, I'm sorry, I forgot, I mean I didn't know. Shit.' She beat at her jeans pockets and pulled out her tin. 'Don't move, I'll make you a joint.'

'It's OK,' I gasped. 'I'll be OK.' I drew my knees up to my face, ignored the nettles, concentrated on breathing, and the pain began to recede.

'Do you think you'll be able to walk?' Phoebe asked anxiously.

'Eventually,' I said. 'Wow.'

'I'll call Stephen,' said Phoebe, pulling my Motorola from my belt.

'And say what?'

'Come and get us. Or you, anyway.'

'Whatever. Sorry, I'm just going to shut my eyes for a while. I feel a bit sick.'

'What happened?' said Stephen, skidding to a halt above us a few minutes later. All that I could see was a pair of old tennis shoes and combat trousers.

'I tripped her up,' said Phoebe. 'And she hit her back on a stone, and smashed the display thing on her phone and tore her beautiful shirt.'

He glared at her and crouched beside me. He smelt of motormowers, of cut grass and petrol.

'Do you need a doctor?'

I rolled slowly on to my knees, he helped me to my feet, and I took a tentative step or two. 'I'm OK,' I said.

'Sure?'

'Sure.'

'Well, I guess you wouldn't be able to walk if anything was broken.'

'Can we take her to the gatehouse and put her to bed?' begged Phoebe. 'And then I can nurse her patiently and selflessly back to perfect health. I could hire a uniform from that Eager Beaver agency in Upton.'

'Phoebe?' said Stephen.

'Yes.'

'Shut up.'

'OK. Will you make us breakfast?'

He turned to me. 'Can you manage the bike? As a passenger, I mean?'

'What about Phoebe?'

'Phoebe can walk.'

I turned to her doubtfully.

'You go ahead,' she said.

Stephen swung a leg over the heavy Triumph, Phoebe helped me clamber on to the back, and the engine coughed into life. Slowly, we bounced through the waves of grass, the Triumph's armchair-like suspension cushioning my back from the bumps, and then we were through the forest gates and into the shadowed cool beneath the canopy of beech trees. Outside the hangar, Stephen stopped, and pulled the bike back on to its stand.

'Can I help you off?' he asked, over his shoulder.

'Please,' I said.

Extricating himself from the seat in front of me, he placed an arm around my ribs and lifted me over the back wheel to the ground. As he did so my shirt rode up and I felt his forearm hard and warm against my stomach. 'Not very elegantly done,' he apologised, settling me on my feet and, a second or two later than was necessary, taking his hands from my waist. 'If life were a Jane Austen novel, of course, I would now bear you in my arms to the *chaise-longue*, but . . .'

'That would be excessively diverting,' I said, prodding experimentally at the southern parts of my spine, 'but Jane Austen heroines tend not to arrive on the back of 750cc Triumph Bonnevilles. Apart from in the roadhouse scene in *Northanger Abbey*, of course.'

He looked at me for a moment, smiled, and wheeled the bike off its stand and over the mossed ground into the hangar. My lower back throbbed; I shifted my weight and tried without success to touch my toes.

'You know about bikes, then?' he said when he returned. 'I

could tell you were an experienced pillion rider.'

'I had a boyfriend once who had a Ducati,' I said. 'You know how girls go through that stage?'

'As opposed to men, you mean, who get stuck there?'

'You tell me,' I said, lifting my arms and twisting at the waist as the hospital physiotherapist had shown me.

'Undoubtedly,' he said, watching me. 'Look, are you sure you're OK? And Phoebe's right. You've torn your shirt.'

I glanced down, saw my armpit through the tear in the sweat-darkened fabric, and lowered my arms.

'I could lend you something,' he suggested.

'I'm sure Phoebe's got some clothes here,' I said.

We made our way in silence to the bright little lawn in front of the gatehouse. The air was heavy with the scent of wisteria, and so still that the soft purple blossoms nodded beneath the weight of the alighting butterflies. To either side of the path, the lavender beds were intent with bees.

'I'll give you the grand tour,' said Stephen, unlatching the studded oak door beneath the gate arch. 'It takes about forty-five seconds.'

We stepped into the small, flagstoned kitchen, sparely furnished, about which hung a faint gamey smell. A rack above the stoneware sink held an unmatched pair of dinner plates, and a few pieces of cutlery stood in a creamware jug, but otherwise there was little to indicate that the place was in use. A single painting of a woodland scene hung on the side wall; at first glance I thought that the subject was a medieval hunt, but when I looked closer I saw that it showed a clearing in a forest, and a stream in which women were bathing. Watching the women was a man with the antlers of a stag.

'Phoebe?' I asked.

Stephen nodded ruefully. 'My last Christmas present.'

'She's really quite good.'

'They both are. Oliver could have been wonderful.'

'Could have been?'

'If he'd bothered. Shall we go on up?'

I nodded, and he indicated the doorway to the stair-tower.

The upstairs part of the gatehouse consisted of a single

rectangular room. At the far end was a large iron bed covered by a plain white counterpane, and beside me as I stepped from the stair-tower stood a grey-painted steel desk and a heavy office chair. The room's decoration, however, was less reserved. Every available inch of wall space had been covered with reproductions of plans and drawings relating to garden design. Most of these were European, but amongst the temperate conceits of Repton, Le Nôtre and Capability Brown I saw cascading Madagascan terraces, hydrological miracles from Kashmir and Alexandria, cigar-label profusions of exotica from Manaus and Curaçao and the Caribbean. There were plans for schemes involving thousands of acres – most of them, I guessed, either unrealised or long since vanished – and there were more practical and detailed illustrations concerning the sinking of wells, the pleaching of limes and the construction of palm houses.

The cumulative effect was dizzying, but after walking around for a minute or two, allowing myself to be drawn from detail to detail, I began to find it almost narcotically soothing. Nothing demanded the attention – humanity, I soon observed, was notable by its absence – but wherever the eye alighted the imagination was engaged. Strangest of all was a series of engravings of automata and hydraulic garden toys. Satyrs disported in fountains, sculpted nymphs rode scallop-shell chariots through flooded grottos, and armoured sea monsters rose from the deeps of ornamental lakes, all of them driven by elaborate configurations of cogs, wheels and screws.

'Salomon de Caus,' said Stephen. 'From his *Raisons des Forces Mouvantes*, published in 1615. I particularly like this little device: it's a fountain designed to wet ladies' underclothes.'

'Yes,' I said. 'I can see that it might well have that effect. Are all of these yours?'

'Yes, all of them. You might say they're my extravagance.'

'There are no human figures,' I said. 'Not one.'

He stepped back, and a small, almost unguarded smile touched his face. 'But they're there all right. They're just waiting to step out from behind those trees, or from the shadow of that bridge, or from somewhere just outside your field of vision. And you're there too, of course, as an onlooker. You're in the frame.' He paused, and surveyed the wall of prints. 'For me there's something, I don't know, almost . . . mystical about these landscapes. They're like stage settings, there's a sense of order and control but there's also a really powerful sense of anticipation: the sense . . . how can I put this . . . the sense that something pre-ordained but at the same time completely unexpected is just about to happen.' He looked at me warily. 'Does that make sense?'

'Yes,' I said. 'Perfect sense. That's exactly what I feel here at Darne.' I moved away from him, towards the window. 'Is that why you stay here, then, because you're in the frame? Because you're part of the picture?'

He dug his hands into his pockets and shrugged.

'Phoebe?' I asked, my gaze shifting to the lawn below.

'Don't underestimate Phoebe. Phoebe and Darne are one. Phoebe *is* Darne.'

I looked at him sideways. 'And you wouldn't leave either of them?'

'I love it here,' he said quietly. 'It's as simple as that.'

I pushed the window open, and the scent of wisteria poured into the long, low room. '"God Almightie first Planted a Garden"' I murmured. '"And indeed it is the purest of human pleasures . . ."'

'That's Francis Bacon, isn't it?' Stephen asked.

'It is.'

'Do you think he wrote Shakespeare?'

'No, I think Shakespeare did.'

'How can you be so sure?'

'Read what Bacon did write. Read *Of Death* or *The Colours of Good and Evil.* Feel his icy breath at your ear and then try and imagine him writing *A Midsummer Night's Dream.* You'll soon be sure.'

'So why do people think he did?'

'Some people are always looking for mysteries and conspiracies.'

'But not you, of course?'

'La Sir, never,' I replied demurely.

'Because you know, of course, what they say about curiosity . . .'

'I know,' I said. 'Poor Pussy. But satisfaction brought her back;

or so I've always been given to understand.' I picked up one of Phoebe's crumpled lace and velvet Voyage tops from the floor and held it up against myself. It smelt of stale smoke and her perfume, and I hung it carefully over the back of the office chair. Interesting, I thought, that he had heard about my MoD enquiry already.

Stephen walked towards the bed, opened a small japanned trunk which stood beside it, took out a faded black rectangle and skimmed it through the air towards me.

'Thanks,' I said, catching and unfolding it. It was a D-Tech T-shirt, identical to the one he was wearing. 'So who are these people, anyway?'

'D-Tech was a private security firm, owned by Bill Duboys. No mystery there, I assure you.'

'Just thought I'd ask; I prefer to know whose private army I'm advertising.'

A phone rang, and he reached into his pocket.

'I'll be right over,' he murmured after listening for a moment. 'Five minutes, OK.'

He disconnected, and turned to me. 'I'm needed for the filming.' He glanced down at the T-shirt in my hands. 'I'll be in the kitchen.'

I took off my torn shirt, whose ripped seam now gaped halfway down my ribs, balled it into my trouser pocket and pulled the D-Tech shirt over my head. A quick scan of the room revealed nothing that I had not already seen, and I stepped into the stair-tower.

I didn't slip on the polished stone, and I didn't fall; I think it was just the twisting motion of the descent combined with the earlier blow. Whatever it was pain exploded through my back yet again and I sank, mewing, to the kitchen floor.

Stephen hurried over. 'You really did hurt yourself by the river, didn't you?'

'I'll be fine,' I whispered.

'You don't look at all fine to me; you've obviously . . .'

'Please, just lie me outside on the lawn.'

Carefully, he manoeuvred his hands under my back and lifted me. I closed my eyes and for a long, long moment, during which he seemed hardly to move, I let my head rest against his shoulder. Pain had made me drowsy, though; when I opened my eyes again I was in bright sunshine, grass was pricking my cheek and Phoebe was kneeling over me.

'What can I do?' she asked.

'Nothing,' I said, closing my eyes again. 'I just need to lie still for a minute or two.' From the forest came the bubbling cough of the Bonneville's ignition.

'Stephen says see you later. He had to go.' Shade slid across my eyelids as she moved to my other side and busied herself with her drugs tin. I heard the rustle of foil and, shortly afterwards, a tiny sizzling sound.

'Here,' said Phoebe. 'Inhale.'

I opened one eye. Acrid smoke was rising from a twist of silver paper, beneath which she was holding a briquet lighter.

'What is it?' I murmured.

'Opium oil.' She pushed the foil towards me. 'Don't waste it.'

I took a dubious sniff.

'Elizabethan paracetamol,' said Phoebe encouragingly. 'Have some more.'

I had some more. Time passed. I lay on my back, and Phoebe sat cross-legged and in silence beside me. When I closed my eyes I was transported to other gardens: to imaginary but graphically exact landscapes whose rides and vistas extended to perspective infinity, to deserted avenues over which sphinxes and griffons crouched in stony vigilance, to the shores of vast black lakes. I had only to open my eyes, however, to return to the gatehouse lawn, to the sunshine and the hum of the bees and the idle swing of the Cabbage White butterflies over the lavender, and for a time I amused myself by moving between the two, between the warmth of the real present and the melancholy chill of the imagined past. After a time, though, the warmth and the chill became confused, and I realised that time had passed, but that I had lost track of it. Dry-mouthed and agitated, I moved to sit up.

'Careful, Belle,' said Phoebe, placing a hand in the small of my back.

'It's not even eleven o'clock,' I said, my voice catching in my throat as I stared disbelievingly at my watch.

'What time did you think it was?' she asked gently.

'At least tea-time.'

'How's your back?'

I twisted experimentally. 'My back seems to be . . . fine again.'

'Sympathetic magic, you see.'

'I should get back,' I said.

Phoebe nodded. 'I've just remembered something I was going to say to you this morning before you started banging on about Eleanor and we got scratchy.'

'What's that?'

'It's about Charles; he's up to something.'

'How do you mean?'

'Well, I was watching him this morning on the set, early, and it was clear from the way he behaved with her that he's still sleeping with Figgy.'

'So why shouldn't he be?'

'Well, he's gone to all this trouble to bring this Dale creature over from New York – paid her a trillion pounds and all the rest of it, and set himself up as her director – and then he makes no attempt to hide the fact that he's sleeping with some off-the-peg bimbo like Duff. When you know the man and how he works, it just doesn't make sense.'

'Perhaps he's fond of Figgy,' I said, bored of the subject. 'She's pretty and nice and . . .'

'Oh, please!' said Phoebe, reaching for her tin.

As I walked back through the valley, devouring a large slice of game pie from Stephen's fridge as I went, I wondered how I could encourage Dale to reveal something of herself to me. I needed her quotes for my piece but I was also genuinely curious; I wanted to unlock her, to know who she was, to know what impelled her.

It was probable, however, that despite my hunch that she would have liked to confide in me, things would simply continue as they were. Even if she did talk, it was unlikely to be on the record. She'd never given an interview in her life, and I had no reason to suppose that she was about to make an exception in my case. What I was going to have to do was to make a virtue out of a necessity, to emphasise her silence, to present her – like Eleanor – as an enigma.

That being the case, I was going to have to find out a bit more about Eleanor. The mystery that Phoebe had mentioned sounded promising, and I was more than a little intrigued by Oliver's Perdita painting. Perhaps this was a good time to visit him; Dale usually locked herself in her room for an hour or two after lunch, and I doubted I'd be missing out on anything.

I continued along the path, the sun sharp at the back of my neck. High above me I heard a plaintive cry, and looked up to see a sparrowhawk turn idly on a wing and plummet to the ground some twenty yards ahead. The action was curiously untidy, as if the bird had suffered some kind of mid-air seizure, but a moment later I saw it lift itself from the grass with a small animal – a mouse perhaps – squirming in its pinions, and I heard a tiny, insistent screaming. The hawk settled itself on the ground, its beak descended in a thoughtful stab, and there was silence. Ahead of me the house looked – as it had looked on that first morning – translucent, depthless.

I knocked at Oliver's door; gently at first and then louder. When there was no answer, I pushed the door open a few inches and looked in.

At first I thought he was dead. He was lying outstretched on an old sofa with his white shirt unbuttoned, his long red-gold hair artlessly disarrayed and one arm outflung towards the floor. Nervously, I crossed the room towards him, and then stopped short. On the floor beneath the trailing hand was a used syringe and needle. Oliver was alive – I could see the pulse beating at his neck – but he was unconscious, or perhaps asleep. He had injected himself, I saw, in the left arm; the sleeve was rolled up to the biceps, and a ligature of picture cord hung loosely at his elbow.

I examined him curiously. I had always imagined that the arms of heroin addicts were bruised and needle-tracked, but Oliver's arms didn't look too bad. There was a junkie gauntness about him, however, that I should have recognised earlier; the drug's pale signature was written in his face.

On impulse, I crossed to the corner and opened the refrigerator door. The shelves held a number of small screw-top bottles of solvents, spirits and acetones, half a dozen rolls of colour transparency film and a six-pack of cherry Coke. Behind these, however, was a white card box printed with a pharmaceutical company logo and a manufacturer's batch number. I reached in and flipped up the lid; inside were several dozen glass ampoules packed in transparent plastic strips and a jumble of disposable hypodermics and needles.

I carefully closed the fridge door, the suctioned gasp loud in the silence, and returned to Oliver. He still appeared to be asleep, and I crossed to the easel, on which the Perdita panel stood angled to meet the light.

It looked very different. In place of the earlier dull black, the upper part of the background was now a deep midnight blue. At the panel's upper corners two winged figures had been revealed, painted in the same simplistic style as the central subject; one was obviously Cupid, the other a skeletal Death. Both figures were armed with bows and arrows, and both appeared to be taking aim at Eleanor, or Perdita, or whoever she was supposed to be. I stood there for several minutes, examining the panel from different angles and musing as to the figures' significance.

'So,' said a quiet voice behind me, and I nearly jumped out of my skin. Oliver was sitting up on the sofa, buttoning his cuffs. He looked refreshed, as if from a good sleep.

'So,' he repeated, ignoring my Miss Muffet-like palpitations. 'What do you think?' The picture cord and the hypodermic had vanished.

'Well . . .' I began nervously, 'the painting looks a lot better for the cleaning. The flying archers have got to be Love and Death, I suppose, although what their meaning is in this context I've no idea. As to the motive for overpainting them, I'd say off the top of my head that some sort of censorship or disinformation is being attempted, if that doesn't sound too paranoid . . .'

He digested my words in silence, and nodded. 'OK. Now have a look at this.'

Climbing a little stiffly to his feet, he took a large bound book from a shelf, and opened it at a marked place. On the right-hand page, beneath a sheet of foxed tissue paper, was an engraved copy of a painting of a young woman. On the left-hand page were a few lines of text.

MARY ROBINSON AS 'PERDITA'. By Sir Joshua Reynolds PRA, born 1723, died 1792.

The property of the MARQUESS OF HERTFORD.

Mary Robinson was born Mary Derby in 1758, in Bristol. As a child she married an attorney named Robinson, who put her on the stage. She was instructed by Garrick at Drury Lane, where she was well received, and in the character of 'Perdita' in *A Winter's Tale* attracted the attention of the Prince of Wales, later George IV. She left the stage to become his mistress, but her royal suitor abandoned her shortly afterwards when, at the age of 26, she succumbed to a sickness which deprived her of the use of her limbs. She turned to writing to support herself, publishing various poems and miscellanea, and died in painful circumstances in 1800.

'A sorry tale,' I said.

'And quite a coincidence. I got it out of the library because it's got an engraving of Eleanor.'

I turned the book over in order to see its title. It was called simply *Beautiful Englishwomen*, and dated 1885.

'Before we go any further,' I said, 'I think you should tell me the full Eleanor story.'

A fly buzzed urgently at the window. Oliver smiled, stretched out his arms and yawned. I glanced covertly at him, amazed at the completeness of his recovery.

'Why not start by looking her up in there?' he suggested cheerfully.

Carefully, I leafed back through the engravings, past a succession of florid Georgians and sleepy, spaniel-eyed Stuarts to the Elizabethans, who were represented by Alice Brandon, Helena Snakenborg and Eleanor Duboys.

ELEANOR DUBOYS IN THE CHARACTER OF A NYMPH OF DIANA. By Robert Peake, born 1551, died 1619.

The Property of GODFREY DUBOYS.

Little is known of Eleanor Duboys beyond the fact that she was born in 1579 to William and Catherine Duboys, all records having been destroyed with the burning of the family's Twickenham house in 1665, the year of the Great Plague. It is thought that Robert Peake's portrait, painted in 1598 at Darne Castle, the family's country seat, may have celebrated her betrothal. A memorial at Darne, however, records that Eleanor Duboys was 'removed from the sight of those who loved her' at the age of 21, a year after the portrait's execution. The equivocally worded memorial, and the fact that no official record exists of her death, has given rise to a number of legends concerning her fate and 'mysterious disappearance', the most fanciful and optimistic of which concern the possibility of a romantic elopement.

'Wow,' I said, ideas tumbling over themselves in my mind. 'Why didn't you . . . I mean, where is this memorial? Does everyone know this stuff?'

'Steady,' said Oliver. 'Hold your horses. Remember, this book was written a hundred and fifteen years ago. The Victorians loved melodramas and ghost stories, but unfortunately there's absolutely no evidence whatsoever to support any kind of "mysterious disappearance" or "romantic elopement" theory. The sad probability is that the poor thing quite simply died young. Scarlet fever, flu, appendicitis, tuberculosis . . . If the disease didn't finish you off, the doctors certainly would.'

'And the family had a place at Twickenham?'

'They originally lived in a house named – ironically, as things turned out – Sands End, of which absolutely no trace remains. William Duboys was a sort of venture capitalist, putting up money for trading expeditions to the Caribbean and the New World. He also fitted up a number of warships – partly for patriotic reasons, and partly to ensure safe passage for his traders – and as a result, through people like Raleigh, he was known to the court. He was a wealthy man, but by the time he had built Darne and received the Queen and her retinue a couple of times I get the impression that things were beginning to get a bit tight. When Sands End burnt down a couple of generations later, the family tightened their belts and moved up here lock, stock and barrel.'

'So where's this memorial?'

'Downstairs, in the Great Hall. Eleanor was born at Twickenham a year or two before Darne was built, but she probably spent most of her life down here. The memorial's just a square stone plaque let into the wall; you probably wouldn't notice it.'

'Do you mind if I go down and see it?'

'I can save you the trouble. It's actually quite hard to read *in situ*, but if you'll just hang on a sec . . .' He rummaged through the books and papers on the shelf, and brought down a small, worn-looking pamphlet. 'My great-grandfather produced this; he was a keen Eleanor buff.'

The pamphlet's cover was illustrated by a photogravure of the rectangular memorial stone. Inside were several short pages of text.

'Do you mind if I . . .?'

'No. Sit down. It'll only take you a minute or two.'

I sat.

Some Notes Concerning the Eleanor Duboys Memorial Stone at Darne Castle, Warwickshire. By Geoffrey Duboys.

I cannot have been more than five or six years old when I first heard the legend of my ancestor, Eleanor Duboys. Thwarted in love, so the story goes, my sad forebear vanished from human sight, to walk the woods and gardens of Darne as a spirit, forever young. It is an affecting story, and one which as a child I accepted without question.

In the early years of the century, I recall, the densely forested area to the north of the lake was always known as 'Eleanor's Wood', and although the landing area was a favourite spot for family picnics (and its ancient stone bear much loved by my late brothers and myself), the woods themselves presented a forbidding and slightly sinister aspect, discouraging of childhood explorations. I suppose that the gamekeepers knew its paths and byways, as did the deer, but I do not recall my family or their guests ever setting foot there.

Before the war the portrait of Eleanor by Robert Peake (later official painter to Prince Henry) hung in the Great Hall, and I passed it several times daily; it was only after the Great War that it was moved to the quieter situation of the Oak Chamber in the west wing, where it remains. Peake painted Eleanor in the character of a nymph of Diana in 1598, when she was twenty years old, and she was without doubt his most beguiling subject. Elizabethan portraits were produced to mark significant events in their subjects' lives, and it is probable, given her age, that the event in question was Eleanor's betrothal. Her brother Nicholas had married Elizabeth Hawthorne the previous year.

Very little is known about Eleanor's childhood, although some Darne household records have survived. In April 1595, for example, the purchase is recorded of, amongst other items, 'fyve bundels bents' (corset-stiffeners made from sandgrass stems), a 'payre bodies' (a bodice) and 'broydered petty coates, pynked and cutte'. In a letter to Sir Thomas Lucy later in the same year, William Duboys describes presenting his 'belovedde childe Eleanor' with 'a carcanett [necklace] of golde enamuled and garnished with smale sparcks of rubyes and divers other toyes'.

Precisely what event or affliction brought this happy young life to a close, we will never know. The inscribed limestone memorial, a copy of which I reproduce hereunder, is undated.

IN MEMORIAM
ELEANORAE,
FILIAE GULIELMI DUBOYSII,
QUAE XXI ANNORUM AETATE
ET IN FLORE PULCHRITUDINIS
E VISU OMNIUM AMANTIUM
SUBLATA EST.
NON OMNIS MORIETUR.

(In memory of Eleanor, daughter of William Duboys, who at the age of twenty-one and in the full flower of her beauty disappeared from the sight of those who loved her. She shall not altogether die.)

One of the factors contributing to the Eleanor 'legend' is that no official record appears to exist of her death. Although the family's principal residence was not Darne Castle but Sands End in Twickenham (which was to burn to the ground in 1665), it is apparent that William and Catherine Duboys came greatly to prefer the air of Warwickshire to that of London. Like Eleanor's brother

Nicholas and her sister-in-law Elizabeth, William and Catherine lie in the churchyard at Upton-on-Arrow, in which parish their demises are duly noted. Of Eleanor, however, no such record exists. Whether the memorial tablet pre-dates the birth of the legend or was struck to confirm it, it is impossible to say. If the inscription reproduced above was intended to serve as her epitaph, however, it is distinctly peculiar that it should be undated.

Scholars have also noted that the choice of the words '*E visu . . . sublata est*' is a curious one in a memorial context, and would seem to exceed by a considerable margin in the euphemism and tact conventional to the medium. The implication is that Eleanor was 'lifted away before the very eyes of her loved ones' as if by some elaborate stage effect.

The inscription's curious final line supports (albeit far from conclusively) the argument that the memorial postdates Eleanor's 'disappearance' by some years. The words are an adaptation of a line by the poet Horace (65–8 BC). Horace was neither well known nor well loved in Elizabethan England: his severe, epigrammatic classicism was antithetical to the romantic spirit of the age. His writing was popularised several decades later, however, by the quintessentially Jacobean Ben Jonson, who in 1640 published a translation of his *Ars Poetica*.

So what does any of this tell us of Eleanor and her mysterious end? Very little, probably, except that the writer of this cryptic memorial wished to excite the curiosity as well as the pity of succeeding generations.

POSTSCRIPTUM. In the library at Darne there exists a copy of Thomas Bright's *Treatise of Melancholy*, written in 1586. The work is in part psychological textbook (Shakespeare, it has been conclusively established, read the Treatise before writing *Hamlet*), and in part Elizabethan book of spells. On the flyleaf of the Darne Castle copy, some unknown contemporary hand has scrawled the following words:

Love, Love no love
No more thou little winged archer O no more as heretofore thou
Love is an eating care a cross. Love is an eating
Quis liberavit me? Lord if thou wilt thou canst make me clean

Could these sad, confused words be those of Eleanor herself? It is certainly tempting to so surmise. We know almost nothing of the life of Eleanor Duboys except that a mystery surrounded her leaving of it. Perhaps it is indeed the case that for as long as this mystery survives, Eleanor Duboys will not altogether die.

Darne Castle, September 1933

'Well,' I said, lowering the pamphlet. 'This is all very . . . edifying. Is this Bright book still in the library?'

'It's been in the British Museum Library for the last fifty years or so,' said Oliver. 'It's easy enough to see if you're interested.'

'That "little winged archer" line is curious, though, isn't it?'

'Under the circumstances, yes, I suppose it is.'

'What kind of a man was your great-grandfather?'

'The brothers he mentions both died at Ypres,' said Oliver. 'Geoffrey was the youngest, and stayed at home because he was lame.'

'Like the boy in the Pied Piper story,' I murmured.

'Yes. Exactly like him. He was an uncharacteristically gentle and cultivated soul.'

'Uncharacteristically?'

'For a Duboys, I mean. Bill, for example, was more of a chip off the old merchant venturer block.'

'And you?'

He frowned at the window's warm glare. 'Oh, I expect the dynasty will limp on one way or another.'

It seemed a curious reply. I fell silent, and when no further comment appeared to be forthcoming, reopened the pamphlet.

'Tell me,' I said, 'I can see why Laurene Forth aren't including all this stuff about dying girls in their press kit, but why did it take you so long to tell me about it?'

'Because I wanted an intelligent outsider's eye cast over the painting, and if I'd told you about the Eleanor legend you would have interpreted everything as pointing to it.'

I felt my hackles rise at his seigneurial tone. 'As it was, I wasn't able to make any sense of it at all.'

'And now you know all there is to know, does the painting make any more sense?'

'Not a lot,' I admitted. 'But tell me something in return: now that you've found those little figures, is the painting worth more than you paid for it?'

'A little more, definitely. How much more will depend on what's waiting under the rest of that paint.'

'Perhaps you're more of a chip off the old block than you give yourself credit for,' I suggested.

'Perhaps I am,' he agreed. 'Do you know what commodity saved the fortunes of this family in the middle of the last century?'

'I don't know, sugar . . . spice . . . all things nice?'

'Close,' said Oliver, looking me straight in the eye. 'It was opium, actually.'

I couldn't get near the Oak Chamber, where they were shooting the portrait sequence. The corridor outside was packed with attendant bodies; all that I could see was the backs of their heads and the bright electric light beyond. Sabrina, the production hairdresser, was trying to shimmy her way out of the mêlée with a tray of brushes and mousses held high above her head.

'Don't even think of it, love,' she said, picking her way over the electrical leads which snaked beneath our feet. 'You won't see anything; they've stuck the camera bang in the doorway for the wide shot and the entire crew's out here in the corridor.'

'How long will they be?'

'My reckoning, at least a couple of hours. They've got the modern to do, and then we've got to change her into the Elizabethan. They all look well settled in to me.'

I was going to miss the whole set-up, I could see. Still, it wasn't vital that I watch every moment of the filming and I had some calls to make. Thanking Sabrina, I turned back to my room.

Kees Reyntiens had left a big A3 photographic envelope on the narrow bed, with the words 'How about this for the cover?' scrawled across it. The print itself, a full-length shot of Dale in the Eleanor costume, was amazing. It had been taken on her first evening, two days ago, as she was stepping from the porch's shadows into the dusty golden light of the terrace. In the background you could see the unfocused outline of the production team: Carlton, Sabrina and John-Paul watching Dale, the cameraman on his crane against the ultramarine sky, the crew crouched around the monitor below. Dale herself, her hands folded over the silk rosettes at the waist of her bodice, was regarding this activity with a kind of wide-eyed, defensive hauteur, as if realising that the step that had taken her from the darkness into the light had also carried her into an era of uncertainty, and possibly of danger. It was a tense, mystical image; I considered it for some minutes and then, marshalling pen and paper, pulled out my phone and rang Directory Enquiries.

It took me an hour to track down Tom Warwick. He had left Exeter several years earlier to take up a post in Colorado, and was now back in England and attached to the English faculty at Durham. His home number there was listed, I discovered – unlike that of anyone I knew apart from my parents – and he was in.

'Sorry,' he began abruptly. 'Just out in the garden mending Dominic's bike. Who's this?'

'My name's Alison MacAteer,' I said. 'Seven or eight years ago I was one of your students.'

'MacAteer . . . Let me see now . . . Dark-haired, rather indolent young woman? Smoked roll-ups? Became a journalist?'

'Sounds like me,' I said.

'My wife reads your stuff from time to time. How can I help you, Alison?'

I got straight to the point. 'Tom, I'm trying to decode a piece of Elizabethan symbolism for an article I'm writing. Cupid and Death, both carrying bows and arrows. Does that say anything to you?'

'Sure it does . . .' The West Country burr suddenly grew faint. 'Dawn, love, get me something to wipe my . . . yes, they're all oily. Kitchen paper or something . . .' His voice returned at full volume. 'Sorry about that; where were we? Yes, Cupid and Death? Well, the story goes back to the old pagan mysteries, Amor as god of death and all that. Alciati published a version, Shakespeare gives it a name-check in *Venus and Adonis*, Ogilby popularised it with his translation of Aesop's Fables in sixteen fifty-something – one, I think – and Shirley wrote a masque called *Cupid and Death* in . . . maybe even in the same year. May I ask what . . .'

'Actually, it's a painting.'

'Anyone we know?'

'Unsigned, but after Robert Peake. Maybe quite a long way after Robert Peake. The figures of Cupid and Death have almost certainly been added later.'

'Right. Well, the story – which is basically the same in all versions – goes as follows. Cupid has been out all day shooting his arrows at young couples, and Death has been equally busy at a battle. Exhausted, they end up staying at the same inn and get drunk together. In the morning, hung-over, Death gets up early to – how does Ogilby put it? – to "breakfast at a massacre", and takes Cupid's arrows with him by mistake. Cupid follows later, taking Death's arrows, and makes his way to a lovers' grove. The results can be imagined: lovers slain, the natural order reversed, blah blah blah. In Shirley's masque the dilemma is resolved by the introduction of a *deus ex machina*: the god Mercury intervenes, the arrows get handed back to their rightful owners and the natural order is restored, but in Aesop and Ogilby's version Death keeps back a handful of Cupid's arrows for himself and slips Cupid others which have been "dipt i'th Stygian Lake".'

'Sneaky,' I said.

'Very sneaky indeed. Death's deceit is thus perpetuated for all time.'

'So what might the figures of Cupid and Death mean if they were included in a painting whose subject may or may not have been Eleanor Duboys.'

'The Wraith of Darne?'

'You know the story?'

'Vaguely. Died young? Disappeared? Something like that?'

'Something like that. What I'm wondering is if the figures might refer to her early death? Death's arrow found her before Cupid's did, that sort of thing?'

'It's possible. But we're not talking about the big Darne Castle portrait, are we? The Gheerhaerts, or whatever it is, where she's got up as a nymph of Diana?'

'The Peake? No, we're not. We're talking about a not-very-good copy, with these Cupid and Death figures added on.'

'OK, Alison, look, the answer is that I can't think of anything right at this moment. Give us a ring this time tomorrow, and I'll see what I can turn up. Can't promise anything, but I'll flip through a few books.'

'That'd be brilliant, Tom.'

'My pleasure. Now, if you'll excuse me, I've a slow puncture to attend to.'

At dinner that night, Dale placed herself next to me. I was beginning to understand how she worked now, and for the first twenty minutes or so I more or less ignored her in favour of Kees, who was sitting on my other side. Eventually, when Sheldrake called Kees's name and he looked away, Dale nudged my thigh with her knee.

'No one's done that to me,' I said, 'since I was at school.'

'Did your parents visit you in hospital?' she asked. We had been served Astrakhan caviar as a first course, and although everyone else had finished theirs she was still nibbling pensively away, egg by tiny egg.

'My dad did a few times. My mum came once, at the beginning, but not after that. She doesn't travel very well.'

'And how was it when they came?'

'Awful. It was very soon after the crash, and I just cried. Do you want some of this wine?'

'No. Did it feel good that they came, though?'

'It didn't feel good or bad. They were just there, along with my brother and his girlfriend, and I cried, and then the nurse took them away, and that was it.'

'Were you worried about . . . your face?'

'That came later, when I was able to think about the future. One of the things about acute physical pain, you see, is that it locks you into the present. You're pretty much incapable of considering anything else. Later, though, yes, I was . . . well, completely terrified, actually. Especially of people like you.'

'I'm trying to imagine how you looked before.'

I shrugged. 'Longer hair. Fewer scars. Couple of pounds heavier.'

'Have you got a guy?'

'Not really.'

'And did you think about dying before you had the crash?'

'Never. I was obviously worried about it at some level, though, because I worked in fashion for six years.'

'But when you were, like you said, looking down at yourself dying on that operating table, where were *you*?'

'Up near the ceiling somewhere, it must have been, given what I remember of my viewpoint. Certainly above the main lighting fixtures.'

'And what do you think would have happened if you had died?'

I closed my eyes and shook my head. 'You've asked me that before, Dale, and I don't know. Perhaps I never even had that experience at all. Perhaps I just read about it somewhere and thought it had happened to me.'

'No,' she said vehemently, placing her hand on my forearm. 'It happened. You know it happened. And when you were lying there in the ice it was the same. You were there, but you were in another place too.'

'Dale,' I said, razor-edging my voice as I turned to face her, 'we either stop this right now, or you start opening up to me. You've helped yourself to my life and my friendship, which is fine, but if you're not going to give anything back, then forget it. I've nothing more to say.'

It was a stratagem of last resort, and it wasn't the first time that I'd employed it. Her eyes froze with shock, and her hands twitched at the linen table-napkin in her lap.

Eventually she nodded. 'Not here, though, OK?'

On the roof the silence was absolute; about us was the faint scent of the night. For ten minutes we stood at the balustrade without speaking, looking down at the terrace, the gardens and the colourless grassland beyond.

'I was six when my father left,' she began abruptly. 'My sister DuToine was five. When he had been gone for a week, Toine asked me where he was. I told her all I knew, which was that he had gone to Seattle. He'd be back any time, I told her, and for some reason I was sure that he'd come back at night. The trailer we lived in was an old single-wide, easy to rob, but for months after he went I didn't allow Ma to lock it, for fear he'd come back and find himself locked out. She'd try, from time to time, and I'd scream and yell and then DuToine would scream and yell and . . . well, you can imagine. The one thing I was certain of, see, was that it was my fault; that it was my badness that had driven him away. There was a dream I used to have all the time where I'd be, like, surrounded by this light, and I'd know that as long as the light was there everything would be all right, and then the light would shatter like glass, and I'd know that if I could just fit the pieces together there was still a chance, but then the pieces would break into further pieces and those pieces into further pieces until they were like the stars in the sky – dust - and I'd give up. And at that exact moment I'd wake up crying, knowing that the thing I'd really given up was the chance of getting them back together.'

I lit a 555. Far below in the valley, in the lamp-black shadow of one of the oaks, something frightened the deer, and they fled away like ghosts.

'Five years ago,' Dale continued, 'a man called Paulie Cvetic shot my mother. People said it was an accident, but I knew that the accident was that it was her and not me that got hit. I was sure, you see, that I was no longer worthy of being alive. DuToine had set up with some guy by that time . . .'

I tried to feel what she had felt but I couldn't. The world was full of people who had suffered similar experiences and would have been able to empathise with her, but I was not one of them. My distress index, I guess, had different entries. I was sorry for her – I wished that she was happy – but I couldn't feel her pain.

Instead, filtering the quotes out of her stream of consciousness, I got on with my job. I had a good verbal memory, and by assigning key words to each quote, and arranging these key words into mnemonic sentences, I was able to store whole racks of conversation. It was a short-term technique, and given that I had the Acu-Sonic right there on my belt I'd much rather have recorded her, but I'd promised to her face that I wouldn't.

Almost the worst of it was that after listening to her for a couple of minutes, I could have written the rest of the script myself. There was a numbing universality about experiences of the kind that Dale had suffered, and they were invariably described in the same numbed, banal terms. I knew long before she told me so that the moment when she first saw herself on film was the moment she had begun to value herself as a person. I knew long before she told me so that fantasy could be real in a way that reality never could. I knew long before she told me that she considered her performing persona to be quite separate from her real self, and that she referred to this performing persona – this other Dale – as 'she'.

Perhaps this was why she had never spoken to a journalist before: because there was nothing new to say. In the end I stopped her. It was clear that there was no catharsis, no relief afforded by the expression of her unhappiness. In addition to which, I needed to get some quotes down before I forgot them all.

So I cut her off short. Dismissed her.

'Will you come down when you've finished your work?' she asked. 'I'm going to walk by the lake.'

'. . . and those pieces into further pieces until they were like the stars in the sky – dust – and I'd give up. And at that exact moment I'd wake up crying, knowing that the thing I'd really given up was the chance of getting them back together . . .'

I closed my eyes. How did the next one go?

'A man called Paulie Cvetic shot my mother. People said it was an accident . . .'

Behind me I heard the cautious opening of the stair-tower door, and closed my notebook.

'Dale told me I'd find you up here,' said Stephen, placing his hands on the balustrade. 'I'm afraid I rather had to race off this afternoon.'

My eyes fell to his loosely rolled white shirtsleeve and the hard, clean line of his forearm, and I felt a crawl of desire.

'It's so hot,' I replied. 'I thought there might be a breeze up here. Do you mind if I just finish what I was doing?'

He shook his head.

'Don't look,' I said.

'I won't,' he promised, moving to the end of the balustrade and folding his arms.

Hurriedly, I scribbled down the rest of the quotes. When I had finished, I saw that he was looking out over the balustrade at the valley, shading his eyes as if from the sun.

'In Elizabethan times,' he said, 'the ladies would gather up here on the roof when the men went out hunting or coursing or hawking. Vistas were cut through the forest so that they could watch the chase.'

'And see returning husbands in plenty of time?'

He smiled. 'Quite possibly. These pavilions are well suited to . . . private business.'

We regarded each other in silence. The night air seemed to shiver electrostatically around us.

'So how's movie stardom?' I asked.

'I wouldn't know. So far I haven't been within two hundred yards of a camera. I haven't had to move yet, either. They could have dressed a shop-window mannequin in my costume and no one would have been any the wiser.'

'I suspect people probably pick up on the vital signs,' I said, lighting a 555. 'Even at a distance.'

'You suspect?'

'I suspect.'

As I smoked, I was aware of his quiet, patrolling tread amongst the columns and the obelisks. For as long as my cigarette burnt, I knew, he would keep his distance. Finally, sensing him behind me, I trod it out, and took a half-step backwards until my shoulders rested against his chest. Soon, although not immediately, I felt the controlled weight of his hands on my shoulders. I closed my eyes, and taking his fingers in mine, drew them to my mouth.

There was no response. His hand remained at my mouth, hard but untensed, a passive gag. I bit, gently at first, and then harder, but he still didn't move. I was sure that he wanted me, though, and unbuttoning my shirt I pulled his hand down to my breast. Again, nothing. His palm overlaid my beating heart as solicitously and uninterestedly as if it had been my own, neither moving nor withdrawing.

This was too much, and wrenching his hand from my breast I bit the ball of his thumb as hard and as deep as I could, bit until I felt the metallic jump of his blood. And even then he made almost no sound, just gasped a little.

'I'm sorry,' I whispered, aghast. 'Your hand. What have I done?' My fingers were trembling, and I couldn't re-button my shirt.

'It's OK,' he said, his eyes watching me with a kind of ravenous desperation that didn't make any sense to me at all.

'I've obviously got it all wrong,' I went on. 'I thought you . . .' I shrugged and shook my head, furious now, although with him or myself I wasn't sure.

'I did,' said Stephen. 'I do. I'm sorry, I just . . .'

'You just what?' I protested. 'I'm here, and all yours, so what's wrong?'

'Phoebe,' said Stephen quietly, half turning.

'*Phoebe*!' I stared at him. 'You're being *faithful* to *Phoebe*? Is that what this is about?'

'She's very fond of you, apart from anything else.'

'So? I'm fond of her, too, but she'll live. I mean . . .'

He said nothing. I circled round to face him, still struggling with my shirt. 'You're worried about her finding out, is that it?'

'I'm going downstairs,' he said very quietly, flexing his thumb experimentally. 'Once again, I'm sorry.'

'Are you frightened of me?'

'Look, Alison, I really don't want us to have this conversation.'

'So what're you going to do?' I asked, moving to block his path. 'Hit me?'

'Is that what you want?' he said, sucking the blood from his hand.

'Maybe,' I said. 'Maybe not. You'll never know.'

'Probably not,' he said. 'Good night.'

I watched him go, appalled at myself. Taking what you wanted without regard to the consequences was not quite as easy as Phoebe had made it out to be. Perhaps you had to be born to it.

I decided to go to bed, to allow Dale to walk the banks of the lake undisturbed. There was such a thing as too much information, and I suspected that, having started, there would be no stopping her. Tomorrow was the final day, the day of the masque, and I needed sleep.

Some thoughtful soul had opened the windows in my room, and as I undressed I heard – or thought I heard – the crunch of the gravel below. When I looked out, however, I saw only the parterre and the dark avenues of yew. My sheets, when I finally collapsed beneath them, were blessedly cool.

12

By ten thirty, breakfast was still in full swing. It was a much larger and noisier affair than any I had so far attended; at least a dozen tables had been called into service, and the air was reverberant with hammering and sawing and the stop-start grumble of trucks.

The masque, Sheldrake had decided, was going to be as extravagant an affair as those of four centuries ago. In line with his 'real people' policy, he had persuaded Phoebe to invite a hundred or so of her closest friends to appear as courtiers and spectators. And despite the fact that she had only started contacting them a couple of days earlier, it seemed that most had accepted and at least half had arrived early.

'It's the blood,' Phoebe had explained to me when I had expressed my surprise. 'And the architecture. It makes them ruttish, Belle, like it does you. They'll suck anything to get at that old money taste.'

The filming, Phoebe had decided, would segue into a costume party on the terrace and the lawn. Very grand, very expensive, very people-like-us. There would be no press, of course, except for me, and I wasn't really *press* press, was I?

As I stepped into the cedar's broad shadows, I paused, reminded of my first arrival five days earlier. I felt something of the same uncertainty now, something of the same sharp terror of the unsympathetic eye. Disposed around the long white tables were at least fifty new faces, a few of which – a scowling novelist and his beach-baby wife, a bad-boy conceptual sculptor, the latest Ophelia, a shrieking trio of heiresses – I recognised at once. *En masse* they were a terrifying assembly, and all appeared to know each other well. I looked around for an ally but Phoebe was nowhere to be seen, nor was Dale, and Gina was surrounded by admirers. At the table in front of me the novelist was holding court.

'Beautiful?' he was saying. 'Models, beautiful? Have you ever looked at their feet? They're enormous, like late-period Giacometti. And those death-march legs and hammocky crutches and crushed-in-at-the-sides heads that they all have . . . If they were animals, it would be considered cruel to breed them.' He looked up at me. 'Wouldn't it?'

The question was not one I was in the mood to answer at that moment, and in some desperation I searched for Stephen. But Stephen, I swiftly concluded, was wherever Phoebe was, re-telling the story of how I had leapt on him with bared fangs in the moonlight. Phoebe, I hoped, would be amused by the story, and it occurred to me that she may even have orchestrated the whole event for my benefit as a kind of lesson in social priorities.

Eventually I spotted Fiona Duff sitting by herself – when not at Sheldrake's side she tended to be left alone – and made my way over. Figgy was subdued, and I guessed that she was wondering whether, at the production's end, she would be dismissed with the rest of the cast. As if in denial of this possibility she had assumed, unasked, a sort of liaison role, and taken to issuing Buckingham Palace-like communiqués. Charles and Fletcher were really pleased by the way things had gone, she told me seriously, and everyone was very excited by the plans for the masque.

'And how have you found Dale?' I asked, pouring myself a cup of coffee and ashing my cigarette into the saucer.

'Oh, we all think she's fabulous. You'd never believe all this was new to her. And that face. Have you seen the rushes?'

'Not yet. But tell me, why are all these guest *artistes* here so early? We're not shooting till tonight, are we?'

'No, but everyone's been told to be here for eleven. There's fittings, and some kind of rehearsal thing, and then we've all got to learn this dance.'

'Dance?' I ground out my cigarette. 'You're kidding!'

'I'm not, but don't worry, they won't make it difficult. They can't afford to.'

'But God, dancing, though, what a grotesque idea.'

'I don't know,' said a familiar voice. 'I don't remember you finding it so bad!'

My heart lurched and I was suddenly and painfully breathless. 'Dan!' I heard myself say. 'What a surprise!' And there he was, and Hermia too, and a woman I recognised from her newspaper photograph as Claudine Le Besque, proprietress of the Prima model agency and Hermia's lover. While the women made a fuss of Figgy – like Hermia, she was a Prima client – Dan Fortess stared straight at me.

'You look . . . fantastic,' he said.

I nodded, unsure what to say. In the course of our last conversation he'd described me, amongst other things, as 'a rattlesnake' and 'a bitch on heat'.

'So do you, Dan,' I managed. And he did. When he'd come to visit me in the hospital two months earlier he'd been at a low ebb, both personally and professionally, but it was clear that those days were now behind him. The wariness had departed his eyes, had been replaced by the cool, searching burn that I remembered from our first meeting. His beauty – so easy, so casually bestowed – made me want to laugh out loud. He blew my defences away like straw.

And his wife, if Hermia was still his wife. Although scrubbed of make-up and wearing nothing more exotic than Levis and a T-shirt, there was a kind of reckless, anti-gravitational shimmer about Hermia that I'd never seen before. 'This is the famous Alison, Claudie,' she announced, wrinkling her nose at me in an ironic, all's-well-that-ends-well kind of a way.

'I've heard a lot about you,' said Claudine Le Besque. She was a sharp, neatly made little thing with the eyes of a nocturnal insectivore and a lot of brushed gold about her person.

'All of it bad, I hope,' I said, a little more defensively than I had intended.

'Not all of it,' said Claudine, flaming a heavy Dupont lighter beneath a pair of Gitanes and passing one to Hermia.

'You're in the film, aren't you, Alison?' said Hermia. 'Phoebe showed us a cast list.'

'That's right,' I said. 'I'm giving up the day job for stardom. Where is Phoebe, as a matter of interest?'

'She was inside five minutes ago. No sign of Oliver, though.'

'He's probably up in his studio,' I said.

'Yes, I expect he'll keep a lowish profile. Phoebe's friends aren't exactly a heavyweight crowd.' She shook her head. 'How funny that it's you writing this piece, though. Of all the people I've ever met I'd have said you and Phoebe were the least likely to . . .'

'Meet? Not really. The moment you upper-class lot start cashing in your assets you meet people like me. We're like enzymes. We're part of the process.'

'Are you sure,' asked Hermia mildly, 'that it's not you who's been processed? That it's not you who's been absorbed into her world?'

'Every story's somebody's world,' I said. 'You check in; you check out.'

'Whip in, whip out and wipe,' said Dan.

'Oh, *écoute*, Dan . . .'

'Oh, *écoute* yourself, Claudie. Alison and I understand each other.'

I was fascinated by this set-up. Were Hermia and Dan still living together? Was Dan still with Tracey? He didn't look ground down by events, that was for sure; in fact, for the first time in our long if irregular acquaintance he looked entirely his own man. He had also not taken his eyes off me since his arrival, which in this company did my confidence no harm at all.

'Could that be Kees Reyntiens over there?' Hermia asked me. 'The last time I saw him was at a house party in Suffolk. I went to my room after dinner – or what I thought was my room – and found him crucified on the back of the door.'

'What did you do?' I asked.

'Well, what *do* you do? As your colleague Jacinta might say: I made my excuses and left.'

'Former colleague,' I corrected her, and there was a moment's silence.

'What projects have you got waiting?' asked Dan.

'Nothing. Like I just said, I'm giving up the day job.'

'So what will you do?' asked Claudine.

'Right now,' I said, lighting another 555, 'I don't even want to think about asking myself that question.'

'So that . . . that business last winter has meant changes for us all, then,' said Hermia, waving away my smoke. 'Even you.'

'I guess,' I said.

At eleven a.m. precisely, Charles Sheldrake walked out of the house, dumped a pile of document folders in front of Figgy, and took his place, radio microphone in hand, against the grey trunk of the cedar. Obediently, we all swivelled round in our chairs, and as he stood there smiling and nodding, Figgy began handing out the folders.

Sheldrake started by welcoming us, thanked us for our punctuality, and apologised in advance for any *longueurs* that might occur over the course of the day. In return, he promised us an event fully worthy of the high summer of the Elizabethan Renaissance. Tonight we were to enact a masque, and he begged our indulgence for a moment's explanation.

The masque in England, he told us, was born of the fantastical spectacles presented to the Queen on her Accession Day or during the court's summer progress. As she moved between the great country houses, their owners fell over themselves to outdo each other in the scale and imaginative power of the entertainments they mounted for her, and the highlight of these festivals was invariably a masque.

So what did these events look like? Well, there was only one known representation of an Elizabethan masque in progress, and this, the *Memorial Portrait* of Sir Henry Unton, painted in 1596, we would find reproduced in our folders, so if we would kindly . . .

Our production tonight, Sheldrake explained, would be loosely based on the Unton portrait. The masquers would proceed to the lakeside where the Duboys family and their retinue would be feasting. They would present themselves, a short ballet would ensue, and there would be general dancing. The intention was to shoot the entire sequence in a single take (applause, cheers) and with luck, rehearsal and a multiple camera set-up, this ought to be just about possible. ('It'll have to be possible,' Figgy murmured to me, reclaiming her place. 'This is a one-take crowd if ever I saw one.')

Which brought him, Sheldrake continued, to the subject of dancing (groans, whistles). Jonet here – and a whip-thin ballerina type stepped to his side and bowed ironically to us – would see us in groups and teach us our steps. Nothing difficult, he promised. One take, right?

One take, we nodded.

Right, if we could turn to the cast list on page three . . .

We had been divided, I saw, into three main groups: masquers, banqueters and spectators. The masque company consisted of Dale, Gina, Hermia, Fiona and Jonet as nymphs of Diana, and various male guests who would be playing the roles of a stag, a barbarian, a fire spirit, a wood spirit, Cupid and Death.

At these last, I stared. Was this pure coincidence, or had Sheldrake perhaps seen Oliver's painting? Was there a connection of some sort, or were Cupid and Death, as Tom Warwick had indicated, simply popular and ubiquitous allegorical figures, as recognisable to today's audiences as they would have been to the seventeenth century's.

I would ask him. Sheldrake's secretive nature and dislike of explaining his work meant that a simple question rarely elicited a simple answer, but I was happy to risk being snubbed. The business of the painting fascinated me, and although common sense told me that any attempt on my part at decoding it was almost certainly doomed to failure, and that I had neither the resources nor the background knowledge required for such a task, the barb of curiosity had been set. Oliver could have confided in Sheldrake or in any number of experts, but he had confided in me. It piqued me not to be able to come up with an answer.

I was a banqueter, I saw from the cast list, as were Claudine, Dan, the novelist, the Duboys family and a dozen others. The musicians were members of a professional ensemble specialising in Elizabethan music, and those guests who were neither masquers nor banqueters nor musicians – some sixty or seventy of them altogether – were to be spectators.

The close focus, of course, would be on Dale, and to a lesser degree on the other masquers. As long as they did what they were meant to do, it probably wouldn't matter too much what the rest of us got up to. Figgy was right, this was a one-take crowd, spoilt, rich and easily bored; they certainly wouldn't stand around patiently like professional extras while the shot was being re-composed.

'Dance class here on the lawn at eleven thirty, then,' finished Sheldrake. 'All banqueters and masquers please to attend. Thank you all very much.'

He came towards us, and Figgy introduced him to Dan, Hermia and Claudine, whom he greeted with elaborate courtesy. There was a general reassignment of chairs.

'Did the talk sound all right?' Sheldrake wondered in the ensuing conversational vacuum. 'Not too boring and academic and generally . . .?'

Yes, we murmured, fine, and no, absolutely not.

'Could I just ask you,' I said, pulling out a notebook, 'are we recreating a particular, named masque?'

'Not as such,' said Sheldrake, pouring himself coffee. 'Elements of several, though.'

I straightened my back and attempted to sound like a journalist.

'Including Shirley's *Cupid and Death*?

'Yes,' said Sheldrake, inclining his head with a small appreciative smile, 'including James Shirley's *Cupid and Death*.'

'But . . . I mean, why incorporate the figure of Death into a perfume commercial? Isn't that a bit counter-productive?'

Sheldrake lifted the apostle spoon from his coffee, allowed it to drip into the cup, sucked it dry, put it down on the linen tablecloth and looked at me appraisingly.

'The product, remember, is called Eternal Summer, which, as you know, is a quote from Shakespeare's eighteenth sonnet whose subject, broadly speaking, is beauty made immortal.

> ' "But thy eternal summer shall not fade,
> Nor lose possession of that fair thou owest;
> Nor shall Death brag thou wander'st in his shade . . ."

'Death, you see, or at least the defeat of Death, is the unstated subject of the commercial. It's only fair that we should get a glimpse of the old boy, don't you think?'

'You don't think he constitutes negative imagery?'

'Negative . . . positive . . . These are strange days, Alison. People are much possessed by death; they see the skull beneath the skin. Have you ever tasted Montrachet?'

'The wine? Probably not, if it's expensive enough to serve as a metaphor.'

'You would remember if you had, because the experience is sublime. It connects – like certain pieces of music, certain lines of poetry – to longings so deeply buried that we have forgotten that we're prey to them. We hear a piece of music, we read a sonnet, we catch a glimpse of a face on an old piece of film, and for a moment – just for a moment – we see the human condition for what it is, and we understand that at the heart of the sublime waits Death.'

There was silence. Sheldrake smiled at me.

'You know, I'm almost tempted to get a bottle of Montrachet up from the cellar and pour you a glass and look into your eyes and watch the moment when you understand that what gives meaning to that golden, celestial taste is the whisper, deep within it, of absolute corruption. I would pay a hundred pounds cash, right now, to look into your eyes and see that moment.'

I looked round. They were all watching me. Hermia smiled and picked up one of the folders. I nodded. 'OK,' I said slowly. 'I take your point. Death, then.'

' "But thy eternal summer *shall not fade* . . ." ' mused Dan. 'Say what you like, the man knew how to write a copy-line.'

'So many of these new perfumes *do* fade,' said Hermia. 'I don't expect this one's any exception. Has anyone tried it, by the way?'

'Will you, my lady?' asked Dan.

'Aye, sir,' I replied breathlessly, planting my hands on his shoulders for leverage as he lifted me by the waist and swung me round. 'I probably will.'

'You're very light.'

'No heart,' I explained. We were rehearsing a dance called a volta, and to my vast surprise I was enjoying myself. I have never been much of a dancer, but for some reason I could manage this Elizabethan stuff. Perhaps it was because, as Sheldrake had explained, you were supposed to remain yourself while you did it, and not worry about mistakes. At any rate I was leaping around in triple time with the best of them as a trio of bearded early instrumentalists piped and sawed and plucked away.

We had been going for over an hour. Jonet had lined up all the masquers and banqueters on the lawn in a rectangle, and had provided us with the basic steps of the volta, the coranto and the measure. When it came to the performance only the masquers would perform the volta; most of us were banqueters, and with our more elaborate costumes were limited to the slower dances, which in truth were little more than sweeping walks. The pace, even so, was beginning to take its toll on the heavier smokers and the harder drug-users: the novelist, I noticed, was in a particularly bad way, as were all three of the heiresses. Oliver and Phoebe, on the other hand, seemed to be bearing up well; they had been placed together by Sheldrake and now circled each other with affectionate and decorous irony.

From a canvas-backed chair in the shadow of the cedar, Fletcher Walsh watched the proceedings like some seersucker-suited Pharaoh. He didn't especially like Phoebe, I had noticed, and he didn't show any sign of especially liking her friends. Perhaps it was the chaos of it all. While Charles Sheldrake appeared completely at home amongst the upper-class anarchy and amateurism, Fletcher seemed strained, and I made a mental note to avoid him.

At twelve thirty, Jonet let us go, and Dan and I sank exhausted to the ground. We didn't really flirt with each other, and we were beyond suggestive conversations. He had asked me before the rehearsal if I was staying on after the performance; I had said that I was, and that had been enough. We would submit to the day's formal structure. We would wait until dark.

'So how's it been?' I asked him. 'All change with Hermia, obviously.'

'Less change than you might think,' he said. 'We still live together, for example.'

'And Claudine?'

'Claudine's about from time to time. The children like her. Life goes on.'

'And Tracey?'

'Tracey sold her story. It was on the inside pages of a couple of the tabloids, ran till the Sunday, and died. After that she modelled 'Mistress Wear' for *GQ*, stripped for German *Playboy*, guested on a couple of TV sports quizzes, and opened a heat-resistant tile showroom in Braintree; I think that's her career arc to date.'

'Have you seen her?'

'No.'

'Miss her?'

'Mmm . . . in ways.'

'The sex?'

'I suppose so. There really wasn't much except the sex. Is that lunch I can smell?'

'It's probably me. I'm going up to have a shower and change.'

'Alison,' he said, 'can I ask you something?'

I touched my finger to his lips. 'Not now.'

'There's something we have to . . .'

'I know,' I said. 'Later, OK?'

At lunch I found myself sitting between Kees and Claudine. I was favourably impressed by the Prima agency's proprietress – being French, she not only smoked between courses, she smoked between oysters, between scallops, between individual *fraises de bois* – and it occurred to me that a quote or two wouldn't go amiss. What did she think of Dale? I asked her.

'For me,' she replied, 'this is a very significant piece of casting. We no longer believe, you see, that a performer comes to each role with a *tabula rasa*. A performer arrives with a history of past roles – some of them played out in real life – and in every new role played is detectable something of this history.'

'So what do you think will be detectable here?'

'Oh . . . a certain genre of despair, perhaps.'

'And is that good?'

'Oh, absolutely. You see, for years now agencies like mine have been providing faces without histories. The girls have life stories, of course – they date rock stars and actors and *prestidigitateurs* – but they don't have histories. What do you know about Gina Tagliaferri, for example, that's more interesting than the fact that she's a beautiful woman? Nothing. What more do you know about

Hermia Page, on the other hand? Well, that's another story because Hermia – *grace à toi*, Alison – now has a history. She is a woman whose sexuality is more interesting than her beauty, and in consequence her career has had a renaissance. People are tired of pretty faces; they want that history – that *reality* – attached to their product. You, Alison, *par example*' – she drew a finger across my mouth and cheek – 'look at you, *chérie*. Your history is inscribed right there in your face. I could get you a fashion shoot tomorrow.'

'Get away!' I said, not displeased.

'She's right,' said Kees, lifting his Nikon to his eye and loosing off a thoughtful half-dozen frames. 'Damage is Beauty.'

As the meal drew to a close, Sheldrake stood up and requested that we reassemble in an hour for a walk-through. I tried to feel blasé, but I had to admit to more than a prickle of excitement concerning the night ahead. The heat of the day, the rise and fall of conversation, the reverberant clang of scaffolding as lighting towers and camera platforms rose from the lawn: all contributed to a mounting sense of event, of occasion.

And for a moment as I sat there, the voices around me seemed to recede, to be replaced by the sound of my own heartbeat. I felt a curious tautness, as if my features were being drawn back over the bones of my face. I could feel Dan's gaze on me, was dizzied by the knowledge of his desire and by the lurching void of my own future. Whom would I see, I wondered, if I were to look in a mirror?

'I think that man's trying to get your attention,' said Claudine.

I snapped to. It was Oliver, pointing interrogatively up at the house.

This time Phoebe came to the studio too. For some reason I had assumed that she had little to do with her brother and his work, but from their conversation as we mounted the stone staircase and filed down the narrow, portrait-lined corridor to the studio, it was clear that she had been following the progress of the painting's cleaning as closely as I had. Oliver himself appeared gripped by a pale, secret excitement, and looked back at me almost anxiously as he fumbled for his keys.

'You locked the studio?' I asked, as he threw the door open for his sister.

'It's those vermin downstairs,' said Phoebe. 'They'd loot the place, left to themselves.' She slowed as she saw the panel and approached it almost warily. For a moment she forgot that I was there, and then, almost unwillingly, stepped aside so that I could see it.

It was still the same painting, just. All of the old varnish had been removed, and the painted surface of the panel was now an unreflective matt. The exposed tempera pigment, however, seemed to absorb the light which poured through the tower's bay window, and to release it as a dull, pulsing glimmer. The skin tones, in particular, emitted a sort of pearly luminescence. Most of this pigment had previously been invisible; an entire layer of overpainting had been lifted away in the cleaning process, and what had formerly looked like a sort of pub-sign version of the Robert Peake portrait now stood revealed as a perfect miniature edition. Whether it was painted by Peake I could not have said, but it was obvious even to my untrained eye that the panel was the work of a skilled and fluent hand. Instead of hovering shapelessly against the darkness, the fair-haired young woman in the green bodice and skirt now stood on the bank of a narrow stream amongst wild grasses and tiny blood-red flowers. From the branches of a tree overhanging the stream were suspended three *impresa* shields, one painted with a flaming heart, one with the head of a stag, the third with a rearing bear.

It was the figure, though, and that familiar heart-shaped face, which held me. There was a sadness in the sapphire eyes, a kind of tender acquiescence, which was absent from the Peake portrait. It seemed to me that she saw – as we saw – the pale figures of Cupid and Death treading the sky. In the bottom right-hand corner of the panel the gold-leaf inscription was now complete: 'ELEANOR DUBOYS PERDITA MDIC AET SUAE XXI'.

' "Lost in the year 1599, aged twenty-one",' read Phoebe. 'And here she is again.'

'It's unbelievable,' I said. 'It's . . . it's just *exquisite*, but . . .'

'It was very, very skilfully done,' said Oliver. 'Opaque glazes to blur the outlines, a deliberately crude overpainting of the face and figure, tinted varnishes and scumbles, a bit of seventeenth-century dirt worked in . . . everything, in fact, to give the impression that this was not a piece of work meriting serious investigation. Just that single word, "Perdita", to engage the curiosity and perhaps stay the hand that might otherwise have slung it on the fire.'

'But . . . *why*?' I said, my eyes following the folds of Eleanor's dress, the jewel-shot lace of her sleeve, the dark-feathered arrow between her fingers. 'What could possibly have been the point?'

'Let me put it like this,' said Oliver. 'Whoever was responsible for overpainting this panel – and we've got absolutely no way of telling whether it was the original artist or not – whoever it was, anyway, knew exactly what he was doing. He was covering it up so that it could be uncovered again.'

'How do you mean?' I asked, watching Phoebe, who was examining the painting with a heavy magnifying glass.

'I mean that thick though it was, every layer and glaze and scumble of that overpainting was designed to be lifted off without damaging the original. It took a bit of nerve to dig as deep as I did, but once I was up and running and it was all coming off, I realised that I was just . . . following the dots. Somewhere between three and a half and four centuries ago, and probably right here in this house, someone sat down and planned this moment of discovery.'

I stared at the painting, at the winged figures of Cupid and Death and the *impresa* shields and the slender, luminescent figure of Eleanor Duboys.

'You should ask Charles Sheldrake,' I said. 'He's an expert on all this.'

'We're rather off Charles Sheldrake these days,' said Oliver. 'We preferred the idea of you.'

'We wanted to ask *you*, Belle,' said Phoebe, slipping an arm round my waist and hooking her thumb in the front belt-loop of my Daryl Ks, 'because you can keep a secret.'

'What on earth makes you think that?' I asked. 'Other people's secrets have paid for everything I own.'

'Oh, we're not worried about other people's secrets,' said Phoebe, lifting my hand to her mouth and giving it an exploratory bite, and then a rather harder one.

'Are you not going to tell anyone about this painting?' I asked Oliver, reclaiming my hand from his sister.

'Not before we know what it means,' he replied.

'What do you think it's worth?'

'More than other people's secrets have bought you,' answered Phoebe. 'I've got rabies, by the way,' she added.

'Is that why you're so afraid of bathwater?' I asked her, and Oliver smiled.

'I told you she was good,' said Phoebe. She turned to me. 'So what do you think, *belle sabreuse*?'

'About the painting?'

'No, sweetheart, about Einstein's General Theory of Relativity; of course about the fucking painting.'

'Will you hand it to me?' I asked Oliver, and he lifted it from the easel. It was warm, and lighter than a child's slate.

'I've never held anything so valuable before,' I said, and they watched me in silence.

'OK,' I said, 'Cupid and Death.' Staring at the painting, I recounted the fable that Tom Warwick had told me.

'Brilliant, Belle,' said Phoebe. 'I *knew* she was right for us.'

'Perhaps,' I continued, 'the figures are suggesting that Eleanor's death was a mistake on the part of the gods? That just when she should have been struck by Love's arrow, she was struck by Death's? Something like that?'

'Makes sense,' agreed Oliver.

'As far as the shields are concerned,' I continued, 'the stag's got to be you lot, and the burning heart is the ascendant spirit or some such. As for the bear, I seem to remember someone telling me that the bear represents the Female Principle.'

'We had a female principal at Winkfield,' murmured Phoebe. 'She was pretty grizzly. The question, I suppose, is was this painted from life at the same time as the Peake, or is it just a copy? Oliver?'

He looked down at the small, heart-shaped face.

'I'd put money on it being an original, painted from life. The expression's different from the big portrait: it's more fatalistic. And if that's the case, then the figures and the inscription – or at least the word "Perdita" – were added later, after her death.' He turned to me. 'That inscription. If there was a *Winter's Tale* connection, would it help us date anything?'

'Not really,' I said. 'The play was first performed in 1611, but Shakespeare based it on a best-seller called *Pandosto* by Robert Greene, which also contains a Perdita – not to mention a father-daughter incest subplot – and was written some time in the 1580s.'

'So actually the truth is that we know nothing,' said Phoebe, her voice hardening. 'We don't know who painted this, we don't know who added the figures and the inscription, we don't know who painted over it all, we don't know when any of this happened, and we don't know why.'

'Look,' I said, 'can I make a suggestion? Suppose we look at the whole thing from a different angle. Let's assume that the covered-up painting was a message of some kind. A message from the past. We don't know who sent it, or when, or why, and we probably never will. So rather than concentrating on the messenger, let's look at the message.'

Oliver nodded. His concentration, I could see, was wavering.

'Supposing you take a portrait of a dead girl,' I said, 'a portrait containing clues as to the reason for her death. You then deliberately overpaint and obscure the whole creation. What message are you sending?'

'That there's been a cover-up?' suggested Phoebe. 'That the truth about the girl and her death have been covered up?'

'Exactly. The overpainting represents the legend. The message is that the truth about her death has been obscured by the legend.'

Oliver looked sleepily doubtful. 'So . . .'

'So clear away the legend – as you've done, Oliver – and see the truth.'

'So what do you think is the truth?' asked Phoebe, touching her forehead to the easel. 'And don't fade out on us now, Oliver, *please*.'

He nodded, heavy-lidded.

'I suspect it's something a little less abstract than a cosmic mistake,' I said to her. 'But tell me something, why the sudden interest? I thought you'd had it with Eleanor.'

'Well, I have and I haven't,' said Phoebe, scratching absently at her armpit. 'I've always had my theories about her.'

'Such as?'

'Look at her, Belle. Look at her eyes. If ever a girl knew how to keep a secret . . .' Behind her, on the sofa, Oliver fell suddenly and heavily asleep.

'Perhaps there is a family resemblance,' I suggested.

'You think I have secrets?' she mused, glancing at her gently snoring brother and winding herself, snake-like, around me.

'I think we're late for this rehearsal thing,' I said, disengaging.

'Oh, fuck that; I'm sure they won't miss us.'

'I want to go.'

'You're a tart, Belle.'

'I still want to go.'

She looked at me sulkily and shrugged.

'Are you and Hermia good friends?' I asked her as we descended the wide stone staircase.

'We were at school,' replied Phoebe. 'Since then it's been a bit off and on. I saw you talking to the new steady at lunch; what's she like?'

'Fairly French, one way and another.'

'So if Hermia's off with Madame, where does that leave Dan?'

I shrugged, Sphinx-like.

'You're *not*!' She stopped dead and stared at me. 'My God, Alison, no man is *safe*. How long have you known him, ten minutes?'

'Seven years,' I said. 'And the really strange thing is that whenever we meet – whenever we collide, really – our lives seem to spin off in new directions. He married Hermia and I became a journalist as a direct consequence of our first meeting. The second time we met he ended up single again and I ended up with a new face. And now here we are again.'

'Best of three falls or a submission.'

'Sort of thing,' I admitted.

'Alison MacAteer?' said the crewcut woman, consulting her clipboard. 'Right. You're over here.'

Murmuring apologies for my lateness, I followed her to the long dining table at the lakeside. Most of the dozen or so seats were already occupied: Dan was there, attended by the heiresses and Claudine Le Besque, and the novelist was deep in conversation with Bridget Duboys. Behind them, unmoving in the glare, lay the lake.

I was directed to a seat between the novelist and an empty chair – Oliver's, I guessed – and I wished that I'd brought sunglasses and a hat. No sooner had I sat down, however, than a phone bleeped, and the crewcut was back at my side. I was Alison, wasn't I? Could I follow her? There had been a change of plan.

Sheldrake and Fletcher Walsh were waiting for me with the masquers, halfway across the lawn. They were grouped about Jonet, who was sitting, clearly in some discomfort, in a canvas director's chair.

'Jonet's having trouble with her knee,' said Sheldrake tersely. 'We need another nymph for tonight.'

'Me?' I asked inanely.

'You seemed to be enjoying yourself this morning,' said Jonet. 'And you're my size, give or take a centimetre or two. Try these on.'

She handed me a pair of low-heeled silk dancing slippers. I looked down at them for a moment, and turned to Gina, who nodded encouragingly. Beyond her, Stephen Faulds raised an amused, interrogative eyebrow.

'Go on,' said Hermia. 'In for a penny . . .'

Conscious of their regard, I lowered myself to the grass, unlaced my baseball boots and pulled the silk slippers on to my sweat-slicked, heat-swollen feet.

They weren't a bad fit. I wriggled my toes experimentally and stood up.

'Good,' said Sheldrake. 'That's settled, then.'

Fletcher Walsh didn't say anything, just watched me with those pale, fastidious eyes and smiled.

After the rehearsal I went to my room and took an aspirin. I couldn't sleep, though. My mind was racing, and I lay there open-eyed as the pillows grew hot beneath my face and the sunlight slowly paled on the French-blue walls. At six o'clock I got up, plunged my face into a basin of tepid water, pulled on my kimono and made my way up to the roof. Others had had the same impulse: Figgy was leaning on the balustrade surveying the lawns, while Gina, a soft-drink can at her elbow, was flicking through *Newsweek* in the long shadow of a chimney stack. There was no breeze, only the faint scent of Gina's hair and of her laundered cotton shirt.

'Hi,' she said. 'Got a cigarette?'

'Not on me,' I said, picking up her condensation-beaded 7-Up can and touching it to my forehead. At the far end of the balustrade, Figgy was as still as the stone.

'Is she OK?' I asked.

'She'll be fine,' said Gina. 'It's just the time of day. You?'

'I'm fine.'

'Looking forward to tonight?'

'Yes and no,' I said. 'I've always been more of a sidelines person. A watcher from the shadows.'

'Not any more,' said Gina. 'As I think you're discovering.'

I digested this for a moment. 'So,' I asked her, 'what will you do next? When this contract is over, I mean.'

She extended her fingers in front of her, and considered them. 'Oh. The next thing on the list, I guess.'

'You sound . . . sort of regretful.'

'I'm not,' she said, picking up the magazine and fanning herself distractedly. 'Not at all. Like I told you, it's just that time of day.'

At six thirty I made my way back down to my room, and seeing the note I had left to remind myself, called Tom Warwick in Durham.

'Alison,' he said, his voice loud at my ear. 'Hello again. Not brilliant news, I'm afraid: I've had a look for you, and I haven't come up with much. There's an engraving of Death stealing Cupid's arrows in Alciati's *Emblematum Libellus* of 1534, and Ogilby's 1651 translation of Aesop has a couple of illustrations, but that's about it. As for their meaning in the context you've described to me, well, your guess is really as good as mine. Some sort of *liebestod*, perhaps. One thing did occur to me, though; have you ever been to Hardwick Hall in Derbyshire?'

'No.'

'You must, you'd enjoy it, and it was talking about Eleanor Duboys that reminded me. Apart from the house itself, which was designed by Robert Smythson, like Darne, there's a very interesting plaster frieze in the High Great Chamber. Bess of Hardwick commissioned it from Abraham Smith around the turn of the century, and there are two sections in particular which might interest you, given our conversation yesterday.'

'Go on,' I said.

'Right. Well, one of them – and it's all the odder when you imagine this vast but rather austere reception chamber built for the visit of the Virgin Queen – is this sado-masochistic scenario showing Cupid being whipped by a naked, big-busted Venus, and the other, tucked away in a corner, shows a nymph of Diana being killed for losing her chastity.'

'What happened to the nymph?'

'Diana turned her into a bear, and she was torn to pieces by hunters.'

I sat there in silence on my bed. I saw from my alarm clock that it was almost time to get changed.

'Hello, Alison? Are you there?'

'Still here. Sorry.'

'It was no picnic, the mythological wild.'

'No,' I said slowly. 'I can see that it wasn't. Thank you, Tom. Thank you very much.'

When I had switched off my phone I opened the leaded window, lit a last 555 and stared out over the knot garden. There was still no breeze.

Crunching out the cigarette on the sill, I made my way to the Long Gallery, where the female masquers were to be made up and changed into costume. The male masquers, banqueters and other cast members had been allocated wardrobe areas on the ground floor, and a kind of damped, distant hysteria crept up the stone river of stairs.

In the Long Gallery, however, all was calm. Carlton and Sabrina were laying out their equipment like ships' surgeons before an engagement, and John-Paul was checking costumes and accessories against a printed list. Five chairs had been placed at the trestle tables, and a jewelled headdress, a pair of silk-rosetted dancing slippers and a hand-written name card stood in each place. My own card was misspelt – Allison, they'd called me – and the name Jonet Dyer was inscribed on the reverse, but I was impressed that they'd troubled to change it. Over the back of each chair hung a long cord of dark olive silk, from which was suspended a tiny bottle of perfume in a gold filigree cage.

'The product?' I wondered out loud.

'The product,' John-Paul confirmed. 'Try it. It's fabulous.'

Like every other fashion or ex-fashion hack I'd ever encountered I was a complete fragrance fascist. For the first six months on the job your dressing table is a department-store counter – free perfume being pretty much the standard lower-echelon press bribe – but then you wise up and either sling the whole lot in the bin or give it to the temp (a thankless gesture, in my case, when it returned to haunt me on Bart's collar, on his skin, in his hair). Thereafter, you use perfume sparingly, and you only bother with the best. By which time, of course, you're beginning to work your way towards the front row at the shows and your bribes are being delivered in carrier bags and on velvet hangers rather than in little cellophane-covered boxes.

Epicure that I was, it had never occurred to me that the Forth product would be anything other than the usual middle-market rubbish, by which I mean an oversweet floral top-dressing over a cloying chemical base. When I had worked the little ground-glass stopper from the bottle and touched it to my wrist, however, I was surprised to discover that Eternal Summer was really very good. It was clever and it was subtle and it was unexpected.

'It's nice,' I said. 'I like it.'

'A kind of dark, mossy green,' said John-Paul.

'Stocks,' said Sabrina. 'Night-scented stocks.'

'Rain,' said Carlton. 'Monsoon rain.' He looked at his watch. 'Are we going to do you, then?'

'Is it time?' I asked.

'It's time.'

Only once had I been made up by anyone other than myself, and that was by Enver Kassapian. I'd never been on a stage, never been on TV, never given a performance of any kind. I'd never even done one of those make-over beauty stories so beloved of the middle-order style magazines because they would have involved close-up photographs and I would have had to sacrifice the invisibility which, in recent years at least, had become part of my stock in trade. In consequence, I found the idea unsettling. How would Carlton react to my re-ordered features? I wondered. What would he make of the corrugations of scar tissue at my eyes and and mouth, of the caterpillar dimpling of my sutures?

In the event he simply studied my face as if it were a circuitry diagram that he had to memorise, adjusted his lights and set to work. It seemed to take a long time – every pore received his thoughtful attention, every lash – and after a few minutes I actually began to enjoy the passivity and curiously distant intimacy of the situation. At intervals I registered the arrival of the others, and heard the murmur of their conversation, but again, as if from a distance. Finally he stood back, and I blinked and opened my eyes. For a moment, as I focused on the mirror at my side, I did not recognise myself. My face was a smooth chalk-white mask, contrasting almost shockingly with the untouched pink of my ears and neck. My mouth was powdered scarlet, fiery suns of blusher had been applied to each cheekbone, and my eyebrows were lamp-black. The transformation was extraordinary. I was a strolling player, a virgin whore, a feral, moon-struck Pulcinella.

'Is that really me?'

'Almost, child,' said Carlton. 'Here.'

It was a small pot of carmine rouge and a sable brush.

'What's this for?' I asked.

'Your nipples.'

'You're kidding?'

'Nope. Director's orders.'

Figgy, Gina and Hermia watched me, amused, as I set to work.

'It's all very well for you lot to smile,' I said ruefully. 'You do this sort of thing every other day. I'm just a simple London girl.'

'Oh yeah?'

It was Phoebe, her hair drawn back in a gold and ruby biliment, her slight, dark form brilliant in a scarlet bodice and flounced silver petticoat. She was carrying a tray, glasses and the largest cocktail shaker I had ever seen.

As John-Paul hooked and eyed me into my masquer's costume I accepted a dry martini. Carlton was working on Dale now, and as he moved around her she sat motionless and silent, her eyes closed. Behind me, the others waited patiently. It was all going to take some time.

In recognition of this fact, perhaps, John-Paul dressed me with almost fetishistic exactitude, perfectly aligning the ribbon ties of my chemisette and my sleeves, minutely adjusting the fall of my chiffon skirts, drawing bodice hook to bodice eye in frowning slow motion. For all its elaborate fastening, however, the costume was so light and insubstantial that at the end of the whole process I felt as physically exposed as if I was standing there in my knickers. More so, in fact, because I was now supposed to be dressed. Lacing my silk chopines, I presented myself uncertainly to Sabrina.

'Not a lot I can do with you, girl,' she said, running her hands experimentally over my tight, two-inch crop. Selecting a band of silver wire fronted by a crescent moon, she fitted it carefully to my head, and threaded it with jasmine flowers from a vase.

'Stay there a sec, could you?' she said. 'I need a Polaroid.'

'Could you do one for me?' I asked her. There were two flashes, and I felt a drop of water trickle behind my ear from the jasmine. As Sabrina gave me the Polaroid, I saw that my hand was shaking.

'You look great,' she said.

'I'm terrified.'

'Have another drink.'

'OK.'

Second martini in hand, I turned to the mirror. I had feared that the costume's transparency would reveal my body and more than my body: that my life and my spirit and my most shameful secrets would somehow be laid bare. In that strange, stomach-emptying moment, however, I saw that the opposite was true, that visibility could be mysterious, that exposure could be a concealment, that transparency could be a disguise. I swallowed the rest of the martini, and an icy recklessness stole through my veins: I was a nymph of Diana now, a huntress, untouchable. I looked into my mirrored eyes, and found power.

*

At eight o'clock, John-Paul's phone rang. It was Sheldrake, to say that the shot was set up and that we should stand by. Slowly, we filed out of the Long Gallery and down the staircase to the Great Hall, where the crewcut woman and the male masquers were waiting for us. They were a bizarre, carnivalesque group. There was a velvet-doubleted gallant wearing the mask and antlers of a stag, a man in a costume entirely composed of oak leaves, a fiery spirit in a tunic of crimson plumes, a woad-painted barbarian, whom I recognised as the conceptual sculptor, a fleshly juvenile Cupid in a pink body-stocking, and at their head, in jet-black watered silk, Stephen Faulds as Death. The nymphs descended to a spatter of appreciative applause, bows and smiles were exchanged, and then the crewcut woman gestured us to silence and led us out to the twilit terrace. There, a dozen torch-bearers were standing around, testing the ignition of their gas-fuelled torches. Briskly, the crewcut woman marshalled them into two files and the masquers into the formation that we had rehearsed that afternoon.

'All torches working? Everybody ready? Yes, Darren?'

'Toilet,' said Cupid.

The crewcut murmured tersely into her headset, strode back into the house and called for a wardrobe assistant.

'His mum's Dale's stand-in,' Figgy explained to Hermia, who was watching with some amusement. 'Charles likes to use real people when he can. I don't mean like you, Alison,' she added hastily. 'You're not real.'

'Darren's pretty real,' said Hermia.

I glanced at Dale, whom I had not heard utter a single word over the course of the evening. Compared to the rest of us, her transformation had been minimal. Her lips had been reddened slightly, and her eyelashes darkened, but that was all. That hint of the synthetic was enough to establish a poignant and almost perverse tension. Cosmetics looked confusing on Dale, as they did on a child. She never quite joined up with them, you could always see the purer line beneath. Seeing me looking at her, she suddenly reached forward, took Hermia and Gina by the hand, and drew them backwards towards Figgy and myself so that the four of us formed a tight, protective square around her.

'Are you all right?' asked Gina.

Dale said nothing, and I smelt the night-scent of the white eglantine flowers in her hair.

'What is it, Dale?' asked Hermia.

She smiled. 'Nothing. I love you all, OK?'

None of us answered; perhaps none of us could. Instead, one by one, we gently squeezed her upper arms and stepped away from her to our original positions.

'Darren's finished,' said Figgy eventually.

'I hope he's washed his hands,' said Hermia, and we all laughed, slightly hysterical.

We led off in a silent column past the topiary garden towards our opening position on the lower part of the lawn. The sun was setting but the heat of the day still lingered; no breath of an evening breeze touched us or disturbed the surface of the lake. It felt strange – and strangely restful – to be an instrument of someone else's inspiration, to know only what I needed to know for my own performance and to have no responsibility for its meaning. For this was not really a masque we were undertaking. Nothing was to be read, no word was to be spoken; instead, all was spectacle. If there was a meaning to the whole thing, that meaning resided only in the head of Charles Sheldrake, and as far as I was concerned, it could stay there. My mind was tired, life was short, and I was happy just to dress up and dance on the grass.

We came to a halt in the shadow of a lime tree. The sun was setting now, its dying fires a thousand-fold reflection in the great bay windows of the house. Ahead of us, the banqueters formed a dark tableau against the drawn gold of the lake.

'Brightness falls,' said Gina.

'One take,' murmured Hermia.

We waited. A curious solemnity seemed to attend the occasion. I glanced across at Dale, but she was far away in some time and place of her own.

'Stand by,' said the crewcut woman, her hands to her headset, and Stephen lifted Darren to his shoulders.

Light bloomed from the light-towers; the banquet was suddenly and brilliantly detailed and all else was darkness.

'Quiet, please. Cameras rolling. On my count, now. *Three . . . two . . . one . . .*'

A dozen torches flared simultaneously, their blue-white flames turning our bodies pale and our costumes to cobwebbed silver.

'*Action!*'

The sound of a lute drifted across the lake, was joined by a viol and other instruments, and drew us into the first long gliding steps of the measure. I had worried about remembering the sequence, but in the event my body remembered for me. We seemed to be dancing inside a corona of light; I was aware of Gina and Hermia in front of me, very white-shouldered and intent, and of the faint susurrus of Dale's hair, and then the music changed from a coranto to a duretto, the light lifted from my face, and we were circling the banqueters.

Although there were thirty or more people grouped around the banqueting table, I was immediately struck by the scene's entranced stillness. The candle flames rose unwaveringly upwards, gilding the immobile faces of the diners, and I saw that the surrounding trees had been hung with *impresa* shields. We were dancing, it seemed, through perfume and saturated colour; through the thick tang of goose-fat and venison; through a gold-stiffened blur of crimson taffeta, moss-green damask, carnation silk and midnight-blue satin. Light-points leapt from sword hilts and signets, from biliments, aigrettes and bodkins, scribbling across the palely materialising faces of the Duboys parents, of Phoebe, Oliver, Dan and the rest of them. All, it seemed, had been mesmerised into an absolute stillness.

The line turned back on itself and we wove between each other to our respective masquing partners. Mine was the velvet-doubleted stag, in real life a trust-funded, nightclub-owning marquis called Charlie Fowey. Charlie had been politely drunk since breakfast time, and tendered me a solicitous if unsteady hand as the duretto's measured cadences rolled vaporously across the water. Darren, as Cupid, had been deposited by Stephen on the banqueting table where, straddling the carcass of a sucking-pig, he was loosing arrows into the darkness from Death's black bow. Stephen was partnering Dale. Charlie and I faced them for a moment, and I saw in Dale's eyes the petrol brightness of the camera lenses that swung to follow her, that moved as she moved, that so loved her.

As the duretto came to a close, trays of gunpowder were ignited on the lawn and on floating platforms in the lake, and the darkness surrounding the banquet was illuminated by a series of noiseless orange flashes. As the sparks rained slowly down and the smoke died away, the musicians struck up the final dance, the volta. Releasing our former partners, we drew the banqueters from their seats. Dan, in buff doublet and white chemise, looked like some jewelled and impetuous lover of Mary, Queen of Scots, some wild-eyed plotter destined for the headsman's axe. He swung me up and around with wordless fluency, locking his eyes to mine and steering us through the angled light, as far as I could divine, by instinct alone. My breath was sawing in my lungs, now, my back was beginning to protest, and I was finding it hard to jump. Ahead of us Phoebe tripped and she and the oak-leaved masquer fell laughing to the lawn, I swerved to avoid them, pulled Dan off balance, heard Figgy's yelp of 'Shite!' and the novelist's curses behind me, and turned to watch the scene's spectacular dissolution into chaos.

'Cut,' came the voice of Charles Sheldrake.

'How exactly does this undo?' Dan asked me, his breath at my ear.

'Wait,' I said, pushing his hands down. 'Please. You'll get this rouge stuff everywhere.'

We were at the lakeside. Behind us, beneath the lights, the set was being deconstructed. Sheldrake had pronounced himself satisfied.

'Dan, let me return this costume to them and change, OK?'

'How long will that take?'

'Less than seven years, I promise. Besides, you've got to change too.'

'Where will I see you?'

I considered. 'On the front terrace, perhaps?'

'Fine. On the terrace, then. Half an hour?'

'Half an hour's fine. And in the meantime, I've got a present for you.'

'Where could you possibly be keeping anything in that costume?'

'Where indeed,' I said, reaching into the lining of the olive silk bodice and handing him a folded envelope.

'So what's this?' he asked, tearing open the envelope and peering at the contents. 'And what's this black stuff all over it?'

'It's a cheque for seventy-five thousand dollars,' I said. 'And that black stuff, as you call it, is my blood.'

His mouth opened and he stared at me. 'You . . . remember what happened, then?' he eventually asked.

'I don't remember anything,' I said. 'But I guess I must have accepted this from you at some point. It was in a plastic bag in my locker at the hospital, along with my lighter and three pounds seventy-five in change. It came out of the trousers I was wearing at the time of the crash, which were Hermia's, if you remember, and are now – unfortunately – history.'

'I do remember. I remember very exactly. So why didn't you cash it?'

'You could have sued me for deception,' I said. 'Or blackmail, or God knows what. The article came out, after all, and you had every reason to hate me. You had nothing to lose at that point, either, so if I'd cashed it you could have made sure that I never worked again.'

'Ah,' he said quietly. 'Right.'

'What's wrong? You sound disappointed.'

'It was purely . . . pragmatic then, your decision?'

I looked out over the lake, where the musicians were being ferried back to the shore. 'Dan, to this day I don't remember what happened in that car.'

'Would you like me to tell you?' he asked, pulling at one of the bows at the back of my chemisette with his teeth. 'Or better still, to show you?'

'You can tell me what you did in half an hour's time,' I said, turning to face him. 'And then you can tell me what I did back. And if I think that what you said I did is what I would actually have done in response to the things that you said you'd done, well, I might just choose to believe you.'

'And then?'

'Who can tell?'

I felt his lips at the back of my neck. 'You smell wonderful,' he breathed.

'It's called Eternal Summer,' I murmured languorously. 'Available shortly at duty-free counters, prestige pharmacies and perfumeries worldwide.'

'Not the perfume,' he whispered. 'You.' He folded his arms round me. 'I don't think I've ever wanted anyone as much as I want you at this moment.'

'Call my agent,' I whispered back.

'Don't be vengeful, Alison. I mean what I say.'

'Do you know what the word "nympholepsy" means?' I asked him, gently lowering his hands from my breasts to my hips.

'Anything to do with nymphomania?'

'Not a great deal,' I said. 'Nympholepsy is an ecstatic state inspired by the desire of the unattainable.'

'I've got it,' he confirmed. 'Is there a cure?'

'That depends on you,' I said.

'Anyone any idea where Dale is?' asked John-Paul, unhooking me from my bodice.

'She's about,' said Gina, rubbing cold cream into her face. 'I passed her on the stairs. I think she was on her way up to the roof.'

'Strange girl,' said Hermia, who was sitting in her dressing gown drinking champagne and smoking a cheroot. 'She told me she remembered a picture story I did for *Harpers* when she was still at school. Made me feel a thousand.'

'She said something like that about me, too,' said Gina. 'Tissues, please.'

'I like her,' said Figgy. 'She's nice.' She turned to me. 'So how did you enjoy modelling? Piece of piss, really, isn't it?'

'What an articulate spokeswoman for our profession you are, Figs,' said Hermia, blowing smoke at the ceiling. 'You're supposed to say what hard, exhausting work it is.'

'Well, she knows it isn't, now, doesn't she? I mean.'

'I enjoyed it,' I said, stepping out of my chiffon skirt. 'Even though I'm sure I'm going to be just a blur in the background. And I didn't think it was easy at all.'

'You sweet thing,' said Hermia. 'Although I should know by now never to trust you when you're being sweet. Have some champagne.'

'Empty stomach,' I said, unwiring the crescent moon and the jasmine flowers from my forehead. 'And I've already had two Phoebe-scale martinis.'

She handed me the tulip glass anyway. 'So what are your plans? Are you staying here tonight?'

'Yes,' I said. 'Are you?'

'No, Claudie's driver's taking us all back to London.'

'Straight away?'

She raised an eyebrow. 'No, I expect we'll drift around for a bit. Why?'

'I was wondering,' I said quietly, 'if I might borrow your husband for an hour or so?'

'Darling, of course. Everyone else has.' She blew a plume of smoke and touched a finger to my cold-cream-smeared nose. 'You will be careful, though, won't you?'

'What do you mean?' I asked her.

'Do I really have to spell it out?'

I didn't answer her, and for a moment I didn't hear her, either. On the display board behind my mirror, John-Paul had pinned a postcard of Elizabeth I being crowned by cherubs, and I was suddenly and forcibly reminded of Darren in his pink sausage-skin, pouring arrows into the darkness. Some vital piece of intelligence, it seemed to me, was dancing just beyond my conscious reach.

'Alison?'

I snapped to. 'Sorry, say that last thing again, Hermia.'

'I said, "Do I really have to spell it out?", meaning that you should be careful.'

I stared at her. 'I'm sorry. I just had something important on the tip of my mind; you know that frustrating thing? It's gone now, though.'

'Think about something else and it'll come back. Think about, oh . . .'

'Don't worry,' I said. 'I'll think of something.'

There were a good fifty people on the terrace when I got down there. The caterers were handing around drinks and canapés, and a second glass of champagne somehow didn't seem quite as imprudent as the first had done. In order to ensure that it wasn't going into a completely empty stomach, I accepted a couple of spoonfuls of caviare on a curl of Melba toast.

'You're looking very scrubbed and minimal, Belle, after your command performance.'

She was back in lace and velvet, her hair slicked back, her eyes dark.

'I've never done anything like that before,' I said. 'So I'm rather pleased with myself. Did you have a good time?'

'I did. The sight of that repulsive little Cupid will go with me to the grave. Talking of which, you've met my mother, haven't you?' She raised her voice. 'Bridget, dear, this is Alison . . .'

When there was no response she waved a hand in front of her mother's face. 'Hello-o-o-o. Anyone home?'

'I know who it is,' Bridget Duboys said tonelessly. 'I've seen her before.'

'I wonder if you'd both excuse me,' I said. 'Some people I have to, um . . .'

Holding my glass before me, I picked my way through the crowd to Dan, who was staring into the darkness over the balustrade.

'Sorry,' I said. 'I didn't mean to choose such a crowded rendezvous.'

'They must have dragged the gene pool pretty deeply to come up with this lot,' Dan remarked as Charlie Fowey and a bleary-eyed female companion attempted to negotiate the stone steps leading down to the gardens. 'He looks as if he was born with a silver spoon up his nose, for a start.'

'I'd never've had you marked out as a puritan, Dan,' I said, surprised.

'I'm not one. There's just something about these aristocratic vampires which gives me the creeps.'

'How about Phoebe and Oliver?'

'They're Hermia's friends, not mine, and I'm not particularly fond of either of them. Phoebe, in fact, I find positively malign.'

'That's what you once called me,' I said gently. 'Or something very like it.'

'Well, you are a bit sinister, you must admit, with your pursuits and your revenges and your blood-soaked cheques.'

I walked slowly round him as if he was a piece of statuary. 'Dan, what really happened in that car?'

'I've told you what happened,' he said patiently, not moving.

I came full circle. 'Will you show me?' I whispered.

'Where?'

'I know a place.'

Our progress was silent, and soon the tick and murmur of the party had died away and we were hurrying along the dark avenues of hornbeam and yew to the gate I had entered by on that first morning. Below it, at the point where the formal gardens ended, a last small terrace of lawn overlooked the river and the lake.

'Here,' I said, throwing down my cigarettes and lighter and sinking to my knees. 'Right here.'

'You looked wonderful this evening. This witchy, white-faced stranger.'

'And you looked like you always do,' I replied, lighting a cigarette and stretching out on my back. Above us, the sky was seeded with stars.

'Tell me one thing,' he said, arranging himself beside me and gently undoing the topmost silk-covered button of my jacket.

'What is it about me that makes you so . . . aggressive?'

'Perhaps it's something I recognise,' I said. 'Some sort of capacity for damage, for causing pain. And a kind of anger at myself for being drawn to you.' I blew smoke at the moon and stubbed out my cigarette. 'I've never been much good at attaching myself to people who'll care for me.'

'I'll care for you,' he said, undoing the second button and touching his lips to my collarbone.

'You left me to die,' I murmured. 'You left me to bleed to death.'

He jerked upright. 'I . . . that's not fair and it's not true, Alison, and you . . .'

I reached a finger to his lips. 'Sssh. It doesn't matter.'

He stared at me in angry amazement. 'Of *course* it fucking matters, I mean . . . if you think that I did that, why are you here?'

'Because you're my weakness, Dan, and because I want you.'

Looking into his eyes I watched the slow collision of suspicion and desire. From the house came the whisper of music.

'I mean it,' I said. 'It really doesn't matter.'

He looked away, but as he undid the rest of the buttons of my jacket, I felt his anger evaporate. He removed my clothes with ritualistic thoroughness, as if performing a task of great complexity.

'You're silver,' he said eventually, studying me. 'Almost blue. There's no colour to you at all.'

'She's watching us,' I said, as he pulled off his shirt.

'Who?'

'The moon. Diana. The cold, cruel goddess of chastity.'

'Keeping an eye on her nymph, do you think? She's not going to be best pleased.'

'And why might that be?' I asked, as his tongue traced slow, cool lines across my body.

'I'll show you,' he murmured. 'What are these marks?'

'They're where the Meccano went in to realign my pelvis.'

'Poor nymph. Let me show you exactly what happened in that car.'

'No. Please. No past tenses. Just be here for me now.'

Even as he made love to me, I think we both knew that we would never see each other again. I didn't mind; it would have ended sooner rather than later, and it would have ended badly. As it was, he made me feel beautiful and I couldn't have wanted or asked for more. I wasn't sure what I could offer him in return, or what I could say to him that he hadn't already been told many times already, and so I held his gaze and said nothing. Afterwards I pretended to be asleep. He studied my face and body very intently for several minutes, kissed the corner of my mouth, and climbed to his feet. A minute or two later I heard the swing of the gate against the latch.

By the time that I emerged from the topiary garden, the production team and most of the guests had gone. A few stragglers, some of them still chalk-faced and rouged from the filming, were talking and smoking on the terrace steps, and they watched me incuriously as I hurried past. From the Great Hall, which was piled high with crates of champagne and with film-lighting equipment, I took a tulip glass and a half-bottle of Dom Perignon. I needed to keep at bay the hangover which was poised to announce itself.

In my room I changed into my kimono, pocketed the bottle and the glass and made my way to the small bathroom at the end of the corridor. It was locked, and seeing Dale's bedroom door ajar, I looked inside. The room was unoccupied, and the lights were switched off. I decided to borrow her bath.

Five minutes later I was lying in the moonlit half-dark with a 555 and a glass of champagne and the blood-temperature water lapping around my shoulders. I had left the lights switched off to avoid luring moths and insects through the open window; instead, the warm night streamed in, carrying with it snatches of laughter, the soft crunch of gravel, the distant departure of cars.

I awoke much later, with the water cold about me. For a moment I was completely disoriented, and then I lifted myself stiffly to my feet, climbed out of the bath and wrapped myself in a towel. Impossible to tell what time it was, except that the stillness and silence were absolute. I dried myself quickly, pocketed my cigarettes, and was just about to pull out the bath plug when I checked myself, remembering the hellish gurgling sounds that this usually caused. If Dale woke up to find me creeping past her bed in the middle of the night she might be a little surprised. Given her generally wobbly state of mind, she might even start screaming, which didn't bear thinking about. Accordingly, I left the glass, ashtray and empty champagne bottle where they were, opened the bathroom door as quietly as I could manage, and tiptoed through.

The curtains of the big four-poster bed were drawn, I saw, except for the one on the window side. Dale, still dressed in her nymph costume, was lying on top of the embroidered coverlet, facing the open curtain and the open bay window beyond. A long bar of moonlight overlaid her face.

She will wake up cold, I thought, cold and stiff, and I looked about for something to cover her with. Finding a blanket folded on top of a chest, I threw it over her. I paused for a second to make sure that I hadn't woken her, and then drew the blanket up to her shoulders.

And gasped in surprise. She was utterly still, her face was inscribed with steel-point clarity against the dark quilting of the coverlet, but her eyes were watching me.

'Dale?' I whispered, jerking upright as if I'd been slapped. 'God, I'm sorry, I . . .'

But there was no reply. There was no reaction of any kind, and as I caught my breath I realised that her eyes stared straight through me, that she saw nothing at all.

'Dale?' I repeated desperately, touching her arm through the gathered chiffon of her sleeve. '*Dale?*' The warmth had not yet left her, but even as I reached forward to search her unresisting neck for a pulse, I knew that I was too late. Dale Cooney was dead.

Panic surged, and with it a dizzying weightlessness. Moonlight burst before my eyes, the floor swung beneath my feet, and I clutched, gasping, at the bedpost. For several seconds I was unable to move, and then, very slowly, the room began to right itself and darkness to reclaim its place.

Stepping tentatively back, I closed my eyes and shook my head. It hurt; a slow bruise beat at my temples, and I felt an undertow of impending nausea, but shock had more or less sobered me. Bracing myself with my hands on my knees, I gulped in the night air and then, straightening, looked around me. On the bedside table, beneath Dale's crescent-moon headdress, lay a sheet of Darne Castle writing paper. I carried it to the stone windowsill.

'Gone to find the people Ive lost. I cant go on alone. Keep me safe. Dale Laurette Cooney.'

I looked back at her. Her chopines were placed neatly together by the bed, and her gauze mantle, unhooked from her shoulders, had been folded and set beside them. Something in this gesture – some last anxiousness to please – seemed to reflect both the hardship of her beginnings and the loneliness of her end, and I felt the tears running down my cheeks.

'I didn't listen,' I whispered. 'I made you talk and then didn't *fucking listen*.'

'It wasn't your fault,' said a quiet voice from the darkness, and this time the shock was so stunning that I almost passed out. For several breathless moments, I could neither hear nor move nor see, and then Charles Sheldrake swung into the half-light, carrying a decanter and a tumbler.

'Drink,' he ordered me, and I drank. It was whisky, and made me gag, but I swallowed it and stared at him, wet-faced and trembling.

Tiredly, he sat down in the bedside chair, leant forward for the tumbler and poured some more whisky for himself.

'It wasn't your fault,' he repeated. 'No one could have stopped her.'

'But . . . why?' I whispered. 'Why did she do it?'

'She had planned it,' he said, tossing me a packet of paper tissues from the bedside table.

'What did she take?'

'Some powerful sedative combined with alcohol, I suspect. She had . . . gone by the time I arrived.'

I blew my nose hard, wiped my eyes, and tried to think coherently. Questions crowded my mind. Faced with the story of a lifetime, needless to say, I didn't have so much as a pencil on me.

'Shouldn't we . . . shouldn't we call the police or an ambulance or something?' I asked.

He leant back, steepling his hands. He looked exhausted but calm. He was wearing a black linen suit and an olive-green shirt. He seemed to have had a haircut at some point during the day.

'Hear me out first, Alison. OK?'

I blew my nose again, stuffed the tissue in my pocket and peered at him in amazement. 'Hear you out? What do you mean, hear you out? Hear you out about what?'

'Before we do anything. Before we call anyone. Are you prepared to do that?'

Talk, I thought. Just talk. Tell me what's happening.

I shrugged. 'OK. I'll hear you out.'

He nodded, stood, and went through to the bathroom. I heard the sound of running water, and he came out drying his face with a hand towel.

'OK,' he said, balling the towel and dropping it to the floor. 'Listen. Sit down or something. This is . . . this is a strange story.'

'I'm listening,' I said.

He looked at me in expressionless silence, as if weighing up a number of conflicting factors, and finally nodded.

'Right. Well, it's eight nights ago. I'm here at Darne, finalising my shot-list, and Fletcher and Nancy are in London at the Connaught Hotel, waiting for Dale Cooney, who's supposed to have taken the midday Concorde flight from New York. Dale doesn't show. Fletcher Walsh calls her apartment in New York, he calls her agent in Los Angeles, but no result. A day passes, by which time she should have arrived here at Darne. Still no Dale; still no word from the States.'

He rubbed his eyes. I watched him.

'Well, no one panics; everyone knows these movieland types run by different clocks. I'm a bit worried that the weather might turn but otherwise . . . *que será, será*. On Monday evening, the day of your arrival, we get word from Forth's London office that Dale's finally arrived in London. I decide to go down to meet her on the Tuesday, only to find that she's locked herself in her room at the hotel and taken her phone off the hook. It's late afternoon before she agrees to speak to me, and when she lets me into her room she's clearly distraught. Someone close to her, it seems, has died recently and she's been thrown off balance. She doesn't want to go into details, but if she can just have a little time to . . .? Of course, love, I say. Take another day off in London. Come when you're ready.'

He poured another splash of whisky into the tumbler.

'She does that, you meet her, filming starts, and all goes well. She's very withdrawn, as you'll have noticed, but her work is wonderful. Very intense, very concentrated, very committed. And then the evening before last I'm down by the lake, working out various things in my mind for the next day's shooting, and we run into each other. She's just spent some time with you, I believe, and she's in a mood to talk. In fact she's more than in a mood to talk: she's desperate. So, we go where Fletcher and I went with you last Monday: to the boathouse. And there, after a number of false starts, the full story emerges. Apparently there was some guy she started seeing when she first came to New York – nobody in particular, she told me, nothing to do with films, just some guy – and eighteen months ago he walked out on her. Didn't give a reason, just said he couldn't see her any more. Anyway, a fortnight ago she found out he'd died of AIDS.'

'Oh, God,' I said.

'Exactly. Oh, God. After a week of wandering round New York in a kind of petrified daze, she had herself tested at a public clinic, and stuck around in New York for two extra days waiting for the result. Didn't let anyone know she was still there, didn't answer the phone, nothing; just stayed at her apartment. On Monday morning she went back to the clinic as she'd been told to, discovered that she was HIV positive, had herself driven to JFK and the Concorde departure lounge. Flight, you see.

'Now, you have to remember at this point who we're dealing with. A volatile, highly strung girl, just out of her teens, who has seen her mother shot to death in front of her eyes and everyone she has ever loved or cared about taken away from her. She's been transplanted, what's more, from a community she can no longer return to, to one she at best only partly understands, and her only escape from all of this is through the process of acting.'

'She could have continued to do that, couldn't she?' I asked, looking at Dale's still, slender, costumed form. 'She could have carried on for . . . well, as long as she . . .'

'That's what I told her,' said Sheldrake. 'She could have a life that was in every sense . . . But get this. The thing that really terrifies her, I discover, the thing that really keeps her awake at night, *is that her father will find out*. This bum, who walked out on her and her mother and sister when she was . . .'

'Six.'

'Six, was it? Anyway, her terror is that this bum – Lunev is his name – will somehow find out about her condition, and never come back to the family. But what family? I ask her, as gently as I can. Your sister's got her own children, and your mother's . . . *He'll find out*, she says. *He'll find out and he'll never come back*.'

Sheldrake leant forward in the chair and shook his head. Dale had tried to tell me all of this, but all I'd heard was a story, a bad-beginnings, broken-childhood story like a million others.

'Go on.'

He threw back the whisky, placed the tumbler on the floor and looked across at me. 'She told me that there was only one way the pieces were ever going to fit back together. Like Eleanor, she had to disappear.'

'Like . . . Eleanor?'

'I understood what she was saying, of course,' Sheldrake continued, ignoring my interruption. 'And I suspect that in some terrible way she even thought that I might be pleased. I'd told her about the legend, and she'd identified with it to the point at which she had actually begun to believe, I think, that she was some sort of reincarnation of Eleanor Duboys. Taking her own life and being buried in secret, deep in the woods, would be the perfect fulfilment of the legend. No one would ever find her, no one would ever know about her condition. The pieces would fit together again. She would live forever.'

Anger suddenly drenched me like a wave. 'And there was no question, of course, of your encouraging her in these fantasies? No question of your realising that your oh-so-brilliant casting coup had blown up in your face and that with Dale alive and talking and HIV positive it was only a question of time before the whole event turned into a complete fucking nightmare?'

'No,' replied Sheldrake levelly. 'There was no question of anything of the sort. And if you don't want to waken the entire household, I'd suggest you lower your voice.'

There was a long silence.

'So tell me,' I asked him, getting to my feet and lighting a cigarette with hands that now hardly shook at all, 'what do you think actually happened to Eleanor? I assume you succeeded in presenting Dale with some exquisite series of parallels with her own situation?'

Sheldrake narrowed his eyes thoughtfully. 'Well, let me put it like this. I have a theory as to the meaning of those Cupid and Death figures in that painting you've been so busy with.'

'You know about the painting?'

'Of course.'

'How?'

'Phoebe told me. Showed me, I should say.'

'I thought you and Phoebe weren't . . .'

He poured a second large measure of whisky into the tumbler and passed it to me. 'You mustn't believe everything Phoebe tells you. She's a habitual liar, apart from anything else. She showed me the painting three or four days ago, in the entirely self-interested hope that I might know what the figures meant. It's true that she doesn't like me much these days, but she is aware that I know what I'm talking about, and anything that might relate to the value of Duboys property is interesting to Phoebe. An estate this size doesn't run itself, and Bill Duboys' money, from what I gather, is running out pretty fast.'

'So what's your theory about the painting?' I asked. The conversation and its circumstances were so surreal that there seemed nothing for it but to continue. The silences when neither of us was speaking were terrifying.

'I realised that I'd seen figures like those before,' said Sheldrake, 'although it took me a while to remember where.'

'Go on.'

'They were engraved on the title page of a book by a celebrated Elizabethan surgeon, a Warwickshire man named William Clowes. The title of the book was *De Morbe Gallico*.'

'*Concerning the French Pox*,' I translated.

'Precisely. Syphilis. Clowes was a brilliant, sardonic man to whom the image of Death shooting Love's arrows as a metaphorical representation of venereal disease would greatly have appealed. You should read Shirley's masque:

> ' "Fly, fly my children! Love that should preserve,
> And warm your hearts with kind and active blood,
> Is now become your enemy, a murderer . . ."

'It's perfect, isn't it?'

I looked at Dale, and nodded.'So you think Eleanor Duboys died of syphilis?'

'No. I think there would have been some record of the fact, medical or otherwise. Put it like this, though: if a young Elizabethan noblewoman of marriageable age had contracted syphilis – a disease whose treatment was excruciating and whose symptoms, as we know from *Timon of Athens*, were all too recognisable – she might well not have wished to live. And by the same token a father who loved his daughter might well have preferred to see her swiftly dead than dying painfully by stages, and the family dishonoured.'

'Is that what you think happened?' I asked, walking through to the bathroom and dousing my cigarette butt under the tap.

'There can be no possible way of proving it.'

' "No more thou little winged archer . . ."?'

'Quite. You've obviously done your homework. But you must draw your own conclusions. In fact it was the painting and those figures which gave me the idea of including Cupid and Death in the masque scene. And when Dale told me all the things that I've just told you, it occurred to me that one chance of diverting her from her course lay in the masque, in the formal and metaphorical enactment of her fantasy. If, as Eleanor, she could literally dance with Death, there was just a faint chance that . . . that that would be enough.'

'So how did you leave it with her?'

'I told her that we would complete the filming and then talk again, and in the meantime I begged her – *begged her* – to do nothing to harm herself, to which she agreed. Shortly afterwards I went and told Fletcher Walsh the whole story, as of course I was professionally bound to do. His immediate reaction was to ask me if I thought she was telling the truth, and I replied that to be perfectly honest I didn't know. Was it possible, he went on, that Dale was making the whole thing up? Yes, I told him, it was. Right, he said. And that was that. End of conversation. He didn't need to say any more; I knew exactly what was going through his mind.'

'Which was?' I asked, although I knew well enough.

'Well, put it this way, the best-case scenario was that Dale was lying. The worst-case scenario . . .' he gestured towards the bed, 'is this one. If it gets out that Laurene Forth's new face was HIV positive and committed suicide on location – and given that there would be an autopsy and an inquest it would be front-page news – the corporation is dead in the water, and Fletcher's career with it. These products are about fantasy, not mortality, and any whiff of an association with anything like this . . .'

'But look' I said, 'what were you doing in here anyway when I came out of the bathroom. What made you come in?'

'Well, the fact is I hadn't seen Dale since we wrapped the filming, and thinking back to what she'd told me a couple of days earlier, I thought I'd check and make sure she was OK before I went to bed. So, once I'd seen the last people off – I was supposed to be hosting the party, amongst other things – I knocked on her door. When there was no answer, well, I stuck my head in, saw what you saw, and sat down to try and figure out what to do.'

'And she was dead when you came in?'

'I'm afraid she was.'

'You're sure of that?' I asked, staring him straight in the eye. 'She's still . . . warm now.'

Our gazes locked, and he nodded. 'You have my word on it, Alison. I came in, and saw that she was dead. You materialised about quarter of an hour later.'

His regard was unwavering, and eventually I looked away. 'So what happens now?' I asked.

Sheldrake took a phone from his pocket and passed it to me. 'What happens now,' he said, 'is that you either ring the police immediately, or you agree to listen to the rest of what I have to say.'

I looked down at the phone, felt its weight in my hand. Carefully, I placed it on the bedside table, and as Sheldrake had done earlier, walked through to the bathroom and splashed cold water on my face. Except that the water wasn't cold, it was tepid, and when I returned to stand at the bedroom window, there was still no hint of a breeze.

'I'm listening,' I murmured to the night. Listening had never been any kind of commitment.

Sheldrake nodded. 'What I propose,' he said quietly, 'is that we respect Dale's wishes.'

'I see. And how do we do that?'

He frowned. 'You're absolutely sure you want to hear this?'

'I'm absolutely sure,' I said. What I wasn't sure, I told myself, was whether I wanted to go through with whatever it was that he had planned.

He nodded. 'Right. Well, the first thing that happens is that you go to your room, take a couple of paracetamol, turn out the lights and go to sleep. I then call Fletcher, show him what has happened here, and put certain suggestions to him, with which he will eventually agree. We will then leave Dale alone here, and this door will be locked.

'In the morning, you will have breakfast in the usual way, and then a car will take you, Gina and Fiona back to London as scheduled. Dale's staying on to do some stills, you'll all be told, and she's sleeping late. Anyone who wants to can catch up with her in London, where she's due to spend a few days before flying back to the States. And that's it. You return to London, write your piece, do what you'd normally do.

'In three or four days you'll probably get a call from the police, and you'll tell them – as about a hundred other people will tell them – exactly how you spent your evening, including coming in here for a bath. When you left the bathroom, you'll tell them, you saw Dale asleep on the bed, and tiptoed out. End of story. And that's it.'

I turned round to face him. 'So you're actually going to do it? You're going to bury her in the forest and pretend she's disappeared, like Eleanor?'

'It's what she wanted. She asked us to keep her safe, and I think we should.'

'You'll never get away with it.'

'I think you'll find that we will.'

'How? I mean who's going to . . .?'

'Choose the place, do you mean? Do the digging? Stephen Faulds is. You know about Stephen, don't you?'

'Only that he was once in some technical part of the army and used to work for Bill Duboys.'

'Stephen Faulds was involved in what used to be referred to as "area-denial". He was a landmines man, basically, and very good at his job. When he left the army he was headhunted by Bill Duboys' outfit, who at the time were involved in some very weird stuff in Cambodia on our Government's behalf. According to Phoebe there were times when Stephen was unsure about the justifiability of some of his work, but one way and another he managed to keep his conscience at bay until, with the anti-landmine campaigns of ninety-seven, the bottom fell out of the market for his particular basket of skills. Somewhere round about that time – it might even have been at Bill Duboys' funeral – he met Phoebe, who was rather taken with him. Having spent his entire professional life planting things in the ground, he told her, he had decided on a sideways move into landscape gardening, and Phoebe, one way and another, decided to take him on.'

'She told you all this?'

'Of course. But the main point that I'm making is that he knows about digging and he knows about discretion.'

'I'm sure he does. But why should he . . .?'

'Because Phoebe will tell him to, and as far as Stephen's concerned, anything that Phoebe says goes.'

'Why involve either of them?'

'If Dale is to be buried here – and there's no question of taking her anywhere else – then they have to be involved.'

'And why exactly should they put themselves at risk of a criminal conspiracy charge?'

'Because what Phoebe needs more than anything else right now is money. Money to keep Stephen in the gatehouse, money to keep Bridget in Bombay gin and Oliver in Chinese heroin, money to keep the house heated and the floors polished and the gravel raked. That's why she leased the house to Forth in the first place; it certainly wasn't for love of me.'

'And who's going to give her all this money? Laurene Forth again?'

'Of course.'

'But why should they?'

'Well, put yourself in Fletcher Walsh's position and look at the options. He can report Dale's death to the police, but that would mean an autopsy and an inquest and huge publicity and basically – in the wake of the Quatrième débâcle – the end of his career.'

'Go on.'

'If, on the other hand, Dale Cooney simply disappears, as Eleanor Duboys did exactly four centuries ago, a great contemporary mystery would be born. Dale would become a cult figure, a romantic enigma. There would be endless "sightings", endless media speculation, endless dinner-party theorising. None of it would cost anything, and all of it would sell Laurene Forth products. Fletcher will work all of this out for himself, and he will see that for the price of two unscheduled payments he can buy himself success on an undreamed-of scale.'

His words begged one more question. I knew the answer, but I still had to ask it.

'If the first payment's for Phoebe, who's the second one for?'

He looked at me, surprised. 'It's for you, Alison. Who else? Knowing what you now know, they could hardly let you leave without, how can I put this, *binding* you to them in some fairly substantial way. I've heard from more than one source that you're ready for a change, so' – he smiled – 'here's your chance. A brand-new life, a brand-new lifestyle. If you're wondering about the actual total amount of any settlement, I think you can probably count on . . . well, certainly the low seven figures. Dollars, that is. If, on the other hand, you're still not . . .' And once again, he held out the phone.

This was it, then. The sticking point. Through the open window, beyond Sheldrake, the first glimpse of light was visible. Slowly, I walked over to the still, pale figure on the bed.

'Good night, angel,' I whispered. 'I'm sorry. I'm so sorry.'

Sheldrake didn't move, but stood there motionless with the phone in his outstretched hand. He had switched it on, and my eyes were held by the dim green glow of its liquid crystal display. Silence roared about my ears, and all the people that I'd ever been – all the parts that I'd ever played – crowded darkly and expectantly around me.

'Well?' asked Charles Sheldrake. 'What are you going to do?'

13

The engine note of the airliner changes. Below us, cloud-blurred, is the amber scribble of New York State. I fold the cuttings away into my briefcase, and within minutes the scribble takes recognisable shape: Jersey City, the beaded grid of Manhattan, the dark channels of the Hudson and the East River. Anticipating the 'No Smoking' sign, I light a 555. The ground rises towards us.

As a first-class ticket holder, I clear Customs and Immigration in less than ten minutes. It still seems like a long time, though; I am impatient for my apartment, impatient for the towers and the verticality of the city. I buy a limousine ticket, and gratefully surrender my bag.

As the limousine crawls through Queens with heater blaring and wipers thumping ineffectually at the slick, snow-blown windshield, I wish that I had accepted my neighbour's offer of a ride in her chauffeured grey Mercedes. The limousine is old and smells of coconut oil and cheap air-freshener, and recently I have become very aware of such things. Near Flushing Meadow there has been a two-car wreck; at the kerb, half-visible through the whirling flakes, the drivers exchange slow-motion gestures of blame. 'Gittin' overheated,' smiles my driver, beating time to the music in his head on the steering-wheel cover.

'Do you mind if I smoke?' I ask.

'Ain't no law says you can't.'

I light a 555 and open the window a centimetre. The winter slides in like a blade. We creep onwards.

When we finally reach the apartment block on West Fifteenth Street the doorman hands me an envelope. I am expecting it, and thank him.

'Good to have you back, Miss MacAteer. Happy New Year.'

In the tenth floor apartment I haul my suitcase on to the bed, unpack, pour myself a drink – I have developed something of a taste for bourbon – and listen to my messages. Although I have been away for the best part of a month there are only half a dozen; very few people have my number here.

Slowly, drink in hand, I walk from room to room. All the walls are painted white, there are no paintings and very little furniture. I have a large television, several shelves of books, and the usual music equipment. There is a better-appointed kitchen than I will ever need, and a large white bathroom. From my bedroom, I can see the river.

Everything has worked out as Charles Sheldrake said it would. On that final Sunday morning Gina, Figgy and I shared a late breakfast under the cedar, signed our commercial release forms and were waved off in a large BMW by Nancy Waller. Neither Charles Sheldrake nor Fletcher Walsh seemed to be around, and Nancy apologised for their absence.

We took the back drive out of the estate, and a few minutes later, undramatically, we were on the main road. We didn't talk much; I think that all of us were tired. By Oxford the sky had clouded over, and by the time we crossed the M25 it was raining hard. The car dropped us off in Mayfair and we went to the Gay Baboon for lunch, but it was very much a Sunday, and no one was much in the mood. At the end of the meal we swapped telephone numbers, ordered taxis and went our separate ways.

When I got back to the flat I sat down at my desk and began writing up my article. I worked fast from my notes and transcriptions, and on Monday evening I e-mailed the piece through to the magazine. Later that night the phone rang. It was Nancy Waller, asking if I had seen or heard from Dale. I replied that I hadn't, and asked if there was a problem. Only, said Nancy, that no one's seen her since Saturday night, and we were wondering if, by any chance . . . Sorry, I said; I haven't seen anyone. Give me a number and if I hear from her I'll call.

The visit from the West Mercia Police came on the Wednesday

morning. There were two of them, a man and a woman, and they gave the distinct impression of having more important things to do than trail about London after missing actresses. They questioned me closely enough, nevertheless. I described talking to Phoebe on the terrace, walking in the gardens with Dan – I left it at walking – and falling asleep in Dale's bath. Yes, I said, I was certain that Dale was not in her bed when I went into the bathroom, and yes, I was equally certain that she was there, asleep, when I left. What had I had to drink? A couple of large martinis and half a dozen glasses of champagne. Would I have described myself as drunk? Well, not falling-down drunk, but certainly . . . I was sure, though, was I, that Dale hadn't been in her room when I went in, and that she had been there when I left? Positive. And she'd definitely been asleep? I hadn't checked. It was dark. Someone was certainly lying there, though, under some sort of cover. But I hadn't checked that it was Dale? Of course not. Why on earth would I? I just wanted to get out without waking her . . .

There was a good half an hour of this, followed by more general questions. I had found Dale pleasant but distant, I told them. She had clearly had an unhappy childhood, which she and I had discussed, but she had seemed to be enjoying her work. Her timekeeping was a bit weird, though. Did they know she'd been several days late arriving on location? They'd gathered as much, replied the senior of the two, a doleful-looking woman in a gaberdine suit.

They eventually left, taking with them a copy of my article and complimenting me unsmilingly on my coffee.

By that afternoon someone had called the papers – one of the party guests, probably, hoping to make a quick couple of hundred quid – and my phone was ringing every ten minutes. I filtered the calls for three hours until, as I had been expecting him to, Sheldrake called. I was to meet him and Walsh at the Connaught Hotel, he told me. He gave me a room number.

At the hotel, all was silence. I took a seat in the lobby, and stood as Sheldrake and Walsh approached. In the lift, I stared through the grille at the passing floors.

'We know why we're here?' asked Walsh, when we were seated

in the suite's pale-lemon antechamber. The question was clearly intended for me. 'Yes,' I said.

His instructions to me were simple: I was to speak to nobody except the police. To any persistent press enquirer I was to say that I had already been placed under contract to write an exclusive report. As time passed, and public interest in the affair escalated, I could explain that I was writing a book on the subject.

And in a way, Walsh continued, this would be true. As a director of the Laurene Forth Corporation, he intended to place me under an exclusive and open-ended contract, and my first task – a task that I could approach in any way I wished, naturally – might well be the preparation of a book relating to the Eternal Summer campaign. The financial settlement, he added, his pale gaze locking carefully on to mine, would be very large indeed, and would reflect the exceptionally high premium placed by the corporation on – and here he paused significantly – loyalty.

Perhaps the best way forward, he suggested mildly, was that I remain in London for as long as the police might need me for questioning – probably for another month or so – and then quietly move to New York. I could stay in a hotel to begin with, and then an apartment could be found; somewhere I could live and work in comfort. How did all of that sound?

Fine, I managed. It all sounded just fine.

Walsh ordered tea. In future, he insisted, there was to be no reference of any kind made to the true facts of Dale Cooney's disappearance. The others who knew the whole truth were Phoebe and Stephen – it had not been thought necessary to inform Oliver.

'Exactly what do the police know?' I asked Charles Sheldrake.

'Apparently several people saw Dale on the roof during the party,' he answered. 'I was looking for her at one point, and John-Paul said he'd just seen her coming down the stairs still wearing her nymph costume but with a T-shirt on top. Other people may well have run into her at other times and in other places during the evening, and some of them may have spoken to her. The last official sighting was yours.

'When we rang the police on Tuesday morning, it was to say that no one had seen Dale for over forty-eight hours. Her room had been locked all Sunday morning, but until midday everyone had assumed she'd been in it, asleep. She wasn't needed, so she'd been left alone. When Nancy got no answer to her lunch-time knock, though, she started to wonder what was up. The caterers had left the night before, and we were all due to go out and eat in Stratford. Anyway, eventually Stephen was found; he got a ladder up to Dale's window, and shouted down that she wasn't there. A bit of a discussion followed, and we agreed that Dale must have gone out earlier and left the door locked behind her.'

'So what did you do then?'

'Took the household out to lunch as planned,' said Sheldrake. 'Dale could have been anywhere. Besides, someone has to have been missing for at least twenty-four hours before the police are interested.'

'And Stephen went with you?'

'No. Stephen stayed at Darne. He had . . . work to do.'

'Ah. So how long before you all came back?'

'Oh, several hours. The general consensus of opinion was that Dale had gone to London.'

'So how did you finally get into her room?'

'Phoebe located a key.'

'And what did you find when you finally unlocked the door?'

'An empty room. A rumpled four poster bed with a nymph costume draped across it. Otherwise nothing.'

'No bag? No clothes?'

'Nothing.'

The storm broke on the Thursday morning. All of the tabloids led with the Cooney story, and all of the broadsheets carried it on the front page. Given that most of Phoebe's hundred-odd guests were avid self-publicists there was no shortage of sources prepared to contribute their impressions of the evening of the masque. I was very grateful to them; they absorbed a lot of the pressure that would otherwise have come my way. From the newspaper Bart left constant messages pleading with me to call him, while Lucy Fane, high on the intrigue of it all, e-mailed me to say that he had tried to access the magazine's copy files to loot my piece for quotes and background but hadn't been able to beat her security system.

On the Saturday, I was asked to go to St John's Wood police station in Newcourt Street to make a recorded statement. I was met by the same lugubrious duo from the West Mercia Division, and we covered exactly the same ground. My article was due out the next day, and that night, not wishing to be besieged by journalists, as I certainly would have been if I'd stayed, I drove down to my parents' house.

I stayed in Camberley for a fortnight. Every morning I bought all the newspapers, arranged myself on the recliner in the back garden with coffee and cigarettes to hand, and worked my way through the mound of newsprint.

Conjecture about Dale Cooney grew increasingly bizarre. The Eleanor Duboys legend was reprised at length, black magic was suspected, and several of the party guests reported having seen strange lights in the sky on the night of the masque. Dale, it appeared, had been in several places at once; at least a dozen of those present that night reported encounters with her – one of them even claimed to have had a ten-minute conversation with her in Latin.

I cut out all the reports, however unbalanced, and filed them. If my parents were puzzled by my behaviour, they knew better than to say anything. All such concerns were swept aside, however, when Wendy and Orde came down for the weekend and announced their engagement. They were perfect for each other. It would be a winter wedding, and I promised to be there.

In July, cautiously, I returned to my flat. The story was still all over the papers, and would certainly remain there throughout the 'silly season' of July and August. Fiona Duff had been persuaded to sell her story, and for the moment the press were feasting on the 'unease' and the 'dark forebodings' that had afflicted her from the first day of the shoot. The West Mercia Police, it seemed, having questioned more than a hundred and fifty people, had got nowhere at all, and the Stratford-upon-Avon incident room had been stood down and the case handed over to Missing Persons. A number of private agencies had involved themselves in the case, including an American outfit hired by Laurene Forth, but none had come up with any answers.

In London I walked, went to films, and enlarged my cuttings

file. The press soon found out that I was back, and I was relieved to receive a call from Fletcher Walsh, a week after my return, suggesting that I come over to New York.

I stayed at a small hotel on Eighth Avenue, near my future apartment building. Fletcher had opened a bank account in my name, and promised that the apartment would be ready for occupancy by Christmas. I accepted these gifts with a kind of dazed gratitude, afraid to test their reality. They were real enough, though; I was shown the unfurnished apartment, and given documents to sign at the bank. I was, I discovered, rich.

Fletcher's team at Forth were preparing for the Eternal Summer launch, which had been brought forward to the end of July. He introduced me to them; everyone was polite, if distracted. A few days before the launch the *New York Times* reported that a newly attributed painting by the Elizabethan master Robert Peake was to be auctioned at Sotheby's Bond Street auction rooms in London. Its subject was Eleanor Duboys – whose legend had recently been revived by the disappearance of the actress Dale Cooney – and considerable interest was expected. In the event, I saw a few days later, the painting sold for a little more than a million and three-quarters sterling.

The launch of the Eternal Summer campaign was, as it had always promised to be, a huge success. America had been as enthralled by the Cooney affair as had Britain, and the commercial acquired instant cult status. Extended 'director's cut' versions were bought and sold like pop videos, to be pored over frame by frame by conspiracy theorists, and authorities on Elizabethan culture were invited to pronounce upon the arcane symbols and references with which the piece was replete. Hundreds of Dale Cooney websites came into being, and I spent hours at a time drifting between them on the laptop computer that had been one of my first New York purchases.

I stayed at the hotel until the end of November, watching the slow death of summer and the coming of autumn. I had always loved New York, and was grateful to be spared the publicity and the questioning that I would have been unable to escape in London. I lived quietly, planning and making notes for the

Eternal Summer book. In the course of my researches I found myself constantly returning to Shakespeare, and in particular to the dark Arcadian forests of *As You Like It* and *A Midsummer Night's Dream*. I often thought of Titania's lines:

> Out of this wood do not desire to go:
> Thou shalt remain here, whether thou wilt or no.
> I am a spirit of no common rate:
> The summer still doth tend upon my state;
> And I do love thee . . .

While I was living at the hotel there was an exhibition of paintings by the eighteenth century French artist François Boucher at the Metropolitan Museum of Art. One painting in particular called me back again and again, and I visited the exhibition so often that the staff began to recognise me. The painting – 'Jupiter in the guise of Diana seducing Callisto' – showed the opening moments of the story whose grim closing sequence was illustrated in Bess of Hardwick's frieze. Diana the Huntress and her favourite nymph, Callisto, are embracing in a woodland setting. The presence on a crag of an eagle gripping thunderbolts, however, indicates that the naked goddess is in fact Jupiter himself, transfigured. Within moments he will reveal himself, have his way with Callisto, and return to the upper air, leaving her to face the terrible consequences of her unchastity. In the painting though, time has been suspended, Callisto has no idea of her destiny, and all is languorous, leafy and calm.

The story, I discovered, did not end with Diana's revenge, with Callisto's transformation into a bear and brutal death on the huntsmen's spears. At the moment of her agony, ashamed of his behaviour (and to the speechless fury of his wife Juno) Jupiter lifted the former nymph in a whirlwind and set her in the night skies where, with the help of a good pair of binoculars, she is visible to this day. Callisto is a moon of Jupiter, and as my handful of lovers have discovered, I bear her mark on my breast.

In December I moved into the West Fifteenth Street apartment, and then returned to London for Orde and Wendy's wedding and to spend Christmas with my parents. When I told them that I was moving to New York permanently, they said that they'd suspected as much.

On Boxing Day morning, with the temperature some degrees below freezing, I decided on impulse to drive to Darne. It took me four hours, and so changed was the landscape that I swept past the gatehouse turning and into Upton-on-Arrow. I found the track eventually, however, and turned the Capri off the road.

The woods were all but lightless, and I was compelled to switch on my headlights to negotiate their twists and turns and frozen puddles. The kitchen light was on in the gatehouse, and parking the car under the arch, I lifted the heavy iron knocker and let it fall.

A stranger answered the door, a heavy-set young man in a sweater and corduroys.

'Is Stephen in?' I asked him, rubbing my ungloved hands together.

'Family's all away on holiday, I'm afraid. Won't be back till April. Can I help you?'

'I'm a friend of Phoebe and Oliver Duboys. Do you mind if I have a quick wander round?'

'Are you a journalist?' he asked, eyeing my coat suspiciously.

'I'm a friend,' I repeated, the cold air catching at my lungs.

'Your name's not by any chance Alison, is it? Alison . . . McManaman or something?'

'MacAteer,' I said. 'Yes.'

'In that case I've got a parcel for you. Hang on.'

He disappeared into the house and returned with a package the size of a phone directory, which he hefted uncertainly in his large hands. 'Look, tell you what, you go and have your walk, and pick it up before you go. How's that?'

'Fine. Thanks.'

Tightening my scarf around my throat, I made my way along the track to the gate, and into the hoar-frosted valley. There, I walked down to the place where Dale had been dropped by the helicopter, and lit a cigarette. Far to my right I could see the black crescent of the lake, and beyond it the grey of the forest. Ahead, the house was vague, spellbound by cold, locked for winter's duration in an icy half-dark. It was not yet two in the afternoon, but it felt like dusk.

'There you go,' said the caretaker, handing me the package a quarter of an hour later. 'Happy Boxing Day.'

'Thanks,' I said.

I drove most of the way back to the road before stopping to open it. The wrapping was plain brown paper, and the twine had been sealed with red sealing-wax and stamped with a stag's head signet ring. Within was the book of engravings entitled *Beautiful Englishwomen* that Oliver had shown me, a folded note, and a tiny hard object wrapped in a silk handkerchief. The object was an aigrette, an Elizabethan gold and ruby hairpin designed as a spray of tiny red flowers. It was a beautifully made thing and obviously very old, and on impulse I turned to the engraving of Eleanor Duboys. I had not noticed the aigrette in the painting, but in the engraving there it clearly was, an inch or two above her hairline. In case I had missed it, some sly hand had dotted in the tiny flowers in scarlet paint. There was also a note, in childishly laboured italics.

Dearest Belle,

The Book is from Oliver, who thanks you for – well, he thanks you anyway. The Pimpernels are from Me.

As you'll have discovered, we have gone Away – I'm afraid we're not very good at The Cold.

I'm told you're moving to New York. Perhaps that's sensible – you always seemed so betwixt and between in this Old Country.

Goodbye, Belle, it was Sweet and so were You, but Best not to write back.

Kisses Always, PHOEBE.

I sat in the car for a long time with the note and the tiny aigrette in my hand. Beyond the smeared windscreen the headlights' beam illuminated an impenetrable wall of beech saplings. I had been deluding myself, I saw, if I'd ever thought that even the smallest niche existed for me in the world of which Darne was a part. For Phoebe and the rest of them I'd represented a diversion, perhaps, and a chance to play a hand or two of *épater la bourgeoise*, but that had been about the limit of it. She was right: I'd always been betwixt and between, and I always would be. Even if I'd wanted to – and I didn't – I couldn't go back to journalism and my old life. The one story that everyone would want from me was the story I couldn't tell.

Laying *Beautiful Englishwomen* on the passenger seat, and folding the aigrette inside the note and slipping the little parcel into my coat pocket, I unwound the window and straightened the wing mirror which had been swiped askew by a branch. In doing so I caught sight of my reflection, and for one terrifying moment had the impression that the regard that held me so unflinchingly was someone else's. I blinked, and the features reassembled themselves. I had changed, everyone had said (well, Wendy and Mum had said). Not so much that I had lost weight, but I had fined down, somehow. And my eyes were different.

*

From my white and silent rooms, I survey the New York nightfall. Snow whirls past the plate-glass windows, blurring the illuminated towers, the jewelled crawl of the traffic, the distant blackness of the river.

Tomorrow, as the letter I hold in my hand confirms, I have a lunch appointment with Fletcher Walsh, ostensibly to discuss the progress of my book, but actually, I suspect, so that he can reassure himself as to my state of mind. He often brings his assistant with him on these occasions, a woman of about my own age named Justine. We get on well enough.

I have visited the Laurene Forth offices a number of times. Nancy Waller is always welcoming and Fletcher has indicated that if I am interested in joining them, interested in the creation of new beauty stories, it can be arranged.

Justine has been encouraging, too. 'You would be perfect,' she said once, and misunderstanding her – or perhaps not – I found my hands stealing to the fading scars at my mouth and eyes. It was at that moment, I think, that I fully understood the old fable for the first time, understood that in a world where Love has become a murderer, Death must be the bringer of joy. Those that are marked out for him, he makes beautiful. The old become young. The dying dance.

At some not too far distant point – in the spring, perhaps – I may take Walsh up on his offer, and then there will be clothes to buy and places to go and people to see. For the moment, though, I need to be alone. I am a child of winter, and the snow is falling.